PRAISE FOR JOHN McFETRIDGE

BLACK ROCK

"Canadian author/screenwriter McFetridge has earned critical praise for *Everybody Knows This Is Nowhere* (2008) and other previous works, but is still looking for a 'breakout book.' With its well-etched family drama and dynamic historical background, *Black Rock* might finally be the one." — *Kirkus Reviews*

"[An] excellent historical procedure . . . Well done history and a really good plot line." — *Globe and Mail*

"[McFetridge]'s prose remains stripped back and forceful, the action propelled by laconic dialogue and the likeable Eddie Dougherty's refusal to allow politics to interfere with his personal pursuit of justice . . . It's a fascinating backdrop, too." — *The Irish Times*

A LITTLE MORE FREE

"Brilliant . . . As a police procedural, *A Little More Free* is superb. As a sociopolitical human drama, it's even better — remember to breathe during those final few pages." — *Winnipeg Free Press*

"This terrific continuation of the narrative McFetridge began in *Black Rock* opens with a bang . . . Working with a deceptively simple style that echoes Joseph Wambaugh, McFetridge has delivered an unpredictable mystery, a fine character study and a vivid snapshot of 1972 Montreal." — *Publishers Weekly*

DIRTY SWEET

"McFetridge is an author to watch. He has a great eye for detail, and Toronto has never looked seedier." — *Globe and Mail*

"McFetridge combines a tough and gritty story populated by engagingly seedy characters . . . with an effective use of a setting, Toronto." — *Booklist*

"If more people wrote the kind of clean-as-a-whistle, no-fat prose McFetridge does, this reviewer would finish a lot more of their books."
— *National Post*

EVERYBODY KNOWS THIS IS NOWHERE

"Sex. Dope. Immigration. Gang war. Filmmaking. In McFetridge's hands, Toronto might as well be the new L.A. of crime fiction."
— *Booklist*

"Amid the busy plot, McFetridge does a good job depicting a crime-ridden Toronto (a.k.a. the Big Smoke) that resembles the wide-open Chicago of Prohibition days with corrupt cops, gang warfare and flourishing prostitution."
— *Publishers Weekly*

SWAP

"[*Swap*] grabs you by the throat and squeezes until you agree to read just one page, just one more page."
— *Quill & Quire*

"In just three novels . . . McFetridge has demonstrated gifts that put him in Elmore Leonard territory as a writer, and make Toronto as gritty and fascinating as Leonard's Detroit. . . . [McFetridge] is a class act, and he's creating fictional classics — maybe even that great urban literature of Toronto the critics now and then long for."
— *London Free Press*

TUMBLIN' DICE

"Dialogue that sizzles and sparks through the pages, providing its own music, naturally of the hard-rocking kind."
— *Toronto Sun*

"John McFetridge is — or should be — a star in the world of crime fiction."
— *London Free Press*

"Like [Elmore] Leonard, McFetridge is able to convincingly portray flawed figures on both sides of the law."
— *Publishers Weekly*

ONE OR
THE OTHER

The Eddie Dougherty Mystery Series

ONE OR
THE OTHER

AN EDDIE DOUGHERTY MYSTERY

JOHN McFETRIDGE

ECW PRESS

Library and Archives Canada
Cataloguing in Publication

McFetridge, John, 1959-, author
One or the other : an Eddie Dougherty mystery /
John McFetridge.

Issued in print and electronic formats.
ISBN 978-1-77041-327-6 (paperback);
ISBN 978-1-77090-884-0 (PDF);
ISBN 978-1-77090-885-7 (ePub)

I. Title.

PS8575.F48044 2016   C813'.6   C2016-902323-0
C2016-902324-9

Editor for the press: Jen Knoch
Cover design: Scott Barrie | Cyanotype
Cover images: front, top photo © Tedd Church/
Montreal Gazette, falling man © Kamenetskiy
Konstantin/Shutterstock, bridge © Michel
Piccaya/Shutterstock; back, man with pistol
© Baibulsinov Serik/Shutterstock
Author photo: Jimmy McFetridge
Printed and bound in Canada
by Friesens   5   4   3   2   1

The publication of *One or the Other* has been generously supported by the Canada Council for the
Arts which last year invested $153 million to bring the arts to Canadians throughout the country,
and by the Government of Canada through the Canada Book Fund. *Nous remercions le Conseil des
arts du Canada de son soutien. L'an dernier, le Conseil a investi 153 millions de dollars pour mettre
de l'art dans la vie des Canadiennes et des Canadiens de tout le pays. Ce livre est financé en partie
par le gouvernement du Canada.* We also acknowledge the Ontario Arts Council (OAC), an agency
of the Government of Ontario, which last year funded 1,709 individual artists and 1,078 organiza-
tions in 204 communities across Ontario, for a total of $52.1 million, and the contribution of the
Government of Ontario through the Ontario Book Publishing Tax Credit and the Ontario Media
Development Corporation.

For Laurie, always.

"Save your neck,
Or save your brother,
Looks like it's
One or the other."

The Band, "The Shape I'm In"

CHAPTER
ONE

Montreal, March 1976.

Standing in line at the bank, middle of the afternoon, Constable Eddie Dougherty was thinking that
he couldn't keep waiting for a full-time promotion
to detective and pretty soon he'd have to propose to
Judy McIntyre anyway — they couldn't stay in limbo
forever.

Two men came into the bank then, both of them
wearing overcoats and red, white and blue Montreal
Canadiens tuques, sunglasses and fake moustaches, and
Dougherty was staring down the barrel of a sawed-off
shotgun. The guy holding it said, "Don't move," and
Dougherty said, "I'm not going anywhere, I have to
cash my cheque."

For once he was glad he wasn't wearing his uniform — that would've changed everything.

The two guys in overcoats and tuques waved their guns around and told everybody in the place not to move. One of them stood by the door, looking at his watch, and the other one went along the line of tellers, holding out a BOAC flight bag for the cash.

Dougherty was pretty sure the guy by the door looking at his watch was Pete McCallum so he figured he was out of jail and back in town, not gone to Toronto after all.

Then Dougherty was thinking if McCallum recognized him that would *really* change everything but when McCallum looked up from his watch he said, "All right, let's go," and Dougherty saw the other guy turn around and head for the door even though he still had one more teller to collect from.

As he rushed past Dougherty, the guy with the BOAC bag looked at him a second too long and bumped into another man in line, dropping the bag. When he reached down to pick it up, the other man started to move like he was going to throw a punch, but Dougherty held up his hand and said, "Don't."

The guy in the overcoat grabbed the bag off the floor and ran out of the bank with McCallum right behind him. The whole thing had taken less than two minutes.

The man in line said, "I could've grabbed him."

Dougherty was running out onto St. Catherine Street then and he turned and called, "Hold my place, that last teller can still cash a cheque."

On the street, a cop car was already pulling up, the

doors opening and two cops jumping out.

Dougherty pointed across the street and said, "They went into Eaton's, overcoats and Habs tuques," and led the way through the department store's doors.

The place was crowded, everybody wearing some kind of overcoat or winter coat. The woman at the perfume counter said, "They went down the stairs, Officer," and Dougherty wondered for a second how she knew he was a cop.

At the top of the stairs, Dougherty moved aside and let the two uniform cops run ahead. He knew they wouldn't catch anybody now. McCallum and the other guy were probably in the Métro by then, probably already caught a train and were long gone. The whole thing seemed well planned and timed and it certainly wasn't their first rodeo.

Then, as Dougherty was walking back out through the main floor of the department store, he saw someone else he knew and said, "Hey, Rod, how you doing?"

An older guy, mid-fifties, turned around looking angry and then softened into a smile and said, "Eddie, man, hey."

Dougherty took him by the arm and pulled him out of the aisle towards a display of new summer dresses, saying, "What've you got in the bag, Rod?"

"Come on, Eddie, you think I'm a shoplifter?"

"No, Rod, I think you're a lookout for a couple of bank robbers." Dougherty had the bag opened and he said, "Shit, you were going to drop these on the stairs. You could've really hurt somebody."

"I don't know what you're talking about."

"Who was it with Pete?"

"Like I'd ever tell you."

"You guys working together, like old times. When did Pete get out?"

"Let go of me, man. I didn't do anything wrong."

Dougherty said, "You can come with me, Rod, or I'll ask that nice lady for a twenty-five-dollar bottle of perfume and I'll put it in your bag and arrest you."

"You're a prick, Eddie, you know that?"

The woman from the perfume counter was walking towards them then and said, "Is there anything I can do?"

"Call the manager," Rod said. "This guy won't let me go."

"Everything's under control, thanks," Dougherty said. He pulled Rod towards the doors and looked back for a moment and thought, Yeah, better propose to Judy soon.

———

Judy said, "I can't believe there was another riot."

"It was a bunch of high school teachers," Dougherty said. "They threw some chairs on the stage, it wasn't a riot."

"You mean the riot squad wasn't called this time."

Dougherty finished his coffee and looked at his watch. "We heard you're going to sue us over the last one, last week, when the riot squad did get called."

"I haven't been hired — I'm not one of *them* yet."

"You will be."

Judy looked doubtful. "With all this going on, the last thing the school board is going to do is hire new teachers."

"They're going to have to, can't have schools with no teachers."

"Are they really going to sue the police?"

The waiter came to the table with the coffee pot and filled their cups and said, "Will there be anything else?"

Dougherty looked at Judy and she said, "No, thanks."

"Just the bill."

They were in the Coffee Mill, a small Hungarian place on Mountain, a couple of blocks from the apartment Judy was sharing with a few other students while she finished up her teaching degree. Neither Judy nor Dougherty had brought up what would happen to their living arrangements when she graduated. For a second Dougherty thought maybe he should say it casually, like it just occurred to him: Hey, what do you say we get married?

Judy said, "I heard someone got beaten up at the meeting last night, taken to the hospital?"

"One of the teachers, union guy, the head of it."

"Don Peacock, is he okay?"

"Yeah," Dougherty said, "the meeting was at Wager so they took him to the Jewish General. He's all right, maybe a mild heart attack."

"Well, I doubt it'll be his last one."

"Looks like it could be a long strike," Dougherty said. "No one's giving in."

"And now the nurses, too."

The waiter put the bill down beside Dougherty's elbow on the table and slipped away. They were the only customers in the place, three o'clock in the afternoon, getting together before Dougherty started his shift.

"Those were my mother's only two career choices," Judy said, "nurse or teacher."

"Is that why you resisted teaching for so long?"

"Maybe."

Dougherty got out his wallet and was thinking that for all her anti-establishment hippie years, Judy would probably want a real wedding and a real engagement with a ring and everything.

Or maybe that's what he wanted, he wasn't so sure now.

"You know you're going to be a great teacher."

"You think so?"

"You're going to be every boy's favourite, for sure."

"I don't know, I'm worried about it."

Dougherty stood up and dropped some cash on top of the bill. "You worry about everything, it'll be fine."

Outside on Mountain a few students walked by, and Dougherty thought how young they looked even though he and Judy had only a few years on them.

She said, "Will you be okay to make Sunday dinner at my parents'? What'll it be for you, breakfast?"

"I'll be fine."

"Get ready for my father to lecture us about the evils of unions."

She took his arm as they walked and it felt good to Dougherty. He was ready, and he was pretty sure Judy was, too.

Give them something else to talk about at dinner.

CHAPTER TWO

The assistant director of the Montreal Police, the man in charge of all detectives, Paul-Emile Olivier, looked over his big desk at Dougherty and then back to the file he was reading and said, "Detective Carpentier tells me you have been very helpful in a number of homicide investigations."

Dougherty said, "Yes, sir."

Olivier was speaking more formal French than Dougherty was used to with the cops and crooks he spent most of his time with but, then, Olivier was wearing a much nicer suit than Dougherty was used to seeing and the office they were sitting in was much bigger and better appointed than any Dougherty had ever seen in a police station. He was starting to understand

7

that at this level the cops liked to pretend they were businessmen or bankers, that they'd always spent time in offices and behind desks and didn't work their way up rolling in the dirt with drunks and bloodying their knuckles on criminals.

"Though you have never been officially assigned to the homicide squad."

"That's right, sir."

Olivier smiled for a moment and it looked like it was part of his duty, like he was following an instruction, and then he said, "*Un vrai joueur d'équipe.*"

Dougherty'd never heard anyone use the expression that way in French, a good team player, and it sounded funny, but he just nodded.

"You have been with us eight years now."

"Yes, sir."

"And you are currently assigned to Station Ten."

"Yes," Dougherty said. "I've been an acting detective-constable a few times."

"Would be nice to make the rank permanent, wouldn't it, Dougherty?" Olivier said slowly, pronouncing it clearly, Doe-er-dee. Then he looked at the file on his desk again and said, "Captain Boisjoli is not displeased with your work."

Dougherty almost said he should be bloody well pleased with my work, the amount of times I saved his ass, but he was learning to keep his mouth shut.

"*Bon.*" Olivier closed the file and then said, in English, "I'm glad we had this little chat."

Dougherty was taken by surprise, the interview, or whatever it was, ending so abruptly but he stood up and held out his hand. The two men shook and

Dougherty said, "*Je vous remercie . . .* sir."

Three floors down, Dougherty walked into the evidence room and saw Rozovsky looking over a spread of eight-by-ten black-and-white pictures and said, "Was that your picture in the *Gazette*, Olympic Stadium going up, looked like an open hand, a bunch of fingers?"

Rozovsky didn't look up. "The story said the workers were not under any great pressure to get it finished in time." Then he looked up at Dougherty and said, "Well, except for the four guys who fell off and died last week, they might have been under some pressure."

"Games don't start till July, right," Dougherty said. "We still have four months."

Rozovsky held up a picture and said, "Do you know her?"

"Is that at the Limelight?"

"She was talking to Colucci; Ste. Marie wants to know who she is."

Dougherty said, "She looks twelve years old."

"You've never seen her in a raid? She could work upscale."

"Since when do we raid upscale brothels?"

Rozovsky leaned back in his chair and said, "Bad meeting? Were you talking to Carpentier?"

"Olivier."

"Shit, you getting fired?"

"I thought it was about a promotion."

Rozovsky shrugged. "That would be better."

"I can't read that guy, though. And at the end he said something in English with the weirdest accent."

"His generation, when they get high enough up in the force they talk like they went to Selwyn House."

"What's that?"

"A private school, like Loyola but for rich Protestants."

"Is there one for rich Jews?"

"Of course."

Dougherty said, "I guess I better get back to work," but as soon as he stepped into the hall he was almost knocked over. "What's going on?"

"Un gros vol, un camion de la Brink's."

"Where?"

Rozovsky was already coming out of the office with two cameras strung around his neck saying, "You have a car?"

"Across the street."

Cops were filing out of the building onto Bonsecours Street, and Dougherty ran to the patrol car he'd driven to his meeting with Olivier. He swung the car onto the street and Rozovsky jumped into the passenger seat, saying, "Royal Bank building on St. James."

Dougherty cut through the heart of Old Montreal on Notre Dame, popping the siren even though no one moved out of the way, the narrow street crowded with cars and delivery trucks, and even a horse pulling a *calèche* ignored the siren.

Rozovsky said, "There," already taking pictures from inside the car, getting shots of other police cars and the crowd starting to gather.

Dougherty got out of the car and said, "Where's the truck?"

A uniform cop standing at the mouth of the lane

between two big old buildings said, "They took it."

"They took the whole truck?"

There was a half-ton moving truck parked at the other end of the lane so all the cops were coming in from St. James.

The cop said, "Those guys went back inside the bank for the last load," he pointed at three Brink's guards standing a few feet down the lane by the side door of the bank, "and when they came out it was gone."

"So maybe it's a joke, the driver went around the block."

"These guys don't joke."

Dougherty looked at the three guards and figured that was true, they didn't look like they'd ever told a joke in their lives. It didn't look like someday this would be a funny story for them. He walked back to his patrol car, where Rozovsky was standing, aiming his camera at the sky. Dougherty said, "What are you doing?"

"I never really saw it from this angle. Look at those columns."

"Yeah, nice."

"Neoclassical," Rozovsky said. "When was this built? Must be twenty storeys."

Dougherty said, "No idea."

"Had to be before the Depression." Rozovsky looked at the buildings lining James Street and said, "All these places haven't changed in decades."

Dougherty said, "Yeah," feeling useless, no idea what to do, and then the dispatch came on the radio saying the Brink's truck had been found, and Dougherty said, "Let's go," jumping into the car and hitting the gas as Rozovsky got in.

"Where?"

"Nun's Island."

Dougherty drove fast, swerving through traffic on the Bonaventure Expressway and heading towards the Champlain Bridge. Dispatch had a couple of updates, saying the truck was near the tennis courts.

Dougherty said, "You know where that is?"

"Yeah, there's a traffic circle. Take the first exit."

Dougherty screeched around the traffic circle, took the exit and said, "I don't see any tennis courts."

"They're in there."

They drove around a big low concrete building and just past the parking lot was an empty field and then the river.

The Brink's truck, the back doors wide open, was sitting there.

"Why would he drive it out here?"

Rozovsky said, "Maybe that had something to do with it," and he was out of the car, aiming his camera at a white van behind the Brink's truck.

The back doors of the van were open, and inside was a big gun on a tripod. Rozovsky had a dozen photos before Dougherty caught up to him.

"What is it?"

Dougherty said, "Anti-aircraft gun."

"Would those bullets have gone through the truck?"

"Armour-piercing, oh yeah."

Dougherty looked in the front of the Brink's truck and saw the radio was smashed. He walked back towards the other cop cars and saw a guy in a Brink's uniform smoking a cigarette and talking to one of the younger cops. The Brink's driver looked to be in his thirties and one of the lenses of his glasses was broken. His eye was banged up, looked like he took a pretty good shot, and there were handcuffs dangling from one wrist.

The young cop said, "*Eille, Dougherty, ici Gilles Lachapelle le driver du truck.*"

Lachapelle spoke French, saying, "You guys got here fast."

"Yeah, you okay?"

Lachapelle touched the tips of his fingers to the spot just above his eye and said, "Like a high stick. I've had worse." He smiled a little.

Dougherty said, "Did they tape you?"

"Yeah." He rubbed his cheek where there was still a little tape and stringy bits stuck to his five o'clock shadow. "My mouth. And they taped my legs. They put me in the back of my truck."

"But you got away."

He held up his wrist with the handcuff still attached and said, "They didn't close them right, the other end."

"How many were there?"

"I don't know," Lachapelle said. "I only saw one, he was wearing sunglasses. The van backed into the lane, and one guy got out of it and came around the side. I honked at him and he opened the back doors, showed me that fucking thing." He motioning towards the white van where Rozovsky was still taking pictures.

"There must've been another guy," Dougherty said, "in the back with the gun."

Lachapelle looked surprised for a split-second but then it was gone and he said, "Yeah, that's right, he was wearing sunglasses, too, and a tuque."

"What colour?"

Lachapelle smiled a little and said, "*Bleu, blanc, rouge. Les Canadiens.*"

"Then what happened?"

"He told me to open the door, so I did, and he shoved me down and got into my truck. He drove it here."

"Did he speak French or English?"

"English."

Dougherty said, "You're lucky they didn't shoot you."

Lachapelle looked serious and said, "They would have."

"For sure." Dougherty saw the ambulance pull into the parking lot, so he started to walk away, then stopped and said, "Hey, there was a half-ton in the lane, too. What was that doing there?"

Lachapelle said, "Must have been so no one else could have come in. That lane is pretty narrow."

Dougherty said, "Yeah, I guess," and walked away as the two ambulance guys got to Lachapelle.

More cars were pulling into the lot then, detectives and a few reporters. Dougherty saw Detective Carpentier and walked over to him.

"C'est arrivé très vite."

Carpentier spoke French, saying, "The guards hit the alarm at two forty and this guy called it in fourteen minutes later."

"He says he was handcuffed in the back of the van

and his legs were taped. And his mouth. Didn't take him long to get out."

"Didn't matter," Carpentier said. "They were long gone."

Detective Ste. Marie walked past Dougherty and Carpentier and said, "You sure you want to work homicide, look at all the excitement in CID."

"If you need any help," Dougherty said.

Ste. Marie said, "I'll let you know," without slowing down on his way to talk to Lachapelle.

"Do you know how much they got?" Carpentier said.

"No."

"Between two and a half and three million dollars."

"Not bad for fourteen minutes' work."

"That kind of money all of a sudden floating around in town," Carpentier said. "There's going to be some homicides to work."

"Well, you know me," Dougherty said, "*un vrai gars d'équipe.*"

Carpentier laughed and said, "You've been talking to Olivier, that's good."

"I've been talking," Dougherty said. "He didn't say anything."

"Now he knows who you are, that's good." Carpentier was looking at Ste. Marie talking to Lachapelle and said, "You believe him?"

"I believe what he says happened."

"But you think he knows more?"

"I asked him about the other truck in the lane, he said it was probably there so no one else could get in from that direction."

"Makes sense."

"Yeah," Dougherty said, "it's the kind of thing you think about when you're planning a robbery."

"He say anything else?"

"He said the guy spoke English."

"You believe that?"

"Why not? There are plenty of English guys robbing banks in Montreal."

"Yes," Carpentier said. "But it is going to send them in one direction."

"Maybe the right one."

"Maybe."

Dougherty said, "Well, we'll see soon enough who has a lot of money on the street."

"Yes," Carpentier said. "And there will be homicides for you to work. I'll put in another word with Inspecteur Olivier."

Dougherty said, "Thanks."

He didn't care if he was assigned to homicide, he just wanted to get out of uniform and be a full-time detective. He was feeling the door closing.

And then all he got was another acting-detective job.

Someone decided that the Brink's job could only have been pulled off by professionals from out of town, probably Boston, and if they had any local help it was some of Dougherty's old friends, the Point Boys.

Still, acting-detective — better than nothing.

CHAPTER
THREE

Ten o'clock in the morning, Dougherty was standing at the back of the room, what they were calling room 4.07 after the meeting room in the courthouse where the cops and lawyers got together to prep witnesses, but this room was in a private club on St. James, donated by someone high up in the Royal Bank just a couple of blocks away.

Up at the front, Ste. Marie was saying that he believed the Brink's job was pulled off by *"Des professionnels de l'extérieur de la ville,"* and Dougherty was thinking that was exactly what they'd said about the FLQ six years earlier, that all the bombs and armed robberies were done by professionals brought in from out of town.

This time at least Ste. Marie added that, "Probably they were working with a local gang."

Dougherty was among about a dozen cops crammed into the room. He didn't have all the details, but he understood he'd been assigned to a special squad of detectives, and he recognized most of them as guys who'd worked out of Station Ten or somewhere else on the west side of downtown. They were all older than Dougherty except for one, Paquette, and it was hard to tell about him with his longer hair and moustache and how comfortable he looked sitting on the edge of the table in his leisure suit as if he'd never worn a uniform.

Then Ste. Marie introduced the man who would be running the special squad, "Detective-Sergeant Marc-André Laperrière from the Bureau des enquêtes criminelles."

Laperrière said, "*Merci, Robert. Bonjour, les gars, bienvenue au* big time."

There was appreciative grumbling in the room, all the detectives glad to be part of it, but Dougherty was wondering how the team was put together.

Laperrière went on to say that because this was now the biggest robbery in North America they weren't taking any chances. "At this stage we believe the local involvement was from the Point Boys and west end criminals," which Dougherty figured was his way of saying Anglos and then the make-up of the room started to make more sense. These were probably all the English detectives left on the force and whatever French guys had worked English neighbourhoods.

"This robbery was very professional," Laperrière said. "It was timed to the second and perfectly carried out. The last time a Brink's truck was robbed like this was in Boston and we know of the connection between the Point Boys and criminals in that city."

Dougherty was thinking, Well, we know they're all Irish but that's not much of a connection. Then he was trying to remember when the Boston robbery happened, and Detective Levine said, "Boston was over twenty-five years ago."

Laperrière looked around the room to see who'd spoken and then said, "Yes, it was." It was quiet for a few seconds and then he went back to speaking French, saying, "It is also possible that there may have been help from inside the bank or even from Brink's." He paused again and looked around the room and then said, "They may even have had help from someone on the police force. For these reasons this squad will meet only in this room, we will use code names on the radio, and only use the radio if absolutely necessary."

Dougherty was hoping they weren't basing all this on the driver of the truck saying the guy spoke English to him and the fact there was also a Brink's robbery years ago in Boston. It could've just as easily been the Dubois brothers or Italians or someone they didn't even know about yet.

"Now," Laperrière said, "what we have so far. This was the seventh drop-off and pickup of the day. The guards loaded ninety-two zippered and tagged leather bags full of cash, bonds and Olympic coins. The gun in the back of the van, the anti-aircraft gun is," he glanced down at his notes for the first time and read, in English, "an air-cooled Browning M2 .50 calibre machine gun with a forty-five-inch barrel mounted on a tripod and a bandolier of three hundred rounds of armour-piercing cartridges. U.S. army-issue weapon."

One of the detectives said, "*Ça marche?*"

"It's being tested," Laperrière said. "But it certainly looks like it does. We're checking to see where it came from." He glanced at his notes again. "The driver, Lachapelle, was in the army in Korea, that's how he knew the gun and knew it could pierce the armour of the Brink's truck."

Dougherty figured that was awfully convenient and expected one of the detectives to say something, but no one did.

Laperrière said, "The van, the white Econoline, was stolen on February 18th in the north end and the licence plate was stolen March 11th. And that's about all we have. Now, you're going to partner up and get assignments. Any questions?"

There weren't any, at least no one asked any, and then Ste. Marie paired them up, calling two names at a time. Dougherty was thinking he might be teamed with Paquette, keep the young guys together, but heard, "*Caron avec Dog-eh-dee,*" and saw an older detective step towards him, holding out his hand.

"I heard you were in the bank that was held up yesterday?"

They shook hands and Dougherty said, "Day before, yeah, on St. Catherine."

"You know me? I'm Denis Caron."

Dougherty said, "Yeah, of course." He was surprised Caron was speaking English, with almost no accent, but that seemed to be this assignment. "You were on the hold-up squad."

"Until I started working exclusively fraud," Caron said. "I guess that's why I'm on this, the bankers know me. Did you recognize the guys in the bank?"

"Pete McCallum was one of them," Dougherty said. "And Rod Kieran was in Eaton's."

"He have his bag of marbles?"

"Yeah."

Caron shook his head, and Dougherty thought he even smiled a little. "Didn't waste any time."

"I heard McCallum was going to Toronto."

"Let's hope this was his stake and he's gone now."

"Yeah, let's hope."

"So," Caron said, looking around the wood-panelled room, "this is going to be interesting."

"Not much to go on."

"We'll shake the trees, something will fall out."

"When are we going to start?"

"Tonight, I think," Caron said. "Probably Peg's, you know it?"

"Sure," Dougherty said, "motel on Upper Lachine Road, no, St. Jacques."

"Have you ever stayed there?"

"Does anyone stay there?"

"Not for more than an hour."

"What are we going to do there?"

"Look around, see if we can find two and a half million dollars."

———

Judy said, "So this could be a good opportunity?"

"For the guys who got the two and a half million bucks it is," Dougherty said.

They were having dinner at a little Portuguese place on St. Urbain, around the corner from Judy's apartment. She poured the last of the red wine into her glass and said, "And it could be for you."

"Yeah," he said. "I guess."

"Not very enthusiastic."

He was thinking that there'd been a lot of these opportunities in the almost ten years since he'd joined the force but none of them ever panned out, why should this one, but he just said, "It's going to be a lot of work, I think."

"Overtime?"

"I don't know. I'm not sure how it's going to be run. They're vague on the details right now."

"This is the biggest armed robbery in North America," Judy said. *"Le crime du siècle."*

"And we've got nothing."

"But you're on the special squad."

"Yeah," Dougherty said. "They've decided it was the Point Boys, and it might be, some of them may be in on it, so they got all the Anglo cops they could."

"How many is that?"

"Under a hundred years old? Me and Levine. And he hasn't been out of the office in ten years."

"Anglos don't join the police anymore?"

"And some guys they're calling bilingual."

"What are you going to do?"

"Knock down some doors, I guess. See who all of a sudden has a lot of extra cash."

"Well," Judy said, "it's close to what you want, it's detective work."

"Another temporary assignment."

She leaned back and smiled at him a little and said, "Yeah, but you like it."

And she kept looking at him until he smiled a little and said, "Yeah, I do, so what?"

"Nothing. It's just," she paused and took a drink of her wine, "I never thought it would make me happy to see a policeman happy about his work."

"Well, this isn't beating up protesters, this isn't bashing hippies," Dougherty said, winking. "This is real bad guys."

Judy said, "Yes." She was still smiling a little, and Dougherty figured she was thinking about her protest days, seemed so long ago now but was really just a few years.

Then he said, "Speaking of opportunities," and let it hang for a moment and then Judy said, "I still haven't heard from the PSBGM."

"So, one of these days you're going to have to apply to the other school boards. South shore, West Island."

"There is no way I'm teaching at the high school I went to," Judy said. "This isn't some *Welcome Back, Kotter* thing, it's not going to happen." She took a drink of wine and said, "Three blocks from my parents' house? No way."

"Those West Island schools are good."

"I'm not going to teach a bunch of suburban kids who don't care about anything I've got to say."

23

Dougherty said, "Okay," and then didn't say anything. He didn't see any point in going over it again, having another fight about Judy wanting to teach in the Point or Little Burgundy, how those kids wouldn't care about anything she had to say, either. He still found it so strange, his own parents had done such a good thing getting out of the Point so his sister and little brother could go to a decent high school.

Then she surprised him and said, "I might apply to the south shore board."

"But you don't want to teach suburban kids."

She shrugged a little, and Dougherty shook his head and said, "Don't tell me you think Greenfield Park is underprivileged?"

"There are parts, those row houses — what did you call them, the terraces? Other parts of the south shore."

Dougherty was laughing now and he said, "Maybe that school in Châteauguay, gets the kids from Caughnawaga. You want to teach on a reserve?"

"I don't know."

He took the last bite of his barbecue chicken and said, "You want some dessert? Cheesecake, maybe?"

"Let's go for a walk, maybe get something later."

"I'm on tonight, we're meeting at nine."

"You see," Judy said, "you're moving up already."

Dougherty said, "Yeah," and he was hoping that was true. Then he said, "Look at you, you like it."

"Don't tell anyone." She leaned in closer and said, "Come on by when you're finished, if it's not too late."

They were smiling at each other, playful, and Dougherty said, "Okay."

By the time he had finished it was way too late.

───

They didn't find two and a half million dollars, but they did find seven revolvers, four sawed-off shotguns, dozens of boxes of ammunition, canvas money bags from the Canadian Imperial Bank of Commerce and the Bank of Montreal, stolen American Express traveller's cheques, blank Quebec driver's permits and a pound of hashish — all in room fourteen.

In the restaurant beside the motel office, Peg O'Reilly told Laperrière she had no idea where any of that stuff came from. "Room fourteen hasn't been rented out in months."

There were three customers in the restaurant at one in the morning when the cops had shown up, and they were still there, sitting at a table drinking coffee with Peg.

Laperrière said, "We're going to keep coming back."

"Could you at least pay for a cup of coffee then," Peg said.

Dougherty was standing by the door to the motel office. He recognized the three guys at the table: one was a Higgins brother, an older one, and Peaky Boyle was beside him, shaking his head with his usual half-annoyed, half-don't-give-a-shit look, and Big Jim Sadowski sat there scowling, looking like he wanted to get into a fight with all eight cops.

Even Peg looked like she wouldn't mind if it turned into a brawl. Dougherty knew her a little from the times he'd come into the motel on the job, but he'd also seen her when he was a kid in the Point. He remembered some ceremony at the Boys and Girls Club where she'd given them a cheque for football equipment.

Laperrière said, "You have no idea what you've done." He was looking at the guys at the table, not the Higgins brother but Boyle, and he said, "This isn't a fucking hold-up, this is big."

"Didn't you get your cut," Boyle said. "Is that the problem? Talk to whoever did it, you're wasting your time here."

Dougherty watched Boyle, trying to see if his casual act was cracking, but he couldn't tell. The guy was, as far as anyone knew, the top boss of the Point Boys. They weren't like the Italians, they didn't have ceremonies and take oaths and give out ranks and Marlon Brando wasn't going to be in any movies about them, but everybody's got to answer to somebody and Dougherty was pretty sure the Point Boys answered to Peaky.

Laperrière said, "You fucked up, Petey. You brought more heat than you can handle."

Boyle just shrugged, and Dougherty looked from him to Laperrière and saw the cop clenching up, looking like he was the one going to snap.

The whole room was tense. It was their first move in the investigation; it was their statement.

Laperrière said, "This the way you want to do it, okay." He turned his head a little and looked at Ste. Marie, and Ste. Marie motioned to Caron.

It took Dougherty a second to realize that was his signal, and when he did he took a last look at Boyle and Higgins and Sadowski and then turned and walked through the motel office to the parking lot.

Two in the morning, and it was quiet, no traffic on St. Jacques, the other motels along the street pretty much empty. Dougherty walked to the car and leaned against it and lit a cigarette. He could see the big buildings downtown all lit up, Place Victoria, the CIBC tower and Place Ville Marie, and the streetlights along the slopes of Mount Royal like a skirt spreading down to the river and the suburbs on the other side.

A couple hundred feet south of St. Jacques was the huge drop down to the expressway below, the 2-20 and the train yards and the Lachine Canal.

"Hey, Eddie, right?"

Dougherty said, "Yeah," and realized he didn't know Paquette's first name.

"Like old friends in there."

Paquette stepped beside Dougherty and leaned back against the car.

"Known each other a long time," Dougherty said. "Came up through the ranks together."

"Different than the guys we see, eh?"

Dougherty wasn't sure what he meant by that but he saw Paquette looking like it was some kind of inside joke and didn't want to be on the outside so he said, "For sure."

Paquette took a drag on his cigarette and blew smoke at the stars and said, "This should be interesting, this secret squad."

"Yeah."

"You been here before?"

"Peg's?" Dougherty said. "Yeah." It was a two-storey building in a horseshoe shape, every room with a view of the pool in the middle. At one time a nice place, not one of those motels thrown up for Expo 67, it was probably built in the '50s, before the expressways when St. Jacques was called Upper Lachine Road or before that when it was Western and it was the road into Montreal from Ottawa and Toronto, but it had faded in recent years and now the restaurant got the most use.

Room fourteen, where they'd found the guns and hash and bank bags, was at the end of the horseshoe on the ground floor. According to Peg the room hadn't been rented out since last fall, five months ago. She had no idea, of course, who could have been using it.

"I knew a couple of the Higgins brothers," Dougherty said. "From the Point."

"That where you're from?"

"Yeah."

"That could help you with this," Paquette said. He took another drag on his smoke and flipped the butt into the parking lot.

Dougherty said, "*If* they did it," and tried to sneak a look at Paquette's reaction.

"Who else could it be?"

"We're probably going there next," Dougherty said, motioning back a little.

Paquette didn't know what he meant, so Dougherty said, "Nittolo's, you ever been there? The Italians."

"No, I haven't worked the west end," Paquette said. His English was good and he didn't seem to have a problem using it with Dougherty even though they were the same rank and probably the same age.

Dougherty said, "You ever work St. Leonard?"

"A little, not much."

"It's the same guys," Dougherty said. "They have the motel and restaurant, Nittolo's, and the garden centre, they do a lot of landscaping and snow removal in the winter, around here and Westmount."

Paquette said, "Nice," but he didn't seem too interested.

"Are you working the hold-up squad now?"

"Yeah, for a couple of months."

Dougherty wanted to ask what he'd been doing before that, how he got to be a detective, but he felt stupid just making conversation, and as the silence dragged on, he realized he was worried Paquette was competition and he didn't like feeling that way.

The senior detectives came out of Peg's office then, and Paquette said, "I wonder what they said to them?" He wasn't expecting an answer, and Dougherty didn't say anything.

They walked across the parking lot and, as they got closer, Dougherty heard Laperrière say, "Run a line on the pay phone."

Ste. Marie said, "You want to start someone on the paperwork?" He nodded a little and Dougherty thought he should step forward and volunteer, but then he realized Ste. Marie meant Paquette.

Laperrière said, "Off the books for now. Okay, let's go."

Caron started around the car, saying to Dougherty, "You know Motel Raphaël?"

Dougherty got in the car and waited while Caron said something to Ste. Marie and then he got in, too, saying, "You know those guys?" looking back at Peg's.

"I know Higgins a little," Dougherty said.

He pulled out onto St. Jacques at the back end of the convoy of unmarked cars.

"The more pressure we put on them," Caron said, "someone's going to want to talk, save his own ass, maybe make a little money — we have some to spend."

"Snitch money?"

"A little more," Caron said. "The bank is going to give us some cash."

Dougherty nodded. "That's good."

"You got any guys you want to talk to?"

"Maybe," Dougherty said.

No one at Motel Raphaël had anything to say, and then Laperrière decided that was enough for the first night, they'd hit Nittolo's and the Cavalier the next day.

Dougherty went home, thinking that somehow he'd lost his spot in the starting lineup.

———

The old man working the night desk at the Cavalier Motel had never heard of any Brink's truck robbery or any bank robberies. They searched all rooms, two floors' worth, and didn't find anything except used rubbers under every bed.

Caron said, "Don't they clean these rooms?"

"In and out," Dougherty said.

Same thing at the West-End Motel and the Belvedere.

Ste. Marie looked at his watch and said, "*Bon, c'est le temps des visites à domicile.*"

In the car Caron was singing, "We've got us a great big convoy, rocking through the night," as the half-dozen cop cars pulled out onto St. Jacques and headed up Cavendish towards Sherbrooke. "We got us a great big convoy, ain't she a beautiful sight."

Dougherty said, "You the rubber duck?"

Caron laughed, "What's your 10-4, Pig Pen?"

Ten minutes later they passed the campus of Loyola

College, now part of Concordia University, and Dougherty wondered if they had evening classes out here in the suburbs like the downtown campus in the old Y building, but he doubted it, not out here with the big lawn and trees and sports fields, trying to look like a real university. Just past Monsieur Hot Dog, the convoy turned into Montreal West and the streets were lined with old red-brick houses, each one with a big tree on the front lawn.

The convoy took up half the block on Percival Street.

Ste. Marie walked to the house and knocked, and a few minutes later a woman opened the door.

Dougherty was surprised the woman was dressed this time of night, wearing tight jeans and a loose blouse, and she stood her ground, saying, "You can't come in."

Ste. Marie pushed past her and said, "Is your husband home?"

The rest of the cops followed Ste. Marie into the house.

Dougherty was the last one in, and he noticed Paquette was near the front, right behind Ste. Marie.

Ste. Marie said, "We have a warrant," and held out a piece of paper.

"That's bullshit. My kids are asleep."

Ste. Marie handed out orders to search the house. Paquette and some of the senior guys got the bedrooms upstairs, a couple other guys were given the kitchen and living room on the main floor, and Dougherty and Caron were told to search the basement.

The woman was in the kitchen then, the phone

receiver in her hand and she was dialling, saying, "If you go in the kids' rooms, we'll sue you."

On the way down the stairs Dougherty said, "At least we don't have to wait in the yard."

The basement had a shag carpet and knotty pine walls and there was a built-in bar in the corner. Lots of framed photos: Montreal Canadiens players, all autographed; fat men and skinny women on beaches and on big boats; black-and-white street scenes of Point St. Charles. Dougherty was thinking, Shit, the Point's only a few minutes away down the hill, what's he need the pictures for, and then he figured it was to remind himself about the mean streets he came from now that he had a respectable house in a respectable neighbourhood.

Caron said, "Maybe there's a safe behind one of these."

"Yeah, and the combination is his birthday."

Caron was behind the bar then and he said, "*Bon, j'ai trouvé.*" He had a bottle of Canadian Club in his hand and was getting two shot glasses from the shelf behind the bar.

Dougherty leaned on the bar and accepted the drink.

Caron reached into his pocket, took a pack of smokes and offered one to Dougherty, saying, "Can you believe it, a buck now."

Dougherty lit his cigarette and inhaled deeply. "It's tax for the Olympics, right?"

"Ten cents a pack," Caron said. "I'm going to quit."

Dougherty said, "Sure you are."

Caron looked at him, serious for a second, and then shook his head. "God damned taxes."

"Hey, we'll get plenty of overtime during the Olympics."

"Like this," Caron said, waving his smoke around. "Chasing our dicks."

"We might get lucky."

Caron walked out from behind the bar and said, "Oh sure, maybe." He looked at some of the pictures on the walls, stopped at one of the Point, a bunch of kids in bathing suits in front of a walk-up, some guy spraying them with a hose. Still looking at the picture, Caron said, "Look at the happy kids."

Dougherty said, "Looks like the street I grew up on."

"You were neighbours."

"My parents moved out when I was in high school," Dougherty said. "Not up the hill, here, though, they bought one side of a duplex on the south shore."

"Brossard?"

"Greenfield Park."

"Oh *oui*, *les Anglais*." Caron looked at more pictures, more kids in the Point, and then he turned around and looked over the rec room and said, "How much you think this house cost?"

Dougherty said, "No idea."

"Seventy, eighty grand?"

"I think my parents paid twelve."

"Cross that bridge every day," Caron said. "No way."

"Drives my father crazy, sitting in traffic," Dougherty said. "It wasn't so bad when they bought the place."

Caron was back behind the bar refilling his shot glass. He looked around the room and said, "Maybe Boyle will move now, he's got even more money."

"Where's he going to go, Westmount?"

"Maybe Toronto."

"We can hope," Dougherty said.

Then he saw Caron looking at him like he was thinking about saying something but not sure, and Dougherty was thinking it was probably something about being an Anglo in Montreal, and Dougherty didn't have anything to say about that, so he looked away and reached across the bar for the Canadian Club and then the shouting started upstairs.

"The fuck you doing in my house!" And a door slammed and feet stomped.

Caron said, "The fun starting."

Dougherty headed up the stairs and by the time he squeezed his way into the living room behind the crowd of cops, Peaky Boyle was already in the kitchen, face to face with Ste. Marie, saying, "All of you, get the fuck out."

A kid was crying somewhere in the house, and Dougherty didn't see the woman in the tight jeans and loose blouse, but he did see Paquette coming down the stairs with a small suitcase in his hands.

"*On y va.*"

Ste. Marie took the suitcase and put it on the kitchen table, open, so everyone could see the money inside, about a dozen packs of bills still with the paper wrapper around them. Then he spoke English, saying, "Well, lookee here."

Boyle said, "My lawyer's on his way."

"You'll need him," Ste. Marie said, "when we find out this came from a Brink's truck."

"You won't."

Ste. Marie was putting the stacks of bills in a neat row, and he looked up at Boyle and said, "You don't think we will?"

"I know you won't, that's not where it came from."

"No?" Ste. Marie was staring now, moving a little closer, and the whole house tensed up, Dougherty could feel it way out at the outer ring of the circle of men. "Where did it come from?"

Boyle said, "I'm not telling you shit."

"You don't have to, but it will help you."

"Get out of my house."

"Come on," Ste. Marie said, "you didn't pull this job by yourself, why don't you get out in front of it?"

"You're fucking hilarious."

Dougherty could feel the tension going out of the room. Boyle wasn't going to say anything and he certainly wasn't going to name a single name. Dougherty knew they could take him down to the old River Road and beat on his thick skull and threaten to drop him in the rapids all they wanted, they were never going to break him.

The door opened behind Dougherty, and a guy came in, saying, "All right, all right, time to go."

Caron said, "Shrier the shyster, you just in the neighbourhood?"

The lawyer, Howard Shrier, pushed past Dougherty and Caron and made his way into the kitchen. "Party's over, let's go." He was wearing pyjamas under his overcoat.

Dougherty stepped out the front door, and Caron and a couple of other cops followed him. They stood on the lawn smoking cigarettes and waving to the

35

neighbours who turned on their lights, but no one came out of their houses.

Caron said, "At least we can leave an impression."

"I think the neighbours already know who lives here," Dougherty said.

"If they didn't, they do now."

A few minutes later, Ste. Marie and Laperrière came out of the house and the convoy headed back downtown.

As Dougherty was turning onto Sherbrooke, Caron pulled a bottle from under his coat and said, "Gin, right? That's what you Anglos drink, gin and tonic?"

Dougherty was pretty sure he'd seen a bottle of Jameson behind the bar, but he was getting tired of explaining the difference between English and Irish so he said, "Thanks."

Caron had a new bottle of Canadian Club for himself. "Don't mention it." He laughed then and said, "I mean, really, don't mention it."

Dougherty nodded, taking up the rear of the convoy.

CHAPTER FOUR

They were getting nowhere. Shaking down every English guy in town who'd ever been anywhere near a bank when it was robbed — and in Montreal that was a lot of guys — but none of them had anything from the Brink's job. Listening to hours of wiretaps from the pay phones at Molly McGuire's and the Country Palace and the Cock 'n' Bull and the Cat's Den Lounge and the Shack Club got them nothing but a lot of guys cheating on their wives and a lot of women cheating on their husbands.

Dougherty needed something to justify his being put on this team, in plainclothes, doing detective work. He could see Paquette and some other young guys passing him by, and he knew this was the best chance he'd ever get — a big job by English guys, guys from his old neighbourhood in the Point. If he didn't score something on this job, he'd be walking a beat the rest of his life.

Then he ran into Fred Bergman.

Driving home from the office, the 4.07 in the bank building, two in the morning in his own car, nothing on the wiretaps again, Dougherty pulled up behind a '75 Monte Carlo on the Bonaventure Expressway. Six lanes and almost no other cars. He followed the Monte Carlo past the Champlain Bridge and Nun's Island exit and up around the bend towards the Décarie, and when it took the Côte St. Luc Road exit Dougherty knew it was Bergman.

Cavendish was quiet, lined with apartment buildings and two-storey storefronts. When the Monte Carlo stopped at the red light at Cavendish, Dougherty pulled up beside it and rolled down the window of his Mustang.

It took Bergman a second, but then the power window lowered and he said, "What do you want, Constable?"

"Pull over."

Bergman shrugged and said, "I'm stopped." Then he looked more confused and said, "And you're not even on duty."

"Pull over." Dougherty pointed to the gas station and when the light changed Bergman cut diagonally through the intersection and stopped in front of the dark garage doors. He cut the engine but didn't make a move to get out of the car.

Dougherty pulled up beside the Monte Carlo and got out and walked back to the trunk. He knocked on it like he was knocking on a door.

Bergman got out of the car then and said, "You look like you want a gold chain. I have some beautiful pieces, just came in."

"I guess gold doesn't break falling off the truck."

"You want a TV," Bergman said, "I can get you one, Sony Trinitron, all solid state, fifteen-inch portable, five hundred bucks."

Dougherty said, "I can get it at Eaton's for five-fifty."

"Three hundred, then, but I don't make anything."

"I'm looking for bonds," Dougherty said. "And Olympic coins. And cash, about two million dollars."

Bergman laughed. He was a big man, had a big belly anyway, but he wasn't as tall as Dougherty. He said, "You think I look like a guy who has two million bucks, Constable?" Then he looked Dougherty up and down and said, "They make you a detective?"

Dougherty ignored that and said, "I think you're smart enough not to start throwing a lot of cash around. I think you'd lie low for a while, pretend like nothing changed for you, go about your business."

"How can I go about my business," Bergman said, "if I keep getting pulled over by the cops?" He put the key in the lock and opened the trunk. "Olympic rings, twenty-four carat." He held up a gold chain and a pendant, the five rings. "Or, you want to party?" The next gold chain had a tiny gold razor blade pendant.

Dougherty said, "I want to know about laundromats."

"I know a good one on Côte St. Luc Boulevard."

"Do they clean money?"

"Come on," Bergman said. He looked at Dougherty and said, "This is out of my league, something like this."

"It's out of everybody's league," Dougherty said. "But somebody did it. Who?"

Bergman shrugged. He had another box in his hand and he said, "What about a watch? Got some nice ones, Swiss."

Dougherty grabbed the box and said, "What about the gun?"

"What gun?" He looked at Dougherty and said, "The big gun from the robbery, what do you think I am?"

Dougherty tossed the box of watches back into the trunk and said, "I know what you are."

"Oy vey, you think I'm schlepping around anti-aircraft guns?"

"You could get one."

"I don't deal in guns, you know that."

Dougherty had heard the rumour that one of the reasons Bergman was left alone to do his business was because he didn't sell guns, but who could tell how hard and fast these unspoken rules were?

"Who does?"

"Look, you want to buy some chains, you want some earrings for your girlfriend, I can help you. Anything else . . ."

"You can get anything."

"No, I can't, really."

"You can find out."

He was looking sad, then, starting to get desperate. "Come on, Constable." Then he looked a little hopeful and said, "How about an engagement ring? Make an honest woman out of that girlfriend." He dug around in the trunk and then held out a ring box, blue like Birks but without the name. "It's a beautiful ring." He opened the box.

"Yeah, it's nice." But Dougherty was mostly struck that Bergman even knew he had a girlfriend. He said, "How did you know I'm not married?"

"Look at the diamond," Bergman said, "it's beautiful." Then he looked up at Dougherty and said, "Come on, Constable, you know me, I know you, we work the same areas."

Dougherty said, "Yeah." He was looking at the diamond ring and thinking the fact he wasn't married couldn't have anything to do with not getting the full-time promotion to detective, could it? He'd heard the term "family man" tossed around but never really thought about it.

"I can let you have it for five hundred bucks. That's a thousand-dollar ring."

Dougherty said, "I might give you two hundred if you tell me who bought the gun. And I might not arrest you."

"You fucking guys." Bergman leaned back against the bumper of his car and fumbled in his coat pocket for his smokes. He took his time lighting the cigarette and blowing smoke at the stars. "How long are you guys going to keep this up?"

"Till we get the money back."

Bergman let out a burst of smoke, almost choked and said, "Way I heard it, that money went straight from Nun's Island to Dorval and got on a plane."

"Where to?"

Bergman shrugged. "Vegas? I don't know. Bermuda?"

"Who was it?"

"For Chrissake, you know who it was, you're shaking them down every day."

"We need some kind of evidence," Dougherty said. "As long as we're looking it'll be bad for everybody."

"It's always bad," Bergman said. "But it's getting worse. These *fercockta* Olympics, they're getting to everybody."

"I might get some overtime."

"That's it exactly," Bergman said. "Everybody sees how much they're spending, they get greedy."

Dougherty said, "So they were a little early with the robbery."

Bergman took a drag and blew out smoke. He watched it rise to the night sky and said, "They're just planning. You know what they want it for."

"The money? They're thieves, they rob banks, it's what they do."

"I didn't think they had it in them, either," Bergman said. "Goyim from the Point." He looked at Dougherty and said, "Never seemed that ambitious to me."

"What are you talking about, Freddie?"

"Nothing, I don't know. You didn't get anything from me."

"I never do."

Bergman smirked at that and shrugged. "Three hundred and that engagement ring is yours. I can see you like it."

"What do you mean by ambitious?"

"We're going to host the biggest party in the world

in a couple of months," Bergman said. "The city will fill up like it did for Expo, more maybe."

"So."

"So," he waved his hands around, "so, so, so, everybody's going to be selling something."

"Yeah."

"They have to buy it first."

"What are you talking about?"

"I don't know, nothing." He paused and Dougherty waited for him because he had the feeling the guy was actually trying to tell him something. "Let's just say, maybe if you really want overtime this summer you should go into narcotics."

Dougherty said, "Shit." It made sense. "They're using the money for drugs."

Bergman shrugged like he didn't know a thing.

"Something big, though," Dougherty said. "Hash by the ton?"

Bergman made a point of looking in the trunk of his car, and Dougherty knew right away what he was getting at. "Coke."

Another shrug. "It's not my business."

The gold chain with the little gold razor blade pendant was still on top of the box Bergman had opened earlier.

"You're sure about this?"

"I don't know anything, Constable," Bergman said. "Or should I call you Detective?"

"That I don't know. But if you want to keep working this summer you have to give me something concrete."

Bergman looked tired. He said, "You know a guy named John Sheppard?"

"Let's say I do."

"You might want to see if he was in Kentucky or Tennessee a couple months ago."

"All right," Dougherty said. "And I want the ring."

"Two hundred and fifty bucks."

Dougherty said, "I thought you said two hundred," but he was willing to go to two-fifty.

Now he was feeling like he had something and he could make a move.

———

Ste. Marie said, "Good work, Detective," and Dougherty said, "Thanks."

What was he going to say, it was just luck he happened to see Bergman on the Bonaventure at two in the morning? And he had an engagement ring Dougherty could use?

He certainly wasn't going to correct Ste. Marie calling him Detective, that felt too good.

Then Ste. Marie said, "We've already checked the serial number with the manufacturer and we know the gun was sold in Kentucky to someone who said his name was John Fuller. Must be Sheppard."

Dougherty thought maybe they would set up some surveillance, get more wiretaps in place, something like that, but Ste. Marie said, "Let's go have a talk with him," and the convoy was on the move again.

It was just before midnight. They hit Molly McGuire's and the Cock 'n' Bull, a dozen detectives walking into the small bars, and this time Dougherty felt a little more resistance. People who had just answered their questions before or who had told them to fuck off under their breath were now coming out and saying it, the bartender leading the way with, "You want to stick your nose up someone's ass, stick it up each other's."

Ste. Marie said, "See you next time," on the way out, and even Dougherty was wondering how long they could keep hitting the same places, shaking down the same guys.

In the car heading out to NDG, Dougherty said, "Maybe we should branch out."

Caron said, "Maybe."

They hit Nittolo's Motel but none of the half dozen Italian guys had ever heard of John Sheppard. Or John Fuller.

Driving to Peg's, Caron said, "If we ask them, they've never heard of the Pope."

Peg's was empty. Which seemed odd to Dougherty. He waited till Laperrière and a couple other cars pulled out and fell in behind them and then he said to Caron, "That seem right to you?"

Caron lit a cigarette and dropped the match out the window, saying, "What's right these days?"

Gunshots went off, loud.

"Holy fuck!"

Caron ducked down behind the seat, and Dougherty turned a hard right, bumping up on the sidewalk. They were just pulling out of the parking lot onto St. Jacques, and there was only one more car behind them, Ste. Marie and Levine.

Dougherty was out of the car and standing behind the open door with his gun in his hand. He could see the other car, the rear window shattered, both doors open and Ste. Marie and Levine with their guns drawn.

There was no sound in the parking lot.

Levine yelled, "On the roof!" and Dougherty started running around the side of the building. In the back it was dark, no lights at all, and Dougherty couldn't see much. The back of the motel, parking spaces, a field and warehouses.

He walked slow, staying close to the wall of the motel, gun in his hand.

There, something moving. Dougherty yelled, "Stop!"

Levine said, "It's me, don't fucking shoot." Coming around the other side of the motel.

"Shit."

"They're gone."

Dougherty said, "You think more than one?"

"Unless it was one guy firing two guns."

Dougherty took a step towards the bushes. Beyond that was the drop, couple hundred feet, down to the expressway.

Levine said, "Come on."

"You think they ran down there?"

"Probably over there," Levine said, pointing at the backs of the warehouses. "Long gone."

"We might get lucky." Dougherty started walking.

Caron came around the side then and said, "Hey, let's go."

Back in front of the motel, the cops were standing in a tight group, the cars in a semi-circle facing the building with their headlights on and doors open.

Laperrière was saying, "This is fucking bullshit."

Ste. Marie said, "Come on," and led them all back into Peg's.

They stayed there drinking till the sun came up. Laperrière and Ste. Marie started the talking but then they got quiet and didn't say much. The rest of the detectives were full of what they were going to do to the bastards when they caught them.

Dougherty sat a little off to himself and watched. He nursed a couple of beers. He didn't disagree with anything they were saying, he just didn't feel like part of this group.

When they finally left, walking out into the sunshine in the parking lot, Ste. Marie said they'd take the rest of the day off, it was Sunday morning then. "We'll get back to it Monday morning," he said, getting into his car.

Dougherty drove Caron home, dropping him off at a bungalow in Ville St. Laurent and then got home and had a couple hours' sleep before picking up Judy and heading out to the West Island for dinner with her parents.

He had the engagement ring in his pocket and he'd been thinking of ways to ask her the question. At first he thought he would just do it casually, maybe even while they were driving, take out the ring and say, "What do you think, should we get married?" But then he thought, no, she wouldn't really like that. She wouldn't say she didn't but it didn't seem to really be Judy these days. Dougherty might joke sometimes that she'd come a long way from her radical days, but he didn't really think that was true. She was still trying to help people, still trying to make a difference in the world, still talking about social justice and working for it but she was living her own life, too.

So Dougherty figured while they were out in Point Claire maybe they'd go for a walk, some park near where she grew up and he'd ask her there.

It was a good plan and it might have worked. But then the last thing Judy wanted to talk about was getting married.

CHAPTER FIVE

On the drive out to the West Island for the once-a-month Sunday dinner, Dougherty started to understand the draw of the suburbs, leaving the city behind, really feeling like you were getting away. Train tracks ran alongside the expressway, and he wondered what it would be like to commute into the city in the morning and ride back at night, reading the newspaper and not thinking about work again until the next day.

Every once in a while, as they passed through Dorval, Dougherty caught a glimpse of the river at the end of a couple of blocks of houses to his left and he thought living by the water could be good.

He said to Judy, "You sure you don't want to teach out here?"

"I'm sure."

They drove through the Dorval circle, passing the exit to the airport, continued on the expressway till the St. John Boulevard exit and pulled off into Point Claire. Near the train tracks the houses were mostly older, pre-war, a couple had once been farmhouses before the housing developments started popping up. Dougherty was thinking it would be nice to move into a brand new house on a brand new street.

He said, "Was your house new when you moved into it?"

"Yeah, the whole street was new. Exactly the same." She was looking straight ahead, not at the houses they were passing as they moved into the newer area. "Well, there were maybe three designs but they weren't very different. At all my friends' houses, I knew exactly where the bathroom was."

Dougherty said, "They look different now, though."

"Not really."

Pulling up beside a station wagon on the driveway, Dougherty said, "It is nice here."

"You think that because you didn't grow up here."

They walked up to the front door of the bungalow, and Dougherty was wondering where Judy's father's Buick was when her mother opened the door and said, "Oh dear, I forgot to call you."

Judy said, "What's going on?"

Her mother was standing in the open doorway and she didn't say anything for a moment, and then Judy's sister Gillian came out, saying, "No dinner tonight, Dad moved out," and kept going, walking down the driveway and along the sidewalk away from the house.

Judy said, "What's she talking about?"

"I meant to call," her mother said, "I've just been so busy. Come on in, we'll order St-Hubert or something," and she turned around and went inside the house.

Judy stood in the driveway looking at Dougherty for a minute, then she said, "Oh, for Christ's sake," and walked into the house.

Dougherty followed and once inside the house he heard rock music playing in the basement and figured Judy's youngest sister, Abby, must be there. He walked into the kitchen at the back of the house, where Judy's mother was leaning against the counter with a drink in her hand, saying, "It was coming for so long, you must have expected it."

"No, Mom, I didn't expect it, why would I expect it?"

"All we did was fight. Or ignore each other."

"He just moved out? Where is he?"

Dougherty had avoided calling Judy's mother by anything; Mrs. McIntyre hadn't seemed right and he didn't want to call her Audrey. He figured it was because of the odd living situation between him and Judy. They weren't living together, or living in sin, as his mother would've said, but the fact they often spent the night at one another's apartment was an open secret their parents just didn't talk about. Up until this moment it had been about the most awkward thing between them. Dougherty had felt like they were in limbo, waiting for Judy to graduate and get a job and then they'd settle down and things would be easier, but now he was thinking he wasn't so sure.

But for some reason it made calling Judy's mother Audrey easier, so that's what he did, saying, "Is there anything we can do, Audrey?"

"Well, I guess you could order dinner. Abby's still here, I think. I'm not sure if Gillian is coming back or not."

Judy held up her hands and said, "What are you talking about? Are we just going to pretend nothing's going on?"

"We're not pretending anything," Audrey said. "This is what's going on."

"Dad just moved out? What happened?"

"Nothing happened."

"Mom, something must have happened."

Audrey drank what was left in her glass, looked like a rye and ginger to Dougherty, and said, "I guess we both finally got tired of pretending."

"What are you talking about?"

"Oh, Judy, you know, you saw it, you felt it."

"No, I didn't."

"We were like two strangers, just going through the motions."

Dougherty was thinking that what Audrey was saying sounded more like something she'd read, or something Judy might have had said to her, than something she came up with herself, but it might very well be the way she felt. He'd certainly felt it, visiting the house for Sunday dinners and birthdays and at other times, but he'd always figured it was because of the situation between him and Judy.

Now Judy was saying, "This just came out of nowhere."

"No, it didn't."

"Mom, I'm sorry, but this doesn't make any sense."

"Do you want a drink?"

"No, Mom."

"How about you, Édouard?"

Dougherty said, "Sure, I'll have one."

Judy turned around and looked at him over her shoulder. He started to move into the living room, saying, "I'll get it."

"It's all right," Audrey said. "It's here."

Dougherty noticed the bottle of rye on the counter next to the toaster and wondered how long Audrey had been keeping it there instead of in the china cabinet in the dining room that Judy's father used for his bar.

"Mom, this is crazy."

Audrey opened the freezer door of the fridge and got out the ice cube tray and with her back to Judy she said, "No, this is the first sane thing we've done in years."

It was quiet in the kitchen while she made Dougherty's drink and topped up her own, and then she turned around and said, "Actually, I thought you'd be happy about this," as she moved past Judy and handed the glass to Dougherty.

Judy said, "Why would I be happy?"

Audrey kept walking into the rarely used living room and sat on the couch. Judy followed her in, saying, "Why would you say that?"

Dougherty thought about staying in the kitchen. If it had been a normal Sunday dinner in Point Claire, then Dougherty and Judy's dad would've been sitting in the rec room in the basement watching golf on TV and not talking, and right now that seemed like a better idea, but Dougherty walked into the living room just in time for Judy to turn to him and say, "Can you believe this?"

She was standing in the middle of the room with her hands on her hips. Dougherty often thought that when they came out here Judy changed a little. He never would've said anything to Judy but he thought when they came into this house she started to be a little more like her mother. She really did now.

Not that he'd ever say that. What he did say was, "I don't know."

Judy stared at him for a moment and kind of shook her head in disbelief and then looked at her mother. "Why would I be happy about this?"

"I'm finally becoming myself, not just Mrs. Thomas McIntyre."

"Yourself? And dad had to move out?"

"He didn't have to, but it's what he wanted."

Abby came up out of the basement then and was on her way to the kitchen when Judy said, "Abby, come here."

"No," Abby said. "Don't talk to me."

Judy said, "I don't believe this."

"Well, I don't believe you." Audrey was leaning back on the couch then, getting out her cigarettes and lighting one and saying, "I guess it was crazy of me to expect a little support from you."

Judy said, "No, it's just . . ."

Dougherty walked into the kitchen then, thinking maybe Judy and her mother could use a little time alone.

Abby was on the phone, twisting the cord around her fingers and letting it go and twisting it again. Dougherty was pretty sure she was sixteen or seventeen, about the same age as his little brother, Tommy, but sometimes he got Abby mixed up with Gillian, who was a year older. There was one more sister, Brenda, between the two girls at home and Judy, but she was out west somewhere, Calgary or Vancouver or something, Dougherty was never sure.

"Okay, bye." Abby uncoiled the phone cord from her fingers and hung up the receiver. "They still going at it?"

"They're just talking now," Dougherty said. "I think it was just the shock — Judy wasn't expecting it."

Abby went to the fridge and opened it. "Why not? Everybody else was."

"I guess we didn't really know what was going on here."

"I'd say you should've come out here more often, but I wouldn't come here if I didn't have to."

"We're not that far away."

"Yes you are."

Abby had a glass of ginger ale in her hand then and Dougherty could hear his own father complaining about the kids drinking his mix. In his father's case, it was Pepsi he mixed with rum but he never called it Pepsi or Coke, just mix. Who drank all the mix? Dougherty almost laughed thinking about it.

"How long has it been bad?"

"It's always been bad," Abby said.

"Really?"

"Really."

"So when did he move out?"

"I don't know. I hardly ever see him — working late was the official story," Abby said. "I guess he stopped coming home a while ago."

"Like a few days or weeks or what?"

"Shit," Abby said, "you're such a cop. I don't know, a while."

"Okay." Dougherty realized he was thinking like a cop in a domestic. He wasn't really interested in the details, they didn't matter at all, he just wanted to get people talking, making conversation, getting people calmed down. But they were calm. He said, "You okay?"

"Sure, what's it to me? I don't care what they do."

"Right, yeah." Now Dougherty was thinking this was the point he usually left, everyone calmed down and talking, the husband out of the house. He never saw what happened next.

Judy came into the kitchen and said, "So, that's it. Crazy." She crossed to the drawer by the sink and got out a bunch of restaurant menus and said, "You want St-Hubert or Chinese?"

"Either one."

Judy looked at Abby and said, "What about you?"

"I'm going out."

"You sure?"

"Yeah, I'm just waiting for Mark and Ralph."

Judy said, "Okay." She still had the folded menus in her hand, and she was just staring at them.

Dougherty said, "Why don't you get the Chinese, there'll be leftovers."

"Yeah, okay."

Abby put her empty glass in the sink and walked out.

Dougherty was trying to think of something to say to Judy but he couldn't come up with anything, and then Audrey came into the kitchen and said, "Have you decided?" She got out the ice cubes and started making herself another drink.

Judy said, "Chinese."

"Get won ton soup, too." She turned to Dougherty. "Do you want another drink?"

"Sure." He drank the last of what he had and handed her the empty glass.

While Audrey was making the drink, she said, "So how are the interviews going, have you picked a school yet?"

Judy was dialling the phone and she said, "I'm going to have to take whatever I can get. Oh hi, I'd like to place an order . . . Yes, dinner number four . . . for six, I guess. And two, no three, won ton soups." She gave the address and then went over the order again.

Audrey handed Dougherty his drink and picked up her own glass off the counter.

Judy hung up and said, "Half an hour."

"Have you applied to all the school boards?"

"All the Protestant ones: Greater Montreal, south shore, Laval."

"What about West Island?"

Dougherty walked out of the kitchen. He was glad they were talking, he was glad it was just normal conversation but it still felt odd, the way they could just move on.

Abby was coming up from the basement and heading to the front door without slowing down. Dougherty followed her and stepped out onto the balcony as she headed down the walk. A couple of boys were standing on the sidewalk waiting. They both had long hair and were trying to grow beards, and they were both wearing jean jackets and jeans and one of them had on a t-shirt that said *Disco Sucks* across the front. They all looked serious, Abby and both boys, no one smiled and they didn't seem to say much to each other as they walked away.

Dougherty looked up and down the street, and now he was starting to see what Judy meant about all the houses being the same. Still, it was quiet.

And it was quiet inside the house. Judy and Audrey were sitting at the kitchen table talking.

Dougherty went down into the basement and turned on the TV. There were album covers scattered on the floor in front of the stereo and the place smelled like cigarettes and pot and he wondered how long the girls had been smoking at home. Since before their dad moved out, he figured, however long that had been.

⸻

Monday afternoon Dougherty stopped in for a cup of coffee at the restaurant a few doors down from the bank building and saw Paquette on a stool at the counter.

Dougherty was thinking about walking out when Paquette said, "Hey, Eddie," looking like he wanted to talk.

"Claude, ça va?"

"Did you hear?" Speaking English.

Dougherty said, "No, what?"

"*Tabarnak*, Gagnon and Levine, they got jumped last night."

"What the hell?"

The lunch rush was over, and there were only a few people in the restaurant. A guy behind the counter refilled Paquette's mug and held up the coffee pot for Dougherty, who said, "I'm going to get a takeout, okay, boss?"

"Sure thing." The guy moved away to get a paper cup.

Paquette said, "At Molly McGuire's."

"They went there by themselves?"

"They were looking for a guy, some guy Levine says he knows. Place was crowded."

"That's the one upstairs, right?"

Paquette drank some coffee, nodding, and said, "Yeah, that narrow stairway, so steep."

"Yeah." Dougherty was thinking how much it reminded him of the staircase at the Wagon Wheel, upstairs from the Blue Bird where there'd been a fire a few years back, a lot of people died, thirty-seven. Dougherty was there that night.

"So they don't find the guy, but then they're leaving, they're by the door, and some guy says to them, 'Leave it alone,' you know."

59

The guy behind the counter put a paper cup with a plastic lid on it in front of Dougherty and said, "On the house, Detective."

"There was another guy at the table and a woman, too, and Levine says to them, 'Leave what alone?' you know, like he doesn't know. And the guy says to him, 'The Brink's thing, leave it alone.'"

"Are the two guys brothers?" Dougherty said.

"Yeah, you know them?"

"O'Donnells, I bet. The woman is Sharon McClusky."

"It's O-something," Paquette said. "A couple of other guys shoved Gagnon out the door, knocked him down the stairs, and then they jumped Levine."

"Shit."

"Busted a couple of beer bottles over his head, slashed his face with the broken pieces."

"Fuck."

"By the time the backup got there they were all gone. But Levine knew them."

"He's okay?"

"Lot of stitches on his face, fractured skull, concussion. They took him to the General."

"Not the Jewish General?"

"I guess they saw he was a cop, they didn't think."

Dougherty had really been kidding but, of course, it wasn't a situation to be kidding about. "He still there?"

"Oh yeah," Paquette said, "he'll be there for a while."

"And now we're going to go get the O'Donnell brothers and Sharon McClusky."

"If that's who it was."

"Well, if they didn't do it they'll know who did by now," Dougherty said. He picked up his coffee and started out of the restaurant, saying, "Thanks, boss," to the guy behind the counter.

Outside on St. Jacques, walking past the big bank buildings with their big pillars and stone walls, Paquette said, "Hey, did you hear about the Brink's car?"

"What now?"

"No, it was a couple weeks ago. Brink's have an unmarked car they use for patrols in the neighbourhood but it was in an accident, a fender-bender."

"So?"

"They never got it fixed, said it would cost too much."

"Yeah," Dougherty said. "Would it have cost two and a half million dollars?"

Paquette laughed.

Dougherty was thinking if they didn't get the money back it was another piece of evidence they'd use to try to claim it was a well-planned job pulled off by professionals brought in from out of town.

"Anyone talk to the driver again?"

"Ste. Marie, every day. Guy isn't changing his story."

Dougherty was thinking they all thought it was a story, no one really believed the guy, and then he was thinking how much more plugged in Paquette was, how much closer he seemed to the top guys on the special squad.

They walked without saying anything for a block, and then Dougherty said, "You married?"

"Why," Paquette said, "you asking me on a date?"

Dougherty didn't want to say, No, I'm just trying to figure out how such a useless brown-noser like you gets promoted, but then he thought he was being too hard on the guy — Paquette wasn't doing anything wrong, he was just in the right place at the right time. And maybe he had the right kind of last name.

"Yeah, I'm married," Paquette said. "We have a baby on the way, another month or so."

"Congratulations."

They were in front of the bank building then and Paquette said, "It's going to mess up my summer vacation."

"That's okay," Dougherty said, "the Olympics are going to do that anyway."

"Overtime, baby," Paquette said. "I need it now."

He held the door for Dougherty, who walked in thinking, Yeah, and you'll get plenty of overtime, for sure.

CHAPTER
SIX

Rozovsky said, "Did you see that TV movie about the Brink's robbery?"

Dougherty said, "Already?"

"No, it was on TV a couple days before this one, with Leslie Nielsen. It was about the Boston robbery twenty years ago."

Dougherty was standing in the doorway to the evidence room and he said, "No, I didn't see it."

"And there was an episode of *Police Story*, did you see that one? They had a bazooka in the back of a van, backed up to a Brink's truck in a lane."

"They get caught at the end of the episode?"

Rozovsky said, "Yeah, they did."

"Maybe these crooks are smarter than TV writers."

"Who isn't?"

Dougherty came the rest of the way into the room and looked over the desk where Rozovsky had spread out a bunch of pictures and said, "This thing was probably being planned long before those shows were on TV."

"The experts coming into town from all over."

Dougherty said, "Are they sticking to that?"

"I don't know," Rozovsky said. "But if you don't catch somebody soon it's hard to imagine what they'll claim it was. Martians maybe."

"They don't care who did it," Dougherty said. "They just want the money back." He looked at one of the pictures and said, "Who's that?"

"Howard Hughes. He just died, didn't you hear?"

"No." Dougherty leaned closer and said, "That looks like a surveillance picture."

"It is."

In the picture a tall man wearing a hat low over his eyes, Hughes, Dougherty figured, was getting out of a limo parked in the shadows of the loading doors of a hotel. Dougherty said, "That's a while ago, look at that Cadillac. Is that the Queen E?"

"Ritz Carlton. Queen E wasn't built till '58. Hughes was here for two months in '57, stayed the whole time at the Ritz. Even then hardly anyone saw him and no one knows why he was here."

"He never left the hotel?"

"Oh yeah, there are other pictures in the file, but not much. He flew his own plane here, something called a Constellation. People figured he was here to see something special Vickers was doing with one of their planes, the Viscount."

Dougherty said, "Never heard of it."

"Hughes ordered meals in the middle of the night, always the same thing, a couple of minute steaks done medium rare, string beans and carrots and Crêpe Suzette. But not really crêpes, he wanted them thick, like pancakes."

"How do you know all this?"

Rozovsky held up the folder and said, "It's all in the file."

"Why was he under surveillance?"

"Who knows." Rozovsky held up another picture, this one of Hughes at the tarmac at the airport, just about to walk up the stairs to the door of a plane. "What do you think of this one?"

"What are you doing with it?"

"Selling it," Rozovsky said. "The tabloid, the *Globe*. 'Hughes Holes Up in Hotel Harem.' Part of a retrospective."

"It's not the *Midnight* anymore."

"I miss it," Rozovsky said. "But the *Globe*'s money is just as good."

"How much shit will you get in for selling a surveillance picture?"

"To give me shit someone would have to admit that they had Howard Hughes under surveillance." Rozovsky slid a couple of photos into a plain manila envelope and said, "What are you doing here?"

"Looking for Carpentier."

"Still trying for the transfer?"

"Have you seen him?"

A loud beeping sounded and Rozovsky said, "Oh man, they got you?"

Dougherty took the pager from the clip on his belt and turned it off. "I gotta go, see you around."

"Not if I see you first."

Dougherty took a quick look around the homicide offices but didn't see Carpentier.

———

Caron was in the lobby and he said, "Come on, we got a tip."

"Number seven hundred."

"But this one is worth checking out," Caron said.

Outside on Bonsecours, Dougherty headed for the parking lot across the street but Caron stood on the sidewalk and said, "We can walk from here." Then he changed his mind and said, "No, let's take the car."

They drove about six blocks farther into Old Montreal, to Rue LeRoyer, and Caron said, "There, with the neon sign."

"The strip joint?"

"Yeah," Caron said. "See what I mean, a good tip."

Dougherty parked in front of the hydrant near the corner of St. Laurent. "*Danseuses nues*, not exactly burlesque."

"You've never seen Lili St. Cyr," Caron said. "You're too young."

"So are you."

They got out of the car and Caron said, "Yeah, but I remember when this went all the way up," motioning to St. Laurent Boulevard, "before they did that," looking at the Ville-Marie Expressway that was like a six-lane wall separating Old Montreal from the eastern end of downtown.

"My father told me about the old days," Dougherty said, trying to get in a dig at Caron, "he was in the navy during the war, said the sailors all walked up the hill for the hookers that cost an extra buck."

"Made a big difference, that buck. Down here, well," Caron looked at the building they were standing in front of, the cheap neon sign that said *Disco-Salon Louis XIV* and said, "It might look different but it really hasn't changed much."

Dougherty was still looking towards the hill and when he turned to walk the half block to the strip joint he saw the building on the corner had a stone carving on the wall, a nun and a young child holding a book. The inscription was in French and English: *Close to this site stood the first school in Montreal established in 1637 by Marguerite Bourgeoys. Founder of the Congregation of Notre Dame.*

Dougherty said, "It's not a school anymore."

"But we can still learn a lot inside," Caron said. "Come on."

Dougherty followed him down the concrete steps.

Inside the music was loud, a heavy disco beat and Caron said, "Is this 'Mon Pays'?"

"Yeah," Dougherty said, "but in English it's 'From New York to L.A.,' Patsy Gallant."

"Mon Dieu."

A big guy stopped them at the door and started to lead them into the club, saying, *"Bienvenue, juste les deux?"*

Caron said, "We can find our own table," and walked past the guy.

Dougherty followed but the guy stepped in the way

with his hand out looking for a tip and Dougherty said, "Police business."

"I don't care."

Dougherty said, "Neither do I," and kept walking.

There was a woman onstage, swaying from side to side, no pasties on her small breasts and her denim shorts cut and torn so much she might as well have been bottomless, too. Dougherty thought she looked stoned. There were a few guys sitting on chairs right up against the stage, as if it were a bar.

Caron led the way through the room. It had been a restaurant, though not a fancy one, but still the coloured lights and mirrors and the disco ball looked garish and out of place. Across from the stage was the bar, no one sitting on the stools there, and there were a few small tables scattered around the rest of the smoke-filled room.

The song ended and another started with no break between them. "Love Is Alive" — Dougherty recognized the synthesizer opening from every disco and strip club he'd been in the last month. The woman onstage turned around, and with her back to the few guys sitting by the stage she bent over at the waist and slid the denim shorts down her long legs. She stood back up, still with her back to the men, and was swaying to the music, moving her hips a lot more now and stepping away from the shorts, barely lifting her stilettos off the stage.

Caron had stopped by the bar and was talking to a waitress who was wearing a see-through nightie and nothing underneath. She was carrying a round tray with a highball glass on it and motioning to a table in the back corner of the bar and saying, *"Peut-être une heure."*

Caron said, *"Tout seul?"* He was looking at a piece of paper the waitress had handed him, turning it over, looking at both sides.

"Juste lui et Melodi et Tom Collins." She looked up at Dougherty and winked and said, *"Je ne suis pas occupée."*

"Tant pis pour moi," Dougherty said. "I'm working."

"You don't work all night, come back."

"You'll still be here?"

"Si tu reviens." Then as Dougherty followed Caron she said, "See you later."

As Caron led the way into the back corner of the room, even darker than the area by the stage, he handed the piece of paper to Dougherty. It was the band from a pile of bills, the words *Royal Bank* printed on it in blue.

In the corner a man was sitting with his back to the wall staring up at a young woman who was dancing — or at least moving a little — her naked crotch inches from his face.

"Okay," Caron said, *"la danse est finie."*

Dougherty put his hand on Melodi's arm and they were eye to eye. She said, "No touching."

"Time for a break."

She got off the little stand and picked it up, grabbing a folded-over bundle of bills from under one of the legs and her high-heeled shoes and shrugged at the guy as she walked away saying, "See you later."

Caron said, "Come with us."

69

The guy hadn't moved. Dougherty figured he was drunk and expected him to come up swinging, but the guy just said, "Come back, Melodi," and smiled a dopey smile.

The bouncer was beside them then, with another guy, a little shorter but wearing a nicer suit, who said, "Okay, boys, take it outside."

Dougherty got himself between the bouncer and Caron, looking at the bouncer and hoping that would be all it took but ready to go if he had to.

Caron said, "Yeah, Maurice, we're going." He had a hand on the drunk's shoulder and said to him, "Come on, buddy, let's go."

The guy in the nice suit, Maurice, said, "Let go of him and get out of my club."

"Didn't you call us," Caron said. "You don't want the reward?"

Then Dougherty recognized Maurice: he'd been a detective at Station Four a few years before, when Dougherty was working there.

"No one called you."

"Then I'll keep the reward." Caron had the drunk on his feet and Dougherty cleared the path for them to get out.

Outside on the sidewalk, the drunk started to come around and get pissed off, saying, "Hands off me," waving his arms around, but Caron shoved him up against the wall of the building.

"You know what this is?" Holding the Royal Bank band in his face.

The drunk started patting the pockets in his sports

coat and he said, "That's mine."

"No, it's the bank's," Caron said. "You stole it out of the truck. Come on," he shoved him towards the car, "you're going to tell us who else was with you."

Dougherty opened the back door of the car and Caron shoved the guy inside and said, "Don't puke." He slammed the door shut and said to Dougherty, "You know him?"

"No, you?"

"No. I'm surprised, I thought I would." Caron leaned against the car and got his smokes out of his pocket and lit one.

Dougherty said, "He might have sold them something."

"Can you see the guys who pulled this job paying someone with a stack of bills, the band still on it?" He was holding the paper band in his hand.

"No."

Caron took a deep drag and blew out smoke. "Okay, let's get his story before we take him in."

Dougherty looked past Caron into the car and said, "You want to let him sleep it off?"

The guy was spread out over the back seat asleep.

"Let's wake him up," Caron said. "But not here."

They drove to the waterfront, along Mill Street until they were in the parking lot under the Bonaventure Expressway by the Lachine Canal. Dougherty pulled the drunk out of the back seat and propped him up against the hood of the car.

The guy was awake and trying to focus. He said, "What the hell?"

Caron stood beside the open passenger door and said, "We're going to give you a chance to walk away from this."

"Where the hell am I?"

"Deep shit," Caron said. "You're in deep shit."

He walked around the car and stood beside Dougherty, the two of them staring at the drunk, and Caron said, "But we can get you out. All you have to do is tell us who else was in it with you."

The guy said, "Who else?" like he really had no idea what they were talking about.

Caron said, "Just one name."

He wasn't getting it and he started to look scared.

Caron spoke softly, like he was talking to a friend, saying, "It's not too late for you, we know it wasn't your idea, we know you're just a small part of it."

"I don't know what you're talking about."

Caron leaned back and Dougherty leaned in and slapped the hood of the car hard.

The guy jumped and closed his eyes, ready to get hit.

Dougherty said, "Tell him what he wants to know."

"I don't know anything."

Dougherty slapped him. He grabbed the guy's face in one hand and shook it till he opened his eyes and then Dougherty showed his other hand now in a fist.

"Tell him."

"It was me, it was just me."

Dougherty pulled his fist back to punch but Caron grabbed his arm.

"Just one name, that's all we need. One other guy who was in this with you."

The guy was crying, now, shaking all over. He managed to say, "J-just me," with Dougherty's big hand squeezing his face.

"I can only help you if you help me," Caron said. "I can't hold him back forever."

"It was just me, Jesus Murphy, I'm sorry, I'm sorry."

Dougherty slammed the guy's head onto the hood of the car and held it there, pressing his face into the still-warm steel.

Caron leaned down close to the guy and said, "Was it Peaky Boyle? We don't have to tell him we got it from you."

"N-no."

"Big Jim Sadowski?"

"Who?"

Dougherty's hand was on the guy's neck then, and he lifted it up a little and then pressed down harder. "Come on."

"I don't know, I don't know, it was just me, I swear." He closed his eyes tight, scrunched up his whole face like he was trying to be a turtle and pull it into his shoulders.

Dougherty looked at Caron for direction.

"Look, no one thinks you did it by yourself."

"I did, ask the old lady, I always work alone, I swear, if there was someone else, I'd tell you."

Caron motioned for Dougherty to let the guy up and he did.

"Here." Caron held out his smokes and the guy looked at Dougherty before he took one in a shaking hand.

Holding the match Caron said, "What's your name?"

"Billy," the guy said, taking a drag and coughing as he let it out. He was still shaking. "Bill. William Greaves."

"All right, Bill," Caron said. He held up the paper band. "You did not hold up a Brink's truck by yourself. Tell me who you work with."

Greaves laughed. He was taking another drag on the smoke and he laughed and coughed and laughed some more and said, "Holy shit, is that what you think I did?"

"Where did you get the money?" Caron said.

Greaves was settling down. He put the cigarette in his mouth and inhaled and tilted his head back, letting out a long stream of smoke towards the traffic going by on the Bonaventure above them.

"I got that from a nice old lady in Westmount. Told her I was a bank inspector."

"Shit," Caron said, "that still works?"

Greaves shrugged. "Sometimes."

They put him back in the car and drove to HQ on Bonsecours Street. Caron told Dougherty to take Greaves into the detectives' office on the third floor and process him, making it sound like a big deal, like real detective work, and Dougherty tried to let him know he wasn't buying it except he was.

It felt good, sitting at the desk, taking the statement, walking Greaves through and making sure he got everything: how Greaves phoned the old lady and told her he was working for the bank, checking into what might be a crooked teller, how she could help by withdrawing two thousand dollars. Greaves met her in Place d'Armes, two blocks from the bank and took the money, thanking her, telling her there was a problem all right, the teller had slipped her counterfeit bills and he'd have to continue his investigation.

"And then you just walked straight to the strip joint?" Dougherty said.

"It was the guilt. It was weighing on me, I had to get rid of the money."

"Yeah, two bucks a dance, it would take a while."

Greaves said, "Two bucks? Didn't you see her, it was five, and another three dances and she was coming back to my room at the hotel."

Dougherty finished up the paperwork, checking it three times to make sure he had everything and then he called dispatch to send a uniform to take Greaves to Parthenais and process him.

When that was done, when the uniform had taken Greaves away, the detective office was quiet. Dougherty felt good, he felt like he could do this job and be good at it and now he was feeling that he really didn't want to go back to uniform. Nothing against it, it was good work, useful work, sometimes it felt like he was doing something really worthwhile breaking up a fight before some drunk killed his own wife or helping people at the scene of a car accident, lots of things like that, but detective work — it just felt better to Dougherty.

He was getting ready to leave when Caron came back into the office, already a couple of drinks in him, and said, "All right, you finished? Let's go give the girls the reward."

"The reward's for information on the Brink's job, nothing for this small-time fraud."

"We can still show our appreciation," Caron said.

Dougherty didn't want to go back to the strip club but he didn't want to go home either, so he said, "Okay, let's go."

They were still there around ten when Dougherty realized his beeper was going off.

He was sitting at the bar with his back to the stage, though he could see the dancer in the mirror, and listening to the song, a girl's name, something like Lorelei, though Dougherty had never heard that name before, and the words, "Let's live together," over and over. He was thinking maybe that's what he and Judy should do, just live together, not get married at all. Judy might go for that. He'd just have to keep it a secret from his mother. And his father.

In the back by the washrooms, Dougherty found a pay phone and called in.

Ste. Marie answered, "Where the hell is Caron? I called him three times."

"I can find him."

"Can you find him in the next five minutes?"

"Yeah," Dougherty said, "he's here with me now. You want us to come in?"

"No, we'll pick him up, where are you?"

"You know the Disco-Salon, on LeRoyer?"

"Should have known you'd be in a strip club. Sober him up and wait out front, we'll be there in five minutes."

Dougherty pulled Caron out from under a dancer and dragged him out to the sidewalk in front of the club. He was thinking along the way how Ste. Marie had said to sober "him" up and that they'd pick "him" up but it didn't really register until the unmarked car pulled up and Ste. Marie, in the passenger seat, said to Caron, "Let's go."

Caron climbed in the back and as Dougherty leaned in he saw Paquette in the driver's seat. Dougherty said, "Where to?" but he had a feeling what was coming.

"It's not the whole squad," Ste. Marie said. "We got a tip on the shooter from Peg's, we don't want to spook him."

"Just you three going?"

"A couple others, they're watching his place now."

"Whose place?"

Ste. Marie said, "We'll bring him in tonight, let him sweat, talk to him tomorrow. Be at the office by ten."

Then Paquette pulled a U and Dougherty watched the car turn onto St. Laurent and gun it. He was pissed off and feeling like he was being pushed out of the special squad but he didn't know what to do about it.

He started to walk back to Bonsecours, thinking he'd just go home, but he saw a pay phone and called Judy.

She said, "Yeah, sure, we can complain about your job and my lack of a job."

CHAPTER
SEVEN

Dougherty got to the bank office at ten but there was no one there, so he went down to the greasy spoon on the corner and had eggs and sausages and toast. He was finishing his second cup of coffee when Caron came in and sat down on the next stool.

"*Tabarnak*, did you hear everything?"

"I didn't hear anything."

"*Juste un café*. To go." He turned to Dougherty. "What a fuck-up, where you been?"

"What happened?"

"It was crazy."

"Have you been up all night? Why didn't you call me?"

The guy behind the counter put a couple of paper

coffee cups with plastic lids on them in front of Caron and Dougherty put down a five-dollar bill.

On the way to the bank office, Caron said, "It was Big Jim Sadowski."

"You're sure?"

"Oh yeah. We had his place staked out last night, apartment building on Sherbrooke, corner of Benny, you know it?"

"Yeah," Dougherty said, "new one, fifteen storeys, all concrete."

They went into the bank building and passed the elevator, taking the stairs up to the fourth floor.

"We waited in the garage below the building. Big Jim was at Peg's, we knew that."

Caron was out of breath by the second floor. Dougherty was a few steps ahead, and he stopped and looked back. He had a feeling what was coming, but he let Caron tell it.

"We waited for a couple hours, it was after three when he got there."

"To the garage," Dougherty said.

"Yeah." Caron started up the stairs again, passing Dougherty. "Fucker started shooting as soon as he saw us."

Dougherty said, "Shit, anybody hurt?" But he was glad Caron was ahead of him then and not looking at his face. Dougherty knew what had happened and he listened while Caron told him how Sadowski got out of his car and Ste. Marie told him to put up his hands and Sadowski said, "Fuck you," and pulled out his gun and everybody started shooting.

"Hit the bastard twenty times," Caron said. "But

we got lucky, he didn't hit any of our guys."

"That's good."

Caron didn't look back and said, "Yes, it is." He pushed open the door from the stairwell and walked down the hall to the office they were using.

Half the squad was there but Dougherty didn't see Ste. Marie or Laperrière.

Caron went over to a corner where a couple of guys were talking quietly.

"Hey." One of the older guys Dougherty didn't know came up to him and said, "Say you see a guy and a girl and she has a black eye, what do you think?"

Dougherty said, "I think he's going to jail."

The guy looked surprised for a second and then he said, "Yeah, you'd think he hit her, right?"

"Right."

"Well," the guy looked back at the other cops he'd been talking to, drawing them in for a kind of audience, and he said, "that's one way of looking at it, sure, but maybe she just wouldn't shut up," and he broke out in a big smile and laughed.

The other guys laughed, too.

Dougherty said, "Funny." He knew there was a time he would've laughed, too, trying to be one of the guys with all these detectives, but he didn't feel it now. Then he saw Paquette leaning against a desk off by himself a little, and Dougherty walked over and said, "That was bad last night."

"Incroyable. The noise in that garage."

"Sadowski just started shooting?"

"Like the punks say, it happened so fast." Paquette finished off the coffee in his paper cup and tossed it into the garbage can. "They say there is a contract out on Ste. Marie and Laperrière."

"Who says that?"

"It's on the street." Paquette shrugged. "All these raids, all the bars we're busting, these guys can't do any business. They're going to fight back."

"You believe that, there's a contract?"

"Fifty grand, they say."

Dougherty said, "Shit." He figured it was possible. It sounded crazy, like a movie, but it could be real. Fifty grand wasn't that much if you were sitting on two and a half million.

"Where are they now?"

"With the chief."

"Shit. And we just wait."

"We need some results," Paquette said. "Soon. We need to find the money."

Dougherty said, "Yeah," but he didn't think very much of that money was still in the city. He was surprised to hear him say that's what they were still looking for, he figured Paquette was a lot closer to the heart of this investigation, all the time he was spending with the top guys, Ste. Marie and Laperrière, and they'd know it was long gone, but Dougherty didn't say anything.

The phone rang and Caron picked up the receiver. He spoke quietly and then didn't say anything for a while, just listened, not looking too happy about it, and then said, "*Bon, c'est correct.*" He put the receiver back down on the phone and said, "Okay, it was a long night — we're not going to get anything done today. Let's meet back here tomorrow morning at ten."

"*Pas ce soir?*"

"No."

Dougherty started to leave, but Caron stopped him and said, "Carpentier wants to see you."

"What does he want?"

"How would I know? He's in the office."

Dougherty walked the few blocks to Bonsecours Street HQ and went up to the fourth-floor homicide office. Carpentier was at his desk talking on the phone, and he waved Dougherty over as he was saying, "*Bon, oui, maintenant.*" He hung up and said, "So, you're not too busy today?"

"Some guys were up all night."

"Everybody's talking about it," Carpentier said.

"What are they saying?"

Carpentier shrugged. "What's to say?"

"What can I do for you?"

"A body was found this morning in the river in Montreal East. It's been taken to the coroner. He won't be doing the autopsy until tomorrow, but I want you to go and see if it's a homicide."

"And if it is?"

"Come and tell me."

"Right."

Dougherty walked out of the office, thinking he wasn't sure if he would rather be Carpentier's gofer or be left on the sidelines of the big moves by the special squad.

"Come on," Dougherty said, "even I can see those are rope marks around his neck."

"Doesn't mean it was homicide."

The body was male, probably between fifteen and twenty years old, and he'd been in the water awhile, but the marks on his neck were clear. He was naked from the waist up but he was still wearing shoes and jeans and the belt was tight.

Dougherty said, "So, what happened, he tried to hang himself and when that didn't work he went swimming?"

The technician said, "You'll find out when Dr. Robillard performs the autopsy."

"When will that be?"

"I don't know, he has a few to do before this one. I don't know how long they will take."

"It would help with the homicide investigation if we could start right away."

"If it's a homicide."

Dougherty started out of the morgue, saying, "Is he in his office?"

A woman in a police uniform was coming in then, and she looked past Dougherty and said, "*Est-ce que c'est le garçon qu'on a sorti de la rivière?*"

The technician was closing the drawer and said, "*Demandez au Docteur Robillard.*"

She said, "*Laissez-moi voir.*"

The drawer was closed.

Dougherty spoke French, saying, "Who are you?" He didn't recognize the uniform.

The woman said, "Who are you?"

"I'm Detective Dougherty."

"Sergeant Legault, Police de Longueuil."

Dougherty figured she was somewhere between twenty-five and thirty-five, it was hard to tell because unlike most of the other policewomen he knew, this Sergeant Legault wasn't wearing any make-up and her hair was short.

She said, "I believe that's Mathieu Simard."

"He's been missing?"

"For three days, yes." She looked at the morgue technician and said, also in French, "You were supposed to call me."

"After the autopsy."

"As soon as the body came in."

"Talk to Dr. Robillard."

"I will." She turned and walked out of the room.

Dougherty caught up with her at the elevator. "He's from Longueuil?"

"Yes, both of them."

"There are two missing?"

The elevator door opened and Legault said, "Yes, him and his girlfriend."

"Is she still missing?"

"No," Legault said as the elevator doors closed. "Her body washed up on Île du Fort yesterday."

Dougherty waited a moment then turned and walked out of the Parthenais building. He was a little disappointed that the homicide would have to be turned over to the Longueuil police, but he was also relieved. Couple of teenagers in the river, unless there was a very good witness, which Dougherty just knew there wouldn't be, it didn't seem likely an investigation would go anywhere.

At the homicide office Carpentier said, "You met

Sergeant Legault, that's good."

Dougherty said, "Why is that good?"

"You'll be working together."

"What?"

"The Longueuil police do not have a dedicated homicide squad," Carpentier said. "And they asked us to lead the investigation."

"They asked us?"

Carpentier stood up from his desk. "Captain Allard and I know each other, he used to work here. He asked me to take it." He picked up his empty mug. "Would you like a coffee?"

"No, thanks."

"I'll coordinate the investigation."

Dougherty said, "And I'll work it?"

"With Sergeant Legault, yes." Carpentier walked back to his desk and sat down.

"What about the Brink's squad?"

"After last night, and Levine still in the hospital," Carpentier said, "they're not sure how it will continue."

Dougherty said, "I heard Ste. Marie and Laperrière were talking to the chief."

"The squad may be reduced. Would you rather go back to uniform at Station Ten?"

"No, I'd like to work this," Dougherty said.

"Good. There's not much information yet, two teenagers went to a concert at —" he checked his notes "— Place des Nations, and then never returned home. Now the bodies have been found."

"So, they went into the river somewhere."

"Sergeant Legault has been working it as a missing

persons, now it's homicide."

"The autopsy's been done?"

"It will be a homicide," Carpentier said. "Go and see Captain Allard this afternoon. Three o'clock."

Driving over the Jacques Cartier Bridge, Dougherty was thinking he was pleased to be working a homicide even if the circumstances weren't ideal. He drove off the bridge past the only tall building, the Holiday Inn by the Métro station, and then through the old Longueuil downtown. Some of the buildings were over a hundred years old, and Dougherty had some memory from high school about Fort Longueuil being built in the late 1600s and occupied by American troops during their revolutionary war.

The police station was a modern two-storey building. Dougherty went in and asked the desk sergeant for Captain Allard and then said, "*Il m'attend.*"

The desk sergeant looked like he didn't believe it, but he picked up the phone and grunted a few words and then said, "Upstairs, down the hall."

A receptionist stood up from behind a little desk outside the captain's office as Dougherty approached and spoke French, saying, "Hello, Detective, would you like anything? A cup of coffee or tea?"

Dougherty said, "No, thank you," and he was surprised she'd called him detective. He figured Carpentier must have referred to him by that rank so he wasn't about to correct anyone.

"All right, you may go in."

Dougherty thanked her and walked into Captain

Allard's office.

"Detective Dougherty, I hope you didn't have any trouble finding us."

"No," Dougherty said, surprised Allard was speaking English and not sure if he was making a joke or not. "I lived in Greenfield Park for a while, my parents still do."

"Oh well, Greenfield Park is not Longueuil, but it's close."

The captain seemed to be smiling a little, and Dougherty figured he was joking. Ingratiating a little, like a politician, which wasn't surprising — Dougherty figured it took a little politics to become a captain.

Then Allard stopped smiling and said, "I'm glad Étienne will be coordinating this investigation, very unpleasant business," and it took a moment for Dougherty to realize that Étienne was Carpentier's first name.

He said, "Yes, very unpleasant."

"When Manon Houle's body was found, we were hoping it was not a homicide."

"You weren't sure?"

"I suppose we still aren't sure," Allard said. He picked up a file on his desk and held it out for Dougherty. "The autopsy report."

The phone rang, and Allard picked up the receiver as Dougherty took the file.

Then the door opened and Legault came into the office, saying, "*Désolée, je suis en retard.*"

Allard switched to French, saying, "Do you have the autopsy report for Mathieu Simard?"

"Yes." She handed a file to Allard.

As he was reading, Allard continued in French, "You've met Detective Dougherty?"

"Yes, sir."

Allard closed the file and said, "*Bien.* So, both of them had water in their lungs and also bruising on their necks."

Neither Dougherty nor Legault said anything.

"Not much else here. You better get started."

Legault said, "Yes, sir," and started out of the office.

Dougherty said, "Thank you, sir," and followed Legault into the hall.

He wasn't sure what he'd expected, but now he felt like he was in charge of the investigation. It seemed sudden, and he felt unprepared even though it was something he'd wanted for a long time.

Catching up to Legault, he said, "Have you spoken to the family?"

"I'll call them, and we should go in person."

Dougherty followed her into the detectives' office, a big open room with a few men working at their desks. None of them looked up as Legault walked to the farthest desk from the door and sat down.

There was a coffee machine, also about as far from Legault's desk as it could be, and Dougherty said, "How about a coffee?"

She had the phone in one hand and said, "I'm calling right now."

"I know," Dougherty said. "Do you want me to get you a coffee?"

"Oh, you go get it?" She looked at him, surprised, and said, "No, this will only take a minute and we'll go."

Dougherty said, "Okay."

Legault dialled the phone and waited longer than

she really needed to and then hung up. "Mathieu's mother must still be at work."

"Where is that?"

"Pratt & Whitney."

Dougherty looked at his watch and said, "She finish at four?"

"Yes."

"Half an hour. Maybe we should talk to the girl's family, let them know."

Legault picked up the phone and dialled. This time it was answered right away and Legault spoke quietly for a few moments and then hung up.

"We can go see the Houles first," Legault said. "The father is just getting up." She stood up and started towards the door.

"Second shift," Dougherty said. "Where does he work?"

"Stelco, the steel mill. He's a machinist."

"I know it," Dougherty said. It was near the Point, where he'd grown up. Some of the dads in the neighbourhood worked there.

They drove a few blocks and Legault stopped in front of a small bungalow barely ten years old and said, "Yesterday I brought them to identify the body of their daughter. We didn't know where Mathieu was so there was a lot of speculation."

"Of course." Dougherty figured the first thing they thought was that the other kid, Mathieu, had killed their daughter and then taken off. Then he said, "We still don't know anything, really."

"We may never know anything," Legault said. "Should we tell them that?"

Dougherty said, "Yes. We should be totally honest with them."

Legault nodded. *"D'accord."*

Ginette Houle and her husband, Albert, were waiting by the door.

Legault stepped into the house and gave Ginette a hug, and Dougherty looked at Albert and tried for understanding and confidence.

"Voici le détective Dougherty de la police de Montréal."

Albert held out his hand and Dougherty shook it, still looking him in the eye. Then Dougherty spoke French, saying, "I'm very sorry for your loss."

"Thank you."

They moved into the living room, and Legault sat on the couch beside Ginette and held her hands.

Albert said, "So, Mathieu is dead as well?"

Legault said, "Yes."

"Did he kill Manon and then himself?"

"We don't know yet," Legault said.

It was quiet for a moment, and then Dougherty said, "There was a rope around Mathieu's neck. It looks like someone strangled him."

"There were marks on Manon's neck," Albert said. "Someone strangled her, too. Not Mathieu?"

"We don't know yet," Dougherty said.

Albert looked at him and said, "So, now it's the Montreal police?"

"Mathieu's body was found in Montreal," Legault said. "We will work with the Montreal police."

Albert was nodding. "You have done this before?"

"Yes. A few times."

Dougherty heard a door open and footsteps, and a girl came into the living room. She looked like the picture of Manon he'd seen in the autopsy file but a couple of years younger. Her eyes were red from crying.

"Mathieu est mort aussi?"

Ginette nodded and the girl started crying. She sat on the couch beside her mother.

After a few minutes, Legault stood up and said they had to go. She said to Ginette, "Call me anytime you want, day or night. I'll tell you everything we know."

Outside, Dougherty said, "How many kids do they have?"

"Just the two girls," Legault said. "The one now."

They got into the car, and Legault said, "Mathieu Simard lived with his mother not far from here." She put the car in gear and pulled away from the curb.

"Just the two of them?"

Legault took a moment and then said, "As far as I know. There are two other kids, boy and a girl, older. The mother says they don't live with her, but I'm not sure."

"She's not cooperative?"

"It may be she doesn't want people sticking their noses in her life."

"That's going to be impossible to stop now," Dougherty said. "There'll be reporters and maybe TV coverage and every neighbour will have something to say."

They were on Chemin de Chambly then, and the bungalows had given way to fourplexes and small apartment buildings. Dougherty was thinking the neighbourhood wasn't exactly what Judy would call underprivileged, but it was getting there.

"Here we are."

Legault parked in front of one of the three-storey red-brick apartment buildings.

The buzzer was answered right away, and Legault opened the door, saying, "She's home."

On the third floor, Legault knocked at the door and a moment later it opened.

"Madame Simard, on a des nouvelles."

She knew right away what news it was, of course, and backed into the apartment. Legault put an arm around the woman and led her to the couch.

Dougherty closed the door and followed them into the small living room just past the kitchenette.

Legault spoke quietly, telling the mother that her son was dead. She used the woman's first name, Paulette, a few times.

The apartment was untidy but clean. There were breakfast dishes on the drying rack beside the sink and a pile of paperback novels beside the couch. A couple of walls had framed prints, Quebec farms and country-side. The furniture was worn.

After a few minutes, Legault said, "This is Detective Dougherty from Montreal, he will be helping."

Paulette looked up and said, *"T'es Anglais, toé? Doe-er-tee?"*

"Oui."

"C'es pas grave, y'a ben des anglais au Pratt & Whitney."

Dougherty continued in French: "I'm very sorry for your loss."

"Who did it?"

"We don't know yet."

"It was not Mathieu," Paulette said. "He did not do this, to Manon or himself."

"No," Legault said, "he didn't." She glanced up at Dougherty, willing him to stay silent, but he wasn't going to say anything. Maybe Mathieu killed the girl and then tried to hang himself and then jumped in the river, maybe he didn't. They'd find out soon enough.

Or never.

But now the mother would have to be taken to the morgue to identify the body of her youngest child.

Legault dropped Dougherty at the Longueuil police station, where he picked up his car. They agreed to meet there later, after Legault brought Paulette home. Dougherty decided not to go back over the bridge at rush hour, even if it was against the traffic, only to have to come back later, so he drove south on Taschereau Boulevard.

Six lanes of bright-coloured signs and neon lights, car dealerships, gas stations, restaurants and bars — not exactly the Berlin Wall but the boulevard separated French Longueuil and Laflèche on one side and English St. Lambert and Greenfield Park on the other. Even the streets changed names when they crossed Taschereau: Boulevard Édouard became Churchill Boulevard and Rue Georges became Gladstone Street. Two hundred years side by side and they were determined to remain two solitudes.

It was just before six when he pulled up in front of the house on Patricia, the corner lot on a block of identical houses — or what had started out as identical twenty years before. Now some had carports added or rooms off the kitchen or big decks in the backyards.

The house looked empty. Dougherty went in through the back door into the kitchen and heard the music coming from the basement. It was so loud Dougherty was surprised he hadn't seen the windows rattling from the outside.

Tommy was on his back on the floor in the middle of what their mother always called the rec room, with its knotty pine walls and indoor-outdoor carpeting. Tommy's eyes were closed, his hands were on his chest and he was so still he looked like a corpse.

The song ended suddenly, the singer yelling what sounded to Dougherty like "Suffragette," and the basement was completely silent.

Dougherty said, "Hey," and Tommy jumped like someone had hit him in the gut.

"Whoa."

"You're not stoned, are you?" Dougherty said.

Tommy was getting up and he said, "No."

The next song had started, guitar strumming steadily, and then the singer came in: "Time takes a cigarette."

Tommy said, "What are you doing here?"

"Mom and Dad not home yet?"

"Any minute." Tommy was at the stereo, then he lifted the needle off the record. "You staying for dinner?"

"Yeah, I was in the neighbourhood."

"In this neighbourhood? Way out here? Why?"

"What do you mean, way out here?"

"Suburbs, boonies." Tommy was putting the record

in a paper sleeve and then he slid that into the cardboard cover. "One of my teachers, Mr. Mardinger, he said to us, 'How can you live way out here?' Like we have some say in it."

Dougherty was shaking his head. "It's nice here."

Tommy wasn't buying it. He sat down on the couch.

"Hey," Dougherty said, "did you hear anything about a couple of kids from around here who went missing a few days ago?"

"From Greenfield Park?"

"Longueuil."

Tommy said, "No," dragging it out like it was the craziest thing he could imagine.

Dougherty was thinking it was like a bubble, this little English town. Tommy was in his last year of high school; Dougherty couldn't imagine him sticking around much longer.

"They went to a concert at Place des Nations and never made it home."

"Gentle Giant."

"What?"

"That was the concert on Monday at Place des Nations, Gentle Giant and, I think, Harmonium."

"Did you go?"

"No, but I know some people who did."

"I guess these missing kids went to the French high school."

Tommy shrugged. "If they were French, I guess so."

"Anyway," Dougherty said, starting to get annoyed and looking to shock his little brother, "they're not missing anymore, they were killed."

Tommy said, "That's too bad," with no emotion.

"Are you sure you're not stoned?"

"Why, you want some?"

Dougherty looked around the rec room and got the feeling Tommy was the only one who ever spent any time there. Their sister, Cheryl, had graduated high school and moved out a couple years before, and Tommy was the only kid left at home. The place felt cold.

"Okay, I'm going to wait upstairs."

Tommy said, "Okay," but didn't make a move to follow.

In the kitchen, Dougherty looked out the back window at the apple tree his mother had planted that never had any apples. He saw she hadn't started any work in the garden, but he wasn't sure if it was time for that yet or not.

Music started up in the basement again, loud and aggressive. When he could make out the words, Dougherty was pretty sure it was something about fly by night, away from here, and then something about my ship isn't coming and I just can't pretend.

Dougherty walked into the living room and looked out the big picture window onto Patricia Street. Both sides of the street were lined with the side-by-side two-storey red-brick houses with flat roofs, small front lawns and driveways. It did feel far from city life, Dougherty agreed with that, but that was the point. He watched a car drive along the street, stop at the corner and disappear up Fairfield, and he thought he could understand Tommy's feeling like he was ready to get out, but Dougherty was starting to think that he was ready to come back to a place like this.

He doubted it was something Judy was thinking about these days, though.

The back door opened then, and Dougherty's mother came in, saying, "Édouard, what are you doing here?"

"I was in the neighbourhood."

Dougherty's father was coming in then, too, and he said, "Well, this is a nice surprise."

"Supper in half an hour," his mother said.

Dougherty's father made a couple of rum and Cokes, and they sat at the kitchen table while his mother put a ham in the oven and got the potatoes on to boil. They talked about work for a while, both his parents with the phone company, his mother working as a clerk in the east end and his father building switchboards and installing them in office buildings. His father complained about the traffic on the bridge and the possibility of another strike.

Dougherty said, "This summer?"

"Maybe in the fall," his father said. "Seems like everybody's on strike. Nurses, teachers, post office."

"Using the Olympics for pressure. I'm surprised you guys aren't talking about going out sooner."

"Too much overtime getting ready for the games." Then he said, "What brought you out here?"

"I'm working," Dougherty said. "On a homicide."

"Detective?"

"Nothing official," Dougherty said. "Acting detective."

Dougherty's mother said, "Like your father, longest-serving acting foreman at the Bell."

His father said, "Not this week."

"It's the union work," his mother said. "None of the ones who started the lineman's union got promoted."

"Was the homicide on the south shore?" His father clearly didn't want to talk about his own job.

"It was two kids," Dougherty said, "high school students. They were at a concert at Place des Nations, and then the bodies were found in the river." He glanced at his mother as he said that, but she was at the sink cutting up carrots and he couldn't see her face. "We're not sure where they went into the river. But they were strangled first."

"So why are you on it?"

"Detective Carpentier is friends with the captain in Longueuil, so I'm here helping out. And one of the bodies washed up on the Montreal side of the river."

"Nasty business," his father said.

"But it's got to be done."

"You want another drink?" His father was already up and going to the cabinet beside the oven where he kept the booze.

"Dinner's almost ready." Dougherty's mother was coming to the table with plates. Then she called Tommy up from the basement, finished mashing the potatoes and brought the food to the table, saying, "So, how is Judy?"

Dougherty said, "She's good." For a moment he thought about mentioning that her parents had split up, but he knew that would just lead to a whole lot of questions and he didn't have any answers.

Tommy came upstairs and grunted his way through the meal, giving one-word answers to every question he was asked. Before he'd even chewed the last mouthful, he got up from the table and left.

Dougherty said, "You don't make him do the dishes? You always made me and Cheryl clean up," and his mother just said, "It's no trouble."

It was almost eight when Dougherty left the house and drove to the Longueuil police station. He got there just as Legault was leaving, pulling out of the parking lot in the unmarked car as Dougherty was pulling in. He rolled down his window and said, "Where you going?"

She said, "We've been replaced," and drove off.

CHAPTER
EIGHT

Dougherty walked into Captain Allard's office and knew right away the two men with him were detectives. Plain dark suits, white shirts, ties and giving off the vibe that they ran the place.

Allard said, "*Bonjour, Dougherty*."

"What's going on?"

"We've decided — I've decided — to bring in our detectives to run this one."

Dougherty said, "That sounds like a good idea, this is a major case. Can I still be any help?"

"Yes, of course." Allard looked relieved. "We will need to coordinate with the Montreal police, of course."

"All right."

"So," Allard said, "this is Detective Boudreau and Detective Lefebvre."

Boudreau was standing up and held out his hand and Dougherty shook it, but Lefebvre was sitting down and didn't make a move.

Dougherty said, "What about Sergeant Legault?"

Lefebvre said, "This is homicide, it's not women's work."

"No," Dougherty said, "it's police work." He regretted it as soon as he'd said it, but he didn't like these detectives. And, he realized, he did like Legault — he liked the way she'd been honest and up front with the families of the victims. He'd been looking forward to working with her.

Allard said, "Sergeant Legault is still working the investigation. She will be the liaison with the families."

Lefebvre said, "We'll call you if we need you."

Dougherty said, "Okay."

He left the office and drove a few blocks to Taschereau and stopped at a strip mall. Found a phone booth and called the pager number on Legault's business card. He punched in the pay phone's number, hung up and waited.

And, as he expected, the phone rang within a minute.

"Dougherty."

There was a pause and then Legault said, "*Oh, c'est toi. Que veux-tu?*"

Dougherty spoke French, saying, "Let's have a drink."

"Not interested."

"We're still working, let's work."

"Do they need someone to bring coffee and dough-nuts to the office?"

"Look, I can see a place, La Barre 500, you know it?"

"Not there, everyone knows it."

Dougherty smiled to himself a little. Legault was negotiating, which meant she was going to meet. He wasn't too surprised, she had a lot to complain about and it would be better to let it all out to Dougherty than to someone she actually cared about.

"There's a bar on Victoria Avenue, that's what Boulevard Lapinière is called on the other side of Taschereau," Dougherty said. "The Rustic Tavern, do you know it?"

"Not in my territory."

"Ten minutes," Dougherty said.

The Rustic was in the end unit of a strip mall next to a dry cleaner and a convenience store, but inside it did a pretty good job of looking rustic: dark wood panelling, heavy wooden bar, low lighting. And it was English all the way.

Dougherty got a table near the door, ordered a draught and waited. Almost half an hour later Legault came in, stood by Dougherty's table and said, in French, "There isn't anything to say."

"Well, you're here now." Dougherty finished off his beer and motioned to the bartender.

102

Legault sat down. Reluctantly. So reluctantly it almost made Dougherty laugh.

A waitress came to the table and said, "What'll it be?"

Dougherty handed her his empty glass and looked

at Legault. She didn't say anything so Dougherty said, "Couple more, thanks."

Legault looked around the bar and said, "It's all English here."

"Our little hideaway."

The waitress brought the beers and dropped a couple of menus on the table. "In case you're hungry."

Dougherty said, "Thanks," and then went back to French, saying, "So, I met Boudreau and Lefebvre."

Legault said, "You will be working with them now."

"No, I'll still be working with you."

"Fine. I work youth services. You're going to love it."

Dougherty drank his beer and waited a moment and then said, "You know there's nothing here at all, nothing. And they're not going to get anything. This is most likely going to be an open file forever."

"So I should just forget it?"

"Yeah, that's right, just forget it."

Legault smirked at him and started to say something and then stopped. Then she said, "Oh, you don't mean that."

"Of course I don't mean it. Look, this is just politics. There's always politics, and it's always bullshit."

Legault drank her beer and didn't say anything.

"Look, you knew you weren't going to head up a homicide investigation from youth services."

"No one cared until now." She put down her glass and looked at Dougherty. "Until you got involved."

"That's what I mean," Dougherty said, "it's politics. The English have an expression, 'it's above my pay grade.'"

"So you don't care?"

"I don't care about the politics, no. Look, I haven't been doing this that long myself, but I've learned a few things. There's always something else going on, there's always something between the inspectors and captains and chiefs and mayors and whatever else, but it all goes on at another level and it's got nothing to do with us. The best thing we can do, the only thing, is deal with what's right in front of us the best we can. We're trying to find out what happened to these kids, and if someone killed them we're going to find out who and we're going to arrest them. None of this other bullshit matters to us."

Legault nodded slowly. Then she said, "Yes, you're right."

Dougherty said, "Okay."

And Legault said, "This time."

He started to say something, and then he saw her sly smile and he said, "Yeah, this time."

After a moment, Legault said, "And you're right, there is nothing. When this was missing persons two days ago, I spoke to their family and their friends, I asked at Place des Nations, there's nothing."

"They were seen at the concert?"

"Yes, they left early, they didn't like it. They didn't make it home."

"They took the Métro?"

Legault shrugged. "As far as I know."

There was a commotion at the door, and then about ten guys came in, all in their twenties, rowdy and loud.

Dougherty said, "Hockey team."

"Yes."

"Okay, so no one saw them on the Métro at Île Sainte-Hélène — did anyone see them at the Longueuil station? Would they have taken a bus the rest of the way?"

"Yes," Legault said. "But I haven't spoken to the bus drivers from that night yet."

"I guess we'll have to start back at the concert, at Place des Nations."

Legault nodded, drank a little of her beer and then said, "They may have walked across the bridge. Teenagers do that sometimes."

Dougherty tried to picture his little brother Tommy walking across the Jacques Cartier, and he figured it was possible. Something he'd ask him about.

"So," Legault said, "they may have gone off the bridge."

"Two suicides?"

"I don't think so. The rope around Mathieu's neck, and Manon was raped."

"They didn't just have sex with each other?"

"The coroner won't put it in the report because there was a lot of bruising and damage to the body that could have come from being in the river, bounced off rocks and so on," Legault said. "But I saw Manon's neck and her wrists. She was raped."

Dougherty nodded, waited a moment and said, "Okay, that's what we go with." He drank a little beer and put down the glass. "When the detectives don't make any progress, if they don't get anything right away, they're going to start bringing in experts, psychologists and psychiatrists and criminologists, and they're going to have theories about water and heights and all kinds of stuff."

"And we should ignore this bullshit?"

"It's not all bullshit," Dougherty said.

"You have some experience with this?"

"I do, yeah," Dougherty said. "I knew a researcher once, she made a lot of sense. But that's not really us, is it? We work the streets."

"Yes."

He held up his glass and Legault touched it with hers. Then they drank what they had left and put down the empty glasses.

Legault said, "You've worked a few homicides?"

"A few."

"They turned out okay?"

"Homicides never turn out okay," Dougherty said. "Someone's always dead. But we caught the guys."

Legault said, "Good."

———

Judy said, "Ulrike Meinhof killed herself."

"Oh yeah, that's too bad."

Judy got out of bed and walked to Dougherty's kitchenette. "Do you know who she is?"

Dougherty said, "No."

"She was in the Baader-Meinhof gang."

"Oh, that Ulrike Meinhof," Dougherty said. "The terrorist."

"She was found hanged in her cell in West Germany."

"She busted the other one out of jail. They went to fight with the PLO."

"Yeah, he's Baader. They're actually called the Red Army Faction."

"I bet they can't play hockey like the Russian Red Army."

Judy came back to the bed, drinking a glass of water, and then held it out for Dougherty. He liked the way she was so casually naked in his apartment after they'd made out, her hair falling loose and her face a little flushed.

She got back into bed, saying, "No, this Red Army doesn't play around at all. Lots of bombs."

Dougherty lit a cigarette. "Terrorists love their bombs. And their kidnapping. Was she involved in the stuff with the Israeli athletes in Munich?"

"I don't think so, but I think at her trial she said she understood or supported the action, something like that."

"Always so understanding." He handed the cigarette to Judy and she took a drag and said, "Do you think there'll be anything like that during the Olympics here?"

"No, there haven't been any bombs or anything like that here in years."

"But the Olympics bring in the whole world, everybody's watching, it could be anyone."

"Security's pretty far up our ass," Dougherty said. "Everybody's getting overtime."

"So, people are worried something might happen."

Judy blew a long line of smoke at the ceiling and handed the cigarette back to Dougherty.

"What's going to happen is people are going to get drunk and get into fights and car accidents. That's going to take up all the overtime. And crowd control."

"So you'll be busy?"

"Yeah," Dougherty said, "but I won't be on any of the Olympic stuff, I'll be working this homicide."

Judy sat up and said, "What? Why didn't you tell me?"

"I just did."

"Before, this is a big deal."

"But it's not something to celebrate."

"It's a promotion."

"Another temporary assignment," Dougherty said, "but it doesn't feel like a happy day. Couple of teenagers killed. I met their parents."

Judy got on her side and pressed up against him and said, "No, I guess it's not a happy day."

Dougherty had left Legault on the south shore and driven back over the Champlain Bridge — he liked that view of Montreal, all the buildings lit up at night clustered together with the mountain and the cross above them — and then was happily surprised to find Judy at his apartment.

Now Judy said, "Puts mine in perspective. After dinner he wanted to go for drinks."

"Thursday's?"

"Some place like that, some place on Crescent. It's like he's trying to relive his youth, or have a youth, I guess. He got married and had me so young."

"He say that?"

"Like that. He was wearing a sports coat and a turtleneck."

"I can't picture that."

"My father, it's unbelievable."

"His new apartment around here?"

"On St. Marc. A lot nicer than this."

Dougherty thought maybe that was a good lead-in to talking about moving in together, getting a nicer apartment, the two of them, but then Judy said, "I hope I get a job soon."

"I was on the south shore today. Maybe they'll call you."

"That's where these kids lived?"

"Yeah. It looks like they went into the river on their way home from a concert. They might have gone off the Jacques Cartier Bridge."

"Oh my god, that's awful."

"If they did, that's not what killed them — they had water in their lungs." He felt Judy pressing harder against his side, and he thought for a moment he shouldn't give her all the details, but then he was thinking she was probably better with that kind of thing than he was. He said, "A boy and a girl. The girl was raped."

"Awful."

"People are worried the boy did it, of course, and then jumped himself."

"That's possible, isn't it?"

"Oh yeah," Dougherty said. "And if we don't find out something different happened, then that's what people are going to believe, that's what the families will live with."

"Then you better find out," Judy said.

Dougherty said, "Yeah."

At five thirty Dougherty's beeper went off, and he called and the phone rang once and a man's voice said, "*Bureau des homicides.*"

It wasn't something to celebrate, but Dougherty did feel good. And he managed to get out of the apartment without waking Judy.

CHAPTER
NINE

The newspaper reporter Keith Logan said, "You forget to put on your uniform?"

Dougherty said, "Temporary assignment."

"You're setting a record for that," Logan said. "You might have to buy more than one suit."

"I'll have to get Yvon Lambert to come with me to Dorion Suits," Dougherty said, "I always get too much as-ole," saying "hassle" in a heavy French accent like the hockey player did in the TV commercials.

"Hey," Logan said, "did you see the Hatfields and McCoys ended their feud? It was in the paper."

"Did you write the article?"

"No," Logan said, "it came in on the wire. They had a ceremony in a cemetery, three hundred people and a couple of ministers, one was a Hatfield and one was a McCoy. They put up a monument."

"A monument to a feud?"

Dougherty was looking past Logan to the group of cops standing around a car parked behind a fairly new drab concrete three-storey apartment building backing onto the lane off Avenue du Chaumont. The other side of the lane was the back of some very nice hundred-year-old brick houses that faced Parc La Fontaine, so it was possible that was where the dead body in the car had lived or was visiting, but if Dougherty had to guess he'd say it was more likely they'd be walking up the winding wrought-iron staircases on the back of the apartment building and canvassing there.

"Yeah," Logan said. "A monument to a feud. They're not sure what started it, probably something in the civil war, and it killed over a hundred people."

"If the guy in that car is a biker," Dougherty said, "we might have a feud to match it."

"I wonder where they'll put the monument when it's all over?"

"How about in there, next to Dollard des Ormeaux, that's a good monument."

"This used to be Logan Park, did you know that?" Dougherty said, "No, I didn't."

"Long time ago. It was the Logan farm before that."

"You get a piece of it?"

Logan said, "Before my time." He leaned over and looked past the backs of the houses and said, "I used to go to the zoo in there."

"I think I only came here in the winter," Dougherty said, "to the ice castle and a little skating."

"So, let me know if he's a biker."

Dougherty started to walk into the lane and said, "I'll let you know when there's an official statement." He saw Carpentier standing by the trunk of the car, a Ford, and walked towards it. The sun was coming up, but it wouldn't hit the lane for a few more hours and the sky was filled with clouds so it was dark enough that Dougherty couldn't make out any features on the dead guy, though it was definitely a guy with long hair and a bushy beard sprawled on the back seat.

Carpentier said, "Do you know him?"

"I don't think so."

"Gaëtane Gagnon."

"Then I do know him," Dougherty said. "Drug dealer."

"Yes, cocaine."

"I thought he only sold hash."

Carpentier said, "They all have cocaine now."

"Was he shot?"

Carpentier started walking out of the lane. "It looks like it, yes." He stopped and got out his cigarettes. As he held the lighter to the smoke, he said, "I was wondering, do you know if he dealt much with the Point Boys?"

"Yeah, I saw him with the younger Higgins a few times," Dougherty said.

"When was the last time?"

"Back in the winter, January, probably. We got that big shipment of hash at the airport, busted the baggage handlers. Streets were dry for a couple of weeks."

"That's when Gagnon started to deal with Higgins?"

"That's the first time I saw him in the west end,"

Dougherty said. "I don't know when he started dealing with them."

"All right," Carpentier said. "Good." He took a drag and blew out smoke, saying, "How's it going in Longueuil?"

"Good. I met the detectives in charge."

Carpentier nodded. "Allard is under some pressure now. From within, you know what I mean?"

"I talked to Legault," Dougherty said. "It doesn't matter to us."

"That's good. This job, *câlisse*," Carpentier said. "It's bad enough with them," he motioned to the dead guy in the car, "and then the office politics? *Merde*." He shrugged. "Keep me posted."

Dougherty said, "For sure," and walked back to his car. He saw Logan was still there, writing in a notebook, and he said, "Now all you need is a fedora and one of those little cards that says *Press*."

"So, is he a biker?"

Dougherty said, "Don't quote me."

"I never do."

"Then, no, he's just a guy."

"So this isn't part of the mob war?"

Dougherty had the car door opened and he stopped. "What?"

"There's talk, haven't you heard it? It's coming out because of the trial, the Dubois Brothers."

"Was that in the paper, too? You should stick to the Hatfields and McCoys."

"Dubois said it's all talk. He said if he's in the Queen E hotel someone says he owns it."

"What's he doing in the Queen E?" Dougherty said.

"Funny. They're saying Dubois is getting squeezed downtown — the Point Boys are moving too far east."

"Did you watch *The Godfather* again?"

"Come on," Logan said. "The Olympics are going to be the biggest party in the world and someone's going to sell a ton of drugs to keep the party going."

Dougherty had his hand on the car door and he said, "Sounds like you already know everything about it."

"Who's the guy in the car? He a dealer?"

Dougherty sat down behind the wheel, but before he closed the door he said, "Off the record, yeah, and you're right about the drugs."

A couple of blocks through the residential neighbourhood, and Dougherty turned onto Papineau and then headed across the Jacques Cartier Bridge to Longueuil. Traffic was heavy and moving slowly coming into the city but heading to the south shore during morning rush hour was quick. Dougherty was thinking that for the newspapers the idea of a mob war was probably exciting, lots to write about, and he might have found the idea kind of exciting himself a few years ago, but now all he saw was dead guys in cars and lanes and talking to mothers and fathers and wives and girlfriends and sadness and anger. Cops would make a lot of gallows jokes and lots of people would find angles to help themselves.

It was almost nine when Dougherty got to the Longueuil police station. He waited in the parking lot until he saw Legault pull in and walked towards her car.

"Good morning."

She got out, saying, "*Déjà?*"

She was wearing a suit, grey jacket and tight grey slacks that flared below the knee, a white blouse and a blue silk scarf, looking like Angie Dickinson on *Police Woman* but her hair was short and dark instead of long and blonde. And she wasn't as confident.

Dougherty spoke French, saying, "My first name's Eddie, by the way."

"Francine."

He figured she was close to his own age, close to thirty, already a sergeant so she must be doing something right.

"All right, Francine, let's get to work."

The meeting with Captain Allard and the detectives went exactly the way Dougherty figured it would. Detective Boudreau and Detective Lefebvre gave out the assignments — they'd be reinterviewing the friends and families of the victims, and Dougherty and Legault would talk to bus drivers, ticket takers at the Métro and the people who were working at Place des Nations during the concert.

Businesslike, polite and, without saying it, clear they thought Legault had missed something. She didn't say anything during the meeting, and Dougherty made sure not to look at her as the detectives did all the talking. Then he and Legault got out of there as soon as they could.

In the parking lot, Legault said, "They've already made up their minds."

"They have." Dougherty stood by his car and said, "I'll drive, if that's okay."

"We're just going to the Métro station, it's not far."

"Maybe we'll go there later," Dougherty said.

Legault looked more interested now and said, "Later?"

"Come on." Dougherty got in and started the car. When Legault was in the passenger seat, he pulled out of the parking lot and headed for the bridge. "You know they're not going to get anything from the friends and families."

"All they'll get is grief," Legault said.

"So, we're going to do what we would have done anyway."

They passed through where the tollbooths had once been and headed onto the bridge.

Legault said, "Yes, but the families shouldn't have to go through the questioning again."

"And they'll feel like no one is actually working on the case," Dougherty said. "I hear you."

As they crested the high point and started down on the Montreal side of the bridge, past the second of the two tall steel spires topped with finials that looked like little Eiffel Towers, Dougherty got into the right-hand lane and slowed down, taking the exit for Île Sainte-Hélène. The off-ramp from the bridge curved around a large five-storey brick building. When the road straightened out at the bottom of the ramp on the island, Dougherty pulled over and stopped.

"Come on, let's see what we've got."

Legault got out of the car, too, and they walked over the grass to the door to the building and the stairway that led up to the bridge's surface.

Inside the wide stairwell it smelled of urine, and as they got to the first landing Legault stopped and looked through a boarded-up opening and said, "Why is this building so big?"

"I don't know," Dougherty said. "I think it used to be a warehouse for the city. I think I smell horseshit, too."

At the top of the stairs, they stepped onto the bridge, and Dougherty stopped. There was a railing about four feet high dividing the sidewalk from the roadway.

Legault said, "Once a month we get a call about a jumper on this bridge."

"You get the call in Longueuil?"

"Harbour Patrol are supposed to respond, but if the jumper is past halfway towards the south shore, they usually call us."

"You've responded?"

"A few times, yes." Legault was looking down over the side of the bridge at the rushing St. Lawrence River. It was over a mile wide at this point. "Some we talk down."

Dougherty said, "That's good."

He walked a few feet along the sidewalk, then stopped and looked around. "They left the concert around ten, so it was dark. It would have been easy for someone to surprise them on the stairs, follow them up here."

"But why?"

Dougherty walked back into the building and looked at the boards covering the old doorway. He pulled it aside easily and stepped through the opening.

The room was big and dark, with a high ceiling and window openings on every wall. There were steel I-beam pillars in long rows but otherwise the place was empty. Dougherty walked to the windows facing east; the openings were covered with steel mesh, like a fence, and there were a lot of pigeons coming and going.

"It's a nice view," Dougherty said.

"Look at this."

Legault was on the other side of the room, in a dark corner, bent over examining something. She looked over her shoulder as Dougherty approached.

He said, "Yeah, that's what we're looking for."

Legault stood up with a length of rope in her hand, maybe two feet, frayed at both ends. "Maybe there will be fingerprints."

"We can hope."

"It won't prove anything."

"It's something," Dougherty said.

He started walking towards the stairs and Legault said, "*Mon Dieu.*" She was staring out the windows overlooking Île Sainte-Hélène and the old Expo 67 site. Many of the pavilions were closed, but some were still operating as Terre des Hommes and the roller coasters and other rides of the amusement park, La Ronde, were still in use.

Dougherty said, "Wow."

A plume of black smoke was rising from the biosphere, the huge geodesic dome that was the American pavilion at Expo.

Legault said, "The fire is spreading so fast."

"The dome is covered with acrylic," Dougherty said. "I worked construction there in '66. The rest of it is steel, it won't burn."

The black smoke continued to rise, looking like a giant tornado.

"The fire is just at the top," Legault said.

Dougherty said, "Yeah," but watched it spread down around the sides of the dome. "We better get going before they close the bridge."

———

"The pavilion on the Jacques Cartier Bridge," Rozovsky said. "It was going to be a casino and a ballroom, there were big plans."

"What happened?"

"The Depression. It was in all the papers, you must've heard about it."

"Yeah, my parents said something about it," Dougherty said. "So it just sat there empty?"

They were in the evidence room. Dougherty had introduced Legault to Rozovsky, but the conversation was in English.

"When the war started, the army took it over. One of my uncles said that's where he had to report when he signed up. Then they used it for storage."

"During the war?"

"And I think afterwards the ground floor was a stable," Rozovsky said. "Might've been police horses."

"It smelled like horseshit. And piss."

Rozovsky came to the table in the middle of the room with the file they were looking for. He spread the pictures on the table and looked at Legault. "You have the rope?"

Dougherty said, "*La corde.*"

Legault was already handing the piece of rope to Rozovsky, and she made a face at Dougherty, shaking her head a little.

"Well, I'm no expert," Rozovsky said, "but it looks like a match to me."

Dougherty looked at Legault and said, "*C'en est un?*"

"*Oui, c'est un match.*"

Rozovsky placed the piece of rope on top of an eight-by-ten picture of Mathieu Simard's face. Now Rozovsky said, "I'll get Morissette to check it for prints."

Dougherty said, "All right, I'll sign it in." He got an evidence form and started filling it out.

Rozovsky got out his camera and put a yellow ruler next to the rope.

"I think this is the first time I've ever seen you take pictures of evidence."

"Very funny." The camera clicked and the flash went off. "And you know I should be at the biosphere getting pictures. That was the American pavilion, they might sell in the U.S."

"There was a plane flying by," Dougherty said. "I'm pretty sure I saw a guy taking pictures."

"That's the one the papers will use," Rozovsky said. "But I could get a better one from the ground."

"I'm sure you could."

Then Dougherty looked at Legault and said, "Come on, we better go talk to Detective Carpentier." Walking up the stairs to the homicide office he said, in French, "He was on a call this morning. Drug dealer killed."

There were a few guys sitting at desks in the big open room that was the homicide office, and Dougherty saw Carpentier getting himself a cup of coffee from the machine in the corner.

As Dougherty and Legault approached, Carpentier said, in English, "Someone just made a fresh pot."

"Detective Carpentier, this is Sergeant Legault from Longueuil."

"You have an update?"

Carpentier walked back to his desk, and Dougherty followed, saying, "We stopped at the Jacques Cartier Bridge, that pavilion by the off-ramp, and Legault found some rope. It looks like a match to the marks on Mathieu Simard's neck."

"I haven't been in that building in years," Carpentier said. "Since the war, I think. Did it look like Mathieu could have attempted to hang himself there?"

Dougherty hadn't thought of that. "I don't know." He looked at Legault and got the feeling she hadn't thought of it, either. "It's possible, we'll go back and check. Right now we're running the rope for prints."

"That's good." Carpentier sat down and said, "Anything else?"

"Not yet."

"All right."

It felt like a dismissal, so Dougherty started walking out of the office. In the hall he said to Legault, "I still think you're right, this wasn't a suicide attempt."

They were at the elevator, and Dougherty pushed the button. "What do you think?"

"Parlez-vous toujours anglais aux homicides?"

Dougherty switched to French and said, "However the boss talks to me is how I answer."

The elevator doors opened, and they stepped on.

"Let's say the bridge is the crime scene," Dougherty said. "Maybe this isn't the first time."

"Not the first murder?"

The elevator doors opened on the ground floor, and Dougherty and Legault walked through the lobby. "Not the first assault, anyway."

"You know of others?"

"Someone might."

"Oh," Legault said. "Harbour police."

Dougherty stopped on the front steps of the building and said, "First let's talk to our guys."

He started walking and looked back over his shoulder and said, "We might talk to some of them in English," and he was pretty sure he saw her smile a little.

Constable Salvatore Galluccio's first language was Italian, his second was French and his third was English. He parked his patrol car on D'Youville Street and walked towards Dougherty and Legault, who were sitting on a bench. To Dougherty he said, in English, "How can you eat that?"

"What are you talking about, it's a hot dog."

"On a mushy white-bread bun covered in cabbage."

"And onions and mustard. Are you telling me you don't eat steamies?"

Galluccio looked at Legault and said, "*S'il vous plaît, dites-moi que vous mangez pas comme ça.*"

She shrugged a little and motioned to the garbage can at the end of the bench, the paper wrapper from her steamie and fries still on top. She drank from her Pepsi bottle and said, "*Deux steamés, une frite pis un Pepsi.*"

123

Galluccio exaggerated his disappointment. Or maybe not. He switched back to English and said to Dougherty, "Sergeant Delisle said you wanted to talk to me, what's it about?"

Dougherty motioned across the street, past the customs building that took up the entire block, a big stone Beaux-Arts building with a dozen steps leading up to three large doorways and columns on the façade from the second storey to the fifth. He said, "You work the port? And the bridges?"

"When the harbour police aren't getting in the way."

"The bridges? You work the Jacques Cartier?"

"And the Victoria, but it's usually just traffic calls."

"What about muggings?"

"Not on the Victoria," Galluccio said. "There's barely room for cars on there."

"The Jacques Cartier. And St. Helen's Island."

"Yeah, we get calls. The bridge is getting more popular. Sometimes there are guys hanging around it at night, the stairwell, you know."

"That's what we're looking at," Dougherty said. "Right there."

"Fags?"

"What?"

Galluccio said, "Sometimes we get calls to roust the fags."

"No, we don't care about that."

Galluccio shrugged and said, "Neither do I, but we get the calls."

"But what about muggings?"

"Sure, yeah, there are some muggings on the island. We got guys working La Ronde all summer, I worked there last year."

"We're looking for someone who might be working the bridge."

Galluccio thought about it for a moment and said, "Not lately. I've heard about a couple of drug dealers, working as a team, one of them sells to kids, teenagers, and the other one robs them when they get there. They probably sell the same nickel bag five times, but no one's made a report, it's just a rumour."

Dougherty said, "That's exactly what we're looking for. Do you have a description?"

"A description? They look like drug dealers."

Standing up, Dougherty said, "Okay, can you put together a list for me, anybody who's been picked up for mugging or pickpocketing or anything like that on or near the bridge?"

Galluccio laughed and said, "Just that? How far back you want to go?"

Dougherty looked at Legault and switched to French, saying, "When was the bridge built, the '30s sometime?"

Legault said, "How about we go back a year? There was probably nothing over the winter, nobody on the bridge or the island, so it's really just last fall and summer."

"She's right, Galloosh," Dougherty said. "It's really just a couple of months."

"I told you, most of the robberies don't even get reported. It's usually someone buying drugs or doing something they don't want to talk to us about."

"You must have picked up some of these dealers. Get those names, too. Even the ones you didn't charge

— I don't care what kind of deals you made with them, this isn't a narco investigation."

"Now I'm your go-boy? I'm not that much younger than you."

"Chain of command. You ever want to get out of that uniform?"

Walking back to his car, Galluccio said, "I don't know about that, the chicks really dig it."

After the patrol car drove off, Dougherty said to Legault, "People are probably starting work at Place des Nations now, there's a concert tonight. We should talk to them before it starts."

Legault stood up from the park bench and said, "You work overtime every night?"

"If I have to."

They started walking towards McGill Street and the parking lot beside the old train station that was now a restaurant, and Legault said, "You're not married?"

"No, not yet."

"You're engaged?"

"No," Dougherty said, "also not yet." They crossed McGill, weaving through the traffic, and Dougherty said, "It's a little complicated, I guess."

"Okay."

At the car, Dougherty said, "You're married, right?"

"Yes."

"Is he a cop, too?"

"No, he's a builder," Legault said. "Houses, reno-vations, additions."

"Sets his own hours."

"Too many hours."

Dougherty got into the car, saying, "Same as us."

Legault said, "Yes."

Pulling into traffic, Dougherty didn't say anything, but he was pleased that there was at least one kind of us that included himself and Legault.

––––––––––

On Île Sainte-Hélène their first stop was the Métro station, where Legault showed school pictures of Mathieu Simard and Manon Houle and got nothing but shrugs. Legault explained, talking through the small circle in the Plexiglas barrier, that Mathieu had longer hair now and Manon wouldn't have been wearing her glasses, but that didn't help.

Dougherty drove slowly around the island, taking the long way around to avoid the mess at the biosphere. The fire had burned for a couple of hours and now the whole side of the island was blocked.

He said, "Did you spend a lot of time at Expo?"

"A little," Legault said. "I was working that summer in the Gaspésie, but I got to Expo." She looked at him and said, "Everybody went to Expo."

"Yeah, it was a great party," Dougherty said. "The whole world came."

Most of the pavilions were still there as part of Terre des Hommes, but quite a few no longer represented the nations they had. Across the small channel on Île Notre-Dame, the Union Jack on the old British pavilion had been repainted as the flag of Montreal with the fleur-de-lis, shamrock, rose and thistle in the four corners, and the rest of that island was being converted for Olympic rowing events.

"Manon and Mathieu would have been seven years

old, do you think they went?" Legault said.

"Yeah, probably. Seems like a long time ago now."

"But not for them," Legault said.

Dougherty said, "No."

He parked in front of the entrance to Place des Nations, and a security guard walked up to the car saying, "*Eilles, tu peux pas stationner ici.*"

Dougherty said, "We're police," and he almost added, We can park anywhere we want, but instead he said, "We need to talk to the manager."

People, mostly young with long hair and wearing jeans and jean jackets with embroidered designs, were streaming into the concert venue. Place des Nations was an outdoor venue, a couple of small cement bleachers and a big open space that held about seven or eight thousand people.

The security guard led the way into the office in the small building beside the entrance gate.

In the office, two men were sitting across a desk from one another and one of them looked up as the door opened. He saw Legault in her uniform and started waving his hand through the cloud of smoke in front of his face and put his other hand down below the desk.

Legault said, "*Bonjour, M. Tardif.*"

"Wow," Dougherty said, "that smells like some good weed. Way better than the kids in the cheap seats are smoking."

The other guy at the desk said, "*Bonjour*, Sergeant Legault. Still looking for those kids?"

"No, we found them," Legault said. "Now we're looking for who killed them."

Tardif, who'd been holding his breath since the cops walked in, exhaled a big cloud of smoke and then said, "That's too bad, I'm sorry to hear that."

Legault took the pictures out of her jacket pocket and put them down on the desk, saying, "So, I ask you one more time. Did you see these kids at the concert?"

The two men looked at each other across the desk, and then the one who still had the joint in his hand, Tardif, said, "Maybe, I'm not sure."

Dougherty was sure. He'd known as soon as they'd walked in that these guys knew something and weren't telling Legault. Now Dougherty was thinking this was Legault's play but he wasn't going to let it go on too long.

"What is it you might know?" Legault was looking at Tardif.

Tardif looked at the other guy across the desk and then at the security guard and then at the clock on the wall. Anywhere but at Legault and Dougherty. Finally he said, "Maybe I saw the girl."

Then no one said anything. The silence got awkward fast and then got worse. Then Tardif said, "Maybe she got backstage."

Legault said, "After the show?"

"Yeah, you know, they bring some girls backstage after."

"I know," Legault said. "And Manon was one of them?"

"Maybe. I can't be sure."

Dougherty was sure. And he knew Legault was sure, too.

She said, "How long did the party go on backstage?"

"Late," Tardif said. "All night."

"When did Manon leave?"

"I don't know, I didn't see her leave."

"And Mathieu didn't go backstage."

"They don't want the boys."

"Was Manon by herself?" Legault asked.

"A lot of girls get invited backstage, ten or fifteen, I don't know."

"To party with the band?"

"Yeah."

Legault looked at Dougherty. He didn't have anything to add.

She said, "You should have told me this sooner."

"I thought she was still partying. Sometimes the girls go with the band on the road for a while — they go to Quebec City or Ottawa or Toronto. It happens all the time. They always come back."

"Not always," Legault said.

———

In the car on the way back towards the bridge, Dougherty said, "So now we have two versions."

"Do we?"

Dougherty took the on-ramp but at the top where it merged with the bridge traffic he pulled over and stopped. To one side was the skyline of Montreal, the old stone buildings by the port, Notre Dame and the Bonsecours Market and then the skyscrapers, the all-black Place Victoria and Place Ville Marie with the searchlight on top, circling the city. Past the buildings Mount Royal and the bright lights of the cross, taller than anything else.

On the other side, across the river, was the south shore, the ever-expanding suburbs, thousands and thousands of houses disappearing into the darkness beyond.

"You talked to Manon's friends, they said she and Mathieu left the concert before it ended," Dougherty said. "This guy says she stayed till the end and went backstage. They can't both be right."

"So, her friends were trying to protect her. They didn't want anyone to know she went backstage."

"Then what happened? She left after the party and was walking back and Mathieu was waiting for her here?"

"Or he was waiting at Place des Nations. They had a fight," Legault said. "By the time they got here it was out of hand."

"Her friends just left at the end of the concert, left Manon here, and she went backstage by herself, does that sound right?"

"It sounds possible," Legault said.

"But you believed them when you spoke to them. You thought they were telling you the truth."

"I guess I was wrong."

"Maybe," Dougherty said. "Maybe not. Do you want to talk to them again?"

"Now that the detectives have talked to them?"

"Yeah, that does make it difficult."

"Difficult?" Legault turned on the seat and looked at him. "And when Captain Allard finds this out," she motioned back towards Place des Nations, "and finds out that someone is lying to me, that everyone is lying to me, what's he going to do?"

"All we can do is follow the evidence."

Legault turned back and faced the windshield, looking out at the south shore. "What evidence?"

"We'll find some," Dougherty said.

He put the car in gear and headed towards Longueuil.

CHAPTER TEN

Rozovsky was right, the newspaper used the aerial picture of the biosphere on fire on the front page. It wasn't very artistic, but it showed the whole thing, a giant black plume of smoke rising from the giant golf-ball-like structure.

Dougherty folded the paper in half and put it down on the lunch counter. He picked up his coffee cup but it was empty.

Legault came into the restaurant and sat down on the stool next to Dougherty. *"Un bon déjeuner?"*

"Oui," Dougherty said. *"Ça fait quelques heures."* He was holding up his mug, looking for the waitress, and he said, "It's almost lunchtime now. You want a coffee?"

The waitress came by with the coffee pot and filled Dougherty's mug. Legault asked for a cup. Then she looked at the newspaper and said, "He was right, your friend."

"He usually is."

"But what would he say about this?" Legault pointed to the other story on the front page, the headline beside the picture of the burning biosphere that read, "Air language war 'racism': Lalonde."

"I don't know, you'd have to ask him," Dougherty said. He'd read the article while he was waiting for Legault, the continuing story of the air traffic controllers in Quebec wanting to speak French instead of English on the job. There was a lot of resistance from the federal government, and now Fernand Lalonde, the Solicitor General of Quebec, was speaking about it for the first time, saying, as the headline screamed, that the issue was really racism.

"What do you think?" Legault said.

"As long as the planes land, I don't really think about it."

The waitress put a mug of coffee in front of Legault, who said, "*Merci*," and then to Dougherty, "But why should we be forced to speak English in a French province?"

He was thinking, So now we're not "us" anymore, us cops, that didn't last long, but he said, "Morissette got a partial off the rope, but there was something else."

"What?"

"Traces of cocaine."

Legault said, "Mathieu did not have any cocaine

in his system. There was none in the autopsy report."

"I bet Manon didn't, either."

"No," Legault said. "Their friends said sometimes they smoked hash, but that was it."

"So, we're looking for a guy who does cocaine, hangs around the bridge."

"There's really no connection between the rope and Mathieu and Manon. You're just guessing."

"I'm not guessing," Dougherty said. "I feel it. So do you."

"I want to," Legault said. "That doesn't make it real."

Dougherty finished off his coffee and put the mug down on the counter. He got a dollar bill out of his wallet and put it beside the mug. "When we get someone who looks good for it, the partial print'll help, give us some leverage."

"It won't be admissible in court, will it?"

"We'll leave that for the lawyers," Dougherty said, starting out of the restaurant, thinking, They're never part of "us." "First we've got to find someone."

In the car, Dougherty said, "Galloosh got us a couple of names."

"You were up early today."

"Who says I went to bed?"

They drove out of Old Montreal and headed west on Wellington, under the Bonaventure Expressway and past the warehouses and factories, past Canada Packers and the smell and through the Wellington Tunnel into Point St. Charles.

Dougherty said, "Might as well start with familiar territory. You ever been to the Point?"

"No," Legault said, "why would I?"

There were a few stores and a couple of banks on Wellington, and churches: English, French and Ukrainian Catholic, Anglican, United and even a Baptist church on the corner of Liverpool Street. And a lot of bars: taverns, brasseries, pubs and blind pigs hidden upstairs through back doors in the lanes.

"Come on," Dougherty said, "it's a tourist attraction, isn't it? Canada's oldest slum."

"It's not a slum," Legault said. "It's working class."

"I guess you're right — since they bulldozed Goose Village to make way for Expo, the place has really gone upscale."

"The Olympics are only bulldozing neighbourhoods in the east end," Legault said.

"I guess that's called progress."

Dougherty turned onto Hibernia and stopped in front of a two-storey red-brick row house, half a dozen apartments on each floor, the front doors right up against the sidewalk. He got out of the car and walked around it, saying, "Maybe you should go around back, and if a guy in his underwear comes running out, you tackle him."

At the front door, he turned the knob and said, "Or maybe he's expecting us," and walked in and up the stairs.

Legault followed closely, and at the top of the stairs they came into the living room that was being used as a bedroom. There was a mattress on the floor and clothes all over the place; it looked like the room had been tossed.

Dougherty stuck out his foot and poked the lump under the sheet on the mattress.

"Hey, Kenny, wakey-wakey."

The lump didn't move, so Dougherty poked it harder.

Legault said, "*C'est ton chum, ça?*"

"*Oh oui, on est des vieux amis, nous autres.*" He kicked the lump again. "Aren't we, Kenny?"

"What are you talking about, asshole?"

The sheet moved and a man sat up. His long hair was a mess, and his beard was scraggly. He held the sheet against his scrawny chest and looked from Dougherty to Legault and back to Dougherty.

"Don't you speak French, Kenny? Come on," Dougherty said, "what happens, you try to mug somebody and they don't speak English?"

"I didn't mug anybody."

"I bet you can count in French. How much is a gram of hash these days, Kenny, *cinq dollars? Dix dollars?*"

"Jesus, Dougherty, what the fuck do you want?"

"I haven't seen you in a long time, Kenny. It's been months since I picked you up, where was that, Atwater Park?"

"I don't know."

"You don't know much, do you? I just want to see how you're doing now, how's business at La Ronde."

"What?"

"You scalping tickets at Place des Nations? Dealing dope at the concerts?"

Kenny dropped his head back down on the mattress and said, "I'm not a dealer."

Dougherty reached down and grabbed him by the

hair with one hand, yanking him up onto his feet. Kenny dropped both hands to try to cover his dick, and Dougherty slapped him hard across the face.

"Last week, you working the concerts?"

"No!" He raised both hands to cover his face and Dougherty made a sharp move like he was going to punch him in the balls and Kenny dropped his hands.

Dougherty slapped his face again, harder. "Selling hash and coke."

"I wasn't, I swear."

Dougherty let go of his hair and Kenny fell back onto the mattress. He wrapped himself in the sheet and sat there looking dazed for a moment and then he said, "What do you care about some hash at the concert, I thought you were a big-time detective now, shaking down the big boys out in the suburbs."

He looked up and flinched a little, but Dougherty had turned away and was walking towards the kitchen, saying, "Don't worry about me, worry about yourself. Those big boys in the suburbs don't give a shit about you, Kenny. They left you far behind."

The kitchen was as big a mess as the rest of the place, the counter and table covered with dirty dishes and empty pizza boxes and beer bottles. Dougherty found half a pack of Export A's on top of the fridge, and he took it back into the living room. Legault hadn't moved from her spot by the door. Dougherty dropped the smokes beside Kenny on the mattress and said, "You remember the concert, it was Gentle Giant."

"Not my style," Kenny said. He got out a cigarette and reached back to get a lighter off the coffee table. "I don't like that prog rock shit."

"Where were you the night of the concert?"

Kenny lit his smoke and dropped the lighter back on the coffee table. He blew smoke at the ceiling and said, "I got no idea."

"So, if I tell you that someone saw you on Île Sainte-Hélène that night, and saw you on the Jacques Cartier Bridge, what would you say?"

"Who?"

Dougherty was walking around the small living room, stepping over piles of dirty clothes and album covers and newspapers.

"And if they say they bought some coke from you?"

"That's bullshit, I don't have any coke."

"Yeah, you the only dealer in town who doesn't?"

"I'm not a dealer," Kenny said.

"What are you?"

"I got laid off, I'm on pogey."

"You expect me to believe you had a job long enough to get pogey?"

Kenny took a drag and blew smoke at the ceiling and said, "I don't give a shit what you believe."

Dougherty was surprised Kenny was sticking to his story so much, he was almost starting to believe him. He said, "Okay, who is working the concerts?"

"I don't know." Kenny shrugged, took another drag. "Fudge is out of jail again. I thought he was going to Alberta, but maybe he hasn't left yet."

"Maybe?"

"I don't know."

"Okay, Kenny, if that's the best you've got."

Dougherty walked back across the living room, and when he was at the top of the stairs Kenny said, "I'm an upholsterer now, an apprentice. That's what I was doing when I got laid off."

"Good for you," Dougherty said. "But I still want to know who's working those concerts."

———

Outside on the sidewalk, Dougherty leaned against the car and lit a cigarette.

Legault said, "Sounds like he doesn't know anything."

"He better find out."

She got out her smokes and lit one herself. She took a deep drag and then motioned back towards the second floor of the row house. "Won't he tell you anything to get rid of you?"

"He'll never get rid of me," Dougherty said.

"Do you believe him, that he lost his job?"

"I don't know," Dougherty said. "I'm worried about my job. Okay, next up is a little farther west, Verdun." He opened the car door and looked over the roof at Legault. "You must've picked up some guys on your side of the bridge."

"We must have," Legault said, getting into the car, "but nobody tells me."

Dougherty pulled a U and headed back to Wellington. He said, "Have you always worked the youth squad?"

140 "I was a matron," Legault said. "When a woman was arrested I would search her and escort her to jail."

"Real police work."

"Not glamorous like this," Legault said, "but we do what we have to do."

"That's the truth."

Wellington continued into Verdun and got a little more upscale, if still working class. There were some bigger storefronts and nicer restaurants and no bars or brasseries or taverns.

Legault said, "Who was that Fudge he talked about?"

"Barry Fudge, another guy from the neighbourhood. Another dealer. These are all small-time guys," Dougherty said.

"We have to talk to all of them?"

"Just till we find the one we're looking for." Dougherty turned off Wellington and parked on Galt in front of more row houses, these ones three storeys with wrought-iron stairs and railings winding up to the second floor on the outside. "I don't know this one," Dougherty said. He pulled a small notebook from his pocket and flipped pages. "Masoud Rahmani. What is that, Pakistani?"

"I don't know."

Dougherty opened the door and got out of the car. He looked up and down the street and said, "There, 142, ground floor."

There was a small patch of grass, maybe five feet long, between the sidewalk and the building and a few flowers under the window of the first-floor apartment. Dougherty knocked on the door and heard footsteps inside and a woman's voice say, "It's about time," as the door opened, then she was quiet.

Dougherty said, "Hey, there, how's it going?"

"What do you want?"

"We want to talk to Masoud Rahmani."

The woman was white, with long brown hair tied in a loose ponytail. Dougherty put her in her mid-twenties but figured a lot of those years were hard living. He looked past her down the hall of the apartment and saw a baby stroller and toys on the floor.

The woman said, "Masi's not here."

"He go back to Pakistan?"

"He's from Iran."

"So, he go back to Iran?"

"What do you want?"

Dougherty stepped back a bit and motioned to Legault, who said, "Are you his wife?"

The woman said, "Yes. Who are you?"

"I'm Sergeant Legault. This is Detective Dougherty. Can you tell us when Mr. Rahmani will be home?"

"You should know, he's in your jail."

Dougherty asked, "How long has he been in?" and the woman started to close the door. Dougherty moved forward and blocked it, saying, "Not yet. Answer the question."

Legault said, "Mrs. Rahmani, we're investigating a serious crime."

"So what are you doing here?"

"Was your husband in jail a week ago?"

"Yes, it's been almost three weeks."

Legault said, "All right, thank you."

The woman glared at Dougherty and started to close the door. He stepped back just enough to let it pass. He stood on the stoop for a moment, looking back at the street, and then walked the few steps back to the car.

Legault said, "Who's next?"

Dougherty took a last look at the closed door and then checked his notebook. "Marc-André Daigneault." He closed the notebook and opened the car door.

"Ville-Émard, other side of the aqueduct."

It was only a few blocks and the row house style was the same but the street names went from being Argyle and Egan and Osborne to Hurteau and Jogeus and D'Aragnon.

The conversation at the door was almost the same, too, except it was in French instead of English and the woman was the mother instead of the wife. But the man they were looking for wasn't there and hadn't been there for weeks. The mother told Dougherty that she wasn't sure where her son was and that she had no idea when she'd see him again.

Legault played good cop and got the mother to admit that her son had been in jail for a couple of months over the winter and since he'd been out she hadn't seen him much. She added that he might be at his girlfriend's, and then spat out the name Louise Tremblay but said she had no idea where that might be.

In the car Legault said, "How many Louise Tremblays do you think there are in Montreal?"

"We can circle back around to her," Dougherty said, "we still have a few more guys to track down."

Dougherty looked at his notebook and said, "Next one is William Garner."

"Another old friend of yours?"

"I don't know this one," Dougherty said. "But I bet he hates to be called Willy."

They drove up to St. Patrick and along the canal. There were no boats on it, of course, there never were since the St. Lawrence Seaway went in almost twenty years before. Dougherty said, "My father said he used to go swimming in the canal."

"In that filthy water?"

"I guess they didn't care back then." Dougherty was driving slowly and looking across the canal at the factories on the other side. A couple of the ancient buildings looked like they still had something going on inside but whole floors looked empty. "My grandfather worked on the canal, at that old crane that's still there, you know it?"

Legault said, "No."

"Unloading the coal boats. I guess that's what most of the traffic was on the canal back then, coal from Nova Scotia."

Dougherty turned onto Atwater and went through the tunnel under the canal and then headed up the hill. He said, "Address we have for Willy is on St. Mathieu, but the building is called Dorchester Place, must be on the corner."

"Nicer neighbourhood."

Dougherty turned onto Dorchester and said, "Yeah, look at that, brand new."

"So ugly," Legault said.

Dougherty parked in front of a hydrant just around the corner on St. Mathieu and got out of the car. He looked up at the building, twenty-five or thirty storeys of flat windows and concrete, towering over the old two- and three-storey stone houses on the rest of the street, and said, "Apartment 2310."

As they were getting out of the car, Dougherty's beeper went off. He found a pay phone and called in for the message: "407-911." Return to the bank office immediately.

Legault said, "What is it?"

"I've got to go back to the office right away."

"The homicide office?"

Dougherty got back in the car. "No, the task force, the Brink's truck squad."

"You're still on that?"

He pulled away from the curb. "I never know where I am."

Legault said, "I've noticed."

"And you're in the passenger seat, so what does that say about you?"

"Good question."

"I can drop you on Bonsecours."

"Where is the robbery squad's office?"

"Top secret," Dougherty said. "They were convinced it was an inside job, maybe even with help from someone on the force, so everything's under the cone of silence."

"Even who's on it?"

"There was a rumour someone put out a contract on the senior detectives. Fifty grand."

"Not bad."

"We did get shot at and a couple detectives got beaten up in a bar, one's still in the hospital."

Legault said, "I heard about that."

"I hope we got someone," Dougherty said. He had to slam on the brakes coming out of the tunnel, the traffic backed up at the red light.

In the parking lot behind the police HQ, Legault got out of the car and said, "I'm going to get addresses for as many Louise Tremblays as I can."

"There may not be a lease in her name," Dougherty said. "But it's worth a shot."

Legault went into the building, and Dougherty continued to Old Montreal.

<hr />

The whole squad was in the office when Dougherty got there, and the first words Ste. Marie said were, "I suppose it's no surprise to you that we can't keep this squad together forever."

Dougherty was standing in his usual place at the back of the office, and he tried to see the reactions from the other detectives. He couldn't see any faces, but he could feel the mood in the room, and it wasn't good. These guys didn't want to give up.

Ste. Marie was saying, "We've been on this now for two and a half months. We've raided more than forty places, businesses and homes."

One of the detectives near the front of the room said, "And we have a lot more to go," and Ste. Marie stopped and looked at him and didn't say anything for a moment.

Then he said, "Martin, I agree, but we have the Olympics coming up in six weeks."

Another detective, Dougherty thought it was Caron, said, "So what?"

Ste. Marie wasn't happy, but he continued. "Many of you will be given new assignments, starting today, right now."

"This is bullshit, Robert."

"This robbery will remain a top priority for the robbery squad."

"*Incroyable.*"

"*Tabarnak.*"

"Bullshit."

"The robbery squad will be expanded, some of you here will be assigned to it right away."

"Fucking politics."

"Who ordered this?"

"We getting too close?"

Dougherty was thinking they weren't really getting anywhere, but he didn't say anything.

Ste. Marie waited till the yelling in the room died down, and then he said, "Look, this money isn't in Montreal anymore, we know that. We're going to catch the guys that did this, mark my words, but now we have to move on to what they spent the money on. We all know what that is."

Some guys agreed and were nodding, but Dougherty felt most of the guys in the room were still pissed off.

"We're still investigating," Ste. Marie said. "If anything, we're expanding. Some of you will be assigned to narcotics — we know that large shipments of drugs have been arriving for the Olympics. Every hotel room in the city is booked, tens of thousands of people are coming to Montreal for a party. We have to be ready for that, and there are only so many of us. We're all going to be busy."

Dougherty figured maybe there was a little more agreement then, and Ste. Marie finished with a bit of a pep talk about keeping the city safe. It wasn't enough to convince many of the detectives in the room that they were doing the right thing, but throwing them the bone of more overtime at time and a half would probably grease the wheels enough to move on fairly smoothly.

As the meeting was breaking into smaller groups, Dougherty saw Paquette standing by himself near the door and he walked over, saying, "Hey, you get an Olympic assignment?"

"No," Paquette said. "I've been assigned to robbery, permanent placement."

"Hey, congrats. Full-time detective."

Paquette was trying to play it cool, but he was clearly pleased with himself. "Not official yet, but looks like it."

"Sure," Dougherty said, "it'll be official soon enough."

Paquette started to say something, but one of the older detectives came up to them and said, "Let's go, some of us are still working."

A few detectives started out of the office, and Paquette looked at Dougherty before he started to follow them. He tried to look like he was unhappy about something, being bossed around or something, but he couldn't really manage it.

Dougherty said, "Go get 'em." The he saw Caron coming over, and he said, "Hey, Detective."

"I'm supposed to give you your assignment."

"I'm already working on something for Detective Carpentier."

Caron said, "Well, you have to report back to Station Ten and see what they have for you."

Dougherty said, "Seriously?"

Caron said, "Talk to Delisle. Tomorrow morning."

Dougherty said he'd do that. Then he drove back to HQ on Bonsecours and found Legault in the ident office on the third floor and said, "Any luck?"

"Yes, I found three Louise Tremblays under thirty years old."

"Good."

Legault was standing up and walking towards the doorway, and she said, "Bad meeting?"

"No, it was nothing. Let's go see Willy Garner."

They walked out of the building without speaking and got into the car that Dougherty had left double-parked on Bonsecours. He put it in gear and stomped on the gas, sending Legualt sliding around in the seat before she'd had a chance to settle in.

She said, "*Tabarnak, là.*"

Dougherty didn't say anything. He swerved through traffic, slowed down at a red, then went through the intersection and changed lanes about five times in six blocks along Dorchester.

Legault said, "*Y'a pas le feu?*"

Dougherty turned sharply onto St. Mathieu and stopped, saying, "We're here."

As they were walking into the lobby of the building two young women were coming out and as Dougherty held the door one of them said, "Thank you."

Dougherty didn't say anything and walked into the building.

On the twenty-third floor they found the apartment, and Dougherty knocked on the door.

From inside a man's voice said, "Hey, I didn't hear you buzz, how'd you get in?" The door opened. The guy was maybe thirty years old with a moustache and shoulder-length blonde hair and wearing a light blue leisure suit with the shirt collar open and no tie. He looked at Dougherty and said, "Who are you?"

Dougherty shoved the guy and walked past him into the apartment.

"Hey, I didn't say come in."

"I'm sure you were going to." Dougherty walked across the small living room to the windows and looked out at the west end, all residential and trees. "What's the best view from this building? Downtown? All the office buildings and the mountain, or looking south, the river and Mont St. Hilaire?"

"Who the hell are you?" The guy looked from Dougherty to Legault, who had come just inside the apartment and closed the door.

"I guess you like the west end, can you see where you're from?"

The guy was standing in the middle of the living room, and Dougherty noticed his platform shoes, but before he could say anything the guy said, "I'm gonna call the cops."

Dougherty said, "We're already here. I'm Detective Dougherty, this is Sergeant Legault. You're Willy Garner."

"William."

Dougherty looked at Legault and raised his eyebrows. She shook her head a little. She looked worried.

"William, of course. You've changed since the last picture I saw. What do you call that with your hair, is that feathered? Do you call it coiffed?"

"What do you want?"

Dougherty looked around the apartment, the chrome and leather couch and armchair and the small dinette set by the kitchen, and then back to Garner in his leisure suit and he said, "Looks like you're going to get down tonight."

"I asked you what you want."

"Do a little dance, make a little love." Dougherty was walking towards him, and Garner didn't notice until they were almost nose to nose and Dougherty said, "I'm going to ask you about some people you sell drugs to and you're just going to answer me."

"Look, man, I don't know who told you what, but it's bullshit."

Dougherty punched him in the stomach and Garner doubled over. Dougherty grabbed a handful of the feathered hair and lifted until they were face to face and said, "How you gonna get down tonight with a busted nose?"

"Fuck off."

Dougherty let go of the hair and punched Garner in the face. He wobbled on his platforms, both hands over his nose and Dougherty said, "You got arrested on St. Helen's Island selling dope."

"You're in so much shit."

Dougherty said, "I will throw you out the fucking window. Tell me about St. Helen's Island."

"That was a long time ago."

"It must seem like it up here, like you've come a long way, but you haven't."

Dougherty took a step and Garner almost fell over backing away. Dougherty turned and walked over to the fancy stereo system and picked up an album, sliding the black vinyl out of the cover. "We're not looking for the guys above you — we don't want you to rat on anyone important. But you sold some coke at a concert at Place des Nations."

"The Peter Frampton concert?"

"Last week."

Garner thought about it for a moment and said, "Gentle Giant. That's more of an acid and mescaline crowd, you know?" He wiped the blood from his nose with a handkerchief.

"The guy I'm looking for bought coke."

"I don't know," Garner said. "I wasn't there."

Dougherty threw the album like a frisbee. Garner got out of the way and the record hit the wall but didn't break.

"But someone you know was," Dougherty said. "Someone you sold to."

"I don't keep tabs on people."

"Give me one name," Dougherty said, "and I'll walk away right now."

Garner thought about it, tapped one of his platform shoes on the parquet floor and after a while said, "Okay, a guy I know may have been selling something at that concert."

"What's his name?"

"Sid."

"Sid what?"

"Gupta."

"Has he ever been arrested?"

"No. He's just a kid."

"Where does he live?"

"I don't know, NDG I think."

Dougherty started walking across the living room and said, "See, that was easy."

Garner said, "This won't come back to me?"

At the door Dougherty said, "You better hope not."

Outside, Legault said, "How did you know he was supplying someone?"

"I didn't, I just guessed. I didn't think he retired from the business after he got busted, and the way he looks now, what else could he be doing, making the kind of money he needs for the rent here and his fancy fucking suits."

The elevator door opened and they got on.

Legault said, "Now we have Sid Gupta and Louise Tremblay. There's always another name, eh?"

"Till we get the one we need."

"Do you want to talk about it?" Legault said as they reached the car.

"About what?"

"Whatever set you off."

"No," Dougherty said. "I told you, it was nothing."

Legault didn't say anything for a moment and then, "Okay, if you say so."

"I say so."

They got in the car and drove, and as they were stuck in traffic on Dorchester, Dougherty said, "I have to report back to my station house tomorrow."

"What do you mean?"

"They broke up the Brink's squad. They're sending us all back to our regular assignments."

"What does that mean for our investigation?"

Dougherty banged the steering wheel and said, "Come on, move." The car ahead of him stopped at the yellow instead of going through and Dougherty had to slam on the brakes. He kept looking straight ahead at the car stopped at the lights and said, "It just means I have to go back in uniform and work this when I can."

"You just give it up?"

"No, I said I work it when I can."

"Well, when can you work it if you have to work a regular shift?"

"Whenever I can. Look, I've done this before."

The light changed, and the car ahead finally moved. Dougherty pulled out around it, passing on the right and cutting off the car in that lane. There was a lot of honking.

Then Dougherty said, "Murder cases are never closed."

"What if they say Mathieu did it, killed Manon and then himself. That's what Captain Allard wants. And the detectives."

"They might do that anyway," Dougherty said. "We wouldn't stop working it then, either, would we?"

Legault nodded slowly and said, "No, we wouldn't stop."

CHAPTER
ELEVEN

Rozovsky said, "Now Dubois says there isn't even a Dubois gang, just him and his brother and they don't control anything."

"I heard." Dougherty was sitting on the other side of the booth, picking at his sweet and sour chicken, honey garlic spare ribs and fried rice.

"Years ago Dubois worked for a loan shark, Harry Schiff, called himself Harry Smith, you heard of him?"

"No."

"He was killed," Rozovsky said, "about ten years ago."

"Before I joined the force."

"Me too, but just barely. So, Dubois and his brothers worked for Harry Schiff, they were the muscle. The word is Dubois took over the business: there was about seventy grand outstanding, and Dubois collected it and went from there."

The waiter came by, a Chinese guy who could have been anywhere from thirty to sixty-five years old. He said, "You want coffee?"

Rozovsky said, "Yeah, thanks," and looked at Dougherty and said, "It's your dime."

"Sure, I'll have a coffee."

The waiter picked up their plates and left, and Rozovsky said, "And like all good loan sharks, Dubois branched out, he started fronting guys money for drugs and a lot of them repaid him and bought more."

"Now it's bikers," Dougherty said.

"Yeah, they're the muscle, and they're buying the drugs from Dubois and he buys it from someone else."

"Italians?"

"They have all the contacts in South America. Rizzuto still lives in Venezuela, right?"

"So I've heard."

"It's a business built on relationships, right? Well, that and money."

"What about your guys?"

"The day of the Jewish gangster in Montreal is coming to an end," Rozovsky said. "It did its job, now all the kids go to McGill and get into legit businesses. Well, not all, of course, but the smart ones. Now your guys are moving up the hill and all over downtown."

"Moved up from the port and put on suits," Dougherty said. "They're into a lot of it. And Dubois being in court all this time has helped."

"And all that money they got from the bank robberies bought a lot of drugs."

"That's the theory with the Brink's truck, that money went straight to Colombia for cocaine."

"More likely it went straight to St. Leonard and from there to Colombia, but there's no doubt the Point Boys are selling the product downtown."

"No doubt," Dougherty said.

"So, why do you want to know all this ancient history?"

The waiter brought the coffee cups and left without saying anything.

Dougherty picked up his cup and took a sip while Rozovsky poured milk and sugar into his. Then Dougherty said, "I don't want to go back to uniform at Station Ten."

"The chicks don't dig a man in uniform anymore?"

"So, I figure I've got to get into narcotics or something."

"I thought you were working homicide with Carpentier?"

"I can't seem to get a permanent assignment."

"So, what do you care? There's no more money in it, is there? You don't get a bonus if you solve a murder. Doesn't affect seniority or pension."

Dougherty laughed and said, "Pension?"

"It sounds like it's a hundred years away, but it isn't."

"It's not my biggest concern right now."

"Okay," Rozovsky shrugged. "So the Point Boys are moving a lot of coke downtown, you know them, you should be able to get into narco, it could be fun."

"I hate all this political bullshit."

Rozovsky drank his coffee. "What're you gonna do, this is Quebec — politics is the national sport."

"Yeah, I guess it is."

"Look, you've been hanging around homicide for years, and you've worked some big cases — you should be able to get in easy."

"Should be."

Rozovsky leaned back in the booth and said, "Anyway, the Olympics are going to keep everybody busy for a couple of months. Who knows, you might meet a sexy Russian gymnast, have to do a little personal security, you know what I mean?"

"The waiter knows what you mean and he doesn't even speak English."

"Don't believe that, he hears everything that gets said in here." Rozovsky drank more coffee and said, "For what it's worth, I say your best bet is talk to Carpentier, tell him what you want and then forget it. At least with the uniform you don't have to worry about what to wear to work every day."

"I've been wearing the same suit every day as a detective, no one's noticed."

Rozovsky drank a little coffee and said, "Well, they're not going to fire you, the rest is just details."

Dougherty said, "I guess." Then he stood up and dropped ten bucks on the table. "You're right." Walking out, he waved at the waiter who was standing beside the cash with another Chinese guy and said, "*Merci*, boss."

Outside on De la Gauchetière Street, there were quite a few people still looking for restaurants and bars, it was only a little after nine.

Rozovsky said, "Look, between you and me, the Dubois trial is going to mean the inquiry into organized crime is going to get extended. Cotroni can't pretend to be sick forever, but he's got enough money to pay his lawyers to drag it out for years. Meanwhile the whole narco squad is going to spend the whole time in court reading old reports. I can talk to Marcel for you, but it's not going to be much fun."

"I appreciate it," Dougherty said. "Nothing seems much fun these days."

"What are you talking about?"

"This city," Dougherty said. "It feels different. A few weeks from the Olympics and all we hear about are the problems. You remember a few weeks before Expo? The excitement?"

"That was ten years ago. A lot has changed."

"And a lot hasn't. But it wasn't just Expo, the whole city feels different."

Rozovsky said, "Yeah, all over downtown, there was so much going on, so much building. Place Ville Marie, Place Victoria."

"The Métro."

"Métro's getting extended now."

"Over budget and behind schedule. We didn't hear that every day about Expo."

"We were too young," Rozovsky said.

"I was working construction then," Dougherty said. "On the American pavilion."

"And now it's burned down."

Dougherty said, "This just feels like a cash grab, people lining up to the trough. And everybody so, I don't know, tense all the time. Pissed off. You feel it?"

"It's not just here," Rozovsky said. "Look at the riots in Boston, that busing stuff, look at New York, it's going bankrupt. 'Ford to City: Drop Dead,' you saw the headline."

"Yeah," Dougherty said, "everybody did."

"I was just in Brooklyn, I've got cousins there. That *Welcome Back, Kotter* is funny but it's not a joke, that place is a dump."

"I hope that doesn't happen here."

"Don't worry," Rozovsky said. "By the time the Olympics start it'll be a party."

"Yeah," Dougherty said, "there's always another party."

He almost believed it.

When Dougherty got to his apartment the phone was ringing. He picked up the receiver and said, "Yeah?"

"Where've you been, I've been calling."

"Working."

He sat down on the edge of the bed and started taking off his tie.

On the phone, Judy said, "Well, I've got news. I got a job."

"Good for you."

"What's that supposed to mean?"

"Nothing," Dougherty said, "just, that's good."

"Why are you so pissy?"

"I don't know, I had a bad day."

"Well, do you think you're going to have a good day soon?"

"I don't know, I guess it depends on the city."

"All right, when the city is more to your liking, give me a call."

She hung up, and Dougherty waited a moment then dropped the receiver into the cradle on the phone.

He looked around his one-room apartment, same place he'd been living since he was first assigned to Station Ten, six years ago now, and that made him feel even shittier. He flopped back on the bed but he knew he wouldn't be able to sleep. Judy was right, he couldn't let it get to him, couldn't let it run his life.

But he could feel something slipping away, coming apart at the seams. There'd always be another party, that was true. St. Jean Baptiste was coming up, that would bring two or three hundred thousand people out to Mount Royal. There would always be work for cops. Especially cops in uniform doing crowd control.

Around four in the morning, Dougherty fell asleep, and when his alarm went off at seven his head was throbbing as if he had a hangover. He was thinking, Great, now I don't even have to get drunk.

He found a wrinkled blue uniform shirt and a pair of pants on the floor of his closet and a plain blue tie hanging over the door. He got dressed and drove to Station Ten.

All the way he was thinking about Judy, thinking how that should be the one thing he didn't let slip away.

At the station, the desk sergeant, Delisle, was hanging up the phone when Dougherty walked in and he said, "You got out just in time."

"What are you talking about?"

"The robbery squad made arrests in the Brink's trunk heist."

Dougherty said, "Shit."

"No, they screwed it up."

"What are you talking about?"

"It was on the radio, you didn't hear? Laperrière gave a press conference, said it was solved, they arrested three guys."

"Boyle?"

"Réjean Duff."

Dougherty said, "Never heard of him."

"Roger Provençal and Michel Pilon."

"Who the hell are they?"

Dougherty was starting to pace in front of the desk.

Delisle said, "It wasn't supposed to go public. The detectives, Caron and the others, they couldn't believe it. They were still going on raids, they heard it on the radio that arrests had been made. By the time they got to the west end there were lawyers waiting at every door."

"They get any of the money?"

"Seventy-five grand."

"That's all? Out of almost three million?"

"Now they're saying the gang was both, east end *and* west end."

"But they didn't charge anybody in the west end, did they?" Dougherty said. "And what have they got that'll stick to these three?"

"You're better off out of it."

Dougherty wasn't buying that, but he said, "Look, I'm working something for Carpentier, something with the Longueuil department. Can you sign off on that?"

Delisle laughed and said, "You think *I* got promoted all of a sudden? Talk to the captain."

"What's going on here?"

"A good assignment for you: we're starting hotel security training. Plainclothes, you meet with hotel staff and explain security measures for the Olympics."

Dougherty said, "That's it?"

Delisle said, "You get to talk to some sexy chicks working the front desks of the best hotels in town."

A few years earlier, Dougherty would have jumped at it. That was almost the main reason he'd joined the police, meeting chicks and driving fast. And not sitting at a desk or going into the same warehouse every day for the rest of his life.

"Anything else?"

"This is it. You work a regular shift for a few days, then go for training yourself, then start meeting with hotel staff." Delisle was picking up the phone then, and he said, "Ride with Gagnon for a few days. The security training will be at a hotel out by the airport. They're bringing in experts."

Dougherty said, "I bet they are."

⸻

Gagnon was behind the wheel, driving slowly through downtown, a beautiful day in early June. He spoke French, saying, "It's not St. Jean Baptiste Day this year."

Dougherty was slouched in the passenger seat. He didn't say anything.

"No, this year it is officially la Fête Nationale du Québec."

Nothing from Dougherty.

"Might be fun this year, there might be trouble. Action. More, more, more."

"No more than usual." Dougherty was thinking about the first St. Jean Baptiste parade he worked, almost ten years ago now, turned into a riot. People throwing bottles and bricks at the reviewing stand, Prime Minister Trudeau refusing to leave, dozens of arrests, probably what Gagnon meant by fun. After that, the parade was cancelled and the celebrations spread out over the city. Over the eastern half of the city, anyway.

"It's a song," Gagnon said. "On the radio all the time. Did you hear about the concerts?"

"On the mountain?"

"Three days, lots of bands, dozens."

Dougherty said, "So, it'll be a party, some people will get drunk and some will get stoned. The usual."

"But all those bands and they didn't invite even one English."

"So?"

"You don't think that will cause some trouble?"

Dougherty said, "You mean with Anglos?"

"Come on," Gagnon said, "they invited bands from all over, from the Maritimes, from France, from Louisiana, all over, but all French. No English acts at all."

"What about Pagliaro?"

Gagnon laughed. "I don't know, maybe if he only sings 'J'entends frapper,' but not 'Rainshowers.'"

"That's his best one."

"I like 'Some Sing, Some Dance,'" Gagnon said. "Anyway, there could be some action."

"Anglos don't riot," Dougherty said. "Haven't you

ever met a WASP? Stiff upper lip and all that. They ignore."

"What about on St. Patrick's Day in the Point?"

"That's the Irish."

"Same thing, no? Irish are English."

"Irish speak English," Dougherty said. "We're not English."

"I don't get that."

"I know you don't."

Gagnon pulled back a bit, surprised, and then said, "Fuck you."

Dougherty said, "Don't worry about it, doesn't matter."

Gagnon shrugged and said, "Not to me it doesn't." He kept driving, the silence bearing down on the car, and then said, "Look, just because you're having a shitty day don't take it out on me."

Dougherty said, "Why don't you let me off right here."

Gagnon pulled over and stopped and as Dougherty was getting out of the car said, "What you want me to tell Delisle?"

"Tell him anything you want."

Gagnon shrugged and drove off.

Dougherty stood on the sidewalk wondering why everyone passing by looked so happy. He thought maybe it was true, what people said, that because of the long harsh winters in Montreal people appreciate and even celebrate the summers so much. Whatever the reason, a beautiful, sunny day in June brought out the best in people.

The only cloud was the one Dougherty was carrying around himself. He walked among the office workers out for lunch, the shoppers and the delivery guys whistling at the beautiful women and didn't lighten up at all. He was determined to be in a bad mood.

He ate lunch at the Rymark Tavern, a smoked meat sandwich and four glasses of draught. The waiter told him if he was going undercover as a drunk he'd want to take off the uniform.

In Dominion Square, Dougherty stopped to read the inscription on the statue of Robbie Burns and was thinking he couldn't explain the difference between the Scots and the English to Gagnon, either, when he heard a man yelling, "*Eille, toâ là, la police, viens 'citte,*" in an accent he didn't recognize.

Dougherty turned and saw an older man, probably in his sixties, coming across Peel Street.

"What is it?"

The man switched to accented English and said, "It's them, right there," turning and pointing back across Peel.

Dougherty was already moving, holding up a hand to stop traffic as he crossed the four-lane street. Cars honked and swerved but didn't slow down. Dougherty rounded the corner of the Windsor Hotel and caught up to the three men as they were running into the parking lot behind the buildings that faced Peel.

Dougherty yelled, "Stop," but kept running towards the parking lot as the men were opening the doors and jumping into a delivery van. He got to the van as it was backing out of the parking space, the passenger side door still open, and he managed to get a hand on the man still climbing in. He pulled and the guy fell out, knocking Dougherty over and landing on top of him.

The van stopped then, surprising Dougherty, and the other two guys jumped out swinging baseball bats, landing hard blows on Dougherty and the guy he'd pulled from the van.

Dougherty managed to get his nightstick off his belt as he rolled away from the guy who'd landed on top of him, and he rolled again, a bat slamming into his shoulder, but he got a good shot in on the guy's knee, enough to buckle him over, and Dougherty swung the nightstick into the guy's jaw.

Then he didn't see the other bat coming, and it landed hard on the side of his face and cracked his nose. Blood poured out.

The three guys were on their feet then and rushing to get back into the van.

Dougherty tried to stand up, but he was dizzy from the beers and the blows to the head, and he fell back down.

The van took off but stopped before it left the parking lot and backed up fast, coming right at Dougherty. He rolled out of the way — barely — and then was almost hit by the cop car coming into the lot.

Doors flung open, there were shouts, punches thrown, and in less than a minute the three guys Dougherty was fighting were face down on the pavement with their hands cuffed behind their backs.

Gagnon said, "Where's the other one?"

Dougherty said, "I only saw these three. What did they do?"

Gagnon laughed, "You don't even know? Why were you chasing them?"

"Someone called for a cop and I saw them running so I chased them."

"They robbed the jewellery store on Peel. Who called you?"

Dougherty looked around and saw the guy with the accent and said, "Him."

"The taxi driver?"

"I guess, if that's what he is."

"The store owner pushed the silent alarm," Gagnon said. "We came right away."

Dougherty stood up, groggy, and said, "That's good."

"You're drunk."

"I had lunch."

Gagnon said, "Okay, get back in the car, shit, we'll take these guys in. You can sleep it off."

"We're okay?"

Gagnon said, "Come on, let's go, forget it."

Dougherty got in the front seat of the cop car and watched as a couple more cop cars pulled into the lot and Gagnon took charge, getting the three thieves loaded into a couple of cars and then coming back and getting in behind the wheel.

They didn't say anything on the ride back to the station, and when Gagnon parked, Dougherty said, "Thanks."

"Hey, don't thank me," Gagnon said, "you taught me everything I know."

Inside the station, Delisle called Dougherty over to the front desk and said, "You got a call, a woman, she wants you to call her right away."

Dougherty took the small pink piece of paper with

the message on it and walked into the detectives' office. The number looked familiar but he couldn't place it. He called and Legault answered.

She said, "I had an idea. Can you meet me here?"

"Where's here?"

"The ident office, Bonsecours Street."

"I'll be right there." He hung up and walked to the front desk, saying, "I've got to go."

Delisle said, "Yeah, you sleep it off, be back in tomorrow morning."

Dougherty said, "Okay," glad that his years of service bought him a couple of mistakes and a few hours.

Ten minutes later, Dougherty walked into the ident office and said, "So, what is it?"

Legault said, "Maybe we should be looking for rapists, not muggers."

Dougherty said, "That's your idea, you think it was a rape? A boy and a girl?"

Legault stood up and walked towards Dougherty. She held out a picture, probably one of Rozovsky's, a bunch of kids at a rock concert. The band was onstage in the background, too small to tell who they were, though they all looked the same to Dougherty, and in the foreground of the picture were four girls in a row, looking at the band, arms in the air and long hair down the middle of their naked backs.

"Maybe he didn't know that," Legault said. "It was dark on the bridge, maybe he thought they were two girls."

She handed another picture to Dougherty, the same four topless girls, their arms in the air, but this time from another angle.

169

An angle that showed two of them were boys.

Dougherty said, "Yeah, that is a good idea, maybe that's what he thought. So now we'll look up anybody picked up for rape in that area."

"Most of the rapes won't have been reported."

"We'll start with the ones that have been."

Legault said, "Going back how far?"

"We'll keep going until we find what we're looking for."

"Don't you have to be somewhere else?"

Dougherty said, "There's no place I'd rather be."

CHAPTER
TWELVE

One more time, Dougherty was sitting at the back of a room full of cops listening to someone tell them a lot of things they already knew.

This time it was about traffic and which streets are busy at what times.

Captain Manseau was speaking English without much of an accent and he said something about morgues and hockey rinks and Dougherty looked up, paying a little more attention.

". . . have been identified as the best sites." Manseau was tapping places on a big map of Montreal hanging on the wall.

Beside Dougherty a guy said, "*Qu'est-ce qu'il dit à propos d'une morgue?*"

"Il veut utiliser les arénas."

"Comme morgues?"

Dougherty shook his head and got out his cigarettes. "It's what he said."

Now Manseau was talking about Munich and the athletes murdered there and the high probability of an attempt at something similar in Montreal, maybe bombs or hijackings, and how they needed to be prepared.

The guy next to Dougherty handed him a lighter and rolled his eyes.

Lighting up and exhaling, Dougherty said, "They'll want to bring in the army again."

The meeting was in English because there were RCMP officers present, officially as liaisons, which hadn't gone over well. Like the rest of the Montreal cops, Dougherty felt the pony patrol should stay in Ottawa and guard the tulips on Parliament Hill. After all, they hadn't lost one yet.

Manseau was tapping the map again, showing the four arenas where the ice would be maintained over the summer and used as morgues if necessary.

A cop near the front said, "Can we bring our skates for while we're waiting, get a few games in?"

"No," Manseau said, as if the guy had been serious. "There will be stretchers on the ice." Then he went on, giving the arenas code names and showing the routes emergency vehicles would take from hotels and games venues to the hospitals and then to the arenas.

Manseau talked for a few more minutes and then said maybe it would be a good time to break for coffee.

Dougherty stood up and handed back the lighter and

said, "You're looking good, Jacques," and motioned to the guy's leg.

Jacques LeBlanc moved his arm up and down and said, "That was a day, eh?"

"I can tell you now," Dougherty said, "I was scared."

"You were scared? I was the one who got shot." LeBlanc laughed and they started walking towards the door, following the rest of the guys into the lobby.

"I had to clean you up," Dougherty said. He hadn't really, of course. LeBlanc and another cop, Maurice Brisebois, had arrived at a bank robbery and there was a shootout. LeBlanc was hit in the arm but he killed one of the robbers and Brisebois shot the other one, who lived.

"It's a long time ago now," LeBlanc said.

"Six years ago, not that long," Dougherty said. "What are you doing now?"

"They put me on a god damned desk. I guess I got okay at it, I'm still there."

"And now you're here."

"All hands on deck."

Dougherty laughed. They were in the hotel lobby then. The conference room was a separate, one-storey round structure that looked like a spaceship from the outside, or at least Dougherty thought that was the idea. The hotel itself was a flat slab about ten storeys high, the whole thing probably put up for Expo and trying to look futuristic.

LeBlanc said, "I think he's hoping for something to go wrong."

"They are." Dougherty motioned to a couple of

guys standing off to the side by themselves, both with crew cuts, looking out of place among the Montreal cops with their slightly longer hair and moustaches, the Charles Bronson look.

"They always get their man, isn't that what they say," LeBlanc said. "Even if there's no man to get."

Dougherty said, "There's always someone to get."

"You got that right," LeBlanc said. "So, you a detective now?"

"Temporary assignment." Dougherty didn't add, another one, but it probably came across.

"Looks like we're all going to get a lot of overtime out of this, might be able to buy a cottage."

"Why should the construction workers get everything?"

LeBlanc laughed and said, "Yeah." Then he saw someone across the lobby and said, "I'll see you back inside, eh."

Dougherty walked a little ways down the hall past the elevators to the pay phones. There were four in a row on the wall with no barriers between them. Not very private, but he picked up a receiver and dropped in a dime.

The phone rang six times before Judy answered, saying, "Hello."

"It's me, how you doing?"

"I'm fine, how are you?"

It was a good sign she was even asking.

"You want to have dinner tonight?"

There was a pause and Dougherty waited. They'd been seeing each other for years, they weren't new at this, but with Judy finally finished school and now getting a job they were definitely heading into something different.

She said, "So, you're having a good day? Everything's okay?"

"I'm having a shitty day," Dougherty said, "but that shouldn't get in our way."

"No, it shouldn't."

Another pause and again Dougherty waited. Looking down the hall, he could see all the cops heading back into the conference room but he just waited.

"I want to go out and look at the school, I haven't seen it yet."

"Okay, why don't we take a drive and then have some dinner there. Where is it?"

"LaSalle."

"Okay, we're working office hours today, what do you say I pick you up around six?"

"Okay."

Dougherty said okay and goodbye, and hung up. He walked back into the conference room, thinking LaSalle wasn't exactly an underprivileged neighbourhood the way Judy had wanted but it also wasn't a West Island suburb, so there was that. A little compromise.

He could learn from that.

———

Judy said, "It's got to be right up here."

They'd driven from downtown on the expressway and took the exit just before the Mercier Bridge that put them in the industrial part of LaSalle, among the big old brick buildings with huge smokestacks, the Seagram's distillery, the Labatt's brewery, General Foods turning coffee beans into instant coffee and smaller plants that made things out of plastic and metal. Made for some interesting smells. Dougherty was hoping coming into LaSalle this way would make it feel very working-class, nothing like the tourist views of Montreal, it was an industrial city, after all, but when they crossed the aqueduct the streets were tree-lined and the houses were mostly newer bungalows.

"There it is."

Dougherty said, "It looks brand new."

"Few years," Judy said. "Opened in '72."

"Same as the one my brother goes to in Greenfield Park."

Dougherty slowed down as they passed. First there was a parking lot and then a big brick building.

Judy said, "Tom at the school board called it the bunker."

"I can see that."

The windows were big enough, but staggered, not in rows, some kind of modern design Dougherty figured. The building was set back from the street a bit and there was a lawn around it, empty now at nearly seven in the evening, but he could picture kids hanging out and smoking.

"Apparently it has an auto shop," Judy said.

As they came up on the sign that said *LaSalle Protestant High School*, Dougherty stopped the car. He said, "It's got some classrooms, too."

"It's not what I was expecting."

"Not too inviting?"

"I mean, the neighbourhood is nice but the school does look a little like a bunker."

Dougherty said, "So, maybe it is a real problem school, lots of drugs and crime and teenage pregnancy."

Judy was still looking at the school and she said, "We can hope."

Dougherty didn't know what to say, but he was finally learning that meant don't say anything.

Judy turned and looked at him. "You think I'm serious?"

Dougherty wasn't sure, but he said, "Of course not." He put the car in gear and drove slowly. Just past the school was an empty field with a large pile of dirt that looked like kids had been riding their bikes on, and past that were some new houses being built. These weren't bungalows, though, they were fourplexes with flat roofs built right up to the sidewalk, no front lawns, small balconies on the second floor and garages underneath.

Dougherty said, "Now you just have to hope there's no teachers strike."

"Maybe a work to rule," Judy said, "but a full strike is unlikely. There's so many strikes now: the pilots, the nurses, the x-ray techs."

"Hydro guys," Dougherty said. "Liquor stores going out soon."

"Is that for sure?"

"Ninety percent, we'll know in a few days."

"Better stock up."

Dougherty said, "I'm sure my father has."

"So it doesn't look like the teachers will go on strike," Judy said. "Not the Protestant board, anyway."

There was a fairly new shopping centre on the left, Le Cavalier, with a Woolco department store and a

Dominion grocery store at each end, and on the very next block another shopping centre, Place LaSalle, looked a little older with a Miracle Mart department store at one end and a Steinberg's grocery store at the other. After the second shopping centre, they came to an intersection with an apartment building on one corner and a round white building that came to a point on the other. It looked like the top of a spaceship. As they got closer, Dougherty saw the sign that said *St. Jean Brebeuf Catholic Church*.

Dougherty said, "We should celebrate. You want to go to the Bar B?"

Judy said, "There's probably a restaurant in the mall."

"Okay."

As they were turning the corner, Judy said, "Places for rent in that apartment building."

"It's a little far from downtown, way out here," Dougherty said.

He was pulling into the parking lot of the mall and driving around to the front of the building, and Judy said, "Yeah, it'll be hard to get all the way out here every morning."

There was a brasserie in the mall, and Judy and Dougherty both ordered the special, hot chicken sandwiches with mashed potatoes and gravy. From their booth they could see out into the mall, teenagers going in and out of the record store and the poster store, middle-aged couples with groceries.

Judy said, "What would you think about getting an apartment out here?"

Dougherty was drinking his beer, and he took an

extra gulp to keep himself from answering too quickly. Then he said, "You and me?"

"We've been talking about it, getting a place together."

"Living in sin, yeah." Dougherty was thinking that for the last few days they hadn't been talking at all, never mind talking about moving in together. "You want to?"

"It would be convenient."

Dougherty said, "Yeah," and Judy said, "More for me, I know, but you work all over the city. It could be a home base."

"I guess so."

"Okay."

That seemed to decide it.

Then Judy said, "So, how's the Olympic security detail?"

"As boring as it sounds."

"What happened to the murders?"

"Officially they belong to Longueuil and we were just helping out."

"Are you still?"

"I'm on the Olympic thing now."

Judy finished her beer and said, "But this is you we're talking about."

The waitress came to the table and asked them if they wanted any dessert, saying, "We have apple pie and lemon meringue."

Judy said, "No, thanks," and Dougherty said, "Just the bill, please."

The waitress did the final tally on her pad, tore off a sheet and put the paper down on the table.

Then Dougherty said, "Okay, yeah, I'm going to keep working with Legault, the Longueuil cop. She had a pretty good idea that the original crime was a rape and not a robbery."

"She had? The Longueuil cop is a woman?"

Dougherty said, "Yeah, so?"

"You didn't mention that."

"If you say so."

Dougherty got out his wallet and looked at the bill. He started getting out some money and knew he was just trying to delay — he knew he'd avoided telling Judy that Legault was a woman and he'd even run over a couple of scenarios in his head about telling her, thinking he might go on the offensive and say something about how he figured she'd be happy to see a woman in the investigation but even he knew how patronizing that would be.

Then he said, "The whole thing is messed up, two police forces, there's all kinds of politics. Legault is actually youth services, so she started it when they were missing kids." He counted out the money and a tip and left the bills tucked under his plate. "There's a good chance the detectives are going to say one kid killed the other one and then committed suicide so they can close it."

"You did mention that," Judy said.

"Look, I'm sorry if I didn't say anything about Legault being a woman."

"No, you're right," Judy said. "It shouldn't make any difference. It should be a good thing, really, that she's still working it."

"They're really just letting her stay on as a gofer,"

Dougherty said, "but I think she may be right."

"She's good?"

Dougherty shrugged. "Sure. She keeps working it, that's good."

"Will she get in trouble?"

"Probably. I mean, if they do close it and we keep working it and they're wrong, they'll look bad."

"But you'll catch a murderer."

"Oh yeah, everybody will be happy in public," Dougherty said, "and then in a couple of months Legault will be transferred to some shit assignment and buried there."

Judy shook her head and said, "The worst part is you're probably right."

"Happens all the time."

"Is that what happened to you?"

Dougherty said, "What?"

"Well, it's just, you know, all these temporary assignments and they keep sending you back to uniform."

Dougherty said, "I can't believe I didn't even think of that." He was thinking about it now, but he said, "Can't be, I never made Carpentier look bad. No, I just do what I'm told."

"Yeah, are you going to stop working this investigation?"

"No one told me to stop."

Judy said, "Right."

"There's not really much we can do," Dougherty said. "We're talking to every guy who was ever picked up near the Jacques Cartier Bridge or on Île Sainte-Hélène."

"It's like Cinderella," Judy said. "But you don't even have a glass slipper for them to try on."

Dougherty said, "That's right." He was thinking they had a partial print on a piece of rope they didn't even know was connected at all.

But he knew when they found the guy who did it, he'd know.

———

They walked through the mall. It was Thursday evening and fairly crowded. The mall was only open past six on Thursdays and Fridays and then only until nine. Judy took Dougherty's arm and he liked that. It felt odd to feel good about it, so suburban.

Dougherty wondered if this was what settling down felt like.

"Look at him," Judy said. "The World's Most Wanted Man."

"I guess he is."

"Looks like they're trying to make him the world's sexiest man, too."

On the cover of *Maclean's* magazine was the drawing of a man who looked to be in his thirties, stylish hair, sunglasses, moustache, turtleneck and a leather jacket. The headline read, *The World's Most Wanted Man, Carlos the Jackal.*

Dougherty said, "Like central casting sent over a bad guy we're supposed to root for."

Judy stepped past the magazine rack and picked up a copy of the newspaper, the *Montreal Star*, and said, "I'm going to check the ads for apartments."

While she was paying, Dougherty looked across the

mall to the poster shop, the teenagers flipping through the racks, passing images of rock stars, bare-chested Robert Plant and Jimi Hendrix and Che Guevara and Fidel Castro. Carlos didn't look out of place on the cover of the magazine.

"Looks like he did in that TV movie," Judy said, "about the OPEC kidnapping."

"He's a star."

"Think he'll be here for the Olympics?"

"I think the Mounties are hoping he is."

They were walking back through the mall towards the parking lot, and Judy said, "That's not funny."

"No, you're right. But the place is locked up tight."

"I hope so."

———

Dougherty had just got into bed when the phone rang. It was Legault, she said, "I've got one."

"Where?"

She said, in English, "It was reported to us, in Longueuil, he rape a woman on our side of the bridge."

Dougherty was standing up then, pulling his shirt back on. "He raped her on the bridge?"

"She walked across from Montreal, he grab her by the building use to be there for the tolls."

"She reported it?"

"Yes, I'm reading the report now." 183

Dougherty looked at the clock radio beside his bed. It was eleven fifteen. "You're in the office now?"

"I've been going through old reports," Legault said. "This is from three years ago. He served twenty-two month in all, he's out."

"Okay, let's talk to him."

"*Bien.* You want to meet here tomorrow?"

"No," Dougherty said, "let's talk to him now. Where is he?"

"Um," there was a pause and then Legault said, "Brossard."

"All right, I'll come out to the station and pick you up, we'll drive to Brossard."

"Should I call the Brossard police?"

"And get them out of bed? No, let's just go talk to the guy."

"*C'est pas l'une des nos juridictions.*"

"Don't worry about jurisdiction," Dougherty said. "By the time they get through the rest of the rules we're breaking, who's going to notice that?"

Legault said, "*Okay, bon, je te revois bientôt.*"

"Twenty minutes," Dougherty said.

———

Legault got into Dougherty's car and said, "I talked to his probation officer, and he's supposed to be at work now."

"You are breaking all the rules."

"It's someone I know," Legault said. "Used to be a cop, he was on the force when I joined." She looked at her notepad and said, "The rapist is André Marcotte and he's working at the Motel du Fleuve, you know it?"

"No."

"Le Boulevard Marie-Victorin, almost under the Champlain Bridge."

"Guy likes bridges."

They passed the Motel des Nations, the Motel l'Oiseau Bleu, the Motel Rideau, the Motel Washington and a few others along the divided boulevard, just a block from the river. More leftovers from Expo 67 getting another run out for the Olympics, Dougherty figured. He pulled into the empty lot of the Motel du Fleuve.

"Is he the night clerk?"

"Yes. He's twenty-two years old, single and was arrested only once."

"And someone gave him this job?"

"I guess so."

They walked into the office, a bell tied to a chain above the door ringing as they did. A man was sitting behind the counter, watching a movie on a small black-and-white TV.

Dougherty said, "André Marcotte?"

The guy said, "*Ouin.*"

Dougherty continued in French, "This is Sergeant Legault, I'm Detective Dougherty. We want to ask you some questions."

He didn't say which police forces they were with, and Marcotte didn't ask. He just said, "Nothing to say."

"You don't even know the questions."

"Doesn't matter, I don't have to speak to you without my lawyer."

Dougherty was walking around the counter then, flipping up the little divider at the end and grabbing Marcotte by the neck. He turned him around fast, twisted his arm behind his back with one hand and slammed his face into the counter with the other.

"Answer Sergeant Legault's questions."

Legault said, "When was the last time you were on the Jacques Cartier Bridge?"

Marcotte said, "Suck my dick."

Dougherty lifted his head up off the counter and slammed it back down.

Legault said, "When was the last time?"

"I don't know."

"How about two weeks ago? Thursday?"

"I was here. I work every night."

Legault leaned down so her face was very close to Marcotte's, and she said, "When you raped Lisette Desjardins you followed her from Île Sainte-Hélène."

"I didn't rape her."

Dougherty shoved his face harder onto the desk.

"It wasn't like that, it wasn't a rape."

Legault said, "What was it?"

"She wanted to."

Dougherty lifted Marcotte's head, but Legault held up her hand and he stopped.

Legault said, "Why did you follow her all the way across the bridge. Why didn't you do it there in the pavilion?"

"I didn't follow her. We walked together."

"You followed her," Legault said, "and then you raped her."

Dougherty was still holding Marcotte's arm behind his back and still had a fistful of his hair, ready to slam his head back into the desk, but Legault glanced up and nodded a little, letting him know she wanted to keep talking.

"Just you two?"

"Yes."

"There was no one else?"

"No."

"No?"

Dougherty started to push his head, and Marcotte said, "Okay, okay."

Legault waited a moment and then said, "Okay, what really happened?"

Dougherty let go of Marcotte's hair but kept hold of his arm.

"We were a gang, some guys, we met some girls. We partied."

"Drugs?"

"Yeah, some. And then Lisette wanted to go home and Martin, he told me to go with her."

"He was the leader of the gang," Legault said.

"It wasn't like that," Marcotte said, "not official like that. I didn't know him that much, a few weeks maybe."

"You wanted to be in the gang."

Marcotte nodded a little and looked at his shoes. "He told me to go with Lisette."

"And to rape her."

His head came up quick. "No."

Dougherty gave his arm one more twist and then let go.

Marcotte started rubbing his wrist where Dougherty had been holding it. He said, "It wasn't like that, I just knew, you know, that when I saw him again I had to tell him we did it, we screwed, you know."

"To be in his gang?"

"I was a kid." Head down again.

"You were nineteen."

"I was in CEGEP."

"Martin still hang out at La Ronde?"

"I haven't seen him since I got arrested and went to jail," Marcotte said. "I've never been back to Île Sainte-Hélène."

"What's Martin's last name?"

"Comptois."

Dougherty walked back out from behind the counter and went to the front door.

Legault said to Marcotte, "How did you get this job?"

"My uncle, he's a plumber, he knows the owner."

"Okay," Legault said. "We won't tell anyone we were here. I haven't spoken to your parole officer. You keep your nose clean."

Marcotte nodded.

Outside in the parking lot, Dougherty lit a cigarette and said, "How did you know it went down like that?"

He held out his pack of smokes, and Legault took one and said, "I didn't. But I felt that the report was, *maigre*, you know, didn't have all the information. There wasn't anything about what happened before, and it didn't seem like a good plan, to stand out in the open on the bridge waiting for a single woman? How long would you have to wait for one to come by?"

"Good point," Dougherty said. "I wouldn't have thought of that."

"So, I just guessed."

"See," Dougherty said, "you are a detective. Got us another name to add to our list."

"What are you going to do if we come across one of these people and you can't just beat the information out of them?"

Dougherty said, "I don't know, I'll cross that bridge when I get to it."

He didn't have to worry about it for a while. First there was the four-day celebration of St. Jean Baptiste, now la Fête Nationale, a couple hundred thousand people partying on Mount Royal and dozens of other parties around the city that kept the cops busy, and then on Sunday a plane on its way from Tel Aviv to Paris was hijacked and taken to Uganda, and suddenly the Olympic security became a lot more serious.

CHAPTER
THIRTEEN

Monday morning, Dougherty was back in the conference room at the hotel listening to Captain Manseau
talk about airport security. Dozens of flights a day
coming and going throughout the Olympics plus the
regularly scheduled flights, dignitaries, charter flights,
everything.

"The airport will be busy every minute of the day,"
Manseau said. "And so will we."

Dougherty was thinking, Yeah, busy watching
planes take off and land.

"The military airport in St. Hubert will also be
busy," Manseau said, "and we will co-ordinate with
them."

Dougherty shook his head, and beside him LeBlanc

said, "More bureaucracy, great."

The plane, an Air France flight, had been hijacked the night before and there was very little information. Captain Manseau said that the plane had been taken to Benghazi, in Libya, and that was all the information they had.

One of the guys near the front of the room said, "If the Olympics still happen."

Manseau said, "You might as well stop reading the papers, nothing they say is true."

"Come on," the guy said. "The IOC said they'd shut down the games over the China thing."

"The games will still go on."

Dougherty leaned over to LeBlanc and said, "What's he talking about?"

"The IOC recognizes Taiwan as China, but Canada recognizes Red China."

"So?"

"Athletes from both countries are coming and they both want to be called China," LeBlanc said.

Dougherty nodded and shared a look with LeBlanc. More politics, politics everywhere.

Manseau was saying that the IOC would be head-quartered at the Queen Elizabeth Hotel, and there would be a lot of extra security. "Pinkertons will supply the guards and also a new metal detector, similar to the ones at airports."

"They're going to walk the big shots through a metal detector?"

"It's mostly for the baggage," Manseau said. "And some of the staff. There will also be dogs sniffing for explosives."

"What if he sniffs out their drugs, do they get to keep it?"

Most of the guys in the room laughed.

A little after ten, they took a coffee break, and Dougherty went straight to the pay phones.

"How's it going?"

Legault said, "Not bad, I found two more Louise Tremblays and a Sidney Gupta in NDG."

"What about Comptois?"

"He's not living at the address we have on file, and they don't know where he moved to."

Dougherty lit a cigarette and exhaled. Then he said, "How's it going in Longueuil?"

"They haven't closed the case yet," Legault said.

"That's something."

"Yeah, that is good. Are they giving you much to do?"

"No, they're leaving me alone. How are you doing?"

"If the Chinese invade, we're ready," Dougherty said.

Legault said, "That's good to hear, I was worried."

"I can't get away until late this afternoon, around five. You want to go talk to some of these people then?"

"I'm going to talk to one of the Louise Tremblays this afternoon. I can meet you later, we can talk to Gupta in NDG."

"Okay," Dougherty said. "We can meet in the west end, do you know Chalet Bar-B-Q?"

"Yes, by Decarie, around six?"

"See you there."

Dougherty hung up and started walking back to the conference room, but LeBlanc caught up to him before he went inside and said, "They took the plane to Kampala."

"Where's that?"

"Africa. Uganda."

Dougherty said, "What for?"

"Idi Amin is welcoming them with open arms."

"Great."

"And look at them." LeBlanc nodded towards the crew-cut Mounties who were in a tight circle with the senior Montreal cops and a couple of guys who might as well have worn their air force uniforms. "Orgasm time."

"Maybe it'll keep them busy."

"At least it will keep them awake," LeBlanc said.

Dougherty said, "Yeah," and then they sat in the conference room for hours listening to guys drone on about procedure and emergency tactics and traffic movement until Dougherty wished someone would burst in with guns or bombs.

He was starting to understand these Mounties.

Dougherty got to Chalet Bar-B-Q at about six thirty, and Legault was already in a booth with a cup of coffee.

He said, "Did you eat yet?"

"No, I didn't even order. What's good here?"

"I've never heard of anyone order anything but the chicken dinner," Dougherty said. "Is there anything else on the menu?"

The waitress, an older woman with a beehive hairdo and an apron, came to the table, and Dougherty and Legault both ordered a quarter chicken dinner with fries, coleslaw and Pepsi.

"So, how was Louise Tremblay?"

Legault finished off what was left of her coffee and said, "She was the right one, she knew Marc-André Daigneault."

"She know where he is?"

"She said California, but she's not sure. He wants to be a biker."

"What do you think, is she telling the truth?"

"I think so," Legault said.

Dougherty said, "Okay," and settled into the booth. The place was busy, as it always seemed to be at any time of the day or night. It had been operating the same menu in the same place for over thirty years, and it looked like nothing had changed in that time. The main business was still take-out from a counter in the back where you could see the rotisseries cooking the whole chickens on skewers and the guys cutting them into four pieces with a few whacks from their cleavers.

The waitress brought them two cans of Pepsi and two glasses full of ice and left without saying anything, moving quickly to the next table.

Dougherty said, "Did you hear about the robbery here?"

"No."

"It was late, just before closing, a guy came to the take-out counter, held up a gun, some kind of pistol, said it was a hold-up. One of those guys cutting up the chickens cut the guy's hand off." Dougherty made a motion with his own hand. "Sliced it off clean like he was cutting off a chicken leg."

Legault said, "Did he just go back and continue cutting up the chickens?"

"I don't know," Dougherty said, "that's a good question."

———

Legault left her car parked half a block down on Girouard. One side of the street was lined with old stone houses. Where the other side used to be was now the Décarie Expressway, twenty feet below. Across the gaping hole of the expressway was one side of another street so the houses still faced each other.

In Dougherty's car, Legault said, "Gupta lives on Melrose Avenue."

"Below the tracks?"

"Is that an expression?"

"Yeah, it is," Dougherty said, "but in this case there are also real tracks." He drove along Sherbrooke and down Regent, checking address numbers until they got to the dead end at the railroad tracks, and Dougherty said, "See, below the tracks." There was a pedestrian walkway through a tunnel, the concrete steps and walls covered in graffiti, and a couple blocks away there was a pedestrian overpass but they had to drive to Girouard to get to the other side.

The Guptas were from India but Sid was born in Montreal and looked to Dougherty like every other pot-smoking student he saw downtown. When they'd parked in front of the two-storey duplex, Dougherty said, "That'll be Sidney," pointing at the guy in the t-shirt and jeans sitting on the front steps with a couple of white guys. Sid was a little darker-skinned and his hair was black but otherwise they all looked alike.

195

Dougherty got out of the car and said, "Hey Sid, how's it going?"

Sid played it cool, smiling, acting like it was no big deal, saying, "It's the fuzz," and laughing along with the other guys on the steps.

Dougherty said, "You want to talk here or go for a ride?"

"I like it here."

Dougherty looked at the two white guys and then back to Gupta and said, "You'll want it to be private, too."

"I don't think so."

"Yeah, you do," Dougherty said. "That way after you cave and tell us everything we need to know you can still tell these guys you were the man and you didn't say a word."

Gupta laughed and said, "Far out, you're cool, man."

"I'm in a hurry."

Dougherty looked back at the two guys and one of them said, "I was going anyway, see you later."

The other guy followed him, and when they were gone Dougherty said, "This is better, just us."

Gupta said, "There will be justice."

"You sell drugs at concerts: the Forum, Place des Arts, Place des Nations."

"What?" Gupta was still smiling but it was starting to fade.

"We're interested in Place des Nations. You remember the Gentle Giant concert?"

"Oh man, yeah," he tilted his head back and said, "the power and the glory."

Dougherty had no idea what he was talking about. He said, "You met two kids on the bridge, they were walking back to the south shore."

"What?"

"At the pavilion, the stairs up to the bridge."

"That old building?" He was starting to focus.

"A boy and a girl, but in the dark they might have both looked like girls."

"No, man," Gupta said. "I take the Métro, man, I don't go near the bridge."

Dougherty glanced at Legault. He got the feeling that Gupta was scared. And not of the cops. He said, "Why not, Sid, what's on the bridge?"

"Heights? I'm afraid of heights?"

"No you're not," Dougherty said, answering the question. "But I believe you, that you're afraid of the bridge. It's not your territory, is it?"

"I don't go near the bridge."

"Who's there?"

"Nobody."

"Just give me his name."

Gupta looked to Legault and said, "Why you gotta hassle me?"

Dougherty leaned in closer and put his hand on Sid's shoulder. He squeezed it hard and said, "Last chance." His free hand curled into a fist.

"There's some guys, I don't know their names."

"Just one."

They were almost nose to nose.

Gupta said, "Comptois. I don't know his first name."

"It's Martin," Dougherty said, standing up. "See, that wasn't hard."

Driving back downtown, Legault said, "You think it was Comptois?"

"We'll find out when we talk to him."

Legault shook her head and said, "This is crazy."

"What is?"

"Do you ever get tired of beating information out of people?"

"Not as long as I keep getting the information."

"And then we just go from one to another. They're all the same."

"Not all of them," Dougherty said. "The glass slipper will fit only one of them."

"What?"

"You know, Cinderella? We keep making them put on the glass slipper till it fits."

Legault said, "You come up with that?"

Dougherty said, "No, it was my," and he paused, not sure of the word to describe Judy. He said, "Girlfriend." But then he said, "We're going to get an apartment together. I think we're going to get married."

"You think?"

"Her parents just separated," Dougherty said. "It doesn't seem like a good time to talk about getting married."

"How long have you been together?"

"A few years," Dougherty said.

"How long have you known each other?"

"Well, let's see, the first time I arrested her was in 1970."

"How many times since?"

"Almost again a couple of years later, that's really when we started going together. She was a political radical."

"She hijack any planes?"

"You remember Milton Park," Dougherty said, "people getting kicked out of their houses? She was protesting that development, stuff like that."

"But not anymore? You set her straight?"

Dougherty laughed a little, thinking about what Judy would say to that. "Oh, she hasn't given up, she's still involved. She's a teacher now." He realized that was the first time he'd said she was a teacher, not going to be a teacher. It felt good.

"Would it surprise you to know I was involved in protests?"

Dougherty shrugged and said, "No," even though it did surprise him a little.

"For an independent Quebec?"

"Oh," Dougherty said, "you're a separatist."

"Does it shock you?"

"No."

"No?"

"It's just politics," Dougherty said. "I don't really care."

"You don't care if we tear apart your country?"

"You won't tear up the roads will you? I'll still be able to drive to the east coast?"

"If you can get through customs. But you would stay?"

"It's my home," Dougherty said. "I was born here. Why wouldn't I stay?"

"People talk about moving, so they can stay part of Canada."

"I haven't thought about it."

"Because you don't think it will happen?"

"Because I don't think it will change anything."

Legault looked surprised. She said, "But don't you think it will be better if we can run our own affairs?"

"*Maîtres chez nous*," Dougherty said, using the expression that was everywhere.

"That's right. Don't you think that would be better?"

Dougherty shrugged and said, "I don't know, I've never known politicians to make anything better."

"We've never tried this."

"No," Dougherty said, "that's true."

He turned onto Girouard and parked behind Legault's car.

She said, "So we have to find this Martin Comptois."

"Yeah, he doesn't have a record?"

"Not in Montreal or Longueuil."

"Okay, I'll make a request with the provincial police and the RCMP. See if they have any information."

Legault let out a sigh and nodded her head slowly. She said, "Sure."

Dougherty said, "Look," and he paused, but Legault didn't look at him, so he said, "not just anyone could do something like this. If we're right about this."

"We are."

"If we are, and there's a guy out there who strangled these kids and threw them off the bridge, if he doesn't get caught he'll do it again."

"You think so?"

"Oh, he was probably all broken up about it when he did it, when he realized what happened, how . . . final it was, that shocked him, sure, but the longer it goes on, the longer nothing happens to him and life just goes on, he'll just go with it. And, yeah, I believe he'll do it again, or something like it."

Legault was nodding, but she didn't say anything.

"As long as we have someone to check out, something to look at, we keep looking."

It was quiet in the car.

Then Legault said, "Okay. We keep trying the glass slipper."

She looked at Dougherty, and he had an urge to hold up his hand to shake on it, but they just nodded at each other, and she opened the car door and got out.

Dougherty drove back downtown, thinking every day this went on the chances of catching the guy got smaller and smaller.

Which just made him more determined.

<hr />

When Dougherty walked into Joe's Steak House Judy was already at a table with her father and already looking like she wanted to get away.

Dougherty said, "Sorry I'm late."

"Don't worry about it," Judy's father said, "just order a couple of these Harvey Wallbangers and catch up."

The waiter was at the table then, and Dougherty said, "I'll have a rum and Coke. Just one, thanks."

After the waiter left, Judy's father looked at Dougherty and said, "You out catching murderers all day?"

"Something like that."

"You're a detective now, right?"

Dougherty had never had much conversation with Judy's father. On their Sunday visits, Dougherty usually stayed out of it, letting Judy and her father argue politics or some world event until her father went into the basement with a drink in his hand and a defeated scowl on his face.

Now Judy's dad was a lot more upbeat, a lot more positive looking, as if nothing could get him down. He also looked like a guy who was trying to score in a bar, and they hadn't even had dinner yet.

"I'm doing Olympic security," Dougherty said. "Spent the day at the Queen E showing people how to lock doors and use the phone."

"That's where the dignitaries are staying, right? There must be some kind of party there tonight for the Americans, big fourth of July thing, the bicentennial?"

Dougherty said, "I don't know, Tom," using Judy's dad's name for maybe the third or fourth time since he'd known him, "probably."

"Maybe we should check it out," Tom said. "Wish them a happy birthday."

Judy said, "Why should we be happy about it?"

"They're our neighbours."

"Nothing we can do about that."

The waiter came to the table with Dougherty's drink, and Tom said, "So, how does everyone want their steaks?"

After they ordered, Caesar salads and steaks medium-rare all around, Tom said, "What better way to celebrate America's birthday than with a steak?"

"I didn't realize we were celebrating it," Judy said.

"Sure, we'll celebrate freedom."

Judy said, "Do you know what *Pravda* said today? The Declaration of Independence has been subverted by American capitalism."

Tom said, "Capitalism is paying for these steaks."

"Yeah," Dougherty said, "but the baked potato is communist."

Judy said, "Lots of places are not cheering for America today."

"Lots of places should take a closer look at the world," Tom said. "Get out of the classroom a little and really look around."

Dougherty could see this was heading straight into the perpetual-student line Tom used to get to Judy. He was going to say something, but the waiter arrived with the salads and that gave them a moment of silence.

Then Tom said, "Look at these hijackers, taking the plane to Uganda, is *Pravda* cheering Idi Amin today, is that the kind of world they want?"

"They let some hostages go," Judy said.

"Yeah, and they kept all the Jews."

Dougherty was a little surprised to hear Tom say that, thinking about how often Tom had been casually anti-Semitic out on the West Island, but then he figured maybe the move downtown was opening him up a little.

"Well, let's hope this ends with everybody safe," Dougherty said.

They ate their salads, and then the steaks arrived on wooden plates.

"Hijackers and terrorists," Tom said, "they should hang them all."

"We're finally getting rid of capital punishment," Judy said.

"Yeah, that'll show them," Tom said. "Look at these guys now, these hijackers, they won't even negotiate."

Judy said, "It's complicated."

"It's not complicated. The Israelis said they'd negotiate, a big change for them. Even Yasser Arafat sent his top guy, and these terrorists wouldn't talk to him. There's nothing to negotiate — they're just going to keep hijacking planes and killing innocent people."

"They're desperate."

"Who's desperate? The main hijackers are German, what do you think this is really about? And Carlos, some South American playboy, they're making him a hero. And you see who they want released? Some Japanese guy killed a bunch of people at the airport in Tel Aviv and some Germans, some Baader-Meinhof gang members who want to kill more people in department stores."

Dougherty saw Judy start to say something and then stop. She was determined not to let her father get to her. Dougherty knew it was really hard, even he wanted to tell Tom to shut up.

Then Tom looked at Dougherty and said, "Must be making things interesting for you guys."

"It's keeping us busy."

"You don't sound too happy about it."

"There are things I'd rather be doing."

"Yeah, well, shit rolls downhill, son," Tom said, all of his boozy cheeriness gone. "You better figure out how to get out of the way."

Dougherty didn't say anything, and he stole a glance

at Judy. She wasn't angry anymore, he could see that, but he couldn't really tell what she was thinking. He thought maybe she felt sorry for her father. Or maybe that was just Dougherty projecting, as Judy called it, his own feelings onto her. He was definitely having trouble taking Tom seriously with his turtleneck and sports coat and moustache and his tough talk, thinking, Really, he's just a guy who was too young for the war but old enough to be in a perfect place to get in on the ground floor with some big company while guys like Dougherty's father were busy getting shot at in Europe. Now he was fifty-something trying to look thirty-something and make up for lost time. Dougherty hadn't seen it but he was willing to bet the guy had on a white belt.

When she finished her steak, Judy lit a cigarette and said, "We're getting an apartment in LaSalle."

"The two of you?" Her father was smiling then, smirking.

"Yeah."

"But LaSalle?" Tom said. "Why not downtown? I'm on St. Marc, it's close to everything."

"This is close to the school I'll be teaching at."

"You sure you want to settle down, way out there?"

Talking about living downtown seemed to revitalize Tom. That or it made him feel superior again. Dougherty thought the smirk turned into a gloat.

205

"Don't settle down too early," Tom said. "Makes it very hard later."

Judy said, "We know what we're doing."

"Yeah, what are we doing? We walking over to Crescent Street for a drink?"

Judy said, "One drink."

Of course, one turned into three in the first bar they went to, and then three more in the next, and then they lost count.

Judy also lost count of the number of times she told her father to stop leering at the girls who were younger than she was, and he kept on winking and buying them drinks.

Two in the morning, Dougherty got Tom into a cab for the four-block ride, and then he got himself and Judy into a cab to head back to her apartment in the McGill ghetto.

The cabbie turned the big handle on the metre and said, "What an amazing rescue."

"What rescue?"

"You didn't hear? Israeli commandos went to Uganda and rescued all the hostages, flew them all back to Israel. It's all over the radio."

Dougherty said, "Well, this is going to change things at work."

Judy said, "How?"

"I don't know, but it can only be bad."

CHAPTER
FOURTEEN

Detective Carpentier looked over everything Dougherty had given him, and then said, "Yes, he is a good suspect."

"Sergeant Legault did good work," Dougherty said. "She suggested rape as the main motive, not robbery."

"But you can't find this guy?"

"I spoke to his mother in Sherbrooke, she hasn't seen him since Christmas."

"Did you tell her why you were calling?"

"No, I just said he might be a witness to something. I got the feeling she didn't like policemen very much."

"Hard to believe," Carpentier said, "but not everyone likes us. He has no record?"

"No. He's twenty-five years old, has no job I can find and never signed a lease."

"Can you find anyone else in his gang?"

Dougherty said, "I don't know that we can really call it a gang, it seems like it was mostly kids. The guy we talked to only knew them for a couple of weeks, says he's never seen them since."

"You believe him?"

"Yeah, I do."

Carpentier was sitting at his desk, and he nodded slowly. "So you want more time to work on this?"

"I'm on the Olympic security now," Dougherty said. "They've got so many guys on it, they won't notice if I'm not there."

"Olympic security is important."

"You think someone's really going to hijack a plane here or kidnap some athletes?"

Carpentier shrugged a little and said, "I think it's possible, don't you?"

"Possible, I guess."

"It could happen," Carpentier said. "And if something does happen during the Olympics and there's even a hint that our security wasn't top rate it will be a huge problem."

"But if this guy kills a couple more kids on their way home from a concert, that can get buried in the press," Dougherty said, "and no one will care."

"Ça suffit."

It was quiet for a moment. Dougherty knew he should apologize, but he also knew he was right so he didn't want to.

Then Carpentier said, "I can make sure you have

access to the records department and to ident and to the labs. The support staff here will process your requests as if you work here. That's the best I can do."

"That's more than I'm asking for," Dougherty said.

"No, it's not," Carpentier said. "But it's the best I can do now."

"Well, thanks."

"How is it going over there? Have you seen Vachon and his squad?"

"Alpha Team," Dougherty said. "That's one I didn't apply for."

"A lot of guys did," Carpentier said, "more than two hundred. They only picked eighty and then only forty-eight made it through the training."

"They showed us around their truck, their Mobile Command Unit. They've been running a lot of simulations, hostage situations, that kind of thing."

Carpentier said, "They have no budget problems."

"I guess not."

"Especially after what happened in Africa," Carpentier said. "You know a few of the hostages were from Montreal."

"I saw that, a woman from Côte Saint-Luc and a priest, I think."

"And a couple of others."

"People keep saying it could happen here," Dougherty said, "and sometimes it sounds like they hope something will."

"We need to be prepared."

Dougherty said, "At the briefing they explained to us that a terrorist attack that includes hijacking and kidnapping is called 'a leverage situation,' because there is a chance for negotiation. But a lone madman with a gun is a 'revenge situation.'"

"So what was Entebbe," Carpentier said, "a hijacking and kidnapping but they didn't want to negotiate?"

"I'm sure there are many strategy meetings going on right now," Dougherty said.

"Yes, that's for sure. I guess it's something new, the rescue situation. What would we do if Israeli commandos came to Montreal?"

"Take them to Schwartz's for smoked meat?"

Carpentier nodded but he didn't smile. Then he said, "But really, they rescue a hundred hostages and lose only one? It's a big deal."

Dougherty said, "Yeah, I get that."

"So," Carpentier said, moving on, "you can still work with Legault?"

"Yeah, working together isn't the problem."

"Sometimes it happens," Carpentier said, "people can't work together."

"No, we can, we just have to find the time."

"Captain Allard will leave her alone as long as the case is open," Carpentier said.

"Legault is worried they'll rule it a murder-suicide and close it."

"That could happen."

"Could we keep it open because the boy, Mathieu Simard, was found in Montreal?"

"It would be difficult," Carpentier said, "if Longueuil has closed the case. There would be a lot of politics. If you feel you're close to something, that would be different."

"I'll know better when I talk to this Martin Comptois. He's a little hard to find."

"Do the best you can," Carpentier said, and Dougherty felt it was a dismissal. He thanked Carpentier again and walked out of the homicide office.

Dougherty wasn't disappointed, he got as much as he was hoping for if he was honest with himself. Which he was, sometimes.

<hr/>

At the Queen Elizabeth Hotel loading dock, Dougherty watched a uniform cop he thought was about twelve years old direct traffic so the trucks could pull in off Belmont Street across from Central Station. There was a lineup of about five trucks.

LeBlanc was sitting on a folding chair beside the shipping office reading the paper, telling Dougherty that the peace talks in Lebanon had been postponed and the civil war continued but he wasn't sure who exactly was fighting, "Christians and Moslems, I think, but it might be communists."

Dougherty said, "On which side," and LeBlanc said, "I don't know."

Then LeBlanc said, "This China thing with Taiwan won't go away."

"The Olympics aren't getting cancelled."

"The IOC says Taiwan is China."

"And a billion Chinese say otherwise."

LeBlanc laughed. "And Trudeau says otherwise — he won't back down."

A truck honked its horn, and then another joined in. Dougherty walked over to the big garage doors that had been open all morning and said to the uniform cop, "What's the problem?"

"No problem, it's just slow going."

The driver hung out the window of the laundry truck and said, "I've got four more hotels to get to today."

"They'll all be like this," Dougherty said. "What can you do?"

"I can lose my job if I don't make the deliveries."

"Sorry, boss, nothing we can do."

The guy threw up his arms and shook his head.

Dougherty said, "You want a cup of coffee?"

"Then I'll have to piss, where'm I gonna go?"

"Cream and sugar?"

"Yeah, okay."

Dougherty walked to the next couple trucks in line and spoke to the drivers, then he pulled over the uniform cop and said, "Four coffees, two cream and sugar and two black."

"I'm not a gofer."

"Come on, not today," Dougherty said. "We're in this together, right?"

The uniform cop stared at Dougherty for a moment then nodded a little and said, "Don't make a habit of this."

"For sure. They've got a coffee machine in the hotel."

The kid said, "Okay."

Dougherty walked back to the shipping office and sat down on another folding chair beside LeBlanc.

"Hospital strike still going."

"Nurses?"

"Fifty-five hundred of them. And x-ray technicians. Says here Hôpital Maisonneuve-Rosemont won't be able to take Olympic athletes, they'll have to go somewhere else."

"Where?"

"English hospitals, the General and the Jewish General, I guess."

"Until they go on strike."

"The airline strike is settled," LeBlanc said. "But people are still mad, some cabinet minister resigned, said the settlement was —" he squinted at the newspaper "— a betrayal of the cause of bilingualism and a blow to federalism in Quebec."

"Who's next to go on strike?" Dougherty said.

He was only joking, but LeBlanc said, "Liquor store workers, might start tomorrow."

Dougherty stood up and said, "I've got to find a pay phone."

He walked into the hotel through the loading doors and passed the uniform cop coming out carrying Styrofoam cups on a plastic tray, and he said, "Cookies, that's a good idea, I didn't think of that." There were a half-dozen packets of chocolate chip cookies on the tray.

"It was the girl at the desk," the cop said.

"Hospitality is her business."

Dougherty walked into the lobby of the hotel, 213 which was very quiet. It was still a week away from the Olimpic opening ceremony and the big shots weren't in town yet. He saw a row of three pay phone booths across the lobby and went into one of them, closing the door. The whole place, the Queen E, felt like something out of the '50s to Dougherty, all the old wood and polished marble.

He dropped a dime and dialled and when the receptionist answered he said, "*Puis-je parler avec le sergent Legault, s'il vous plaît?*"

"*Un moment.*"

Dougherty was sitting on the little seat in the booth, and he looked out into the lobby, watching the two women behind the counter chatting. One of them lit a cigarette and tilted her head back to blow smoke at the ceiling and she laughed at something the other woman said.

Legault came on the phone then and said, "*Ici Sergent Legault.*"

Dougherty spoke French, saying, "Hey, it's me, how's it going?"

"Well, I'm in the office."

"Is that good?"

"I've been given another assignment, I'm writing a report about the youth centre downtown."

"Downtown Montreal?"

"No," Legault said, sounding a little impatient, "downtown Longueuil."

Dougherty was about to say he didn't realize Longueuil had a downtown, but he let that go and said, "They didn't take you off the homicide?"

There was a pause and then Legault said, "It's still open. I think Detective Carpentier spoke to Captain Allard."

Dougherty was surprised to hear that. "Can you still get away when we need to?"

"I think so. Have you got an address on Martin Comptois?"

"Not yet. You still have a Louise Tremblay to see, right?"

"Yes. Maybe later today."

At the hotel desk a couple of men were checking in and one of them was starting to get upset, waving his arms and raising his voice. Even from behind, from across the lobby, Dougherty had a very good idea what the guy looked like and what he was upset about.

"Okay, will you be back in the office around five? I'll call you then."

"Okay."

Dougherty hung up and walked across the lobby towards the front desk. By the time he got there, a man had come out of the office and was talking to the guy who was upset. Dougherty hung back a little and then took a few steps to the side of the counter, just beside the second guy, who wasn't as upset as his friend but who Dougherty figured would certainly jump in if they didn't get everything they wanted.

The man from the office was saying, "As Mlle. Daoust has said, there is no problem for the first two days but after that there are no rooms available."

"I have stayed at this hotel for years."

As the guy went on about how important he was, Dougherty looked at the other woman behind the counter, a little older than Mlle. Daoust, maybe thirty, and she looked back and said, "May I help you, sir?"

Dougherty said, a little too loudly, "I'm Detective Dougherty. We're doing the hotel security prep, one of the other cops said there was coffee around here?"

"Oh yes," the woman said, "this way." Her name tag said *Amalia*.

Dougherty said, "Thanks." He walked slowly around the front desk and figured that just announcing his presence would be enough to settle these guys down. They looked like businessmen in their forties, both of them wearing suits and carrying briefcases. Dougherty didn't see any luggage, and he wondered about that, but he kept following Amalia into the coffee room.

She was ahead of him, saying, "Cream and sugar?"

"Just black, thanks."

She poured the coffee into a Styrofoam cup and handed it to him. "It's really just beginning."

"I guess so. Are you ready for it?"

"Oh yes." She smiled. "I started working here during Expo. We were full every day for months."

"At least this'll only be a couple of weeks."

"Yes," Amalia said. "But to tell you the truth, it's different."

"Yeah," Dougherty said. "It's more tense, isn't it?"

Amalia nodded. She was leaning back against the table and she said, "Would you like a cookie?"

Dougherty felt the flirting and he said, "No, thanks." He didn't feel like a married man, he didn't think, but he had lost interest in flirting. He said, "I better get back to work."

Amalia said, "Me, too. I'm working until six o'clock," giving it one more try.

They walked out of the break room together and saw that the two men at the front desk had left. The younger woman came over to Amalia, and they were deep in conversation immediately.

When Dougherty finished his shift at the hotel, he

phoned the Longueuil police station for Legault and was told she was at the hospital.

"Why?"

"I can't say."

He was in the phone booth in the lobby of the hotel, and he closed the door and said, "I'm Detective Dougherty from Montreal, I'm working with her on an investigation. What's going on?"

After a pause the receptionist said, "There was an incident on the bridge, the Jacques Cartier. I don't have any details, I just know Sergeant Legault was hurt and was taken to the Hôpital Charles-LeMoyne."

Dougherty hung up and ran to his car.

⸻

"I had him," Legault said.

Dougherty spoke French, saying, "What happened?"

She was lying on the bed, one arm and one foot in a cast, and she said, "I don't know."

Dougherty was the only other person in the room. He was sitting on the edge of the empty bed next to Legault's and he waited.

She said, "I was coming back to Longueuil — I went to see Louise Tremblay."

Dougherty wanted to ask if she had any information, but he didn't want to interrupt.

"I saw him, up on the . . ." She paused and then said, "La Tour Eiffel, you know?"

"The ironwork," Dougherty said. "The spires."

"He was climbing up when I stopped. I called to him, but he didn't hear me, he was too high, there was too much noise, the traffic, the river."

"Yes."

"When I climbed up it was so quiet."

Dougherty realized she must have climbed very high up the spire.

"But then I didn't know what to say."

"I know."

Legault turned her head and looked at Dougherty. She said, "Have you ever seen a suicide?"

"A couple times I've been first on the scene," he said. "In the Métro, a guy jumped in front of the train at Guy station. And one time, a British guy, a war veteran, shot himself in the head and I was the first one into the apartment where he did it."

Dougherty was looking down, and when he lifted his head Legault was nodding.

Then she looked away and said, "I spoke to him. I even tried in English." She almost smiled.

"Was he English?"

"I don't know, I don't think so."

Again, Dougherty waited.

"He stopped climbing and looked back at me. I tried to say something, I tried to get him to talk to me, just to talk. I guess I didn't say the right thing."

"Maybe there was no right thing," Dougherty said.

"He wasn't young," Legault said. "He wasn't a boy, he was a man. He was maybe forty or forty-five. He was wearing a white shirt and a tie but no jacket."

"You always think there's something you can do," Dougherty said, "that there's something more you can do. It's why we join, isn't it?"

Legault nodded and said, "I thought if I could just talk to him I could get him to climb back down, but he just looked at me." There were tears in her eyes. "And then he just let go." She was crying then, tears running down her cheeks. She lifted a hand to her face.

Dougherty saw a box of tissues on the table by the bed and pulled out a handful. He said, "It's the worst thing to see."

Legault took the tissues and wiped her eyes but she was really crying now, barely able to speak, the words coming out broken. "He, he . . . passed right by me . . . looked right at me . . ."

Dougherty sat back down on the bed.

"I tried to grab him," Legault said. "I reached out, we were so close. Then I fell."

Dougherty didn't say anything. He thought about reaching out and taking her hand but he didn't. He figured he and Legault worked together, he wouldn't reach out and take LeBlanc's hand.

But Dougherty also knew that if he'd been on the bridge and reached out as the guy fell into the river so far below he'd be crying, too. He didn't think he'd ever admit that to anyone but he knew it was true.

Legault's husband walked into the room then, carrying a couple of paper bags from St-Hubert BBQ and Dougherty stood up and held out his hand, saying, "*Salut, tu dois être M. Legault.*"

They shook hands, and Legault said, "This is my husband, Réal," and then to her husband, "this is the Montreal cop I told you about."

219

Still holding Dougherty's hand, Réal looked at Legault and said, "*Anglais?*"

Dougherty continued speaking French. "I just stopped by to see how she was doing."

Réal held up the bags and said, "I didn't know you were here, I only got two. She didn't want hospital food. I can share with you." Réal was still wearing his work clothes, jeans and a t-shirt covered with white plaster and paint.

"No, that's okay," Dougherty said, "I should be going." He was thinking it was funny that he hadn't told Judy he was working with a female cop and Legault hadn't told her husband she was working with an Anglo cop.

From the bed, Legault said, "Thank you for coming."

"No problem. I'll come back tomorrow." He looked at Réal and said, "My parents live in Greenfield Park, I'm visiting them."

"Okay, sure. Nice to meet you."

They shook hands again and Dougherty left.

Instead of taking the busy Taschereau Boulevard, Dougherty drove through the quiet residential streets of Greenfield Park. His parents liked it out here in the suburbs: the Park had a small-town feel even though it was just across the bridge from Montreal. They moved there from Point St. Charles when Dougherty was in his last year of high school and he commuted to Verdun High rather than enrolling in the local Royal George High School. At the time it was a small school, and it went all the way from grade one through to the end of high school, but a few years ago the new English high school was built.

The street Dougherty drove down was lined with identical red-brick side-by-side duplexes surrounded by green lawns, exactly like the one his parents had bought. The whole area was a housing development that went in at the same time as the Greenfield Park Shopping Centre, which still bragged it was the biggest indoor mall on the south shore, though Dougherty wasn't sure if that was still true. He never really spent any time in the Park: the day they moved in, it felt too small for him, too isolated, but he was starting to see the appeal of that small-town feel, not quite twenty thousand people and almost all of them English-speaking, surrounded by a couple hundred thousand French speakers in Longueuil, St. Hubert and Brossard. Even in the suburbs it was the two solitudes.

He parked in front of his parents' house on the corner and went in through the back door that led into the kitchen. His mother was at the sink putting the last dish on the drying rack, and she said, "Eddie, I didn't know you were coming. Do you want some supper?"

He didn't want her to go to the trouble so he said, "No, that's okay, I just ate."

"You sure? It's no trouble."

His father had stepped into the kitchen from the living room then and said, "Of course, if you're looking for dessert there isn't anything."

"That's okay, I'm fine." It was a running joke when Dougherty was growing up: after every dinner his father would ask if there was anything sweet and his mother would say no. By the time Dougherty moved out, they were still saying it, but it had long stopped being funny and had taken on an edge. Dougherty held up a bottle in a paper bag and said, "I got you this. There's going to be a strike."

His father said, "You didn't have to do that," but he took the bottle. "How much do I owe you?"

"It fell off the back of a truck. I'm working at the Queen E, watching them unload."

His mother said, "What happened?" She looked stricken.

Dougherty laughed. "No, I'm still on the force, that's what they've got me doing, looking for mad bombers and hijackers hiding in laundry trucks."

"You getting overtime?" his father said. He was pulling the bottle out of the paper bag and looking at the label, Captain Morgan's dark, his drink. "I'll make us a couple." He looked at his wife and said, "Do you want one?" and she said, "Just a small one." Another running gag that wasn't funny anymore.

Dougherty sat down at the kitchen table and said, "I was out here visiting someone at the Charles-LeMoyne, a Longueuil cop I'm working with. Tried to stop a jumper on the bridge and fell, ended up in the hospital."

"Is he hurt bad?"

"She," Dougherty said. "Yeah, she broke an arm and a leg."

His father brought a rum and Coke, Pepsi really, to the table and handed it Dougherty. He took a sip — just enough Pepsi to give it some colour.

Going back to the counter, his father said, "What are you working on in Longueuil?"

"Didn't I tell you, a couple of kids were killed. Well," he said, "we think they were killed. They washed up downriver — one on the Montreal side and one on an island."

Dougherty's mother sat down and said, "Île du Fort?"

"No, I don't know that one, it was Île Charron."

His mother said, "*La même chose*, they change the name."

"You think they were killed?"

"The bodies were in the water for a while," Dougherty said, "so it's hard to tell. They were strangled, but they were alive when they hit the water."

His mother closed her eyes and said, "*Mon Dieu, quel âge ont les enfants?*"

"Dougherty said, "Fifteen, sixteen."

"*Le même que Tommy.*"

Dougherty nodded. He drank his rum and Pepsi and got out his cigarettes. "They were coming back from a concert on Île Sainte-Hélène. They walked over the bridge."

Dougherty's father handed him a lighter and got out his own Player's Plain.

His mother looked at his father and said, "Does Tommy go to concerts there?"

"I don't know."

Dougherty said, "Where is he?"

"Out. Around, somewhere."

For the first time, Dougherty started to feel the emptiness in the house. He hadn't spent a lot of time there even when he'd lived there, a couple of years after high school and the first couple of years after he joined the police force, but all his friends were still on the island in the Point and Verdun. Although with these days of being more honest with himself he'd have to admit he didn't really have many friends from high school. He

223

was thinking maybe the move to the south shore was more of a break than he'd realized at the time, but then he thought, No, it had a lot more to do with joining the police. The police were the enemy in the Point and Verdun.

Dougherty's mother said, "He gets in trouble at school."

"It's July," Dougherty said, "he's not getting in trouble now."

His mother shook her head and said, "No."

"So, he only has one more year, right?"

His mother got up from the table and started dragging a dishcloth over the sparkling clean countertop.

His father said, "He's got no idea what he's going to do then."

"Does he have to know that now?" Dougherty said, "He's got plenty of time." He wanted to say compared to the teenagers he arrested Tommy was completely fine, but then he realized he didn't really know Tommy that well — he still thought of him as ten years old.

"How's Judy?" his father said, changing the subject.

"Good," Dougherty said. "She got a job."

"That's great."

His mother turned from the counter and said, "Where is it?"

"It's in LaSalle, at the Protestant school."

His father said, "Full time?"

"Yeah, it looks good." Dougherty finished his drink and his father picked up the empty glass and went to the counter to make another one.

Dougherty said, "So, she's getting an apartment there, in LaSalle."

With his back to Dougherty his father said, "That's good, is it near the river or in the Heights?"

"Near the river. Between the river and the aqueduct. It's a nice neighbourhood."

His father put the glass down in front of him, and Dougherty said, "I'm going to move in, too."

His mother said, "To LaSalle."

"Yeah, LaSalle. To the apartment."

"Vivre ensemble?"

"Yeah, I guess."

"Not married?"

"Her parents just broke up, I told you that, remember? Her father's got an apartment downtown. It doesn't seem like a good time to get married."

"Mais c'est bien de vivre ensemble." It wasn't a question.

Dougherty tried to laugh it off and say, "It's not a big deal, we're going to get married. I got a ring."

His mother walked out of the kitchen.

"I really didn't think it would be such a big deal."

His father spoke quietly, saying, "Why would you think that?"

"I just figured after Cheryl did it."

And then he realized his parents still didn't know Cheryl was living with her boyfriend. After graduating from Concordia University, his younger sister had moved to Calgary, two thousand miles away. They both found work there when they couldn't in Montreal, and that was bad enough for his parents. Now Dougherty felt guilty for letting the living arrangements slip. But really, he couldn't believe anyone still believed Cheryl's story about living with a girlfriend.

His father just said, "Don't tell your mother."

Now he was laughing out loud, the nervous tension driving it but he also was starting to find the whole thing ridiculous. "All right, sure, if you don't want to know, we'll keep secrets."

"It's been hard enough on her with Cheryl so far away."

"How's she going to feel when she finds out?"

"She doesn't have to find out."

"The truth always comes out," Dougherty said. "That's what my whole job is based on."

His father said, "This isn't a police investigation, it's family."

"That's what most of them are."

Then his father didn't say anything. He drank his rum and Pepsi and lit another Player's Plain.

Dougherty said, "If Cheryl was here she'd be giving you a hard time for still smoking, especially unfiltereds, after the open-heart surgery. You don't miss that, do you?"

He was hoping for a laugh but his father just said, "Yes, I do."

"Okay, fine." Then Dougherty didn't say anything for a moment. When it started to get awkward he said, "We're going to get married. I really do have the ring."

"Why don't you stay in your apartment until then? Just keep the apartment."

"I don't know," Dougherty said. "We went out to look at the school and we saw an apartment for rent, it just kind of happened."

"It hasn't happened yet."

"I didn't think it would be such a big deal, we're not kids."

His father didn't say anything.

Dougherty let out a sigh and stood up, saying, "All right, well, I better get home. Big day tomorrow watching the maids make the beds."

"All right."

Dougherty walked to the back door and stopped and said, "It's going to be okay."

"I know."

Outside it was starting to get dark, and the streets were quiet. Dougherty drove through town again instead of heading straight to Taschereau. It was all flat, must have been farmers' fields before it became suburbs, though there were also older houses in Greenfield Park, wooden houses that probably dated back a hundred years. Dougherty passed Royal George School, an old red-brick building that was now Royal George Elementary and had a few portable classrooms in the parking lot for the last of the Baby Boomers.

Without thinking about it, he realized he was taking Victoria Bridge into the city instead of the newer Champlain that hooked up to the expressways. This was more like driving through town. What he was thinking about was the way people were committing to one another these days. Did it make a difference if Cheryl and her boyfriend got married or if he and Judy got married? They'd still be together, they'd still be committed to one another.

227

As he crossed the bridge, going over the section that lifted for the locks so the roadway was always close to the river, so different from the Jacques Cartier Bridge, he was thinking about Legault in the hospital and how she said she was a separatist. The politics didn't really mean anything to Dougherty, what flags flew, what areas called themselves a country, where the borders were. He crossed into the United States often enough — going camping with his parents when he was a kid, going to the drive-in when he started dating, he and Judy had been to Vermont so many times it didn't feel like another country.

Anyway, it really didn't seem like separation was going to go anywhere, it felt like another thing leftover from the '60s.

But marriage seemed like the right thing. Dougherty was thinking it did make a difference, it wasn't the same as living together. He was going to ask Judy to get married. They weren't anything like her parents — it was totally different.

Then the Olympics started and he was working twenty-four hours a day.

CHAPTER
FIFTEEN

First there was the dismantling of the Corridart, a four-mile-long art installation by sixty artists along Sherbrooke Street leading from downtown to the shiny, almost-finished Olympic Stadium.

The exhibits had taken months to put up along the street, and a few days before the opening ceremony the mayor ordered them taken down and hundreds of cops stood guard in the middle of the night while all the art was thrown into dump trucks and taken away.

Dougherty was one of a few dozen detectives walking the street and sitting in unmarked cars looking to see who came by to protest. There was a lot of shouting and a couple of people had to be kept away by uniform cops but no one was arrested.

In the car, watching what looked like a three-storey building being pulled down, LeBlanc said, "Why is that art?"

"I don't know, it looks just like that building," Dougherty said, pointing to a real three-storey brick building on the next block. The real building and the façade on the front of aluminum scaffolding looked exactly the same. Except the façade was being ripped down and tossed into dump trucks.

LeBlanc said, "Why is it being torn down?"

"I don't know." No one did, the order was simply to take it all down. Dougherty heard rumours that the mayor, after years and years of constant praise for everything from Expo 67 to the Métro to the expressways, was finally being criticized. Corridart had been up for six days and was supposed to be up throughout the Olympics. There were even two stages set up along the way that were supposed to have hundreds of performances. But some of the art pointed out how much money was being spent on a two-week sporting event hardly anyone really cared about and some of it was about housing, but most of it was too abstract for Dougherty. He thought there was probably some truth to the criticism, but he also figured the mayor was probably due for some pushback. All that building that went on the past few decades wasn't all sunshine and roses.

Dougherty met Judy when she was protesting a plan to kick thousands of people out of their homes that were then going to be bulldozed to put up huge apartment buildings and condominiums, and while they had managed to stop some of the development —

only phase one got built — that was one small victory in years of losses: Griffintown in the Point was lost, a bunch of the east end was torn up to make way for the Ville-Marie Expressway and a lot of houses in NDG were lost for the Décarie Expressway. There were protests, of course, but the people were tossed out and the new buildings and roads were built.

Now the Olympics felt like the final straw, the last big build that people were willing to put up with, and the artists of Corridart were going to let everyone know.

"We'll be getting overtime every day now," LeBlanc said. "From now till the end of the Olympics."

"Yeah, probably."

"It's good. We're not getting a raise this year. We can't go on strike like everyone else."

"No."

"I might get a new car," LeBlanc said.

It was starting to get light out, and Dougherty was watching a few people coming towards them down St. Famille Street looking like they were ready to make trouble.

"Maybe a Datsun. You ever drive a Datsun?"

"No."

"Or a Peugeot, my uncle has a Peugeot, it's all right. Maybe a Renault. You ever work youth services? They drive Renaults."

There were three people coming down the street, and Dougherty tensed up as they turned onto Sherbrooke.

"You like American cars? Maybe a Duster."

"Those guys look like trouble to you?" Dougherty pointed at the three men, all of them maybe twenty years old, skinny with long hair and wearing t-shirts and jeans.

"Yeah," LeBlanc said, "if you're a plate of bacon and eggs. They look like they worked all night and they're going to breakfast."

"What did they do all night?"

"They look like a cleaning crew."

Dougherty watched the three young men cross Sherbrooke and head farther south towards St. Catherine. They glanced at the destruction going on for miles along the street and kept walking.

LeBlanc said, "Are you back this afternoon, four to midnight?"

"No," Dougherty said, "I'm off for a couple of days."

"You took time off now, with all this overtime? You crazy?"

"What about those guys," Dougherty said, pointing. "What are they doing?"

"The bus driver?"

"No, those guys beside him."

Three people standing by the open door of the bus, the driver with a cup of coffee in his hand.

LeBlanc said, "You do need some sleep — you're starting to sound like the Mounties, you see bogeymen everywhere."

232   Dougherty looked at his watch and said, "What time will they be done?"

"Supposed to be by seven," LeBlanc said. "Doesn't look like they'll make it."

It was nine when the destruction finally finished and the last of the dump trucks headed to wherever they were going. Dougherty dropped LeBlanc off at the Métro and then drove to Station Ten to drop off the car.

When he walked in, Delisle said, "You got a phone call from downtown." He held out a small piece of pink paper.

"Who was it?"

"I'm not your receptionist."

Dougherty took the paper; it had the words *While You Were Out* across the top and boxes to check off for *telephoned, came to see you, returned your call* and a few other options. Delisle had just written a phone number across the bottom, and Dougherty was thinking it sure looked like he was a receptionist, but he didn't say anything. He dialled the number and waited while it rang.

"Bureau des homicides, bonjour."

Dougherty spoke French, using his official rank, "Constable Dougherty. There was a call for me?"

"Oh yes," the woman's voice said, "just a minute." There was a pause, and Dougherty could hear papers being moved around on a desk, and then, "We received a call from the Cornwall Police in Ontario. You were looking for a man named Martin Comptois."

"Yes, that's right."

The homicide receptionist gave him the phone number and the cop's name in Cornwall and then said, "Constable?"

Dougherty said, "Yes?"

"Well, it's just they asked for Detective Dougherty."

"Yeah, it's not official yet."

"I see."

"Thanks." He hung up and dialled the number she had given him. When it was answered he spoke in English, saying, "This is Detective Dougherty in Montreal. I'm looking for Sergeant Meekins."

He was put on hold and waited a few minutes and then a man came on and said, "Meekins."

"Yeah, this is Dougherty in Montreal. You picked up a guy named Martin Comptois?"

"Couple days ago. We just finished processing and we saw you were looking for him."

"I want to talk to him," Dougherty said. "Will you be holding him for a while?"

"He gets arraigned tomorrow, then out on bail if someone pays it. Otherwise he gets transferred to Kingston until his trial. What do you want to talk to him about?"

"He might have been a witness to a murder, a double murder."

"Shit. Okay, well he'll be here until tomorrow."

"What did you pick him up for?"

"He was on a boat that was smuggling. We get a lot of that through the Indian reserve here. We're hoping to get more out of him, but he's not saying anything."

"He have a lot of dope?"

"Not as much as we were hoping for — now it's going to be a conspiracy to import. It's getting complicated."

"If I drive out there today can I talk to him?"

"Sure," Meekins said, "he's in our cells until he goes to court tomorrow."

Dougherty thanked him and hung up. He'd been planning to go home and get some sleep and then go

234

to dinner with Judy, show her the ring and propose. He wasn't thinking about finding the right place or the right time, now he was just thinking about getting it done. Of course, that made it more likely she would say no, but then he could say he asked. Then he laughed a little, thinking, As if that would satisfy my mother.

"Hey, Delisle, how far is Cornwall?"

"Couple hours, why?"

"Can I take a car?"

"You're not on duty."

"It's official business."

Delisle had come down to the end of the dispatch desk, and he tilted his head to one side and said, "Really? Official?"

"Yes."

"Keep the radio on, in case we need the car back."

———

Dougherty kept the radio on, but he also cranked up the AM, top forty from CKGM, heard all about getting some afternoon delight and how moonlight feels right and knockin' on heaven's door and all about the Olympic breakfasts they would be broadcasting every day during the Games. The morning man, Ralph Lockwood, was going to be the host, and Dougherty imagined there would be plenty of practical jokes and prank phone calls to delegates from countries where they don't speak English.

The Dylan song made Dougherty think of the concert he and Judy went to at the Forum a couple of years back. They were still feeling out the relationship, and Bob Dylan at the Forum seemed like a kind of compromise: it was the folk music Judy liked, but it wasn't at the Yellow Door or some really intimate place, it was sixteen thousand people at the Forum, where Dougherty figured he could just blend in. He knew Dylan's songs, the famous ones, but he wasn't really a fan. And then it was a strange evening because he'd enjoyed the concert as much as Judy had. Dougherty liked the part with just the Band the best, "The Night They Drove Old Dixie Down" and "Stage Fright" and even most of the Dylan songs when the Band was onstage with him, and he liked to see Judy singing along to songs when he couldn't make out the words. It was a cold January night, and they'd gone back to his place, a short walk from the Forum. Now that he was thinking about it, Dougherty realized it wasn't really a compromise or finding common ground or something that sounded like the Paris Peace Talks, it was what couples did, they found things to do together.

Heading west on the expressway, he passed the factories and breweries in LaSalle and then the rows of apartment buildings in Lachine and then the backs of post-war detached houses in Dorval. The houses got bigger and farther apart from one another in Beaconsfield and then Dougherty could see only the trees in Baie-D'Urfé, the houses on big lots too far from the highway.

Dougherty was thinking it had gone without saying that after the war people had wanted to move farther from the city, away from the noise and congestion where they were stacked on each other in three- and four-storey flats, out to where there could be a little space between houses and some grass under people's feet. It's what Judy's parents had done, what his own parents had done, but it was the last place Judy wanted to live.

Then he crossed the bridge off the island of Montreal and an hour and a half later he was in Cornwall.

It was a small town on the St. Lawrence River and on the other side was New York state. Driving along Montreal Road, Dougherty had the window down and the place smelled like sulphur and something burning. The big industry was pulp and paper; there was a huge Domtar plant and a lot of smaller factories.

He found the police station, a nearly brand new four-storey brick-and-concrete building that also had cells in the back. The receptionist at the front desk called upstairs, and Sergeant Meekins came down to the lobby a few minutes later.

Meekins was older than Dougherty, probably mid- to late thirties, and he had a thick head of hair, long sideburns and a moustache. He wore a light blue suit with a checkered tie and Dougherty thought he could as easily be selling furniture as booking criminals.

He held out his hand and said, "How was the drive?"

Dougherty shook hands and said, "Fine."

"It's okay coming this way," Meekins said, "but I don't like going back — too much traffic when you hit Montreal."

"I guess I'm used to it."

"Don't know how you can get used to sitting in traffic. Anyway," he started walking towards the big winding wooden staircase and said, "what do you want to talk to Comptois about?"

Dougherty followed and they walked up to the second floor. He said, "Couple of kids were killed, strangled and thrown off a bridge."

"Holy shit," Meekins said, "that's huge." He stopped and looked back at Dougherty. "You're here by yourself?"

"Comptois may be a witness, that's all."

"All right, well, I'll get him brought up to an interview room."

Meekins turned into his office and sat down behind the desk, picking up the phone and saying, "Yeah, bring him up now." He hung up and said to Dougherty, "Just be a minute."

Dougherty nodded. He was still standing by the office door and he didn't sit down. "So, he was smuggling dope?"

"He was with some guys, yeah." Meekins motioned out the window and said, "We've still got jurisdiction for the island, but it's an Indian reserve. It's right on the border so there's a lot of smuggling."

"What do you mean you've still got jurisdiction?"

"It's all changing," Meekins said, "OPP taking over, some kind of joint taskforce with New York and the Mohawks. You don't want to know."

"No, I don't," Dougherty said, last thing he wanted to talk about was more politics. "The other guys, were they Americans?"

"No, locals. Pretty junior members in the local club. Comptois was the only one from out of town. He was probably here to pick up the drugs and take them back to Montreal."

"They bikers?"

Meekins shrugged. He got out a cigarette and said, "Probably higher up the chain of command they come into it, but they aren't based here now. Yet." He lit his smoke and said, "It looks like your boy Comptois is just a runner, came here to look over the organization and make a pickup."

"But he's not saying a word."

"Claims he doesn't speak English."

"Maybe he doesn't."

Meekins shrugged, and Dougherty figured Meekins, like every other Anglo, probably believed that every French person in Quebec actually could speak English if they wanted to. Or if you spoke to them in English slowly and loudly enough it would rub off.

"Well, if we can make the conspiracy case he might start talking Swahili — it's real jail time, three to five for sure." Meekins looked at Dougherty and said, "You think he threw those kids off the bridge?"

"His name came up in the investigation. It's a long shot."

"It always is," Meekins said, "until one of the long shots comes through."

A man was at the office door then, and he said, "He's in one."

Meekins stood up, saying, "Thanks," and then to Dougherty, "This way."

They stopped a little ways down the hall at the door to interview room number one, and Meekins said, "You want to be interrupted, hold up your hand," and he pointed to the observation room next door where he was planning to wait.

Dougherty said, "It's okay, I'll just talk to him."

"I have to listen in," Meekins said. "You know how it is." He walked into the observation room and closed the door, and Dougherty nodded at the other cop who opened the door to the interview room.

Martin Comptois looked about exactly the way Dougherty had expected him to: defiant, trying to look bored now that the initial shock of being arrested had worn off and he hadn't been beaten and thrown into a pit.

Dougherty sat down and said, in French, "I'm Detective Dougherty from Montreal. How you doing?"

Comptois shrugged, looked away.

Dougherty got out his cigarettes and held out the pack, and Comptois took one. Then Dougherty held up the lighter and said, "I almost missed you, you're getting bailed out tomorrow."

"Yeah." He was holding up his hand for the lighter.

Dougherty figured Comptois was in his mid-twenties, a few years younger than Dougherty, and he also figured they were at about the same place in their stalled careers. Comptois was likely looking to impress a boss by not saying anything during his incarceration just as much as Dougherty was looking to impress his by working this investigation.

He said, "I don't care what happens in Ontario, I'm looking to find a friend of yours in Montreal."

Now Comptois was staring at Dougherty with the cigarette dangling from his lips, waiting for the light. He didn't say anything.

"A guy named André Marcotte." No recognition from Comptois. "He got arrested for rape a few years ago. You were with him on the Jacques Cartier Bridge before it happened."

Comptois made a face, *you expect me to remember that*, and said, "A few years ago?"

"But you still work Île Sainte-Hélène, you still sell drugs there, at the concerts and at La Ronde."

Comptois didn't say anything.

"And a few weeks ago, after a concert by Gentle Giant, there was another rape."

"I don't know anything about any rapes."

"Just drugs."

He shrugged. "If you say so."

"I say you know about the rapes, too. I say you know who was there and you know who did it. I say you did it."

"Say whatever you want," Comptois said. "You're wrong."

But Dougherty didn't think he was.

"You saw a couple of girls headed for Longueuil so you grabbed them, but it turned out one of them was a boy. You strangled him and threw him off the bridge."

Comptois smirked and looked away like this was the craziest thing he'd ever heard.

"Then you raped the girl and strangled her and threw her off the bridge. Her name was Manon Houle. The boy was Mathieu Simard. They both lived in Longueuil."

Comptois said, "I don't know what you're talking about."

Dougherty was still calm, not raising his voice. He had all the time in the world. He said, "I didn't pick you at random, Martin. I know you were on the bridge. I know you were selling dope. I know you raped Manon and killed her and Mathieu."

"I didn't kill anyone!" Comptois slammed his hand on the table and glared at Dougherty.

Dougherty looked back at him, calm and now a little understanding, nodding slightly. He handed the lighter to Comptois and said, "You didn't mean to, you were just going to talk to them, sell them some dope."

Comptois took the lighter and said, "I never saw them. I wasn't there."

"You were surprised Mathieu was a boy, and he said something to you, he laughed and you got mad."

Comptois lit his cigarette and exhaled smoke at the ceiling.

Dougherty said, "It was an accident."

"It wasn't me."

"Who was it?"

There was enough of a pause that Dougherty knew — Comptois knew who it was. He knew all about it.

Dougherty said it again, "Who was it?"

"I don't know anything about it, this is the first I heard of it."

"If you don't tell me who it was," Dougherty said, "I'll pin it on you."

Now Comptois looked scared. It passed, though, and he said, "Bullshit. I don't know nothing."

Dougherty took a moment, took a drag on his own cigarette and blew out smoke, flicked some ash in the tiny tinfoil ashtray and then said, "I've got plenty of time. You'll be doing three years in the Kingston Pen for this, and one of your boys will give you up."

Comptois didn't say anything.

"You think you're moving up," Dougherty said. "You think if you do what your boss wants, you do your time inside and keep your mouth shut, you'll get something for it. You think it matters what you do.

"But everybody moves on, Martin. Nobody waits for you. You fall behind, you get stuck where you are. You get out of jail, you go back to what you were, you start over." The way Dougherty felt every time one of his temporary assignments to detective ended and he went back into uniform. What he knew was waiting for him when the Olympics were over. "So when you get out, you won't have anything Martin, you won't have any friends. Why protect them now?"

"I wasn't on the bridge."

"Who was?"

"I don't know."

Dougherty was sure he did. He wasn't sure if Comptois was actually involved in the rape and the murders, but he was sure the guy was there and knew who did it.

"This won't go away," Dougherty said. "I won't go away."

Comptois looked at him and shrugged. He didn't believe it.

Dougherty wanted to punch him in the face. Punch that fucking smirk right off him, but he also knew he was screaming mad inside because what Comptois believed might be true.

243

Now Dougherty wished Legault were here. He'd been used to working by himself on the fringes of these investigations, but after a few of these interviews with

Legault he was starting to see the benefits of a partner, of a good one.

He said, "All right, have it your way."

Dougherty stood up and stubbed out his smoke in the ashtray. He took two steps to the door and knocked.

The door opened and Meekins was standing there. "You done?"

Dougherty looked back at Comptois and said, "Yeah, he's done."

They walked down the hall back to Meekins's office and the Cornwall cop said, "I didn't realize you could speak French like that."

"In Montreal," Dougherty said, "you have to. What do you think about Comptois?"

Meekins turned into his office, and Dougherty waited by the door.

"From what I got, he knows something."

"He does, doesn't he."

"You rattled him, that's for sure. But he still thinks he can beat this."

"He thinks he's part of something bigger that'll protect him. From what I can see he's been selling drugs on St. Helen's Island for a few years. He's probably moved up and he expects to keep going."

"If he didn't do it," Meekins said, "whoever did is probably long gone, out to Alberta or something, cooling off. They all think they're tough guys, but actual murder? It's something else."

Dougherty said, "Yeah, for sure." He nodded towards the desk and said, "What did he give you for an address?"

Meekins picked up the file and opened it. "1388 Rue Overdale. No phone number."

"Thanks, I appreciate this."

"Don't worry," Meekins said. "I'll call you if there's anything you can do for me."

———

On the drive back to Montreal, Dougherty started to wonder if he wanted to solve these murders for some kind of justice or if he was really just after a promotion. Or did he want to be a hero? Didn't all men want to be heroes?

He turned up the radio, hoping to think about something else, but the pop song, something about fooling around and falling in love, didn't take him away. Then he was thinking about "Knockin' on Heaven's Door" again, the scene in that movie, Slim Pickens shot in the stomach, trying to be a good guy, helping Sheriff Pat Garrett bring in Billy the Kid. Slim staggers down to the river, his wife coming after him and that song starts playing. Seeing that movie was another one of the things Dougherty and Judy did together, but that one was his idea, a Hollywood western. But a good one. Guys trying to be heroes.

At Station Ten, Dougherty phoned Legault in the hospital to tell her about Comptois and she said it didn't matter now.

"What are you talking about?"

"The detectives found someone who told them Mathieu Simard was selling drugs," Legault said. "It's a different investigation now."

"No, it fits," Dougherty said. "Mathieu started working for Comptois and something went wrong, he owed him money or something."

"No, he was working for someone else, someone from Longueuil," Legault said. "They picked him up, the dealer, and he told them everything — that Mathieu was selling drugs, that he was using drugs. They believe Mathieu killed Manon and then himself."

"But you don't believe it."

There was a long pause and then Legault said, "I would like to talk to this drug dealer myself."

"All right," Dougherty said. "Then that's what we'll do."

He hung up and headed out to the parking lot.

Now he was certain he just wanted to find out who really killed the two kids.

CHAPTER
SIXTEEN

Dougherty parked in the driveway beside the house and walked up to the front door. Legault was already starting to come out and he grabbed the screen door and held it.

"Hold on."

She said, "I've got it," and came out onto the concrete steps.

The front porch was under construction, the two-by-four frame in but nothing else. It looked to Dougherty like it may have been like that for a while and he said, "The cobbler's kids have no shoes, right?"

Legault was making her way down the steps, hopping a little, the cast on her ankle looking like a ski boot, and holding her crutch. "Every time he starts to work on it he gets another job."

The house was an older wood-framed two-storey building, but the roof looked new and so did the picture window in the front. A work in progress.

Dougherty said, "Hang on," and started around the car to the passenger side but Legault said, "I got it," and had the door open and was getting in before he could get there.

"Nobody signed it yet." He motioned to the cast as he was backing out of the driveway.

"It wouldn't look professional."

Legault gave him directions, and Dougherty drove through the residential streets of Longueuil. On a busy street, Legault said, "I spoke to her yesterday," and motioned to an apartment building as they passed.

It took Dougherty a moment to recognize it as the one where Mathieu Simard's mother lived, and he said, "How's she doing?"

"Awful," Legault said, "terrible." Then she pointed and said, "Turn left here."

"She doesn't believe it, does she?"

"No, of course not."

They drove a few more blocks, a few more turns, and ended up in a newer part of town, mostly bungalows with carports or a garage.

248

Dougherty was thinking, Of course she doesn't believe it, it's her son we're talking about, and he didn't want to believe it, either. He wanted it to be a homicide, he wanted to arrest someone and have them confess and go to jail.

Legault said, "This guy's name is Benoît Cloutier,

he's twenty-three."

"Where does he work?"

"He doesn't, he goes to university, *à l'UQAM*." She pointed and said, "There, number seventy-nine."

Dougherty parked on the street and said, "Are you going to be okay?"

"To walk to the house?" Legault said. "Yes, I'll be fine."

Dougherty wanted to go around the car and open the door for her, but he stood and watched as she got out and managed the crutch with her one good arm and made her way up the walk to the front door.

"Nice house." Dougherty was walking slowly beside her.

"His parents', of course."

Legault knocked, and a few minutes later a man's voice came from behind the door, speaking French, saying, "What do you want?"

"Police, we want to talk to you."

The door opened and a guy in his twenties stood there looking at them. Dougherty figured the guy was just waking up: he was wearing a t-shirt with the Pink Floyd prism ironed-on and jeans but he was barefoot.

"What is it now?"

Legault said, "Can we come in, Benoît? We just want to go over the details again."

"Again? I think I'm supposed to call my lawyer, hang on."

249

Dougherty shoved the door hard, knocking it into Benoît and knocking him off balance.

Legault hopped over the doorway and into the house. She said, "Have a seat."

Benoît was scared and didn't know what to do. Legault motioned with her crutch to a stuffed chair in the living room and said, "Right there."

He walked into the living room and said, "Where are the other cops?"

"Sit down."

He sat down.

Legault moved farther into the living room, and Dougherty stayed by the doorway. He was the threat, waiting, watching how it went. Benoît seemed to get this, and he looked from Dougherty back to Legault and said, "I told them everything."

"So this won't take long. You sold marijuana and cocaine to Mathieu Simard, that's right?"

"Yes."

"At the concert at Place des Nations?"

"Gentle Giant, yes."

"Both drugs?"

"Yes."

"How did he pay you?"

"What?"

"How did he pay you? One-dollar bills? Two-dollar bills? Tens?"

"I don't remember."

"How much did he buy?"

"Couple of grams."

"Couple grams of each?"

"I guess, I don't know," Benoît said. "He wasn't my only customer."

"Did you sell to him before the concert or after?"

"Before."

"Was Manon with him?"

He thought about that and then said, "Yes, she was."

"They were together?"

Now he was certain. "Yes."

"Did you sell drugs to Mathieu any other time?"

"Yes, many times."

It sounded rehearsed to Dougherty, but he didn't say anything, he didn't move, he just kept staring at Benoît as threateningly as he could.

"Where?"

"What?"

Legault said, "Where did you sell drugs to Mathieu? You go to UQAM, do you usually sell drugs at school?"

"No, not at school. Here."

"Longueuil?"

"Yes."

"At Mathieu's school, Monseigneur Parent?"

He looked at Legault and considered it, and then said, "No."

She said, "But you sold to Mathieu before?"

"Yes."

"Where?"

"I can't remember."

Legault stared at Benoît and didn't say anything for a long moment, then she looked at Dougherty and said, "You hear this?"

"Yeah."

"Okay." Legault looked back at Benoît and said, "That's enough for now." She turned, using her crutch maybe more than she needed to, and made her way to the doorway. She turned back and said, "We'll talk again."

251

Outside by the car, Dougherty said, "Wasn't even close."

"Why would they do this? Just to close a case? It's crazy. That guy never met Mathieu in his life."

"Your sources for drugs are more reliable at high schools," Dougherty said. "If Mathieu was using drugs, especially cocaine, you would have found the source."

"This guy," she motioned with her crutch, "might be selling weed and coke, but not in high schools. They must have picked him up and shown him Mathieu's picture. Just to close this case."

"It happens all the time," Dougherty said.

"At least you didn't punch him." She started getting in the car.

"I would've if I'd had to," Dougherty said. "But he wasn't a good enough liar."

They pulled away from the curb, and Legault said, "I wonder what they offered him?"

"Guy like that, easy to make a deal with."

"What do you mean, guy like that?" She was accusing.

"Because he's got something to lose," Dougherty said. "Look at him, living in a nice house with his parents, going to school, he's got a good future ahead of him."

Legault relaxed a little. "That's what you think?"

252

"Sure, he's not like the guys we busted in the Point or Ville-Émard — dropouts, losers."

Legault said, "You see it all the time?"

"Well, to be honest," Dougherty said, "my girlfriend explained it to me — she was studying sociology. But it makes sense."

He was thinking of the song then, one of the ones Judy would play on her old record player, Janis Joplin singing about freedom being nothing left to lose, but he didn't think the guys he was talking about saw it that way.

"So what now?"

Dougherty said, "I think we should keep doing what we're doing. Somebody was on the bridge that night, they saw Mathieu and Manon and they killed them."

"I think so, yes."

"So, we keep talking to anybody who might have been there."

"Louise Tremblay," Legault said. "She had some information."

"What was it?"

"She was the girlfriend of Marc-André Daigneault, we spoke to his mother in Ville-Émard."

"Oh yeah," Dougherty said, "I remember. She *was* his girlfriend, she isn't anymore?"

"That's right. Daigneault was in jail for a few months last winter, his mother said, remember?"

"Right."

"She said when he got out of jail she didn't see him much. He spent his time with his girlfriend, Louise Tremblay."

"Yeah."

"So, I spoke to Louise. She said he moved in with her when he got out, but it didn't last. She said he was back to dealing drugs, hanging out with some bad guys, and she didn't want him to. They fought, he moved out."

Dougherty said, "She told you that?"

"Not right away."

"You think it's true? Or is she just mad they broke up?"

"I think she was sad. Disappointed. I think she really liked him."

Dougherty said, "That's good work, getting her to talk like that."

"Took a while," Legault said.

"Well, it's good work." Dougherty pulled into the driveway of Legault's house. "Did she have any idea where he is now?"

"I'm going to go see her again in a couple of days, she's going to try and find out."

"You really did get through to her."

"Well," Legault said, "I didn't punch her."

"Wait till next time." Dougherty looked sideways at Legault, who was almost smiling at him. She had the car door open and was getting out. Again Dougherty wanted to run around the car and help her, but he felt she didn't want that.

She looked back inside the car and said, "I'll let you know what she says as soon as I can."

"All right."

Dougherty watched Legault make her way up to her front door and go inside her house.

He drove away thinking they were going to do it, they were going to keep on it until they found the guy who did it. Someone was going to talk, he was sure, they just had to keep asking.

⸻

The apartment was on the second floor of the three-storey building and from the balcony off the living room Dougherty could see the top of the round white church across the street. He thought it really did look like the top of a rocket ship that at any moment could rise up out of the ground and take off.

He'd been surprised the place was still available when Judy had called. July first was moving day, changed a few years earlier from May first, what his mom and the other women working in the assigning office of the phone company had always called the May Move, and it seemed like half the city of Montreal packed up and changed apartments. Dougherty and Judy paid the full month's rent for July, 235 bucks, and moved in the second week. Dougherty brought his bed and kitchen table and two chairs and Judy brought a pullout couch and a dresser and a few cardboard boxes marked *kitchen stuff*. When they spread it out all over the apartment Judy said, "This place is huge." A one-bedroom, with living room/dining room and kitchenette — what was called a three-and-a-half in Montreal.

They'd moved in without anything to mark the occasion, no ceremony, no speeches, no party. It didn't really feel to Dougherty like it was a life-changing event, like it had any permanence or significance — no matter how much his mother tried to make him feel it did — and he hadn't talked about that with Judy, so he wasn't sure how she felt about it.

Now Dougherty was standing on the balcony, looking at the rocket ship church across the street, and he saw Judy coming across the street, Bishop Power, carrying a couple of paper grocery bags from Steinberg's in the mall, and he went back into the living room and lifted the cover off the turntable he'd just set up. He turned on the receiver and slid the new album out of its sleeve and put it in place. He waited a few minutes, and when he heard the apartment door opening, he lifted the arm and moved it over the edge of the record, which started turning automatically.

Crowd noises filled the apartment, a huge arena of people cheering and then Bob Dylan singing, "Don't Think Twice, It's All Right."

Judy said, "What's this?"

"Housewarming present."

She put the grocery bags down on the table and came into the living room. Dougherty handed her the album cover, *Before the Flood*, the live recording of the same tour they'd seen at the Forum a couple of years earlier.

"Nice stereo."

"I got a great deal. Remember that store on St. Catherine that was robbed a few months ago? We caught the guys and the owner was so happy."

"Not so happy," Judy said. "They were employees, weren't they?"

"Relatives, too, I think. Anyway the guy gave me a deal."

Judy was looking at the record cover and said, "Somebody rob Sam the Record Man, too?"

"All the time, but I had to pay full price for that."

"You know I'm going to play a lot of Janis Joplin and Jesse Winchester."

"I know."

Judy was smiling. "It's like a real apartment." She walked back to the table and started getting groceries out of the bag. "I got a barbecued chicken and some salads from the deli counter — I wasn't sure you'd be home."

"Yeah, I went with Legault to talk to a guy, didn't take long."

"Your day off."

"Crime never sleeps."

"How did it go?"

"Good." Dougherty walked over to the dining room, really just the end of the living room by the kitchenette, and said, "About what we expected. The guys in Longueuil, they're saying the kid killed his girl-friend and then himself."

Judy said, "You were worried about that."

"Now they've got a guy who says he sold the kid some drugs, weed and coke."

Judy closed the fridge door and said, "You don't believe him?"

"No, I don't. The kids who were killed, their bodies had been in the river a couple of days so the coroner says he can't be sure about what drugs they took, but I doubt it was cocaine."

"So why are they saying this guy sold them some?"

"To explain the behaviour, I guess. And we found a rope in the pavilion there, where the stairs go up to the bridge, that building, and it had traces of coke on it. I think that was from the guy who did it."

257

Judy came out of the kitchenette and said, "You're going to keep working it?"

"You sound like a cop. I bet you never thought that would happen."

"I never thought I'd know one this well."

She sat down on one of the kitchen chairs and got her cigarettes out of her purse.

Dougherty said, "Yeah, we'll keep working it."

One of the guys in the Band was singing then, how out of nine lives he'd spent seven.

Judy said, "Unofficially now?"

"It's like that," Dougherty said, listing to the music coming from the two stereo speakers on the floor of the living room. "'Save your neck or save your brother, looks like it's one or the other.' We keep going after these guys, one of them is going to tell us what really happened."

"If they know."

"Yeah, if they know." Then Dougherty said, "How's the mall?"

"It's okay. I saw the pinball arcade where my students will go when they cut class."

"Good to know."

Judy took a drag on her cigarette and said, "I'm nervous."

"Why?"

"Standing up in front of a classroom full of kids."

"You could sit down behind the desk."

"It's not that . . . oh, very funny."

Dougherty said, "You stood up in front of lots of classes in your placement."

258

"Not lots. And there was another teacher in the back of the class."

"You're going to be great, and you know it."

"Weren't you nervous? The first time you drove a police car by yourself?"

"Yeah, but I was no good at it. You're good at this."

She blew smoke at the ceiling and said, "What do you know?"

Dougherty sat down in the only other chair and said, "I know you."

He reached for the pack of smokes on the table, but Judy put her hand on top of his and said, "Can that wait awhile?"

"Why?"

She stood up, still holding his hand, and led him to the bedroom.

When they finished and were both having a smoke, Dougherty felt good, he felt like they were living together and that it was something.

Then the phone on the wall in the kitchenette rang, and he thought about just letting it ring, but he got up and answered it and the shit hit the fan.

CHAPTER
SEVENTEEN

Dougherty walked into Toe Blake's Tavern through a thick cloud of blue smoke and saw Detective Carpentier sitting by himself, a glass of draught on the table and a newspaper in his hand.

Dougherty said, "I got here as fast as I could."

"I thought you lived just around the corner?"

The waiter was at the table then, a middle-aged guy in a white shirt, like the waiters always wore at Toe Blake's.

Dougherty ordered a draught and sat down. "I moved to LaSalle a few days ago."

"You didn't move to Longueuil?"

Dougherty knew from the second he'd heard Carpentier's voice on the phone — "I need to talk to you right now" — that it was something serious but all the way downtown, driving too fast, he had no idea what it was about. Now he was starting to figure it out, but he didn't say anything.

Carpentier put the newspaper down and said, "You've been spending a lot of time in Longueuil."

It wasn't a question so Dougherty didn't say anything.

"They're pissed," Carpentier said. "Captain Allard called me."

Dougherty wanted to say he was working the case, he was doing good work, but he knew this wasn't the time.

"You overstepped, you shouldn't have talked to that kid."

Dougherty nodded.

The waiter set the glass of beer down on the table and Carpentier motioned to a small pile of change. The waiter counted the cost of the draught and a good tip for himself.

"They had already talked to the kid."

Dougherty wanted to say, Yeah, but they . . . and there was nothing he could say after that.

"You were supposed to help," Carpentier said. "Do what you were told."

To keep from saying something he knew he'd regret, Dougherty picked up the beer and drank.

261

"Okay, I know," Carpentier said, "that you had some good leads, some of those drug dealers and those losers, they look like maybe they could have done it."

Dougherty looked over the top of his glass and said, "Yeah, they do."

"I know you want to work this, you've never been afraid of hard work." Carpentier drank some of his own beer and put the glass down on the table. "You want to be so bad on the first line, you want to be on the power play." He motioned to the pictures of the old Habs on the walls — Maurice Richard and Doug Harvey, Dickie Moore, Jacques Plante — and said, "But I'm your *entraîneur*, I'm your Scotty Bowman. I make the lines."

Dougherty nodded. He drank the rest of his beer and put down the empty glass and said, "I know."

"This Longueuil cop, this woman cop, she said it was her idea, she was going to talk to the kid and you went along."

"That's not true," Dougherty said. "I took her along, have you seen her? She's got a cast on her foot."

"You made it look like we don't trust them, like we think they can't even interview a witness."

Dougherty nodded. When Carpentier had first called him he'd been scared he was in trouble for something but now he was getting angry. He wanted to order another beer, mostly just so he'd have something to do with his hands, but he didn't want to say anything and he didn't want to look away from Carpentier. He wanted to argue with him, to say he was right to talk to the kid and he wanted to keep talking to the dealers, but he didn't. He just sat there.

"This is their case, this is how they're going to handle it."

"Even if they're wrong?"

Carpentier took his time and said, "I need to know that you can play on the team, on whatever line you're told to play on."

"That kid didn't sell any cocaine to Mathieu Simard."

"You don't know that." And then, before Dougherty could say anything, he said, "It doesn't matter, this is what they want to do."

"They just want it to go away."

"It's done," Carpentier said.

Dougherty said, "Okay."

"This isn't *Dirty Harry*," Carpentier said. "This is your job. You have your Olympic assignment?"

"Yeah, I'm working the Forum. Gymnastics first and then boxing."

"That's good, you can see that Cuban everybody's talking about. See if he's really any good."

"He might be for three rounds," Dougherty said. "Scoring points with punches, doesn't matter how hard they are."

"It's the Olympics," Carpentier said. "That's the rules."

Dougherty said, "Yeah."

Carpentier picked up the newspaper and said, "You might get some action, some terrorists escaped from prison in Germany."

"In Germany?"

"Four women from the Baader-Meinhof gang. One of them," he looked at the article and said, "Inge Viett was on the list of prisoners the guys who hijacked the plane to Uganda wanted released. Probably connected to the guys who killed the athletes in Munich."

"You think they can really get to Montreal?"

"I think no amount of overtime will be spared."

Dougherty stood up and said, "Thank you."

"Keep your head down for a while," Carpentier said. "We'll talk after the Olympics."

Out on St. Catherine Street it was a warm summer evening, about ten o'clock by then, and Dougherty walked back to where he'd parked his car. He was mad, he wanted to scream and punch something, well, someone, really — himself most of all. He knew Carpentier was right, he'd overstepped. He should have known there'd be consequences.

He got into his car and started driving back to LaSalle. He wasn't sure what to do but he was looking forward to talking to Judy. Maybe they wouldn't even talk about it, they'd talk about something else, play the record he bought, the side with "Lay Lady Lay" and "Knockin' on Heaven's Door." Forget about all this work shit.

———

Saturday morning was controlled panic. There were hundreds of uniform cops at Olympic Stadium trying to keep the crowd moving as 75,000 people all seemed to show up at the same time. Everyone had to be inside the stadium by two thirty when the doors would close and the thousands of athletes would make their way from the village. Even those few blocks were lined with tens of thousands of people.

Dougherty was across town at the Forum.

Most of Station Ten was set up in what they were calling the security office, a room at the end of the hall past the dressing rooms and coaches' offices, next to the media room. The *Hockey Night in Canada* signs were still on the walls, covered up by black curtains, and the same big TV cameras would be used for interviews.

The security room was small with bare concrete-block walls and a cement floor. Sergeant Delisle had set up as if it were Station Ten except his desk had half a dozen phones instead of two and there were two TVs mounted on the wall, one showing the Canadian broadcast in French and one the American broadcast on ABC, though the sound was turned down on both.

There were half a dozen cops in the security room, all dressed casually, which meant slacks, sports coats and shirts but no ties. Another two dozen uniform cops were on duty around the building, including two on each door. There were no athletes, they were all at the opening ceremony at Olympic Stadium, but even when Dougherty had arrived at nine that morning there were quite a few support staff making last-minute checks to the gymnastics equipment, all the parallel bars and pommel horses and balance beams and a few other guys were still working on the electronic scoreboards and making a few last-minute light bulb replacements.

Now, at two thirty in the afternoon, the ceremony was starting and Delisle turned up the volume on the small black-and-white TV.

One of the cops said, "*Eille, le Radio-Canada, okay.*"

Delisle turned down the volume on the ABC broadcast and turned up the volume on the French broadcast, saying, "*C'est la même chose.*"

"*Oui, maintenant, mais pas plus tard.*"

When the World Youth Orchestra finished "O Canada," Delisle said, "*Bon, ça commence.*"

Dougherty was sitting on a stool by the door with his back against the wall, thinking after everything that had gone on in the six years since Montreal had been awarded the games, all the fears after Munich, all the politics with China and Taiwan, all the construction problems putting together so many buildings and the giant stadium, after all that and so much more it did feel good to see it all coming together. He was proud of his city, the eyes of the world on it for a moment and it looked good.

The team from Greece was the first into the stadium, as always, and there was another huge cheer from the crowd.

Dougherty was thinking he could slip out of the security room and no one would notice. Or he could say he was doing a patrol and no one would say anything and he could take off for a few hours, go watch the rest of the ceremony with Judy at her parents' place. Her mother's place, he could hear her saying, just her mother's now.

Delisle said, "*Il n'y a pas du tout de pays Africains?*"

"*Quelques-uns,*" one of the other cops said, "*mais pas beaucoup.*"

"*Et pourquoi déjà?*"

One of the cops said something about the African nations boycotting because New Zealand had sent a rugby team to South Africa and another cop interrupted to ask if South Africa was here and the first guy said, no, they've been kicked out of the Olympics, that's why the other countries are boycotting, because everybody is supposed to boycott South Africa.

"*Pourquoi?*"

"Apartheid."

Then Dougherty was thinking he could just slip out to a bar, just across the street in the Alexis Nihon Plaza, he could grab a pint at the Maidenhead, but then he'd just be watching the same thing on a different TV.

"Eilles, Tabarnak, c'est les États-Unis pis y'a une annonce!"

On the French broadcast, the American team, the biggest one in the Games, was coming into the stadium but the ABC broadcast was showing a commercial for Budweiser. The cops in the security room were laughing, and Dougherty realized the Americans hadn't realized that their team wouldn't be the United States, they were les États-Unis, much earlier in the alphabet. It was kind of funny, but Dougherty wasn't laughing.

The American team was still coming into the stadium when the commercial break ended, so they caught some of the athletes waving to the crowd.

A few minutes later the biggest cheer so far rang through the stadium and Delisle said, "That's for Entebbe," and motioned to the TV where the small Israeli team was coming into the stadium. The TV announcer said that the flag-bearer, sprinter Esther Roth, was a survivor of the Munich attacks and the flag she carried had a small black ribbon at the top in commemoration. The rest of the team had black ribbons on their lapels.

267

Delisle said, "Shit, I hope no one tries anything here."

Dougherty said, "Yeah, I hope not, too," and no one else said anything. Now that the Games had started, now that it was real, Dougherty didn't get the feeling that anyone really wanted to see any action, least of all himself. Even though being in on the action was the reason he'd joined the police force almost ten years earlier: he'd wanted to drive fast cars and break up bar fights and stop bank robberies. If he was really honest with himself he'd have to admit he'd wanted to be John Wayne, he'd wanted to be a hero.

He still did, really, but his idea of what that was had changed. He didn't want to be Dirty Harry, like Carpentier had said, he didn't want to break all the rules and do it all on his own and run around chasing people and shooting at them, that had definitely changed.

On the TV the Soviet team was coming into the stadium and a barrel-chested guy was carrying the flag — holding his arm straight out parallel to the ground and not moving it. Dougherty couldn't imagine holding a flagpole like that for a minute, never mind the entire ceremony like this guy was doing it.

Then he was thinking what had changed was meeting the families of victims. When he'd been looking for the guy who'd killed Brenda Webber and he talked to the Webbers, that was personal because he'd grown up a few streets over from them, he was in Brenda's sister Arlene's class in high school, but even if it hadn't been personal it still would have had the same effect. Dougherty was sure of that now. When someone gets killed, no matter who it is, the family suffers, no matter what kind of relationship they had before, no matter how strained it was or how distant they seemed. People always feel there's time to save a bad relationship, things will change and people will see eye to eye. He'd heard that so many times, how people thought they had more time. But death was final. That was why he wanted to work homicide. Sitting there watching the ceremony on TV, he started to understand it himself for the first time.

There was a huge cheer as the Canadian team came into the stadium, and Dougherty stood up and said, "I gotta go to the can." No one said anything as he walked out of the office.

Down the hall Dougherty found a row of phone booths. He dropped in a dime and dialled.

A teenage girl answered, "Hey."

"Hey yourself. Can I talk to Judy?"

"I don't know, can you?"

"Is she there?"

"One minute."

Dougherty was thinking maybe it was playful, maybe it was Gillian joking around, saying what her mother would say to her if she used "can I" instead of "may I." But there was an edge to it.

Judy said, "Hi."

"How's it going?"

"About as well as can be expected, I guess."

"I wish I could be there."

Judy laughed and said, "No you don't. You'd rather work a night shift downtown by yourself than spend five minutes in this house."

"Yeah, that's true."

269

"My mom's doing her best stiff upper lip but she's had too many stiff ones."

"Tense?"

"The sarcasm is."

"Gillian's there," Dougherty said. "That's good."

"I think she's stoned, her and the boyfriend."

"Well, everybody else in town is, it seems like."

Judy said, "Yeah, you'll probably arrest my father later. He asked me if I knew anyone who could get him cocaine."

"Has he tried any bar in the city?"

There was a pause and Judy said, "I used to think they were happy, my parents, happily married."

"They probably were," Dougherty said. "At the time."

"I guess so." There was another pause, and then Judy said, "How do people do that, how do they go from being happy to being so unhappy."

"I don't know. Why, you worried it could happen to you?"

"No," Judy said, "I've never been that happy."

"I don't know about that, I've seen you pretty happy."

"How do you know I'm not faking it?"

"Good enough for me," Dougherty said. "I'm gullible that way."

"You're the least gullible person I've ever met," Judy said. "No one ever gets away with lying to you."

"People lie to me all the time."

"But you always know," Judy said.

Dougherty wanted to keep joking around, say something like, So you better watch your step, but it didn't feel right. He said, "You want me to pick you up in Pointe-Claire when this is over?"

"No, I'll catch a bus, meet you back at the apartment."

"You sure? Once I'm on the highway it's no problem. We could grab a bite somewhere."

270

Judy said, "My mom will insist on some kind of dinner, but if you don't mind driving out here."

"I don't mind. It'll probably be seven before I get there."

There was some talking in the background, Judy's mother saying something to her and then Judy said, "Yes, I see it," and then to Dougherty, "Do you see that? The torch is coming into the stadium."

"No," Dougherty said, "I'm at a pay phone, who did they get to carry it?" Another one of the potential controversies about the Olympics, who would be the torchbearer, everything getting so political.

"My mom's saying I should be excited because it shows equality, it's a boy and a girl."

"Two of them?"

"Yeah, and now they're explaining that he's French and she's English."

"No Indians?" Dougherty said.

"Or Eskimos. All right, I'll see you later."

Dougherty said bye and hung up feeling pretty good.

He walked back to the security room and watched the end of the ceremony, the queen declaring the games officially open, Mayor Drapeau waving the flag handed to him by the mayor of Munich, and then a few athletes started dancing and then that spread throughout the stadium.

Delisle said, "Okay, that's it, going to be non-stop now for two weeks. Everybody get some rest, it may be the last you sleep for a while."

On the way out of the Forum, a couple of the other cops said they were going to head over to Crescent

271

Street and see what was going on, and they asked Dougherty if he wanted to go, too.

"I know what's going on," he said.

"Hey, you're not an old married man yet."

"No," Dougherty said, "but I need my beauty rest. See you tomorrow."

He felt good driving out to the West Island to pick up Judy. He didn't want to have to go into the house but he did, and it was awkward, of course, but it didn't bother him as much as he thought it would.

As they drove back to LaSalle, Judy said, "I feel bad leaving Gillian and Abby there."

"Gillian didn't seem to notice where she was."

"Should we be worried?"

"Probably."

Judy said, "And it probably won't be long until Abby is just as stoned."

"You never know," Dougherty said. "She might go the opposite way and become a nun."

There was a parking garage under the apartment building, but Dougherty pulled into the lot in the back. He parked facing the pool and got out of the car.

Judy said, "Maybe I'll ask Abby if she wants to come hang out with me for a while."

"What for?"

"Just to get away for a while. Maybe we'll go see some of the Olympics."

They were walking to the back door of the apartment building and Dougherty said, "We should've got the two bedroom."

Judy took his hand.

The next day Dougherty was walking down the hall-way outside the security office and a middle-aged guy stepped in front of him and said, "You cop?"

Dougherty said, "Yes."

The guy's dark hair was in a kind of bowl cut and he had a bushy moustache. He was wearing a track suit and had an ID badge hanging around his neck.

He just stood there and didn't say anything so Dougherty said, "Can I help you?"

The guy said, "No," and turned and walked away.

Dougherty waited a minute and then walked in the same direction, down the hall and then through the tunnel onto the floor, what would have been the ice surface during hockey season. There was a young uni-form cop standing there and Dougherty said, "That guy who just came through here, who is he?"

"I don't know."

"Didn't you look at his ID badge?"

"I just looked to see that he had one."

To Dougherty the cop looked like a teenager, all the new recruits did, but he had to be at least twenty years old. Dougherty said, "Which way did he go?"

"I don't know."

Dougherty almost said, What do you know, but he kept his mouth shut. A huge cheer went out from the crowd and Dougherty looked up into the seats. It felt so strange to him, nine thirty on a Sunday morning and there were almost eighteen thousand people in the Forum. Cheering for gymnasts.

The cheer faded out and the place was eerily silent.

Then a murmuring started, grumbling, and it spread throughout the crowd.

Dougherty turned to the young cop and said, "What's going on?"

He didn't expect anything other than, I don't know, but the kid said, "That girl there just had an amazing routine on the uneven bars but they scored it a one."

"That's not good?"

"It should be a 9.8 at least."

"You know a lot about gymnastics?"

"I've been standing here for a week watching them set up, I picked up a few things."

"Yeah, I bet you did."

The young cop leered and said, "My Romanian is getting a lot better."

An announcement came over the PA system then, which Dougherty didn't catch, but the whole building cheered.

Dougherty said, "What is it?"

"It's a ten, a perfect ten," the young cop said. "The first time that's ever happened, it's history." He was excited, practically jumping up and down, and he took a few steps forward, looking through the crowd of gymnasts and coaches and TV announcers who were all trying to get a look at the girl who'd scored the perfect ten.

Dougherty saw her then, and he saw the man with the bowl haircut and the moustache was with her, hugging her and kissing her on both cheeks.

If he'd wanted to talk to a cop, he didn't anymore.

Dougherty walked back down the tunnel and into the hallway. He was almost at the security office when he noticed a kid standing by the door. This guy really was a teenager.

Dougherty said, "Can I help you?"

The kid said, "Are you Canadian official?"

"Yeah, I am, I'm a police officer."

The kid nodded. It seemed to take him a few seconds to decide what he was going to say next, and then he nodded again and said, "I want defect."

Dougherty said, "Okay, well I guess this is the place."

The kid said, "Yes?"

"Yes, come on." Dougherty opened the door to the security office and motioned the kid inside. He started to follow him but stopped when a man's voice yelled, "Halt."

Dougherty turned around and said, "Halt?"

A bunch of men were coming towards him, practically running down the hall. A couple of them were wearing track suits though they had big bellies, and the rest all wore dark suits. One of the suits said, "He must return, open that door, send him out."

Dougherty said, "No can do."

The same man said, "He must come with us."

"We have a protocol," Dougherty said. "We spent weeks bored out of our minds learning it, we're damn well going to use it."

The man who was doing all the talking for the group said, "We will not leave."

Dougherty shrugged and said, "I've got ten hours left in a twelve-hour shift. I can stand here all day."

He didn't have to, though, ten minutes later the place was crawling with diplomats and reporters.

CHAPTER
EIGHTEEN

"He's seventeen years old," Dougherty said. "He's got an aunt and uncle in St. Catharines, it's in Ontario somewhere. He's going there."

Judy said, "He's just a kid."

"I thought he was twelve when I first saw him."

They were finishing off a late dinner at Centrale Pizzeria, spaghetti and Caesar salads, and Judy said, "Is it going to be a big diplomatic event?"

"I don't know. We were prepared for it, well, I mean we knew who to call to come and take over right away. We were told there were over a hundred defections in Munich four years ago so they figured there'd be some."

"Was it a lot of Germans then, trying to get back together with their families in the West?"

Dougherty used a piece of bread to mop up the last little bit of meat sauce and said, "I don't know. There was another guy just before the kid, an older guy, I thought he was going to try, but he seemed to lose his nerve."

"You didn't say anything?"

"We're not supposed to. If they ask us we're supposed to help them, get them somewhere safe and call the diplomats, but we're not supposed to assume anything."

"Well, you know what happens when you assume."

"Yeah."

Judy finished off her glass of wine and said, "I hope the kid's okay. Wait till he finds out it's not blue jeans and rock 'n' roll all the time."

The waitress came to the table and asked if they'd like any dessert.

Dougherty said to Judy, "Rice pudding? Apple pie?"

"No, thanks, that's all for me."

"Okay, me too."

The waitress tore a page off her pad and put it on the table. Then she cleared the empty plates and glasses.

Dougherty slid open his cigarette pack and held it out to Judy. She took one and leaned forward as Dougherty flicked his lighter.

"Did it make you think about the kids on the bridge?" She leaned back and blew smoke at the ceiling.

"It does now."

Judy said, "You were thinking it."

"I guess I was."

"That's good, you don't want to just forget about them."

Dougherty took a drag and blew rings. Then he said, "Carpentier told me to move on, you know? But he doesn't. He's got open cases he goes back to sometimes."

"So he knows you won't just move on."

"I could, though. I don't think I'm ever going to get assigned to homicide. I'm probably going to be driving patrol forever."

"No you're not."

"The way I'm making friends?"

"It's not about making friends."

"It's office politics," Dougherty said. "Like anywhere else, you have to play the game."

Judy inhaled on her cigarette and then exhaled a long thin stream of smoke. She started to say something, stopped and then said, "I'm not exactly one for giving career advice, here I am almost thirty and starting my first real job." She looked at Dougherty and he was nodding slightly, and she said, "You're supposed to say I've been busy with worthwhile things."

"You're still busy with worthwhile things."

She made a face, kind of dismissive that but not completely, and said, "But when I finally figured out that I could teach, that I *should* teach, it felt really good."

"I remember."

"But then when I had my first placement, and I walked into the teachers' lounge and it was so awful?"

"I remember that, too."

"I just about quit on the spot," Judy said. "The tension in that room, the cynicism, the, I don't know . . . disdain for the kids. It was unbelievable."

Dougherty said, "I believe it, I remember those teachers."

"I had no idea so many of them hate it so much. How burnt out they are."

"It's a tough job."

Judy nodded and said, "Yeah, well, I'm not going to get like that."

"I never thought you would."

"So you're not going to get like that, either."

"I wasn't planning on it."

She raised her eyebrows at him.

"Okay, I get it."

Walking home through LaSalle, past the old row houses with the wrought-iron staircases winding down the front, they held hands and talked about what a nice night it was, how beautiful Montreal was in the summer.

Dougherty said, "Until it gets humid."

"It'll be nice here by the river," Judy said. "Get a nice breeze."

When they got back to the apartment the phone was ringing and Judy answered it. She listened for a little and then said, "*Un moment, s'il vous plaît,*" and held out the receiver for Dougherty. "It's a woman. French."

Dougherty took the phone. "*Oui?*"

On the phone Legault said, "I have a line on Marc-André Daigneault."

"That's good."

"Louise Tremblay, remember, I told you I was talking to her."

"Yeah, right," Dougherty said. "But didn't Captain Allard talk to you?"

Legault said, "Sure, so?"

Dougherty said, "Well, maybe you should listen to him."

There was a pause and then Legault said, "Oh, you don't want to do this?"

"I want to," Dougherty said. "But maybe we shouldn't."

"I'm going to."

Dougherty squeezed the receiver till his fingers hurt. "When?"

"Tomorrow, she said when she finishes work, four thirty."

"Where does she work?"

"UPS, it's near the airport."

Dougherty said, "I know where it is, off the thirteen."

"We're going to meet at the Lafleur on Côte de Liesse."

"Okay," Dougherty said, "I'll pick you up at your place at three thirty."

Legault said, "Good," and hung up.

Dougherty turned away from Judy as he hung up. He said, "I think I should do this."

"It sounds like you've already decided to."

Judy's French wasn't as good as Dougherty's, but he never offered to translate or asked her if she understood everything, and this was a time she didn't need to know the words to know what was being said.

"It's a good lead."

"After Carpentier told you not to?"

"No one else will do this."

Judy was nodding. She said, "So, I finally decide to join the establishment and now you're going to be the rebel, breaking all the rules?"

"You didn't join anything," Dougherty said. "You're just working it from the inside."

"That's what I'm telling myself."

The next day the Romanian girl, Nadia Comăneci, scored another perfect ten and the place went crazy. There were more reporters showing up at the Forum all the time and Delisle was going crazy in the security office trying to get all the credentials approved.

Dougherty decided it would be easier to just slip away rather than ask for the time off, so at a quarter to three he was in his own car heading for the Champlain Bridge. He was scheduled to finish his shift at four anyway, though most of the guys working days were also working the four to midnight and Delisle was surprised when Dougherty turned down the overtime.

Legault was waiting in her driveway when Dougherty pulled up, and she jumped into the car.

He said, "You're getting around pretty good on that cast."

"I'm about to tear it off," she said. "So itchy, it's driving me crazy."

"Have you tried driving with your left foot?"

"Didn't work."

Dougherty laughed a little. "But you did try?"

"Of course."

They were heading back onto the Champlain Bridge and he slowed down at the tollbooths and tossed a quarter into the basket.

Legault said, "You don't have tokens?"

"I don't cross often enough. I usually take the Victoria."

"My husband usually throws in a slug."

Through the tolls Dougherty stayed left and got onto the expressway heading west. On the left was the Lachine Canal lined with big factories and warehouses that had been there a hundred years or more. There was an old crane still standing from the days when coal boats came up the canal, before the St. Lawrence Seaway was expanded and LaSalle Coke had closed and a couple of the huge old buildings were empty. On the right were dozens of rail lines coming into Montreal from the west and beyond them the steep hill up to NDG.

Dougherty said, "Tourists coming for the Olympics don't get out here much."

"Montreal is an industrial city," Legault said. "A port city. All these factories, the oil refineries in the east end. It's not all Expo and Olympics and parties."

There wasn't much traffic and they made good time, getting to Côte de Liesse a little after four. It was a wide four-lane boulevard mostly used by trucks coming and going to the CN train yards and Dorval Airport.

Dougherty pulled into the Lafleur Restaurant parking lot and said, "You want a hot dog?"

"Sure. *Tout garni.*"

There were picnic tables beside the small building

and Legault sat down at one while Dougherty went inside and got them a couple of coffees, steamed hot dogs with mustard and onions and chopped cabbage, and fries. Afternoon shifts were finishing all over the industrial area and traffic was picking up and people were lining up at the bus stops.

"She said she might be late," Legault said. "I don't think she wanted anyone to see us together."

"I'm starting to get a complex," Dougherty said. "Nobody ever wants to talk to us."

They finished the food and sipped their coffees and watched people get on buses. Dougherty kept checking his watch and at five o'clock he said, "This is too late."

"We should give her ten more minutes."

It was a beautiful day, sunny and hot and even a table in a parking lot beside a busy four-lane boulevard was nice but not where Dougherty wanted to be. He said, "Five."

Then he didn't check his watch for a while and almost fifteen minutes later said, "She's not coming, let's go to her."

"She won't want her boss to see her talking to cops."

"We're not in uniform, how's he going to know we're cops?"

Legault gave him a look, but she stood up and made her way to his car. "All right, but don't be pushy."

"When am I ever pushy?"

283

They drove a few blocks to the big concrete UPS building, and Dougherty pulled up at the security gate and held up his ID so the guard could see it. "Police business."

"Who do you want to see?"

Dougherty looked at Legault and she said, "Someone who works in sorting."

The guard said, "Building B," and lifted the gate.

Dougherty drove around the side of the building to where there were fifty or so garage doors and parked by the office door.

Inside the building it was a giant maze of conveyor belts and big white plastic bins on wheels being pushed around by people in brown uniforms.

Dougherty flagged down a guy in a turban who was pulling a stack of packages on a pallet jack and asked him in English where he could find the supervisor.

"Shipping office." He pointed.

Dougherty tried to see what he was pointing at but there were too many boxes piled everywhere.

The guy said, "This way," and led them between the packages like they were rows of corn in a field. After enough turns that Dougherty was pretty sure he'd never be able to find his way back, the guy said, "There," and pointed at a closed door.

"Thanks."

Dougherty knocked on the door and a voice from inside said, "What is it?"

Legault said, "*Bon, encore un anglais.*"

Dougherty opened the door and said, in French, "Are you the supervisor in sorting?"

A man was sitting behind a desk, looking up at them, and he said, "*Oui, c'est moi, le boss.*"

Dougherty glanced at Legault and then held the door while she made her way into the office and the conversation continued in French. Legault said they were the police and she introduced herself as Sergeant but didn't mention being from Longueuil. She added, "This is Detective Dougherty."

The supervisor said, "What can I do for you?"

"We're looking for Louise Tremblay."

"So am I."

"She works in sorting."

"She didn't come in today."

"Did she call?"

"Nothing," the supervisor said.

Legault said, "Is that unusual?"

"Yes, she never misses a shift. I was very surprised today when she didn't show — she's been trying to get off the night shift onto days for quite a while, and she finally does and now she doesn't show up. What's going on, is she in trouble?"

"No," Legault said. "We just wanted to talk to her."

"Detectives? It must be something."

"It's about a family member," Dougherty said. "Nothing to do with Louise directly."

"People have to have clean records to work here," the supervisor said. "If she's in trouble with the police we need to know."

"It's not her," Dougherty said as forcefully as he could without making a scene. "Don't even mention that we were here."

"It doesn't matter," the supervisor said. "If she doesn't come in tomorrow morning with a good excuse then she doesn't work here anymore."

In the car driving back out past the security gate, Legault said, "That guy has too much power."

"He just likes to use what little he's got," Dougherty said. "Okay, do you have an address for Louise?"

"You want to go now?"

"Yeah, let's find out what's going on."

Legault got out her notebook and said, "8445 Boulevard de l'Acadie. You know where that is?"

"Yeah," Dougherty said. "I know it, do you?"

"Not really." Legault shrugged. "I don't come into the city very often."

"You're going to love this."

———

Dougherty looked sideways at Legault as he drove around the traffic circle getting off the Metropolitain Expressway and onto l'Acadie.

Legault was looking at the apartment buildings that lined the east side of the street, most of them three storeys or more, brick buildings without any real character or anything very inviting other than being a place to live. Cheap urban sprawl.

"There is it."

Dougherty pulled a U and stopped in front of 8445, a yellow-brick building with balconies, identical to the buildings on either side. He got out of the car and went around to help Legault, but she was already getting out. She stood up and got her crutch under her arm and was starting to move towards the apartment building when she looked back over the roof of the car to the west side of the street.

She said, "Oh, I see what you mean."

"TMR."

But before the big single-family suburban homes of the Town of Mount Royal, there was a tall hedge and, Dougherty knew, behind that a fence. He was thinking there probably couldn't be a more obvious example of the divide in Montreal than the green wall on l'Acadie: cramped apartment buildings and row houses on one side and tree-lined winding streets, big front lawns and bigger backyards on the other.

Legault said, "So, let's see if Louise Tremblay is home," and started towards the front door of the apartment building.

Dougherty followed thinking, Yeah, ignore it, what else can you do? On the way over he'd expected Legault to say something, make some kind of comment, sarcastic or biting in some way, and he realized he'd been looking forward to it. But standing on the sidewalk in front of the apartment building and looking at the backs of the big houses — of course it was their backs — even he didn't find it funny.

Legault pressed the buzzer for apartment 312 and they waited.

After a few minutes Legault pressed the buzzer again, and Dougherty said, "Let's talk to the super."

Legault pushed the buzzer marked *Superintendent*.

Through the big glass front-doors they saw an apartment door on the first floor open and a middle-aged woman stick out her head and say, "*Oui?*"

Legault spoke French, saying, "Can we talk to you for a moment?"

The woman came out of the apartment and walked down the hall towards them, saying, "No vacancy."

Legault said, "We're police."

"Ya?"

Dougherty figured the woman's first language was Greek or whatever they spoke in Yugoslavia, around there. She was looking at the casts on Legault's wrist and ankle.

Legault said, "Open the door."

The woman looked at Dougherty and said, "Ya?" He didn't want to answer, make it look like he was overruling Legault, but he did want the woman to open the door.

Then Legault was holding up a leather wallet with her badge on one side and an ID card on the other and saying, "Police, open the door."

Dougherty liked the wallet, the kind he planned on getting when he finally made full-time detective, though now he was thinking that would probably never happen.

"Okay, okay," the woman opened the door and Legault stepped into the apartment building.

It was a lot like the building Dougherty had just moved into with Judy, but it smelled a lot different: cabbages and beets and a lot of stuff he didn't know but recognized from these kinds of buildings filled with recent immigrants.

Legault said, "We're looking for Louise Tremblay, apartment 312."

"No, no Tremblay," the woman said.

"Maybe she's not on the lease, but she lives here. Young woman, twenty, twenty-two years old. Long hair, dark blonde. Skinny."

The woman shook her head, nothing.

"French," Legault said. "She's French, Louise Tremblay."

"I never seen her."

"All right, maybe your buzzer isn't working, we'll

knock on the door."

Legault walked to the elevator and pushed the button. The door opened immediately.

"Buzzer works," the woman said. "Everything work, my husband fix everything."

In the elevator Dougherty said, "It's a good thing her husband keeps everything working, how were you going to get up three flights of stairs?"

"Easy," Legault said. The elevator doors opened and she walked down the hall until she found apartment 312 and banged her crutch on the door.

No answer.

Legault banged again.

Dougherty said, "Looks like she's not home."

"It's not right."

"Happens all the time," Dougherty said. "People say they'll talk to the cops but then they change their minds."

Legault was still looking at the door, waiting for it to open, willing it to open. "She was scared, I had to talk her into meeting, she didn't want to."

"So she didn't."

"She didn't go to work." Legault turned slowly and looked at Dougherty. "I asked her about Marc-André, I pushed her to tell me. She didn't know anything, she hadn't seen him in months."

"So she said."

"I practically threatened her," Legault said. "I made her go looking for him, she didn't want to."

"It's what we do."

"It's what you do."

Dougherty said, "Watch it."

"You're just a thug."

She turned and started walking down the hall to the elevator.

Dougherty stood and watched her press the button and saw the door open right away. He watched Legault get on the elevator and the door close.

Dougherty said, "Fuck."

He walked to the elevator and pushed the button. He could hear the motor start, groaning and clanging its way up. When the door opened he didn't get on and the door closed.

"God dammit."

He paced a little in the hall, thinking they should talk to the neighbours, find out the last time anyone saw Louise, get the super to let them into the apartment and have a look around.

Then he pressed the button for the elevator, the door opened and he got on.

In front of the building Legault was leaning against the car, and as soon as Dougherty walked up she said, "Okay, I'm sorry."

He didn't slow down, walking around the car and opening the driver's side door, saying, "Don't be, you're right." He looked over the roof of the car. "I am a thug, that's what works for me." He got into the car.

Legault got into the passenger seat and said, "Yes, it's true, it works. Most of the time."

Dougherty started driving. He didn't want to talk about it because he knew where it was going. He'd been avoiding it for a while himself, knowing it and not wanting to face it.

What would he do when being a thug didn't work?

It's what was holding him back, why he couldn't get to the next level.

Legault said, "It's just sometimes maybe we need a different approach."

"I know."

She looked at him and said, "You do?"

"I do."

"That's good."

They didn't talk much the rest of the drive and when they pulled up in front of Legault's house she said, "I'll keep trying to find Louise Tremblay."

"Good."

"I'll call you when I find her."

Dougherty said, "Okay."

"Will you keep looking?"

"Yeah, of course. I'll be on this Olympic security but like today, I can get away."

Legault said, "Okay, good," and got out of the car.

Dougherty drove back into Montreal, over the Champlain Bridge, a great view of the skyline reflected in the St. Lawrence River, the searchlight on top of Place Ville Marie sweeping over the other tall buildings and behind them the mountain with its cross lit up on top. Dougherty had always loved this approach to Montreal — it was his city, his home, he was proud of it.

Now, for the first time, he wasn't sure about his place in it.

CHAPTER
NINETEEN

The sergeant in charge, a guy Dougherty didn't know named Latulippe, started the briefing by saying that in the first week of the Olympics they'd arrested two hundred guys for scalping and seized over three thousand tickets.

"So, you men," Latulippe said, "are going to put a stop to it."

They were crowded into a room at headquarters on Bonsecours Street, twenty guys at least, all looking pleased to be on this assignment. It was straightforward: they were going out undercover to all the Olympic venues to buy tickets and pick up scalpers. Because Dougherty had been working at the Forum, he got assigned across town at the Olympic Stadium.

Other guys were sent to the Maurice Richard Arena, the Claude Robillard Centre, even Molson Stadium, though Dougherty couldn't imagine anyone would be selling scalped tickets to a field hockey game between India and Australia — he figured they must be giving those away.

As the meeting broke up and they all headed to their assignments, Dougherty saw Galluccio coming across the room towards him. He waited till he was close and said, "Nice shirt. You going to be looking for tickets to the disco dance final?"

Galluccio wiped the lapels of the light blue suit jacket, even though it was shiny clean. "You should talk."

"What?"

"You don't look like you could afford a ticket to the peewee Olympics."

"Maybe you could lend me a gold chain, you wouldn't notice one or two missing, how many you have there?"

Galluccio touched the bare chest exposed by his white shirt unbuttoned halfway to his waist, and he said, "Tickets for the closing ceremony are going for five hundred bucks, gotta look like we can afford them."

"You sure you don't just like dressing like that?"

Galluccio laughed. "You got Olympic Stadium, too?"

"Yeah, you going now?"

"Let's get started."

They left Bonsecours and headed towards the Place d'Armes Métro station. Galluccio said, "Did you ever find any of those dealers?"

293

"Yeah, we did, thanks."

"They weren't who you were looking for?"

"No, we're still looking."

"That's why you took this job? Talk to the ticket scalpers?"

They got to the Métro station and Dougherty said, "Yeah, see what's what."

"They figure there are about a hundred guys working at the stadium but only about fifty are pros."

"Amateur athletics, amateur scalpers."

Galluccio said, "Funny," in a deadpan.

The train arrived in the station, quiet on its rubber wheels, and they got on. Standing, holding on to the pole, Dougherty said, "You still working the port, the islands?"

"Oh yeah, but I'm doing a lot of these special assignments. I've been working a little narco, hanging out in the discos."

"You going to be a detective?"

Galluccio said, "Yeah, maybe. But the chicks dig the uniform, you know?"

At Berri they switched to the green line heading east towards Olympic Stadium and Dougherty said, "Maybe we should split up."

"Yeah," Galluccio said, "we really don't look like we belong together." He looked Dougherty up and down and shook his head pityingly.

"Hey, this is what I would wear to the Games, jeans and a t-shirt."

"Yeah, you probably would."

The train was crowded and a man pressed up against Galluccio turned awkwardly to face him and said,

"Excuse me, do you know which stop is the stadium?"

Galluccio said, "Yeah, sure, it's Pee Neuf."

The guy said, "What?" and Galluccio pointed to the map above the door of the train and said, "Right there, see, Préfontaine, Joliette and then Pee Neuf."

"Pie IX?"

"Pie nine," Galluccio said. "Pee Neuf. It's the Pope, you heard of him, right? Pope Pius the Ninth."

The guy was already turning away, back to his wife and saying, "It's coming up, Pie Nine," and she said, "Why isn't it called Olympic Stadium?"

Galluccio rolled his eyes. Then he said, "Hey, you were on that Brink's truck robbery, right?"

"Yeah."

"They shut that down?"

"It went back to the robbery guys. They needed the rest of us for Olympic security, for this kind of thing."

"You were looking in the west end?"

"Yeah, mostly. Why?"

Galluccio shrugged and said, "No reason, really. Just, a lot of the cocaine in the clubs, there are a lot of English guys making deals, you know."

"Yeah, the boss said the money was being reinvested in the local economy."

"So you were on the right track."

Dougherty shrugged. "They really wanted it to be someone from out of town. It's hard to believe some locals pulled it off."

"Especially Anglos."

"Irish," Dougherty said.

Galluccio said, "Whatever." Then, "Here we are, you coming?"

"I'll get off at Viau," Dougherty said. "So we don't look like a team."

The Métro stopped and the doors slid open. Galluccio waited till most of the crowd had gotten off and then started towards the door, saying, "No one would believe I hang out with a guy dressed like that." He winked and stepped off the train as the doors closed.

Olympic Stadium was pretty much halfway between the two Métro stops but Pie-IX was built to handle the crowds. It was the first one people would get to coming from downtown.

There were people all over the concourse. Dougherty walked through the crowd and looked up at the unfinished tower rising above the stadium, the concrete bowl he'd seen made fun of so much, cartoonists almost always drawing it as a huge toilet bowl.

But now, with the crowds and the athletes and the excitement of the whole thing it felt pretty good. Dougherty almost wished he was actually buying tickets to see an event.

It was easy to find a scalper: just like a hockey game or a concert at the Forum, there were guys standing at the edges of the crowd saying, "Tickets, who needs tickets?" Dougherty thought he even recognized a couple of them. He walked up to a young guy who looked like he'd cleaned up for the occasion and said, "You got tickets?"

"For the stadium? Track and field today, semifinals. Or the Vélodrome, it's judo today."

"The stadium."

"How many you need?"

"Four."

"Yeah, I got four."

"You have any for the closing ceremony?"

"Yeah, I can get those."

"Four?"

"If you have two grand."

Dougherty handed over the cash for the four he was buying then and the guy handed him the tickets. He only had a couple more.

"I can get it this afternoon."

"I'll be here."

Dougherty walked away thinking, No you won't be, buddy, you'll be downtown in a cell. Then he tried to blend in with the crowd and still keep an eye on the young scalper. A minute later the kid was selling more tickets, this time to a white guy who looked like a boxer and a big broad-shouldered bald black guy. They took their tickets and headed straight for the stadium.

After one more sale, the scalper turned and walked away, and Dougherty followed him.

A few blocks away the guy went into a tavern. Dougherty waited a moment and then went inside and sat down at the bar, not looking at the back where the young guy had gone. The bartender came over and Dougherty ordered a beer and was thinking this was exactly what his father made fun of, getting paid to sit in a tavern and have a beer — a dream job.

Why did he want to be a detective?

He glanced to the back and saw the young guy standing in front of a booth. An older guy, maybe mid-forties, dressed like a tourist in a colourful short-sleeved shirt and a straw hat, was sitting in the booth and he didn't ask the young guy to join him. They did have a transaction, though: Dougherty saw the tourist take money and hand the young guy more tickets.

Then the young guy left without noticing Dougherty. He nursed the beer for twenty minutes and during that time two other young guys came and three more while he had another. They all went to the tourist in the back booth for less than a minute and then left.

Dougherty walked to the pay phone by the door and called the number of the special squad at HQ and asked for Sergeant Latulippe.

"*Oui?*"

Dougherty told him that he'd followed one of the runners to a drop point and gave the address of the tavern on Rue Hochelaga and said, "He's sitting in a booth in the back like it's his office desk. He looks like a tourist."

"Can you stay until we get someone else there?"

"Sure, but I'll have to order another beer."

"We appreciate your sacrifice, Constable."

Dougherty hung up and went back to the bar. The TV mounted on the wall in the corner was playing a soap opera, and Dougherty called over the bartender and said, "Can you put the Games on?"

The bartender walked over to the TV and turned the dial, clicking it a few spots until the inside of Olympic Stadium came on. Then the bartender brought Dougherty another beer and walked away.

A few minutes later two men came into the tavern and Dougherty recognized one of them, Gabriel Dion, a constable he'd worked with a couple of years before.

Dion and the other guy sat in a booth at the back, the one beside the tourist, and ordered rum and Cokes.

Dougherty settled his bill and left.

Back at Olympic Stadium there were still thousands of people milling around. There were musicians and people who had set up to sell their paintings and other crafts. Dougherty made his way through the crowd and spotted a couple more guys selling tickets.

"So what did you do, quit?"

Dougherty turned and saw a man with a red beard wearing an Expos cap and two cameras strung around his neck and said, "I'm working right now."

"I bet you are."

"What are you doing here?"

Rozovsky held up one of his cameras and said, "I'm working."

"Since when are you in the sports department?"

"The women's hurdles, hundred metres."

"Pervert."

"It's human interest," Rozovsky said. "The girl who finished sixth is a story."

"She must be a beauty queen."

Rozovsky said, "No." He paused, looked back at the stadium and said, "She's the only one here who survived the attack in Munich." He looked back at Dougherty. "But she doesn't want to talk about it."

"Can't say I blame her for that."

Rozovsky nodded. "She did say she feels safe here."

"It's all the overtime we're getting."

"And those don't hurt, either." Rozovsky pointed to the entrance where half a dozen cops were holding big German shepherds on leashes. "Can they sniff for explosives?"

"That's what they tell me."

"You looking for terrorists?"

"I was, now I'm looking for ticket scalpers."

"You need a ticket? I can get you in with my press pass."

"I'm looking to arrest them," Dougherty said. "It's a crime you know."

Rozovsky said, "It is? Has a ticket scalper ever been arrested in this city?"

"First time for everything."

"We want the world to notice us," Rozovsky said, "but not the real us."

"Maybe we're just like everybody else."

"I don't know if that's a compliment or an insult."

Dougherty said, "Neither do I."

He spent the rest of the day buying more tickets from young scalpers and watching them head to the tavern on Hochelaga. He asked a few of them about tickets to rock concerts, especially to shows at Place des Nations, but none of them knew anything about that. Dougherty was beginning to think it was possible the story the brass was putting out on this one was true, these might actually be professional scalpers from out of town.

When the final event was starting inside the Big O, Dougherty went to HQ and made a report to Sergeant Latulippe. They'd done well, found a few rungs on the ladder, and Latulippe was optimistic that over the weekend, the final days of the games, they would get the whole scalper ring.

It was a little after nine when Dougherty got to the apartment in LaSalle and Judy was on the couch reading a paperback.

She said, "There's some lasagna in the fridge, you

can heat it up."

Dougherty got out the glass tray and left the tinfoil on it and put it in the oven. He walked into the living room and said, "How was your day?"

"Good. I'm just about finished my class prep. It's a lot of work."

"What's that?" He motioned to the book.

Judy was holding the paperback in one hand, her thumb holding it open and she seemed to have forgotten it. "My mother, she's crazy." Judy held up the book so Dougherty could read the title, *When I Say No I Feel Guilty*.

"At least it's not *I'm Okay, You're Okay*."

"Oh she has that one, too," Judy said, sitting up. "She's got a stack of them. She's a changed woman."

"I bet she is."

"You can see for yourself on Sunday, she invited us over to watch the closing ceremony. She's having a party."

"Can't make it, I'm working."

"You said you were getting the weekend off?"

Dougherty was back in the kitchenette getting a beer out of the fridge. "I got a new assignment." He walked back into the living room. "Scalper squad."

"All weekend?"

"Closing ceremony tickets are going for five hundred bucks."

"So, who cares? The tickets aren't stolen."

Dougherty put the beer bottle to his lips and took a long drink. Then he said, "I really just took it so I can talk to the scalpers. I'm still looking for those guys from the Jacques Cartier Bridge."

Judy said, "The murderers?"

"Yeah."

"But you really don't know if those kids were killed."

"No, I don't."

"And there isn't even an investigation going on."

"Just mine."

"Do you really think doing exactly what they told you not to do will get you a promotion?"

"I don't know," Dougherty said. "I don't care. I don't think I'm getting a promotion anyway."

"Oh great, so what are you doing?"

"You know what I'm doing."

"No, I don't. I don't have any idea what you're doing."

Dougherty shrugged and drank more beer.

Then he said, "We talked about this."

"We talked about doing a job. What we both have to do now."

"Yeah well, this is it."

"No," Judy said, "this isn't your job."

"I'm not going to explain it to you again."

Judy was standing up. "Yeah, if you could." She threw the paperback on the couch and walked out of the living room. "I'm going to bed."

The bedroom door slammed.

302   Dougherty sat at the table eating the still-cold lasagna out of the glass dish. Through the living room window he could see the top of the church across the street, the round white top that looked like a rocket ship.

Then he slept on the couch and left for work before Judy got up.

All day Friday at the stadium Dougherty bought tickets and followed scalpers. He asked more of the kids about tickets to concerts and a few offered to find some for him, but he could tell it wasn't something they'd done before so it wasn't any use to him.

Inside the stadium the big excitement was an American, a guy named Bruce Jenner, winning the decathalon and becoming the world's greatest athlete. One of the young scalpers said, "He'll be on a Wheaties box before we get home," and Dougherty said, "Where's home?"

The kid said, "You know what I mean," but Dougherty was pretty sure the kid's accent was American, not quite Boston but somewhere in New England.

Saturday afternoon Dougherty bought tickets to the gold medal soccer game that night. The scalper really didn't know much about it, "Poland and East Germany," the guy said, "I guess they're good."

"Sure they are," Dougherty said. "East Germany beat the Russians and Poland beat Brazil to get into this game."

"Hundred bucks a ticket is a steal then."

"Hundred for two is better."

The guy said, "Okay," and Dougherty made the buy. Then as he was headed into the stadium he ducked into a security office and made his report.

Galluccio was in the office and he said, "We're picking everybody up in half an hour. Looks like sixty guys."

Dougherty said, "Holy shit."

"Yeah, we'll be processing them all night. All this overtime, I'm going to buy a Camaro. What are you going to get?"

"I was thinking the down payment on a house."

"Oh yeah, I forgot," Galluccio said, "you're an old married man."

"I'm not married."

Galluccio shrugged, "You might as well be. If you were Italian you'd have the ceremony and get the down payment at the party."

Dougherty didn't want to tell Galloosh he'd probably be living by himself again in a few days. He hadn't talked to Judy since their fight. Moving in together may have been a mistake.

Late in the afternoon they started picking up the runners and the next level up, the guy Dougherty had spotted in the tavern on Hochelaga and a couple of other guys like him. They used the whole twenty-one-man scalper squad and twenty more uniform cops. The entire force was working the final weekend of the Olympics, and from what Dougherty saw of the young guys he figured Galloosh better get his Camaro quick before they sold out and there wouldn't be one on a lot for a hundred miles around Montreal.

Almost sixty guys were taken into custody, and when the processing started Dougherty realized he still had the two tickets to the gold medal game in his pocket so he slipped away and found a pay phone and called his father.

"It's short notice, but would you like to go see the gold medal soccer game?"

"You got tickets?"

"A bonus for all the overtime. We can meet at the stadium." Dougherty looked at the tickets and said, "Gate twelve, it's on the east side."

Dougherty knew his father wouldn't take the Métro. He'd been driving that phone company van all over the city for thirty years, he knew every street and every lane and every parking spot there was. Sure enough, half an hour after he got off the phone with him, Dougherty was standing outside Olympic Stadium and his father came walking up from Viau Street.

They got a couple of beers and found their seats. Dougherty was glad he hadn't really paid a hundred dollars for them, they were pretty high up and in a corner, but once they were sitting he looked around and said, "This place actually looks pretty good."

"It's worth a billion dollars, easy," his father said and they laughed.

The place was packed, seventy-one thousand people according to the notice on the big scoreboard, and loud.

The game was East Germany; they hit the post in the first minute, scored in the seventh minute and again in the fourteenth.

Dougherty's dad said, "Looks like a rout. And Poland won the gold last time."

In the second half the Germans took their foot off the gas and Poland scored but the Germans pulled themselves together and started using long passes over the top to keep the ball in the Polish end. Germany scored one more and that was it, 3–1 final and another gold medal for East Germany.

"It's been good for the commies," Dougherty said when the medal ceremony ended and people starting filing out of the stadium. "The Soviets and East Germany, one and two in the medals."

"West Germany won a lot of medals, too," his father said. "If they were one country they would've finished first."

"Lucky for us that'll never happen."

They stopped for one more beer at a tavern a couple of blocks from the stadium.

Dougherty's father said, "Are you working tomorrow?"

"I thought I was but we made all the scalper arrests today. Turns out the ring was from Boston, or near there, someplace called Somerville, Massachusetts. Guy running it is a travel agent and he had a connection in the organizing committee, got a few thousand tickets two years ago."

"Thinking ahead."

"Back then we didn't think the stadium would be finished or the Games would really happen."

"Now Bourassa's a hero for saving the day."

"I wouldn't call him a hero," Dougherty said, and his father smiled. The premier of Quebec was sure trying to take the credit since his government had stepped in and taken over the Olympics from the city. "But he might call an early election."

"That's the rumour. Quick before the separatists get ahead in the polls."

The tavern was full but Dougherty felt it was oddly quiet for the end of the Olympics.

His father said, "So, tomorrow, you and Judy want

to come over for dinner? Even though you're living in sin, your mother still likes Judy."

Dougherty said, "We got the same invitation from her mother, but I said I couldn't make it."

"But now you can?"

"I don't think so, not the way we left it."

"You have a fight?"

"Yeah."

Dougherty's father leaned back in the small wooden tavern chair and drank some beer. Then he said, "It's none of my business, but you two have a lot going on."

"We do?"

"You moved in together, you're working all the time, Judy starts a new job in a couple of weeks."

"She was in a classroom for months last year as a student-teacher, it's not like she's never done it before."

"It's a new job in a new school," his father said. "And before she even starts they're talking about going on strike. It's got to be getting to her."

"Why?"

"And her parents splitting up, that's got to be tough."

"That doesn't have anything to do with Judy."

"Nothing?"

Dougherty finished off his glass of draught and said, "Yeah, okay, I didn't think about it like that."

"Usually when you fight it's not about what it's really about."

Dougherty nodded. "Maybe you're not just a pretty face."

His dad finished off his own beer and put the empty glass on the table.

It was just after eleven when Dougherty got to the apartment in LaSalle.

Judy was sitting at the dining room table with a bunch of textbooks spread out, making notes. She looked up when he came in the door and then went back to the books.

Dougherty said, "Look, I'm sorry."

Without looking up Judy said, "I thought love meant never having to say you're sorry."

Dougherty said, "You thought that movie was as stupid as I did."

He opened the fridge and got out a beer. "You want one?"

She looked at him and said, "That's it, that's your whole apology?"

He got another beer and brought them both to the table. "Are we really mad at each other?"

"I'm really mad at you."

"Okay, but not because I'm still working the homicide, because I was acting like that's the only thing that's important."

"If you say the words 'self-actualized' or anything else out of my mother's stupid self-help books I swear I'll hit you with this bottle." She picked up the beer and took a drink.

Dougherty said, "I'm not working tomorrow, you want to go to your mother's?"

"No, I don't want to, but we're going to."

"Okay, sounds good."

They went to bed and made out.

And Sunday night when they got home from Judy's mother's house the phone was ringing. Dougherty answered it and Legault said, "I found Louise Tremblay. Marc-André found her first."

CHAPTER
TWENTY

Legault got into Dougherty's car and he said, "When do you get the casts off?"

"Two more weeks."

Dougherty backed out of the driveway and said, "So, we're going to Sorel?"

"Yes, I have directions, it should take about an hour."

If it wasn't police business it would have been a nice summer drive along the St. Lawrence River passing through some beautiful countryside. Another month or so and people would be doing it to see the spectacular fall colours.

As they approached the town of Sorel, Legault said, "Do you know it at all?"

Dougherty said, "No. I played hockey here a few times, but I don't think I could even find the arena."

Legault gave directions that took them through the centre of the city and over the bridge where the Richelieu River joined the St. Lawrence. There were a couple of big ships docked at a steel foundry that looked to Dougherty like it was a hundred years old.

On the other side of the river was the town of Tracy. Legault said, "Turn right here," and they drove past some old industrial buildings, and after a couple more turns they were on Adélaide, and she said, "This is it, number forty-nine." The house was one in a row of two-storey clapboard houses. Number forty-nine, in Quebec style, had a wrought iron staircase winding down the front. "Top floor."

Dougherty said, "Of course it is," and followed Legault as she made her way up the stairs, the cast on her foot banging on the iron steps. She knocked on the door and it opened right away.

"*Entrez.*"

Legault went in and Dougherty followed, nodding at the young woman who quickly closed the door. He figured she was Louise Tremblay. The black eye and bruises on her face a real giveaway.

In the small kitchen she said, "*Voulez-vous un café?*"

Legault said no, but Dougherty had the feeling that Louise wanted to be doing something so he said, "*Oui, merci.*"

Louise filled a kettle with water and put it on the stove. Then she said, still speaking French, "My mother is out, she won't be back until this afternoon."

"We thank you for talking to us," Legault said.

Louise shrugged.

Dougherty sat down at the table with his back to the wall, trying to take up as little space as possible.

Legault said, "Are you okay?"

Louise put a couple of fingers to her face and said, "Yes." Then she shrugged and said, "It's happened before."

"That's why your mother is upset?"

"She didn't know that I was back with Marc-André. She didn't approve."

Dougherty said, "No kidding."

Legault gave him a look, then said to Louise, "You knew Marc-André before he went to jail?"

"Yes. He wasn't like that, he wasn't . . ."

Dougherty exhaled a little too loudly. He'd seen this so many times since he'd become a cop, so many women who said the man wasn't really like that. The man was always like that.

The kettle whistled and Louise turned off the heat and said over her shoulder to Legault, "You don't want one?"

"No, thanks."

Louise got two mugs from the drying rack next to the sink and a jar of instant coffee from the cupboard. She made two cups and brought one to Dougherty saying, "Would you like milk and sugar?"

"No, thanks, this is fine."

Louise got the milk out of the fridge and poured some into her mug then added a generous spoonful of sugar. She sat at the table holding the mug in both hands and said, "He was different when he came out of jail."

"His mother told us she didn't see much of him then."

"No? I don't know about that," Louise said. "I don't know where he went. He wasn't . . . perfect, before he went to jail, you know?"

Dougherty said, "Yeah," and Legault looked at him again, making a motion for him to be quiet.

Then she looked back at Louise and said, "I know, but jail is hard."

Louise nodded.

"Was Marc-André involved with drugs before he went to jail?"

Louise was looking down at her mug and she nodded. She spoke quietly, saying, "Yes, we both were."

"You were both selling drugs?"

"A little. We were both using drugs."

"He was selling drugs?"

"Yes. That's why he went to jail."

"Do you know where Marc-André is now?"

Louise shook her head. Still staring at the mug.

"There is no way he will ever find out that we talked to you," Legault said. "You don't have to worry about that."

"I don't know where he is."

"When was the last time you saw him?"

"On the day . . . the day I was supposed to see you." She looked at Legault.

Dougherty squeezed his mug and took a drink to keep from saying anything.

Legault said, "What happened?"

"I was leaving for work, going to the bus stop. A car stopped and Marc-André got out."

"What did he say?"

"He said, 'Here I am.'"

"Why would he say that?"

"Because!" Louise slammed the mug down on the table, spilling coffee. "Because I was looking for him. Because you asked me to!"

Dougherty was still and so was Legault. The yelling and the banging was startling but the silence that followed was, too.

After a moment Legault said, "I'm sorry, Louise."

"I . . . I wanted to see him, but I didn't think . . ."

"What happened?"

"He told me to get in the car."

"Was he driving?"

"No, it was someone else I don't know, I never saw him before."

"You got in the car?"

"Yes. We drove somewhere, I don't know where. Behind a warehouse."

"And he hit you?"

Louise nodded. She put a hand on her throat and said, "He choked me. He told me to stop looking for him, stop asking people about him."

Legault said, "I'm sorry, Louise."

"We're going to catch him," Dougherty said. "You can make a complaint against him."

"Oh, no," Louise said, "I don't want to do that."

Dougherty said, "Course not."

Legault turned on him and said in English, "Enough." She looked back to Louise and spoke French, "We really appreciate you trying to help us. And we will arrest him. It's for something else, you don't have to make a complaint if you don't want to."

"Thank you."

Dougherty shook his head, sighed heavily.

Legault said, "Do you have any idea who he would be with?"

"No."

Dougherty said, "Do you know Martin Comptois?"

"No."

"You sure? He lives downtown, near the Lucien-L'Allier Métro station."

Louise was looking into her coffee mug, she hadn't drank any of it. "No."

Legault said, "That's okay, Louise."

"What about the car," Dougherty said. "What kind was it?"

Louise shrugged. "I don't know."

"Was it a four-door or a two-door?" Dougherty asked. "When you got in the back, was there a back door or did they push the seat forward?"

Louise looked up and stared at Dougherty and said, "I didn't get in, he pushed me in. He grabbed me by the throat and pushed me onto the back seat, pushed my face into the seat. I thought he was going to kill me."

"So a four-door," Dougherty said.

Legault turned to Dougherty and said, "Would you be quiet." Then she turned back to Louise and said, "When you and I spoke on the phone, and you agreed to meet with me after work at UPS, at the Lafleur Hot Dog, do you remember?"

Louise nodded.

"What were you going to tell me then?"

It took a moment and then Louise said, "It doesn't matter now. That was before I saw Marc-André."

Legault spoke like she was just making conversation, like it wasn't important, saying, "I'm just curious, what were you going to tell me?"

"Not much, I had been asking around about Marc-André, calling some people we knew. No one knew where he was, he was gone." She shrugged and drank some coffee. "He always talked about going out west, maybe to California."

Legault nodded and waited for Louise to continue.

Dougherty wanted to jump in and say something but he didn't. He realized where Legault was going: Louise wouldn't have agreed to meet if she had nothing to say and now she was even more scared. He waited.

Legault said, "Did he go to California?"

Louise shook her head no. "I think he went to Toronto. I think he took drugs to sell there."

"Is that what you were going to tell me, that he'd gone to Toronto?"

"Yes."

"Is that all you were going to tell me?"

It took another minute and then Louise said, "I was going to tell you that Marc-André was not a bad guy."

Dougherty leaned forward and almost said something but stopped himself.

Legault said, "But now?"

"I don't know now." Louise stood up and paced in the small kitchen. "He wasn't . . . like this. His mother threw him out when he was young, a kid. He had no father, you know?" She looked at Dougherty and he managed to nod. He thought it looked sympathetic.

Louise said, "It's hard, you know, there's no work. He met some guys."

Legault said, "In jail?"

"He sold a little hash," Louise said. "It was nothing. But then he went to jail. When he got out he was different."

Dougherty said, "And he had new friends?"

"Yes." Louise looked at him. She wasn't angry, she was hoping he understood and she looked doubtful.

Dougherty said, "I've seen it before."

"I was going to tell you that, I was going to tell you he wasn't bad."

Legault said, "I understand. Did you know where he was?"

Louise shook her head. "Some people I talked to said they had seen him so I knew he was back. I thought if you found him you should know."

"Thank you." Legault stood up and was close to Louise. "We're still going to find him so this is good to know for when we talk to him."

Louise was nodding. "I don't think he's here," she said. "I think he went back to Toronto or out west."

Dougherty said, "Who did you talk to that had seen him?"

Louise looked up sharply and said, "I don't know exactly, just some people."

"You don't know their names?"

"I spoke to a lot of people." She looked at Legault, glared at her and then at Dougherty. "I don't remember who said what."

Legault said, "Okay, Louise, thank you."

As they were walking out the front door and starting

317

down the stairs to the street Dougherty turned back and said, "If you do hear from him again, call us right away, okay?"

Louise was looking down at him and she said, "Yes."

"Or if you remember who you talked to who saw him."

Louise nodded and Legault pulled Dougherty by the arm and said, "Come on."

In the car on the way back to Montreal, Legault said, "You pushed her too hard."

"You didn't push her hard enough."

"Now she won't tell us anything."

"She will if we keep asking."

"She doesn't know anything."

"She knows he's a good guy."

Legault lit a cigarette and rolled down the window a little.

Dougherty said, "He'll get picked up again, we'll get him."

"How will we know?" Legault said. "This case is closed, remember? If he gets picked up he'll get processed and we'll never know, you and me."

The highway was flat and straight along the St. Lawrence River and Dougherty drove too fast. He said, "You think the other guy was Martin Comptois?"

Legault shrugged. "Could be anybody."

"Yeah, but what do you think? They met in jail?"

"Is Comptois in jail now?"

"He's out on bail," Dougherty said. "I have the address he gave the cops in Cornwall, you want to go see?"

"Sure, why not?"

Dougherty was thinking, Because we could both get fired for it, but he didn't say anything, he just drove even faster. He took the Jacques Cartier Bridge into the city and they were both quiet driving past the exit to Île Sainte-Hélène, both of them looking at the spot where Mathieu and Manon probably went over the guardrail.

In the city Dougherty took Dorchester Boulevard and headed towards downtown, past the big office buildings of Hydro-Québec and Place Ville Marie. Overdale Avenue was a one-block street wedged in between Dorchester and the Ville-Marie Expressway. At one end was the Guaranteed Milk building, with a big milk bottle on the roof, and at the other end an old hotel that Dougherty had been to plenty of times breaking up fights and throwing out drunks since it'd become a gay bathhouse. The owners were decent guys.

One side of Overdale was taken up by a few old solid stone apartment buildings, and on the corner of Lucien L'Allier was the Lafontaine mansion, once a stately home, now divided into a dozen or more units, not very well kept. The other side of the street had a row of two-storey homes and a big warehouse building. Dougherty parked in front of the warehouse.

Legault said, "How did you even find this street?"

"Yeah, it's a little hidden," Dougherty said. "But it's on my beat."

They walked along the row of houses to 1388, and when Dougherty knocked on the front door it pushed open a little. He said, "Okay," and pushed the door wide open. Directly ahead was a short hallway with two doors on the right and on the left were stairs going up to the second floor.

Dougherty knocked on the first door but the second one opened. A young guy, maybe twenty years old, stuck his head into the hall and said, "Yeah?"

Dougherty took a couple steps towards the guy and said, "I'm looking for a guy named Martin Comptois."

The young guy shrugged and said, "Don't know him."

"Maybe he lives there?" Dougherty pointed to the door he'd knocked on.

"No, it's the same place." The young guy stepped back from the door and motioned inside his apartment.

Dougherty looked inside and saw it was all one room. There was a kitchen — or at least a fridge and stove and sink — at one end and windows looking onto Overdale at the other. And in between were both doors to the hall.

"Why does it have two doors?"

"I don't know. I think it used to be a rooming house or something. I think it's been a few things over the years."

Dougherty noticed the maroon and yellow flag on the wall and said, "Do you go to Sir George?"

"Concordia, yeah."

"Right." Dougherty always forgot the new name since Sir George had merged with Loyola College out in NDG. "Have you lived here long?"

"I'm in my third year," the guy said. "I've been in this place for two."

"And no Martin Comptois?"

"I don't know him. Maybe he's in the basement, I never see them."

"What about upstairs?"

"They're from India," the guy said. "There are quite a few different guys but I don't think any of them are named Martin."

Dougherty said, "Okay, thanks."

He stepped back into the hall and walked towards the stairs, saying to Legault, "You might as well wait here."

She said, "That was my plan." She tapped her foot, the one with the cast, on the floor but even without it she may have stayed by the front door. The building wasn't a slum, exactly, but the light bulbs hanging by wires from the ceiling above the stairs looked to have burned out years ago.

Dougherty felt like he was going into a cave. He went down the stairs and banged on the door. Nothing. He banged again and listened but there was no sound coming from inside.

When Dougherty got to the top of the stairs Legault said, "What now?"

"We could talk to the landlord."

"What are the chances Martin Comptois is the name on the lease?"

"Slim to none," Dougherty said. "He may never have lived here, he may have lived here years ago and given this address to the cops in Cornwall."

"Right."

"Or he may actually live here," Dougherty said.

They were walking back to Dougherty's car.

"This is pointless," Legault said.

"This is police work."

Legault slapped her hand down on the roof of the car, making a loud bang. "It's bullshit."

"What do you think we should do?"

"What should we do?" She banged on the roof of the car again. "We should be pulling these guys in, we should have every cop going after them, after everyone they know, we should find them!"

Dougherty waited a moment and then opened the car door. He started to get in but he stopped and looked back along the street. "And what do we do if we find them? We don't have any evidence."

Legault said, "They will confess."

Dougherty nodded. Then he said, "Then we'll have to find them."

Legault said, "Yes," and got in the car.

————

A couple of weeks later Dougherty was back working in uniform at Station Ten. The new law making wearing seatbelts mandatory had come into effect, and although there had been a lot of press to get people ready for it, Dougherty and the other cops were sent out on a ticket blitz.

It gave him a chance to pull over every four-door sedan driven by a long-haired guy he saw, but he didn't find Martin Comptois or Marc-André Daigneault.

August ended and after Labour Day weekend things seemed to settle down in the city. Judy started teaching at LaSalle High, and Dougherty was mostly working days. He was the senior constable at Station Ten and spent some time helping Delisle with desk sergeant duties. "Being trained," Delisle said.

And then at a Sunday dinner at his parents' place in Greenfield Park, of all places, Dougherty got the best lead yet.

CHAPTER
TWENTY-ONE

Dougherty was standing on the balcony, watching people coming out of what he still thought of as the rocket ship church across the street.

He took the small jewellery box out of his pocket and opened it. The wedding ring he'd bought from Fred Bergman. Dougherty was thinking that was when he was working the Brink's truck robbery, back in the spring. It seemed like years ago now. And that investigation had gone nowhere. Well, not really nowhere. Dougherty shook his head thinking about it: they all knew it was the Point Boys, they just couldn't pin it on anyone. Yet.

Judy walked into the living room and said, "We going?"

Dougherty snapped the jewellery box shut and said, "Yeah, you ready?"

"In a minute."

She went back into the bedroom and Dougherty put the box back in his pocket. He was thinking there would never be a perfect time to ask so he might as well just do it now. Just hand Judy the ring and say, "What do you think?"

Not much of a proposal.

And, really, was it just so they could have a Sunday dinner with Dougherty's parents that didn't end with another fight with his mother?

On the drive to the south shore Judy said, "I hope there's no strike."

"You think there will be?"

"I don't know, it's hard to say."

"My dad's union settled," Dougherty said.

"They're talking about a day of protest, a province-wide walkout. Not just teachers, all kinds of unions."

"One day wouldn't be too bad."

Judy said, "I feel like I just learned all the kids' names. I finally stopped mixing up Dawn and Denise just because they both wear glasses."

"It sounds like you're doing fine?"

"I have to admit, I like it more than I thought I would."

"That's good," Dougherty said. "Someone should like their job."

"How bad is it?"

They were coming off the Champlain Bridge and turning onto Taschereau Boulevard. Dougherty said, "It's fine. Paperwork, schedules, you know, important stuff."

"Someone does have to do it."

"Could you imagine working as a teacher without the classroom stuff, without talking to the kids? Just the meetings and the administration stuff."

"The older teachers," Judy said. "They talk about that all the time, how much they hate the meetings, how they're more childish than the kids."

Dougherty nodded.

Judy said, "It won't be forever, though, will it? You can still get into detective work?"

"Sure."

As they were driving on a quiet street past well-kept lawns and flower beds in front of the houses, Dougherty said, "It is nice here."

Judy said, "Yeah, it is."

Walking up to the back door of the house Dougherty said, "Sounds like your parents' place."

"My mother's place."

Loud music coming from the basement.

Dougherty shouted, "Hello," as he walked into the kitchen but it was empty. He saw through the window both his parents in the backyard. He opened the fridge and got out a beer. "You want one?"

Judy said, "No, thanks."

They went to the backyard and Dougherty's father said, "Good, you found them."

Dougherty looked at Judy and said, "See, I could be a detective, I can find a cold beer in a fridge."

Judy said, "You could be a captain."

Dougherty's father said, "Something going on?"

"No, everything's fine."

They sat in the backyard for a while and then moved

inside for dinner.

Once the food was on the table, they managed to coax Tommy out of the basement, and he sat down and stared at his plate, his long hair obscuring his face.

Judy said, "So, how's school?"

"Fine."

"Teachers good?"

"Yeah."

"Schedule okay?"

"Yeah."

Dougherty laughed and said, "Did you want to law-yer up?"

His mother said, "This is the most he's talked in weeks."

Judy said, "Everybody makes such a big deal of your senior year but really it's the low point. Things get a lot better when you finish high school and move on."

"If he had any idea where he was moving on to," Dougherty's dad said.

"It's only September," Judy said, "you don't have to decide now."

"But some vague idea might be good."

"Maybe you'll get lucky," Dougherty said, "maybe the school bus will get hijacked like the one in California."

"*Édouard!*"

His mother glared at him, and Dougherty said, "Well, come on, all he does is grunt."

"Those poor children," his mother said. "They were buried alive."

"They got out," Dougherty said. "And we got one of the kidnappers, picked him up in Vancouver."

"It's not nice to talk about."

"It's a happy ending."

Tommy stood up and said, "I'm done," and went back into the basement. The music started up right away.

After they'd eaten the pie Judy had picked up at Steinberg's on the way over, they cleaned up and Dougherty's father made himself a rum and Pepsi and Dougherty had another beer.

Sitting in the living room, Dougherty's mother said to Judy, "Are they all like that, the students these days?"

"Most of the boys are," Judy said.

"None of them have any ambition?"

"A few, I guess, but most of them have no idea. They are just kids."

"When you were a kid, you had no ambition?"

Judy smiled and said, "Well, according to my parents I had too much ambition, always trying to change the world."

"I wish Tommy would change his underwear."

Dougherty laughed. "He's fine."

"He's not." His mother really looked worried. "He never talks to us. He's out so late."

"He's home today."

"He'll go out later, stay out so late. Some nights he comes home after midnight, we don't know where he is."

Dougherty looked at his father and said, "Have you asked him?"

"He just says he's out."

Dougherty stood up and said, "I'll talk to him."

He went down the basement stairs, like going into a cave, and switched on the light.

Tommy said, "Hey." He was lying on the floor in front of the stereo.

Dougherty said, "Mom's worried."

"So."

"So's Dad."

Tommy got up on his knees and moved towards the stereo.

"Apparently you don't talk. And you stay out late."

"What?"

"They don't know where you are."

"Where am I going to be?"

Dougherty said, "You tell me."

Tommy was flipping through his records. "I'm just around, come on, what's she thinking?"

Dougherty drank some of his beer and said, "She's worried about you, you're going to CEGEP next year and then university. Have you thought about what you want to do?"

"You, too?" Tommy looked over his shoulder at Dougherty and then back to his records. He slid one out of the cardboard sleeve and carefully put the black vinyl down on the turntable. He said, "I have no idea," as he lowered the arm.

Dougherty could see the cover of the album on the floor, a man's face took up pretty much the whole thing and it was all green and trying to look demonic.

"You have no idea at all?" The music blasted out of the speakers and Dougherty said, "What's this?"

"'Go to Hell.'"

"What?"

Tommy said, "Not you, that's the song." He held out the album cover and Dougherty took it.

"Nice."

Tommy turned the volume down a little and said, "This album's not as good as *Welcome to My Nightmare*."

Dougherty said, "No, of course not," and Tommy almost smiled.

"I'm not even out that late," Tommy said. He thought for a moment, nodding along to the music, the words about how you were something that never should have happened and you should go to hell. "I went to the Nazareth concert and we were late coming back from that."

"Was it at Place des Nations?"

"No," Tommy said, "the Forum." He did smile a little then and said, "We did get off the Métro at Île Sainte-Hélène, though, that was a blast. The place was so quiet and it took so long for another train to come. We were freaking out."

"How stoned were you?"

"We weren't," Tommy said. He shrugged. "I wasn't, anyway. It was like a horror movie, I kept imagining something coming out of the tunnel, out of the darkness. It was like *Willard*."

"Yeah," Dougherty said, "there are rats in the tunnels."

Tommy was smiling now. "Cool, I've never seen one. I want to get a movie camera."

"A movie camera?"

"Yeah, a Super 8. I want to make a horror movie."

"Rats in the Métro?"

"Yeah. Just standing around in that empty station is scary."

"It was built for big crowds," Dougherty said. "For Expo, and there were huge crowds."

"Yeah, but now on a winter night, when all of Île Sainte-Hélène is empty, that place is creepy."

Dougherty said, "It can be."

"Oh yeah, add a little scary music, it'd be cool."

"I thought you wanted to be in a band?"

Tommy shrugged. "It's not so fun anymore."

"But you went to the concert?"

"Yeah, Kim sold me her ticket." Tommy was nodding to the beat again, now the song was about how you gotta dance, you can't stop dancing, and he said, "She should be in a band, she goes to every concert. Well, she used to."

"What do you mean?"

"She used to go to every concert, but now she doesn't want to go to any. She sold me her ticket to Nazareth and she offered me the one she bought for the Doobie Brothers. She slept all night at the mall to get the tickets first."

"At Alexis Nihon?"

"No, at the Greenfield Park Mall, the ticket counter's at the Miracle Mart. But now she's getting rid of all her tickets."

"Just like that."

"Yeah," Tommy said. "I heard something happened."

Dougherty said, "What happened?"

The cop was seeping into his voice, and Tommy looked at him and said, "I don't know."

"But you heard something?"

"Not really, just a rumour."

"What was the rumour?"

Tommy looked nervous. "I don't know, just something happened to her after the last concert she went to."

"Where was that?"

"I don't know."

"Think, Tommy!"

"Shit, I didn't do anything."

Dougherty took a breath and said, "Sorry, it's just it might be something. Do you know which concert it was?"

"Yeah, I guess." He thought for a moment and then said, "It could've been ELO."

"Was it or not?"

"I think so, yeah."

"Where was that concert? Did you go?"

"Yeah, I went, it was," he closed his eyes and then opened them and said, "that one was at Place des Nations."

Dougherty nodded and spoke quietly and calmly, trying to sound casual. "So, what happened to Kim?"

"I don't know, she didn't leave when we did."

"She stayed behind?"

"Yeah, her and . . . some other girls, they tried to go backstage."

"Did they get backstage?"

"I think so. Dawn said they did."

"Who's he?"

"No," Tommy said, "D-a-w-n, Dawn Stark, a girl at school."

Tommy was looking away and Dougherty figured

this Dawn was a girl Tommy liked. He said, "That's all you know? After that concert Kim didn't want to go to any more?"

"Yeah, she sold all her tickets."

"Did Dawn say anything else?"

Tommy looked up and said, "No."

"When did she tell you this?"

"Friday," Tommy said. "We went to see a movie, *The Man Who Fell to Earth*." He looked at Dougherty and said, "At the York, all right?"

"I'm sorry," Dougherty said. "But this might be important."

"Important?"

"It's probably nothing," Dougherty said. "But, did she say anything about the bridge, the Jacques Cartier?"

Tommy said, "Hey, that would be another good location for the movie, way up on the bridge, that would be cool."

"Did she say anything about that?"

"What? No." Tommy slid on his butt back to the stereo and lifted the arm cleanly. It didn't make any scratching sound. He put the vinyl back into the sleeve and started flipping through the records again.

"Okay," Dougherty said. "Well, thanks, this might be helpful. What's Kim's last name?"

"Cunningham."

Tommy put another album on the turntable. This time the music was spacier, more psychedelic. He said, "This would be creepy in an empty Métro station, wouldn't it?"

Dougherty stood up and said, "Yeah, it would."

Tommy said, "Ummagumma."

Dougherty had no idea what he was talking about. He went back upstairs.

In the kitchen, Dougherty's mother was wiping down an already clean counter. The kitchen was spotless, it practically glowed it was so clean.

He said, "Tommy's fine, Ma."

She stopped wiping and looked at him, and for a second Dougherty was worried about her. She said, "You sure?"

He tried to laugh it off and said, "Yeah, I'm sure, it's just a girl."

"Really?"

"Don't look so surprised, he's not that ugly."

"No, it's just, he never said."

"Well there you go," Dougherty said, "maybe one of your kids will get married."

She punched him in the arm. *"Commence pas ça, c'est pas drôle."*

But Dougherty was laughing. He walked into the living room where his father was in his usual spot at the end of the couch, rum and Pepsi in his hand, and Judy was in the La-Z-Boy. She was saying, "Wait, this is here in Montreal?"

"Yes, it is."

Dougherty said, "What is?"

Judy said, "Guy with Legionnaires' disease."

"Here? How many guys died in Philadelphia?"

His dad said, "Twenty-six so far."

"Yeah, but not for a while," Dougherty said. "It's over, isn't it."

"We'll see what happens to this guy. He's in the

General, they say he was in Philadelphia right after the Legionnaires."

Dougherty said, "This is why you don't hang out at the Legion?"

His father said, "I go to the Legion sometimes."

Dougherty said, "Right." Then he said to Judy, "You ready?"

She stood up saying, "Sure."

Dougherty's father said, "You want one for the road?" holding up his drink.

"I better not, gotta work in the morning."

"You're on days again?"

"I may be on days forever," Dougherty said.

"That's good."

Dougherty said, "Yeah, sure."

His father was walking towards him then, saying, "You've been working a lot of overtime, it would be good to work straight days for a while."

"I don't remember you ever turning down any overtime."

"Maybe I should have." He reached out and gave Dougherty's arm a squeeze.

Dougherty said, "I think we needed the money." He was surprised. It wasn't like his father to talk like that, that kind of regret.

His father looked at Judy and said, "I hope your parents are okay. Anything can happen, you know."

Judy said, "I guess so."

Dougherty said good night to his mother, and when they were in the car he said to Judy, "What was all that about your parents?"

She rolled the window down a little and blew out

smoke. "Your dad thinks they might get back together."

"What do you think?"

"I don't know what to think. I was hoping they'd both be happier."

"Aren't they?"

"Honestly, I don't know. I mean, that's the idea, right? You split up and it's better for everybody. But what if it isn't?"

"I guess you get back together," Dougherty said.

"You really think that's possible?"

"I don't know."

Judy was looking out the side window, looking at the river in the darkness. After a few minutes she said, "I guess we'll see, who knows."

Dougherty didn't say anything, but he was pretty sure it wasn't the right time to get the ring out of his pocket.

And then he was thinking about whether he should call Legault when he got home or wait till morning, and then he was trying to figure out how they were going to set up some kind of interview with the girl at Tommy's school.

He called Legault as soon as he got into the apartment and Judy went straight to bed. She was asleep by the time he got off the phone.

CHAPTER
TWENTY-TWO

Dougherty pulled into the empty parking lot of Centennial Regional High School and said, "Must've been designed by an American, thought there'd be student parking."

Legault said, "I'm surprised you could find it."

A nearly new building, maybe four or five years old, two storeys, long and flat, red brick with vertical concrete on either side of the windows, squatting in the middle of a new residential neighbourhood filled with bungalows and laid out like a maze. There was a second parking lot full of teachers' cars.

"My brother goes here," Dougherty said.

"He talked to the girl?"

They got out of the car and walked towards the main doors. "He heard something. I told him we wouldn't mention his name."

Dougherty pulled open one of the glass doors and held it for Legault. She said, "Even here, someone might figure it out."

He was still a little surprised by Legault's dry humour, her sarcasm. It was familiar to him, a lot like what he was used to on the Irish side of his family but it wasn't one of the stereotypes that Anglos usually saw in the Québécois. Dougherty was thinking maybe it was too subtle for most Anglos to see and then he was thinking about Anglo stereotypes.

Legault held open a door in the second set about six feet in, and Dougherty said, "Thanks, you okay?"

She fanned her fingers and made a fist, saying, "Skin is still a little raw, maybe I scratched too much, but it's good to get the casts off."

It was just after lunch and the hallways of the school were empty and quiet. Dougherty could imagine the comedy voice saying "too quiet."

They walked into the main office, an open concept space with wall dividers around small desks but no people. Dougherty said to Legault, "This place is a lot different than Verdun High."

"Yes, a lot different from my high school, too."

A young woman came down the hallway from the offices beyond, the ones with walls around them, and said, "May I help you?"

Dougherty said they were there to see the vice-principal.

"Mrs. Norris or Mr. Desjardins?"

"Mrs. Norris."

The young woman said, "Is she expecting you?"

"Yes."

A middle-aged black woman came down the hall then and said, "Thanks, Nancy," and then, "This way, please."

Dougherty and Legault followed Mrs. Norris the few steps down the hall to her office. When they were inside she said, "Would you mind closing the door?"

Dougherty had to move one of the chairs out of the way and take a pile of files off it to sit down. Legault had already sat down in the other chair facing the desk and Dougherty said, "This is Sergeant Legault, from the Longueuil police."

The vice-principal said, "I'm Evelyn," extending her hand and shaking theirs before sitting down behind her desk. She looked at Dougherty then and said, "You look a little familiar, did you go to Richelieu Valley High?"

"No," Dougherty said. "I just have a common look."

"I thought maybe you were in my class when I was a teacher."

"No, we didn't live on the south shore when I was in school," Dougherty said.

"But Tommy has been at Centennial for a few years?"

"Since grade seven," Dougherty said. "Since the school opened."

"Well, I don't really know him."

"That's good, I guess, he doesn't spend much time in the vice-principal's office."

Mrs. Norris said, "Mr. Desjardins handles discipline, he knows him."

Dougherty was thinking, Yeah, probably not nearly as well as Mr. Richardson knew me in high school, but he didn't say anything, just smiled a little.

"Now," Mrs. Norris said, "you said you'd like to talk to Kim Cunningham?"

"That's right," Dougherty said. "It's a little delicate. We were hoping she could help us with some information about something she may have seen."

"All right, well, I'll talk to Kim, and if she's willing to talk to you I'll need to be there as well."

Dougherty said, "Okay."

"We'll be changing classes in a few minutes. I can catch Kim then. Why don't you come with me." Mrs. Norris stood up and Dougherty and Legault followed.

They left the main office and walked down the hall to a kind of open area with a wide staircase in the middle and carpeted areas around the edge. There were posters on the wall for an upcoming dance and other notices.

At the top of the stairs, Mrs. Norris stopped in front of the library and said, "We can talk in here." She pushed open the glass door and Dougherty and Legault followed.

A woman stood up from behind the desk, and Mrs.
Norris said, "Helen, I'm going to bring in a student and we're going to talk over there. This is Mr. Dougherty, Tommy's brother."

The librarian, Helen, shook hands with Dougherty and said, "I see quite a bit of Tommy."

Dougherty said, "Really?"

"You sound surprised."

"I've never seen him reading a book."

"Oh, he likes to read."

Mrs. Norris said, "Have a seat and I'll go get Kim."

Helen saw Legault looking at a table set up beside the circulation desk with a display of books about Vietnam and said, "This month's topic. We have quite a few students from Vietnam."

Dougherty said, "Boat people?"

Helen said, "Yes, I guess you could say that. They arrived last year."

Legault said, "They go to English schools?"

"They're not Catholic," Helen said. "I don't think there are any French Protestant schools on the south shore."

"Are they Protestant?" Legault said.

The librarian had an uncomfortable smile frozen on her face, and she said, "I don't know."

Dougherty said, "The Protestant school boards aren't very religious, they're really just everybody who's not Catholic."

Legault said, "I see."

There was tension, Dougherty could tell that, but he didn't really get what it was about.

The bell rang then and the hall outside the library filled with students.

Dougherty said, "Come on," and found a table behind the last row of stacks near the windows overlooking the empty parking lot.

A few minutes later, Mrs. Norris came into the library with a girl who looked about sixteen or seventeen.

"Kim, this is Detective Dougherty and Sergeant Legault."

Dougherty had stood up and was holding out his hand. "Hi Kim."

She shook his hand and said, "Hello."

Legault also stood up and said, "*Bonjour*," also shaking hands.

Dougherty said, "Have a seat."

Kim looked at Mrs. Norris, who nodded and sat down, so Kim sat down as well.

Dougherty looked at her and tried to be as friendly as he could, but he had the feeling it was coming across as creepy. He was looking Kim in the eyes and he noticed she had make-up, eye liner and eye shadow and even some lipstick. She had long straight dark blonde hair that was parted in the middle and fell past her shoulders and she was wearing a white peasant blouse and jeans.

He said, "You know you're not in any trouble, right?"

"Yeah, I know."

Dougherty nodded. He felt the girl seemed confident. He had some doubts about himself, this was more delicate than his usual interrogations. He told himself it wasn't an interrogation and said, "We were wondering if you could tell us what happened after the concert you went to last week."

"I didn't go to a concert last week."

Now Dougherty was worried. He was really acting on rumours, third and fourth hand at that, and high school students. Still, he didn't think his brother would have brought it up if there hadn't been something to it.

He said, "A concert at Place des Nations?"

Kim glanced sideways at Mrs. Norris and said, "ELO?"

"It's all right, Kim, you don't have to talk about it," Mrs. Norris said.

"Is that who it was?" Dougherty said.

"Yeah but it wasn't last week, it was quite a while ago, it was before Labour Day."

Dougherty said, "That's not important."

"Is this because I sold Tommy the ticket? I just didn't want to go. I only charged him what I paid for it."

Dougherty smiled and said, "No, it's not about that." He paused, trying to pick his words, and then he said, "When I was talking to Tommy he said that you bought this ticket a while ago but then you didn't want to go to the concert."

"That's right."

"And you have another ticket for a concert in November, for The Doobie Brothers, that you said you'd sell."

Kim nodded.

Dougherty said, "The thing is, I was wondering if something happened at the last concert you went to that made you not want to go to another one?"

Kim was looking at her hands then, squeezing them together. Quietly, she said, "No."

"After the concert at Place des Nations, did you go to the bridge, the Jacques Cartier?"

"No."

She was still staring at her hands, and Dougherty wasn't sure what to do. He didn't want to press her too much, but this wasn't his kind of interview. He looked over at Legault, and she nodded and moved forward a little.

She waited a long moment, until the silence was becoming too much for everyone, and then she said, "Kim, please excuse my English, it's not so good."

Kim looked up a little, relieved to be talking about something else and said, "It sounds good. It's way better than my French."

Legault smiled and said, "Thank you."

Mrs. Norris, taking the cue that they were going for more casual conversation said, "You aren't in French immersion anymore, are you?"

"No, I was failing math and science," Kim said. "And English." She laughed then, a quick nervous laugh.

Legault said, "I understand." She paused and then said, "Kim, we are looking for a man and we think he sometimes sells drug on Île Sainte-Hélène."

"I don't buy drugs."

Dougherty noticed she didn't say she didn't use drugs but he let it go.

"We don't care about that," Legault said. "We are trying to get to know what the man looks like."

Kim shrugged.

They were getting close to it. Dougherty could tell already that it was true, Kim had met the guy and something bad had happened. He said, "You can tell us, Kim."

She said, "Did Dawn tell Tommy?"

"No," Dougherty said. "Tommy doesn't know what happened."

Kim looked back at her hands in her lap but didn't say anything.

Mrs. Norris stood up and said, "Maybe we should go to my office."

Legault stood up and looked at Dougherty and said, "We'll meet you back at the front door."

It took him a moment to realize they were going without him, and by then they were walking out of the library.

Dougherty waited a few minutes then got up himself. As he started to walk out, the librarian stepped up and held out a book.

She said, "This is one Tommy read." She seemed very pleased, so Dougherty took the hardcover book from her. There was a picture of a cop in uniform on the front and the title, *Walking the Beat*, in yellow letters. Under that Dougherty read, *A New York Policeman Tells What It's Like on His Side of the Law*.

"This could be pretty boring."

"It's not." She took the book back. "It seems like a very interesting job."

"It has its moments," Dougherty said, and he thought about adding, But this isn't one of them, but he didn't. He said, "I was kind of hoping Tommy wouldn't have to know I was here."

The librarian looked doubtful. "Not many secrets in a high school."

Dougherty said, "I guess not." That's why he was there, after all, chasing down a rumour. "Well, thanks. I'm supposed to meet them in the front office."

He left the library and walked down the stairs, but instead of heading towards the front office he walked down the hall in the other direction. He passed the doors to the auditorium and then the cafeteria, empty

345

in the middle of the afternoon, and at the end of the hall he came to the gym. He wasn't really looking for anything, just killing time until Legault and the vice-principal were finished talking to Kim. Walking back down the hall, lined with lockers, he admitted to himself that he was upset not to be in on the interview, or really, that he was upset he didn't have the skills needed for that interview.

It's not like anyone was needed to punch a teenage girl to get her to talk.

Dougherty turned down another hall and followed the sounds of power tools. When he'd been in high school he'd certainly been a lot more comfortable in the wood shop than in the library. In fact, he couldn't remember a time he'd gone to the library, except for photo day, maybe.

At the end of the hall, past the wood shop and the auto shop, the back doors of the school smelled of cigarette smoke and a little weed. Dougherty knew that if he'd gone to this new school this is where he would've hung out, having a smoke at lunch and talking about cars and being a tough guy. It was an attitude that had served him well at Verdun High, made him at least as popular as he'd been and most of all gave him some security. These were things he'd never thought about before, and probably never would have if it hadn't been for Judy. She understood these things, the kinds of group dynamics that went on in high schools and at work and in families.

Judy would be able to explain to Dougherty how his skills were perfect for walking a beat, for wearing a uniform and keeping the peace — with a nightstick and his fists — and for dealing with the tough guys, the street hoods and low-level gangsters and bikers dealing drugs in the bars, but when it came to a real investigation, a homicide, where evidence had to be collected and presented to a prosecutor and taken into court, his skills might not be the right ones.

Dougherty checked his watch and figured he'd better get back to the front office. He walked down the empty hall, listening to the sounds of the power tools and a couple of guys' voices, and he was thinking that's the way Judy would say it, too, something that didn't really sound like a limitation or make him feel like he was heading for a dead end, just something he needed to work on, like taking a CPR course.

His fear, though, was that he was good at being the good thug who dealt with the bad thugs. If that wasn't needed he might not have anything to offer.

As he approached the main office, the bell rang and the halls filled with students, so Dougherty kept walking out the main doors and waited in the parking lot. He lit a cigarette and looked at the bungalows across the street and wondered if that was the kind of house he and Judy would end up in. Could he live like that, mowing the lawn on the weekend, shovelling the driveway in the winter? Coming home from a call in the middle of the night? Maybe Delisle was right, maybe he shouldn't try for detective, maybe he should become a desk sergeant and work a day shift, run a station.

Maybe he wouldn't have a say in the matter.

Legault came out of the school then and said, "Did somebody die?"

Dougherty said, "No, I was just thinking about living here."

"It's not that bad," Legault said. "Too English, maybe."

They walked to the car, and Dougherty said, "Listen to yourself, this is the most English I've heard you speak."

Legault said, "*Elle était très . . . serviable.*"

"So something did happen?"

"*Oh oui.*"

Dougherty pulled out of the parking lot and drove through the winding streets of the neighbourhood and switched to French himself. "Coming home from a concert?"

"Yes," Legault said. "Electric Light Orchestra. You know them?"

"Sure, 'Evil Woman.'"

"Yes, that's right. So, after the concert some of Kim's friends went backstage."

"She's sixteen?"

"Yes," Legault said. "But the band had left and Kim wanted to leave as well."

For a moment Dougherty thought he must have taken a wrong turn and was going in a circle, but then he saw the back of a grocery store and followed the road around until he saw the way to Taschereau Boulevard.

"Did she?"

Legault nodded. "Yes. But her friends stayed. It was late by then and the rest of the crowd from the concert was gone. She walked to the Métro station."

At Taschereau there was a Chinese restaurant

on the right, Kenny Wong's. Across the four lanes of Taschereau was the rest of Greenfield Park, old Greenfield Park, and Dougherty wondered how it had managed to spread onto the other side of the boulevard.

"There was a man standing by a car," Legault said.

"Near the bridge?"

"Yes."

Dougherty turned right and headed towards Longueuil. "If she was walking from Place des Nations to the Métro, she wouldn't need to go near the bridge."

"You think that's important?"

Dougherty said, "I don't know," and he didn't. "But if she's not telling the truth about one thing how do we know she's telling the truth about anything?"

"She is."

"How do you know?"

Legault said, "In youth services I have talked to many teenagers, many girls."

"Are they all the same?"

"When the girls talk about how they were raped, I can tell if it's true."

Dougherty didn't think that would go over well with Carpentier and the other homicide detectives, and he didn't even want to imagine taking that to the prosecutors, but he could see how serious Legault was so he didn't say anything for a moment, and then he said, "That's what happened?"

349

"Yes."

They were taking the on-ramp to the bridge then, passing over a huge ship in the seaway.

"Two men?" Dougherty said.

"Yes. At first she only saw one man, standing by a car. He's young, maybe twenty-five, long hair, not much of a beard."

"Of course."

"He offered Kim some drugs."

"Cocaine?"

"No, just marijuana. She said he held out the joint."

"He speak English?"

"Yes. But he had an accent."

They were going over the crest of the bridge, the skyline of Montreal off to the right.

Dougherty said, "And the other one?"

"He didn't speak. Kim took the joint from the first one and he offered her a ride. She said no. The other one grabbed her from behind and forced her into the car, the back seat."

"Did they do it there?"

"No. They drove somewhere. The one who pushed Kim into the car, the one who didn't speak, he held her down, pushed her face into the seat."

Dougherty changed lanes, jerking the steering wheel, and the car behind them honked. He said, "Where did they drive to?"

"She doesn't know. They drove to the south shore."

"How does she know that?"

Legault said, "It's where they left her," with an edge to her voice. She took a moment and then continued in the almost monotone she'd been using. "They drove for a while and when they stopped they pulled her halfway out of the car but kept her face pushed into the seat. They took turns. Then they left her and drove off."

Dougherty drove along Taschereau, still lined with a lot of motels that had been thrown up for Expo, past La Belle Province hot dog place, the Greenfield Park Shopping Centre and pulled into the parking lot of the Champion Lanes bowling alley.

"Where did they leave her?"

"Not far from where we just were. The train yards across Boulevard Wilfrid Laurier."

"How did she get home?"

"She walked."

Dougherty said, "And she didn't tell anyone? She got home in the middle of the night and no one noticed?"

"No, no one. She said there is trouble at home, her parents are separated, they may have to sell the house."

"So she didn't tell anyone."

"Not until today. But you heard rumours, your brother did."

"He really had no idea, I was just guessing."

"You guessed right."

Dougherty said, "Are you going to make a report?"

"She won't."

"What?"

"The vice-principal is going to arrange for something, some kind of counsellor, but Kim, she doesn't want any police."

"She talked to you?"

Legault said, "Yes."

Dougherty turned and looked at Legault. "You don't seem surprised."

"They never want to involve the police."

Dougherty said, "Why not?"

"She thinks it was her fault."

"It wasn't her fault."

"People will say that. She'll be treated like the criminal, not the victim. She was walking by herself after midnight, she took drugs, she was a . . ." Legault searched for the word and then said in English, "a groupie."

"*Elle a seize ans*," Dougherty said.

Legault looked at him.

"Okay, maybe you're right," he said. "Maybe that's what would happen."

It was quiet for a minute, and then Legault said, "Do you think it was the same guys?"

Dougherty was angry. "Of course it was, it's Comptois and Daigneault."

"Maybe."

"How many guys you think are raping girls on Île Sainte-Hélène?"

"More than you know."

Dougherty slammed the steering wheel. "We know these two."

"This case is closed," Legault said.

"We'll reopen it."

"Who, you and me?"

"You don't want to?"

"*Câlisse*, of course I do." Legault paused and then said, "But you know we can't."

Dougherty balled his hands into fists and tapped the steering wheel. "We can keep doing what we're doing."

"What are we doing? We're getting nothing."

"We know who did it."

"You have any evidence? Eh? Do you?" She didn't wait for an answer that wasn't coming. "We have nothing, nothing we can use. You want to go to your *chef des homicides*, what's his name, the friend of Captain Allard?"

"Carpentier."

"You want to go to him with this? These girls, Louise Tremblay, *tabarnak*, what happened to her was *my* fault!"

"It wasn't your fault."

"Be quiet! These girls, Louise and this one today, Kim, you think we can help them? We can't help them any more than we can help Manon."

"You want to give up? Just let them go?"

"I want to kill these fucking bastards!" She slammed her fist into the dashboard and then it was suddenly quiet in the car.

Dougherty realized he was squeezing the steering wheel and he loosened his grip. He knew Legault was right, everything she had said and everything she hadn't. There were no more official channels to go through, she was back on youth services, lucky to still have a job, and Dougherty was sitting at a desk at Station Ten or driving patrol.

He said, "I'll drive you home."

Legault opened the car door and said, "It's okay. It's not far, I'll call my husband. We have to go grocery shopping anyway." She got out of the car, and before she closed the door she leaned back in and said, "They're criminals, they'll do something else, you'll catch them."

Dougherty said, "Yeah."

Legault slammed the door and walked towards the pay phones by the door of the bowling alley.

Dougherty waited a moment then pulled out of the parking lot. He drove back the way he'd come, along Taschereau, not thinking about it but avoiding the Jacques Cartier Bridge and taking the Champlain. Not passing the scene of the crime.

One of the crimes.

He knew Legault was right, he knew criminals. They'd do something else to someone else. There'd be another victim, maybe a lot more victims, but they'd get caught. But maybe not for years, maybe not even in Montreal, maybe in Calgary like Wayne Boden, the guy who had killed three women in 1970 who Dougherty had chased around the city. Seemed so long ago now, but it was only six years. Dougherty had spent that whole time thinking he'd get promoted, make detective, it was only a matter of time.

Now it seemed like it would never happen.

By the time he pulled into the parking lot behind the apartment building, he was feeling okay, glad to be coming home to Judy.

As soon as he walked in she said, "We're on strike."

"You've only been on the job a month, you won't even get strike pay, will you?"

"No." She stood up from the couch and said, "It could be long, we're really dug in."

"That's what it looks like?"

"Yeah. How'd it go?"

"Not good." Dougherty opened the fridge and got out a beer. "You want one?"

"No, thanks."

"Well, it's a good thing I have a job."

Judy said, "Yeah."

They started making dinner and Dougherty was thinking he was lucky to have a job.

A couple weeks later, the government ordered the teachers back to work and the next day called an election.

And then, shocking a lot of people, the PQ, the party that wanted Quebec to separate from Canada, really started to gain a lot of traction.

Dougherty kept his head down and did his job, but he also kept an eye out for Martin Comptois and Marc-André Daigneault.

He might spend the rest of his career driving patrol, but he'd always be working these murders, Manon Houle and Mathieu Simard.

CHAPTER
TWENTY-THREE

The call came in the morning, just after ten. Dougherty was in the squad room looking at arrest reports from the past week, pulling out anything that mentioned narcotics or rape.

Delisle hung up the phone and said, "Hey, Dougherty, take a drive. Woman says her daughter is dead."

Dougherty paused for a second and then stood up, saying, "How old is the daughter?"

Delisle held out a piece of paper and said, "She's hysterical, that's all we got."

"Is there anybody else here I can take?" Dougherty took the paper, glancing at the address, and headed out the back door of the station.

Delisle called after him, "I'll send Gagnon as soon as I find him and Bernier when he finishes the call he's on."

In the car on the way down the hill, Dougherty was thinking he hadn't planned on leaving the station all day, but when Delisle said the daughter was dead he hopped on it. He was hoping she wasn't just a baby.

He drove fast but didn't put on the siren. There wasn't much traffic. A couple of minutes later he pulled up in front of the row of houses on Coursol Street and saw a woman standing on the sidewalk looking like she had no idea where she was.

"*Madame, avez-vous appelé la police?*"

"*L'ambulance.*"

Dougherty was standing beside the woman then, and he realized she was older than he expected, in her forties or fifties, not a young mother at all.

He continued in French, "Is it your daughter?"

"Inside."

She pointed vaguely, and Dougherty saw the door to the ground-floor apartment was open. He walked towards it.

Inside the door was a long hallway. Dougherty took a step in, looking into the living room but not seeing anyone. He moved farther into the apartment and came to the bathroom. It was empty. The kitchen was at the very back of the apartment, but before he got there Dougherty looked into the bedroom and saw the girl on the bed. It wasn't what he'd expected.

The call had said the daughter was dead so Dougherty had thought it was a baby or very young child, the kind of call he'd seen a couple of times, the

357

baby just didn't wake up, stopped breathing. Later, sometimes, they found evidence of shaking or sometimes they never found anything and the tragedy went on forever.

This daughter looked to be in her twenties. And she was tied up. Hands behind her back, electrical wire wrapped tight and then wound around her ankles and back up to her neck. There was a gag in her mouth.

Her eyes were open. Ringed in blood. Dougherty touched her neck but he knew she was dead.

He unclipped his radio and called it in, told Delisle the victim was in her twenties and had been murdered. Something seemed off in the room, strange, and it took Dougherty a moment to realize it was that the room was so neat. Nothing had been disturbed. There were bottles of perfume and make-up on the dresser in front of the mirror and clothes neatly folded. There hadn't been a struggle at all. And she was dressed for work, a dark skirt and a blouse, buttoned up all the way. Dougherty lifted the skirt and saw white panties. She probably hadn't been raped.

As he was walking out of the room, he stepped on something that made a rustling sound and he saw it was a large empty bag of Humpty Dumpty salt and vinegar chips. He picked it up and it wasn't empty. He reached in carefully and pulled out what he thought was a dark blue tuque but when he had it in his hand he realized it was a ski mask. He put it back in the chip bag and put that on the dresser.

Then he closed the door to the bedroom and went back outside.

The ambulance had arrived and Dougherty told the

two guys that the girl was in the bedroom and asked them not to disturb too much, it was a crime scene.

One guy said, "We do what we have to," and they went inside with their gear.

Dougherty took the mother aside and asked her what her name was.

"Yvette Dionne."

"Do you live here?"

She shook her head no. "In Verdun. She didn't go to work, my daughter. She didn't phone me. I came to see if she was sick."

"What's her name?"

"Madeleine Dionne."

"Do you have a key?"

"Yes."

"Was the door locked when you got here?"

Mme. Dionne thought for a moment and then said, "Yes."

"Who else has a key?"

"No one."

"Is there anyone she would let in? Is she married?"

Mme. Dionne shook her head again. She was crying and holding a tissue to her face, but she was holding it together.

"A boyfriend maybe?"

"No, they broke up."

"When?"

"A couple of weeks ago, I think. He's useless, a bum."

"He's not working."

Mme. Dionne shook her head, "He never works, he's too lazy."

"What's his name?"

"Stéphane Roberge."

"Do you know where he lives?"

"No, I think downtown."

"You said your daughter didn't go to work today, where is that?"

"At the bank, the City and District. She works hard."

"On St. Catherine?"

"No," she thought for a moment and said, "on Notre Dame, past Atwater."

A crowd had started to gather on the sidewalk, neighbours coming out of their apartments, and a couple more cop cars arrived.

Dougherty saw Gagnon and waved him over, saying, "Keep people out of the apartment. The tech guys will be here soon, it's a homicide."

An unmarked police car pulled up and a woman got out. She was wearing a suit jacket and a skirt and said, "I'm Constable Benoît with Family Services."

Dougherty stepped closer and explained the situation, and Benoît said, "I'll talk to Mme. Dionne."

"The homicide detectives will probably want to talk to her," Dougherty said, "but I have a preliminary statement so she doesn't have to stay and watch all this."

"I'll see if she wants to go to a hospital," Benoît said. "Or I'll take her home." She walked over to Mme. Dionne and Dougherty watched her take charge, dealing with a grieving parent, something she'd probably done dozens of times before.

Dougherty unclipped the radio handset from his

collar and asked Delisle which homicide detectives were on the way and Delisle said, "What do you care?"

"Who is it?"

"It's Carpentier."

Dougherty said great under his breath and heard a voice say, "Doesn't sound great."

"Rozovsky, how you doing?"

"Better than you."

"Wait till you get inside."

"Is it bad?" Rozovsky asked. He had one camera bag in his hand and another over his shoulder. "I heard the mother called it in."

"It's not a baby," Dougherty said. "She looks to be in her twenties."

"Is she a mess?"

Dougherty shook his head and said, "No, she's tied up, you'll see. The place is clean."

"No robbery?"

"No, and no rape."

"So what was it?"

Dougherty said, "I don't know. The mother said she didn't go to work today."

"Where does she work?"

"Not far from here, the City and District on Notre Dame."

"A bank?"

"Yeah."

Rozovsky said, "Remember the extortion last year, that bank manager was tied up?"

"No, where was that?"

"North end, maybe you don't know. Couple of guys broke into the bank manager's house, tied him up. They called the bank, got them to hand over fifty grand."

"They didn't kill him."

Rozovsky shrugged. "They said they would."

"They get caught?"

"Yeah, I think they did. They both bought cars right away."

"So, it's not them."

"No." Rozovsky said and started into the apartment. "Maybe it's someone smarter."

Dougherty doubted that but thought it could be someone who heard the story.

A couple of minutes later, a grey four-door sedan pulled up and Detective Carpentier got out. He saw Dougherty and said, "Constable."

Dougherty quickly briefed him, giving him all the information he had, and when he finished Carpentier said, "You think it's an extortion?"

"It's possible."

"But that was the manager they had, she's not the manager."

"No." Dougherty paused, then said, "But it wasn't a rape and it wasn't a robbery. No one broke in."

"Yes, so maybe she's the one they could get," Carpentier said. "Have you called the bank?"

"No."

Carpentier looked around and said, "Well, if they've contacted the bank they won't come back here." He motioned at all the cop cars and the ambulance. "Not now."

"Maybe they haven't made the drop."

"City and District on Notre Dame?"

Dougherty said, "That's right."

"Come on."

Carpentier drove. It was about ten blocks west. They stopped at a Fina gas station on the corner of Notre Dame and Atwater, and Carpentier got out and walked from there.

Late afternoon. A beautiful day in October, the neighbourhood was busy.

Dougherty got out of the car and walked around, got in behind the wheel. A couple of minutes later the radio jumped to life and he unclipped it from his collar. Through the static he heard Delisle say, "Carpentier says you were right, whatever that means, over."

"Roger, over."

Delisle said, "The manager left a few minutes ago, he's going to Atwater Market. He's walking."

Dougherty figured that was so Roberge and whoever was with him could see if the guy was being followed. Into the radio he said, "I'm on my way."

"Wait for Carpentier."

"Roger that."

"And stay out of sight, you in your uniform."

"Why?" Dougherty said. "The girl is already dead."

"But not the manager."

Carpentier was back then, getting into the car and saying, "Let's go."

Dougherty put the car in gear and pulled out onto Atwater.

Carpentier said, "The bank was crowded and someone gave an envelope with the manager's name on it to a teller. There was some confusion, they aren't sure how long it was before the manager got it."

"They're not sure?"

Dougherty pulled into the parking lot of the market. The building was almost fifty years old, a long narrow brick building with a clock tower at one end.

"It could have been delivered hours ago. It said to put fifty thousand dollars in a briefcase and bring it here, to the market. The manager just left the bank ten minutes ago."

"What does he look like?"

"Like a bank manager," Carpentier said. "Carrying a briefcase and filling his pants with shit."

"Should be easy to spot then."

Dougherty parked and they both got out of the car.

"If they see you in the uniform it will spook them," Carpentier said. "So stay back as far as you can." Carpentier started towards the building.

Dougherty followed, thinking if Carpentier thought he looked like anything other than a cop he was fooling himself, but he stayed back.

It was getting close to lunchtime and the market was crowded. Carpentier walked past the stalls without looking at any of the fruits or vegetables or fish or any of the baked goods. He looked like a man on a mission, and Dougherty followed as far back as he could.

In the middle of the market were tables and chairs filled with people eating lunch and drinking coffee. Carpentier turned slowly in a circle. Dougherty figured he might as well be holding up a sign.

There were a lot of people but no middle-aged men in suits. Except for Carpentier.

Dougherty turned around to go back to the car and

he saw a young man, mid-twenties, with long hair and a beard, wearing jeans and a t-shirt and carrying a brief-case. The guy was heading for the doors so Dougherty started after him, hoping the guy wouldn't look back and see the uniform.

But of course he did, and he started running.

Dougherty said, "Shit," and started running after him, calling back over his shoulder, "This way!"

The guy pushed through the doors, and Dougherty was right behind him in the parking lot.

Instead of running towards the street, the guy ran through the lot towards the canal. Dougherty was gaining on him, and the guy turned a little, saw him, and threw the briefcase. Dougherty raised his arm to block it and got knocked off balance but stayed on his feet and kept running.

The guy jumped the low fence and ran towards the footbridge over the canal but Dougherty caught up to him and got a hand on the guy's shoulder. He turned and swung, but Dougherty ducked and kept moving forward, slamming into the guy like he was making an open-field tackle. Coach Brown would've been pleased.

Dougherty's momentum carried them and they both went over the edge and into the canal with a huge splash.

When he came up for air the guy sputtered, "*Je sais pas nager.*"

Dougherty said, "Then drown." He let go and the guy went under, wildly waving his arms. Dougherty managed to make his way back to the stone wall of the canal and grab hold, but it was about ten feet up to the ledge.

Carpentier was there then, and he looked down and said, "Hold on, we'll get you out. Get him."

Dougherty swam back a few feet, reached under water, grabbed hold of the guy's long hair and pulled him up. "You Stéphane Roberge?"

"How do you know?"

"Madeleine Dionne is dead. You killed her."

"No, she's not dead."

Roberge was kicking his legs, trying to get away, so Dougherty let go and watched him flail and go under the water. When his head came up again, spitting water and bug-eyed, Dougherty grabbed him and held on.

The fire truck arrived a few minutes later, and Dougherty and Roberge were pulled out of the canal.

Carpentier was waiting and he said, "Good work, Constable."

"He said he didn't mean to kill her."

"They always say that, don't they?"

Dougherty said, "Yeah."

Carpentier told Dougherty to get dried off and make a report and then took Roberge to Bonsecours street.

Back at Station Ten, Dougherty changed into a dry uniform and when he walked back into the squad room Delisle said, "Hey, there he is, Mark Spitz."

"Funny."

366   "We picked up another guy and now the two of them are giving each other up."

Dougherty said, "I figured they would."

"And look at this," Delisle said, "you're still finished at the end of your shift, no working late."

"Yeah, that's good."

Delisle laughed and said, "You got someone waiting for you at home, you bet it's good."

Dougherty knew he was right. Still, as he drove back to LaSalle, he did wish he could have gone to Bonsecours Street and taken the guy into the interrogation room, get the confession out of him and charge him with murder. It would have felt good.

It felt good going into the apartment building while it was still light out, too.

Judy said, "I made dinner."

Dougherty said, "You sound surprised."

"I never thought I'd say that to some man coming home from work. Look at me, I'm June Cleaver."

"You're not wearing pearls."

Judy patted her jeans and said, "Or a dress."

"Should we have a drink?" Dougherty said. "Is that what we're supposed to do?"

"That's too much like my parents."

"Yeah, I guess it is. You have a good day?"

"It's good to be back at work." Judy went into the kitchenette and added noodles to a big pot. "It's goulash, it'll be ready in ten minutes."

Dougherty followed her and opened the fridge. He got out a beer and said, "You want one?"

"No." She reached out and he handed her the bottle and she took a drink. "That's enough. I just wish we were really back and it wasn't work to rule."

"Why, were you going to coach a team?"

She was stirring the pot and she said, "I was going to help with the school newspaper."

"Oh right," Dougherty said, going back to the table. "Start a new generation of radicals."

"That's the dream," she said. "And we prefer to be called activists."

"Yeah, that's what we call you down at the station."

Judy looked at him over her shoulder and smirked a little, but she wasn't upset and she said, "Ha ha."

"You've got your work cut out for you, all the kids I see these days, all they want to do is get high."

"How was your day?"

"I was at a murder scene."

Judy was still and she hesitated for a second. He said, "Don't worry, I just took the call."

"I'm not worried."

"Look, I'm home at dinner time."

"And that's nice," Judy said. "But I'm not worried."

Dougherty drank some beer and said, "Couple of losers tried to rob a bank. Well, one of them was the ex-boyfriend of a teller. They went to her house and tied her up and took a note to the bank, said to give them fifty grand or they'd kill her."

Judy had stopped stirring and she was looking at Dougherty.

"Turns out they tied her too tight. Or she passed out and her legs relaxed and that pulled the rope on her neck. Not rope, actually, they used electrical cord — there was no give." He drank some more beer. "And they probably pushed the gag too deep into her mouth. Whatever they did, she suffocated. She was dead before they got to the bank."

Judy stood there quiet for a moment, and then she said, "I'll be honest, I'm not going to miss this."

"Talking about my work?"

"This part of your work. This awful stuff. People killed."

"Well, there won't be much of that," Dougherty said. "Don't worry."

Judy got a couple of bowls out of the cupboard and said, "You want to butter some bread?"

They ate dinner and Dougherty started to relax. He hadn't even realized how tense he had been and he was thinking it was because he'd been afraid of sitting down to dinner and not having anything to talk about, but once he was there and doing it he realized they had plenty to talk about.

He was starting to think it was something he could do every day.

When they finished eating and were doing the dishes, Judy washing and Dougherty drying, she said, "My father said if the PQ win the election his company is going to move to Toronto."

"Might as well move to the Arctic."

"But I've been hearing a lot of that," Judy said, "people talking about moving."

"Do you think anyone would really do that, move because of an election?"

"If Quebec separates."

"That's not going to happen."

"My father is pretty worried about it. If the company moves he'll have to go with them. It's not like he could find another job here."

"A lot of talk for nothing," Dougherty said.

They finished the dishes and went into the living room and sat on the couch.

Judy said, "You want to watch TV?"

"What's on?"

Judy said, "I don't know." She didn't make a move to turn on the TV. "It is good, you working days all the time."

"Yeah, we can sit around and watch TV every night if we want."

"That's right," Judy said. "And it would make it easier if we ever had kids."

Dougherty leaned back on the couch and looked at her. She was expecting something, waiting for it, almost daring him and he said, "You'd make a great mother."

Wasn't what she expected and she laughed. "I doubt that."

"No, you would. It's not the worst idea I've ever heard." He stood up and said, "Hang on," and went into the bedroom.

When he came back into the living room he had a small box in his hand and he said, "Here."

Judy tilted her head to one side as she took the box, saying, "Is this a . . .?" She opened it and said, "Oh my God, it is? When did you get this?"

Dougherty sat down on the couch and put his arm across the back, not quite around Judy, but ready. "Months ago, actually. When I was working the Brink's heist, one of the guys I questioned, Fred Berger, he deals a little in jewellery."

"Is it stolen?"

"Not from a person," Dougherty said. "It wasn't from a burglary or anything like that. It might not have passed through customs coming into the country."

She was laughing. Then she said, "Were you going to propose?" And then, it suddenly hit her and she pulled up her legs and turned sideways on the couch to face him and said, "Is this a proposal?"

Dougherty said, "Yeah, it is."

"You want to get married?"

"Well, you're the one talking about having kids."

"Yeah, but I never said anything about getting married."

"Well, come on, kids are a lifetime commitment. If you're willing to do that with me, you should commit to this, too."

She was shaking her head but she was smiling. "Édouard James Dougherty, I never imagined you were the marrying sort."

"I'm pretty sure you never imagined that you were the marrying sort."

She turned back facing forward and leaned into him. "Oh yeah, that's right. I'm the one who corrupted you. I thought I did a better job." She was still looking at the engagement ring.

"Well, you think about it," he said. "We don't need to rush into anything."

"That's true, we've got all the time we want, don't we."

She turned and leaned close to him and kissed him.

He said, "That's right, we can watch TV every night if we want."

She kissed him again and said, "Maybe later."

They went into the bedroom.

Later, after they made love and then really did watch some TV, Dougherty couldn't sleep. He was a little worried that Judy would actually want to get married, and he was just as worried that she wouldn't want to. But then he knew it would work out, it felt too good to be together. Whatever they did, he knew they'd do it together.

What he was really worried about was work. He wasn't so sure about that. He knew he could take over from Delisle, he could be a perfectly good desk sergeant, run a perfectly good station house. Go in every morning and come home for dinner. Maybe he and Judy would have kids, maybe buy a house, have a backyard and a finished basement. They could go camping in the summer. It would be a good life.

So why was he really disappointed he wouldn't be on the homicide squad? Why did he want to do that, anyway? He lay in bed staring at the ceiling, thinking about it. He felt he could talk to Judy about anything, but he wasn't sure about this. Maybe because he was worried that he wanted to do it for the wrong reasons. Maybe he wanted to do it for the prestige, to be a big shot on the police force.

Because he knew it didn't make much difference to the families of the victims, it didn't bring anyone back or make the pain any less for the people left behind. Did he just want it to feel better about himself?

Maybe.

But he didn't feel bad about himself. So maybe it was something else.

He was thinking about the homicides he had worked, really just running Detective Carpentier's errands, but he did see the murderers and he knew there was something about them — they were different than other people, they crossed a line. It wasn't something just anyone could do, it was extreme. It was final.

People get mad and say, "I'm going to kill you," but they don't do it and they don't go home and plot it and work out the details and think about how they're going to get away with it and actually do it. Normal people don't.

But the ones who do cross the line, rapists who strangle their victims, guys who kill their wives or the criminals who see it as the best way to solve a problem, if they don't get caught, they might do it again.

Men who throw teenagers off bridges.

CHAPTER
TWENTY-FOUR

For a while the election was all anyone could talk about. It turned into a three-party race; the Liberals said they were the only chance to keep Quebec a part of Canada, the Parti Québécois played down separatism and talked about the poor economic record of the Liberals and the Union Nationale was reborn with a charismatic young leader and made a late charge for the middle ground.

Dougherty worked day shifts, and in addition to the usual calls, he took a lot of calls about defaced election signs and broke up a few near-brawls at all-candidate events. One of the calls, at the Hall Building of Concordia University, looked like it was going to turn into a riot — Dougherty hadn't been to a riot at Concordia in almost ten years, since it was called Sir George Williams University, and the Hall Building was brand new — but this time there were no cops in riot gear, no smoke bombs and no one set fire to the building.

There was a lot of shouting, and from what Dougherty could make out there was a group of English students who supported the PQ, trying to shout down another group of students who looked to Dougherty like they were Greek and Italian and Chinese and were waving Canadian flags. Dougherty got five cops in uniforms — short-sleeved blue shirts and hats, not body armour and riot helmets — to form a line between the two groups and waited it out.

It seemed unreal to Dougherty that people in Canada, in Montreal, would come to blows over politics.

That kind of tension was really the exception, but there was no escaping the politics. It was definitely a different kind of election.

On Saturday night, Dougherty and Judy went downtown to see a movie. He suggested *Two Minute Warning* with Charlton Heston and she said, "You really want to see a terrorist in a big stadium shooting people," and then she said, "How about *All Screwed Up*, the new Lina Wertmüller?"

"You think it'll be as good as the last Lina Wertmüller?"

For a second Judy looked like she was going to answer that and then she said, "It's Italian, there might be naked chicks," so they went to the Snowdon Theatre.

After the movie they stopped at a deli for cheesecake, and Judy said, "Did you like it?"

"You know how I love subtitles."

"Really, did you like it?"

"It was okay. I mean, it's kind of nice to see that everybody has the same problems, trying to make a living, trying to get by."

"Yeah, puts things in perspective." Judy reached across the table and put her hand on Dougherty's and said, "We can appreciate what we've got."

He squeezed her hand and said, "Yeah, it's good."

The next morning they had a late breakfast, coffee and croissants, and read the paper. Next to the endless election coverage — too close to call — there was a story about four men who had escaped from the Leclerc medium-security prison in Laval, north of Montreal, and Judy said, "Are you going to have to work overtime on this?"

Dougherty read the article and said, "Little Johnny Wisnosky."

"Who's that?"

"One of the Point Boys, or he wants to be. He went in for armed robbery. Remember that one, the bank in NDG? We got him downtown, in the Holiday Inn. He was beating up a hooker and some tourists in the next room called."

"No," Judy said, "I don't remember. Sounds like a real winner."

Dougherty put the paper down on the table and said, "And the other geniuses, Sylvio Lamoureaux and Andre Poitras, they'll be caught before my next shift."

"But look at that," Judy said, "English and French working together."

"Better tell your father."

"What about your folks, they talking about moving?"

"They're talking about retiring. It's still five years away, four maybe, but that's what my dad's talking about." He finished his coffee. "They might retire to New Brunswick, but it's hard to picture my dad living in the country."

"Or your mom," Judy said. "She talks about it like she spent her whole life there sometimes, but she's been in Montreal since she was eighteen."

"Maybe earlier," Dougherty said. "She's vague on exactly when she got here. During the war sometime."

"She might be the one to have trouble moving to the country."

Dougherty stood up, saying, "Still, hard to imagine people moving across the country for politics. Giving up their jobs and houses." He walked to the kitchen and put his mug in the sink.

"But what if it's not the same country," Judy said. "What if Quebec does become a country?"

"Can you really see it happening?" He leaned back against the counter. "But anyway, what would really change? I'd still have my job, you'd still have your job. What difference would it make?"

"You do need to hear my father talk about it."

Dougherty started out of the kitchen and said, "No one needs to hear that."

They went for Sunday dinner in Point Claire at Judy's mom's place and tried not to talk about the election but it kept coming up. There was even talk about the American election, how did a guy named Jimmy get elected president?

On the drive back to LaSalle, Judy said, "My mom seems to be adjusting to single life."

Dougherty had no idea what she was talking about and said, "What?"

"She sounds like she's going to start sleeping with half the men in the neighbourhood."

"Where did you get that?"

"Didn't you? The way she talks."

Dougherty laughed. "Sorry, I didn't get that."

Judy was shaking her head. "I don't know, it's like *Peyton Place* out there."

"Yeah, *Peyton Place*, not *Love American Style*. It's not *Bob & Carol & Ted & Alice*."

"I'm sure it is," Judy said. "For some of them. My mom said she's making up for lost time. Did you see all the self-help books? One of them was called *Open Marriage*."

"I think that's about the election," Dougherty said, "that's what we're going to do about separation, Quebec can date other countries."

Judy said, "I'm serious."

Dougherty was laughing a little. "How can you take that seriously?"

"What about Gillian and Abby? What's it doing to them?"

Dougherty shrugged. "Your sisters are all right, you worry too much."

"I worry just enough." Judy turned her head away from Dougherty and looked out the side window of the car. They were pulling off the expressway and passing the big General Foods plant and the Seagram's distillery. "They're like the kids in my classes, people think they don't know what's going on but they feel everything."

"No one knows what's going on," Dougherty said.

"It feels like everything is falling apart."

"But it's not really, it's business as usual. It's just a lot of talk."

"Except my parents," Judy said. "They're really getting a divorce."

It was quiet for a moment and then Dougherty said, "Yeah, that's true."

Judy was still looking out the window, and Dougherty wanted to say something reassuring but he didn't want to say something that sounded trite and that's all he could think of at the moment. So he didn't say anything.

When they got home he was surprised that Judy wanted to make out and even more surprised by how passionate it was. Like they were holding on to each other for dear life.

The next morning, Monday, Dougherty was putting on his uniform and Judy said, "You working late tonight?"

"Yeah, a double. Election day. First overtime they've approved since the Olympics. They think there could be trouble."

"Well, someone's going to be really disappointed," Judy said.

She was sitting up in bed, not needing to get ready for another hour. Then she just walked a few blocks to the high school.

Dougherty came over to the bed and leaned down and kissed her and said, "But not me."

He started to stand up and she grabbed his tie and pulled him back down and said, "And not me, either. This is good."

"I'm glad you like it."

He started out of the room and Judy said, "So, we should get married."

"Well, I'm working the double shift today."

"Let's do it next spring. Just a small ceremony."

Dougherty said, "Okay, let's do it."

He felt good all day. There was an accident in the early afternoon, a guy in a sports car cut off a bus and got nailed, the back end of the car was banged up but no one was hurt. There was a lot of yelling, of course, the guy driving the sports car screaming about separatists and the bus driver yelling about turn signals and brakes.

Dougherty got in between them and said, "Right now you two need to separate," and the guy driving the sports car seemed to take it personally but the bus driver started to laugh. When the bus was towed away and the sports car was loaded onto a flatbed, the bus driver said to Dougherty, "All day like this," and Dougherty said, "It'll be over soon."

The driver said, "You think so? Maybe it's just starting."

Dougherty said, "Let's hope not," but he still wasn't too concerned. He was thinking about getting married, maybe he and Judy would have kids. It was looking good.

At eight o'clock the polls closed, and the early results starting coming in.

There was a TV in the squad room, and most of the guys sat around watching.

At ten o'clock a call came in that as the hockey game was ending in the Forum a brawl broke out. There were cops on the scene, but it was getting out of hand, so Dougherty and Gagnon got into a squad car and headed down de Maisonneuve to help.

Gagnon said, "I still don't believe it, *mon Dieu*, the separatists won?"

"Don't worry about it," Dougherty said, "it's just politics."

As they pulled up in front of the Forum, Gagnon said, "You tell them that."

The brawl had spilled out onto St. Catherine Street, a few dozen guys punching each other.

"It's probably because the Habs lost," Dougherty said. "They were playing the Blues."

Gagnon said, "I don't think they lost."

Dougherty blasted the siren a couple of times and most of the crowd took off, but a few guys came towards the car looking like they wanted to keep fighting.

Gagnon said, "What should we do?"

"What do you mean? Get out of the car."

Dougherty got out and was about to yell something when he stopped. He wasn't sure if he should yell in English or French. The wrong choice could turn it from a little brawl into a big riot.

One of the guys coming towards them yelled, "Fucking seppie bastards."

Dougherty yelled, "Okay, take it easy," and held up both his hands showing them he wasn't holding his nightstick and this could still end now. "Everybody just settle down."

"They won! They fucking won! Can you fucking believe it!"

Another cop car pulled up, coming down St. Catherine Street the wrong way on the one way and also fired off its siren and a couple of cops got out.

Dougherty said, "Okay, time to go, come on."

By then the crowd was breaking up anyway. There weren't really that many brawlers and the rest of the hockey fans were coming out of the Forum then and heading for the Métro and the parking lots.

Dougherty was moving into the crowd, looking for anyone who still wanted to throw a punch but those guys had moved on. As he was coming back to the car, he saw a guy getting into a four-door sedan in the parking lot across Closse Street, and he thought he recognized him.

When the car pulled out of the lot Dougherty was sure of it, and he jumped into the squad car and started after it. As he pulled away from the curb, Gagnon jumped in front and he slammed on the brakes and yelled, "Get in, quick."

The sedan headed down the hill on Atwater and Dougherty followed.

Gagnon said, "What are you doing?"

"I've been looking for that guy."

"How can you even tell who it is?"

"I'm pretty sure."

"Pretty sure?"

The sedan turned onto Notre Dame and then turned again onto a street lined with three-storey row houses.

Dougherty turned the corner and saw the sedan was stopped and a guy was getting out of the driver's side. Then Dougherty was sure.

It was Martin Comptois.

Then a guy got out of the passenger seat and Dougherty said to Gagnon, "You get him," and pressed the brakes and opened the door. Dougherty moved fast and was almost beside him before Comptois turned. Dougherty said, "*Eille, bouge pas.*"

Comptois smiled and said, "*Qu'est-ce que tu veux, man?*"

Dougherty glanced over and saw Gagnon had his hand on the other guy's arm so he said to Comptois in French, "Don't you remember me? I came to see you in Cornwall. I knew you were out."

"You keeping tabs on me?" Comptois was still smiling, and Dougherty grabbed his arm, twisted him around and had his hands cuffed before Comptois knew what was happening.

"Another girl got raped," Dougherty said. "So, I knew you were back in town."

The smile was gone. Comptois said, "Fuck you."

"No," Dougherty said, "someone's going to fuck you. Lots of guys."

He shoved him into the back of the squad car and saw Gagnon doing the same with the other guy.

Back at Station Ten, the place was full of cops still staring at the TV in disbelief. The three parties had split the vote and the PQ ended the night with a majority government. Most of the cops were like Dougherty, they didn't have strong feelings about it one way or the other, they still had jobs to do, but everyone knew it wasn't just an election like any other. It was big.

The cells were empty when Dougherty and Gagnon dumped in Comptois and the other guy. Dougherty hadn't even asked him if he was Marc-André Daigneault, but he was pretty sure. The thing was, he really had no evidence at all.

He went back into the front of the station and found Delisle and pulled him aside.

Delisle said, "Holy shit, what's going to happen? Are we going to be our own country?"

"We've been our own country for a hundred years," Dougherty said.

"Shit, you know what I mean."

"Yeah," Dougherty said. "That's for the politicians. Right now, look, I put a couple guys in the cells."

"You didn't process them?"

"I'm going to. In a while. Look, can you just keep them for a while."

"What are they charged with?"

"Nothing right now," Dougherty said. "Just let me work something out."

"You can't just leave them there."

"They won't say anything." Dougherty started out of the station and said, "Like you said, it's a big night, no one knows what's going to happen. They can wait a few more minutes."

Dougherty got back in the squad car and drove over the Champlain Bridge to the south shore. As he drove along Taschereau, he wondered how his parents were doing, if they were as shocked as everyone else. He drove into Longueuil and stopped in front of a small house with a half-finished front porch.

There was a party going on inside.

Dougherty knocked on the front door and a moment later it swung open and a man was standing there with a beer in one hand and a smile on his face, saying, "*Salut, mon ami, bienvenue dans notre nouveau pays!*"

Dougherty said, "*Salut, Réal, Francine est là?*"

"*Oui, oui, entre. Comment ça va?*"

"*Bien.*" Dougherty stepped into the living room full of people and pushed his way through until he saw Legault in the kitchen. As he walked towards her she saw him and smiled. She had a beer in her hand and Dougherty figured she'd had a few before this one.

She spoke French, saying, "Dougherty, did you come to join our side? The winning side."

Dougherty got close to her and said, "I arrested Martin Comptois and Marc-André Daigneault."

Legault was still smiling — it didn't seem to register with her for a moment — and she said, "What for?"

Dougherty half-smiled and said, "Nothing. I just saw them and I grabbed them. They're in the cells now. Look," he paused and then said, "there's never going to be any evidence against these guys."

Legault said, "I know."

"They're going to have to confess."

She said, "Yeah, so?"

"So, I don't think I can get that myself. I need you."   385

Legault nodded and put down her beer and said, "Okay, let's go."

On the way into Montreal, they made up a game plan where Legault would offer each Comptois and Daigneault immunity if they testified against the other.

They didn't expect either one would take it so then Dougherty would go in and "do what you do," as Legault put it.

Dougherty had been feeling that because all he could do, all he was good at, was smacking guys around, his career had peaked and he was where he was going to be forever, but now he was thinking if it worked to put these two bastards away, that was enough to make being a desk sergeant for the next thirty years worthwhile.

He said, "I did see some rope in their car, we could say it matches the piece you found in the pavilion on the Jacques Cartier Bridge, and we could say the partial print matches, but I'm worried if we try that they'll know we don't really have anything and they'll clam up."

"I think you're right," Legault said. "I think we talk to them, we play good cop bad cop and we get one to turn on the other."

Dougherty said, "Save your neck or save your brother, looks like it's one or the other."

"Is that a song?"

"Yeah," Dougherty said. "The guys who back up Bob Dylan, I saw them at the Forum a couple of years ago."

"I was at that concert," Legault said. "Réal is a big fan of Bob Dylan."

Dougherty said, "I wouldn't have guessed that."

"Nothing but Gilles Vigneault in our house?"

"Well, tonight anyway."

Legault said, "How many houses do you think will be playing 'Mon Pays' tonight?"

"All the ones that aren't packing."

Legault turned and looked at Dougherty and then saw the look on his face and smiled. Then she was serious again and said, "*Bien*, let's do this."

And when they did, it was much easier than they expected. Legault made them both the offer, and Dougherty smacked them both, and the next time Legault went in to talk to them Comptois said it was all Daigneault's idea and Daigneault said it was all Comptois.

They had been selling drugs for a while and sometimes women, girls, would offer them sex instead of money. When they moved from pot to coke not all the girls they knew wanted to make the change, and the first time Comptois forced it Daigneault was surprised and just watched. After that it happened more easily. "I didn't want to," Daigneault said, "it was the drugs."

And Legault said, "Then you shouldn't have taken them."

He said, "Once you start . . ."

Legault waited a moment and then said, "Tell me about Manon and Mathieu, what happened?"

And it was almost exactly what Dougherty had said it was. They thought it was two girls and they stopped them on the bridge, on the sidewalk, and when it turned out one of them was a boy they got mad. "It was the drugs," Daigneault said. "The coke."

387

"No," Legault said. "It wasn't the drugs it was you. You and Comptois."

She got them both to write it all down, full confessions, and they both did.

It was almost dawn then, and Legault said she was

going home. She phoned her husband and he came and picked her up. When she was leaving, she said to Dougherty, "What happens now?"

"I give all this to Carpentier. It's up to him."

Legault said, "I will tell the parents. If there are charges or not, at least they'll know the truth."

Dougherty said, "Yes, but it would be better if there are charges."

"Yes."

Dougherty stood on the sidewalk and watched Legault and her husband drive away through the empty streets. The parties — and the mourning — came to an end. Then he went back into the station.

CHAPTER
TWENTY-FIVE

Detective Carpentier said, "You know, without the confession you have nothing."

Dougherty said, "I know."

Carpentier tapped the paper and said, "It may not be accepted into court, they could get good lawyers."

Dougherty didn't say anything.

"It is very detailed," Carpentier said. "You got them to say all this?"

"Honestly," Dougherty said, "Sergeant Legault came in from Longueuil and handled most of it. She would appreciate it if we didn't mention that."

"We may have to," Carpentier said.

"Understood."

Carpentier shook his head and let out an exhausted sigh. "It's been quite a night."

"Yes, sir."

"This is good work, Dougherty."

Dougherty didn't say anything.

"Very good police work."

"Thank you, sir."

Carpentier stood up. It seemed to Dougherty that the overcoat must weigh a thousand pounds. "This is going to cause a lot of problems for Captain Allard and his detectives in Longueuil. It's going to cause a lot of problems for Olivier, too, with the chief."

Dougherty nodded. It had been months since his meeting with the assistant director of detectives, Paul-Emile Olivier, and that hadn't gone all that well.

"I'll talk to him," Carpentier said. "And when this blows over in a couple of months I'll see to it you are transferred to the homicide squad."

Dougherty wasn't sure he heard right and said, "Pardon me, sir?"

"You're going to be a homicide detective," Carpentier said. He was walking out of the squad room then, and he stopped at the door and looked back. "Don't worry, you'll hate it as much as you hate working patrol soon enough."

Dougherty said, "I don't hate working patrol."

Carpentier winked and said, "I know."

He walked out, and a few moments later Dougherty realized he'd been holding his breath and let it out in a long exhale. He looked around the squad for someone to shake hands with but there was no one there.

Outside the sun was coming up.

As Dougherty drove to LaSalle he started to wonder what he'd say to Judy. They were settled into such a good routine, they were both working days and having dinner together.

They were going to get married.

He had no idea what he'd say to her.

But when he walked into the apartment and saw Judy sitting at the dining room table eating breakfast he knew it would be okay.

AUTHOR'S NOTE

These days if someone brings up the 1976 Summer Olympics in Montreal, the conversation usually quickly becomes about the debt incurred, the lack of a gold medal for the host country and the unfinished stadium. But from my vantage point as a sixteen-year-old living in LaSalle, the Olympics were great. I attended one event, with my father, a soccer game between Iran and eventual silver medalist Poland, and I watched many hours a day on TV. I also saved the daily insert section in the *Montreal Star* for years afterwards. The highlights for me were Nadia Comăneci, Caitlyn Jenner (then known as Bruce Jenner), Sugar Ray Leonard, the Spinks Brothers, and Greg Joy's silver medal in the high jump.

But in researching *One or the Other* I looked at the summer of 1976 in Montreal as an adult and it seemed quite different. Yes, it was a big party, but big changes were in the air.

The Brink's truck robbery happened very much like it is described in the book and the perpetrators were never caught and the nearly three million dollars never recovered. Whether or not the money was used to purchase cocaine to be sold in the city that summer is speculation, but there is no doubt someone brought in a lot of cocaine and sold it in Montreal that summer.

Bob Colacello, the editor of *Interview* magazine, wrote that by the mid-1970s "cocaine suddenly was everywhere . . . It went from something people tried to hide, except among close friends, to something people took for granted, and shared openly . . . None of us thought cocaine was really dangerous, or even addictive, back then. Heroin was off limits in our crowd, but coke was like liquor or pot or poppers, fuel for fun, not self-destruction."

In 1976 a book came out called *Cocaine Handbook*, with lots of useful information like "testing for purity." The intro said, "Now that it has come into everyday use . . ." Another phrase that came up a few times in my research was, "Some people have a rule about cocaine: Never buy it, never turn it down."

Along with cocaine, disco arrived in a big way. Of course, like cocaine it had been around for a while but suddenly that summer it was everywhere. Writing about the large number of discos that opened, the *Montreal Gazette* said, in a way that seems very Montreal to me, "Saying a street is fashionable may sound derogatory but Crescent Street handles it with elegance and spark." Seeing something fashionable as a negative may be one of the most striking examples of the gap between the two solitudes in Montreal at the time.

Disco did not arrive in the suburbs in 1976. As a teenager I was firmly in the "disco sucks" camp even though sometimes, when no one else was around, I slipped my radio from CHOM-FM to CKGM-AM to hear "Play That Funky Music" or "Car Wash." Rediscovering and re-evaluating disco was one of the most fun things about writing this book. Dorian Lynskey's book, *33 Revolutions Per Minute*, has a great chapter on disco as protest music, bringing gay rights to the forefront. In retrospect this is easy to see. At the time it was not. And the movie *Funkytown* gives a very good idea of what the club scene was like in Montreal in 1976.

Ulrike Meinhof, of the Red Army Faction (Baader-Meinhof gang), really was found hanged in her maximum-security prison cell in West Germany. Her death was ruled a suicide but immediately many people questioned the circumstances. In July 1976, a member of the RAF, Monika Berberich, and three members of the 2 June Movement, Juliane Plambeck, Gabriele Rollnik and Inge Viett, escaped from prison in West Germany. With the memory of the Munich Olympics still fresh, these events added to the security tension at the Montreal Olympics.

After the Olympics, I headed into my final year of high school, the teachers went on strike (there were a lot of strikes in the 1970s) and Quebec headed into an election. It's usually remembered as the Parti Québécois upset victory, but the real surprise was probably the strong showing of the resurgent Union Nationale party under the leadership of Rodrigue Biron, which led to a three-way split and the PQ majority.

Two teenagers were murdered in 1979, strangled and thrown from the Jacques-Cartier Bridge by two men who had committed many crimes before that night. The two men were picked up quickly by the Montreal police and convicted of the two murders. They are still in prison.

As always, I rely on a lot of people for help with the research, though of course, the mistakes are entirely mine.

My father, though he passed away in 1985, was a Montrealer his whole life and my first guide to the city and I have used a lot of his insights. My uncle Bob, Robert S. McFetridge, though he passed away in 2008 also provided me with a lot of insight into his city (and picking up my tickets for the Olympic soccer game at his corner office on the top floor of Place Ville Marie was a thrill). My cousin Mike Powell took me to the Bob Dylan and The Band concert at the Montreal Forum mentioned in the book. Sadly, Mike was killed in 1990.

Randy McIlwaine, Keith Daniel and Dawn Stark from LaSalle High continue to try to correct my foggy memories of those days, but I resist. Jacques Filippi has once again taken on the task of making my awful French readable. Once again, the mistakes that remain are mine.

Thanks to everyone at ECW Press. I could not imagine writing these so very Canadian novels without the support of a truly Canadian publisher. And especially to Jen Knoch, who once again provided thorough and thoughtful editing.

And, of course, thanks to my wife, Laurie Reid.

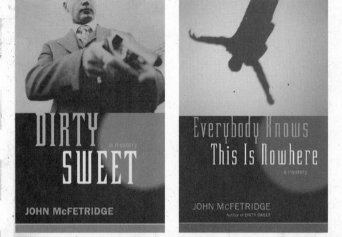
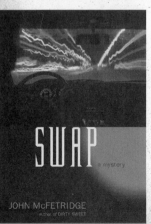
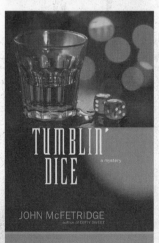

GET THE
EBOOK FREE!

At ECW Press, we want you to enjoy *One or the Other* in whatever format you like, whenever you like. Leave your print book at home and take the eBook to go! Purchase the print edition and receive the eBook free. Just send an email to ebook@ecwpress.com and include:

- the book title
- the name of the store where you purchased it
- your receipt number
- your preference of file type: PDF or ePub?

A real person will respond to your email with your eBook attached. Thank you for supporting an independently owned Canadian publisher with your purchase!